Aurora knocked tenta[...]
the study. "You wa[...]

Slayde rose. "No, actually my visitor wanted to see you." He inclined his head toward the sideboard where Julian lounged, watching Aurora's entrance. "You remember the duke of Morland?"

Twin spots of color stained her cheeks, but she met Julian's gaze without flinching. "Yes—I remember. Good afternoon, Your Grace."

Julian grinned at her formal acknowledgment. Straightening, he crossed over until he stood before her, close enough to make out all the vibrant hues of her red-gold hair. "Lady Aurora," he replied, capturing her hand, slowly raising her fingers to his lips. "How are you?"

She inclined her head, myriad emotions flashing across her face. "The same as I was when you last saw me," she managed. "One doesn't change overnight."

His lips brushed her skin. "Doesn't one?"

Andrea Kane delivers sensuality, suspense,
and a tale to treasure in
LEGACY OF THE DIAMOND

Books by Andrea Kane

My Heart's Desire
Dream Castle
Masque of Betrayal
Echoes in the Mist
Samantha
The Last Duke
Emerald Garden
Wishes in the Wind
Legacy of the Diamond
The Black Diamond

Published by POCKET BOOKS

ANDREA KANE

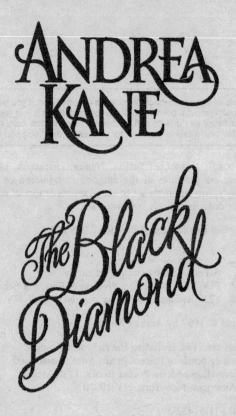

The Black Diamond

POCKET STAR BOOKS

New York   London   Toronto   Sydney   Tokyo   Singapore

This book is a work of fiction. Names, characters, places and
incidents are products of the author's imagination or are used
fictitiously. Any resemblance to actual events or locales or persons,
living or dead, is entirely coincidental.

An *Original* Publication of POCKET BOOKS

 A Pocket Star Book published by
POCKET BOOKS, a division of Simon & Schuster Inc.
1230 Avenue of the Americas, New York, NY 10020

ISBN: 0-671-53482-3

First Pocket Books printing November 1997

10 9 8 7 6 5 4 3 2 1

POCKET STAR BOOKS and colophon are registered trademarks
of Simon & Schuster Inc.

Cover art by Gerber Studio

Printed in the U.S.A.

To Mom and Dad,
for teaching me what life's blessings truly are,
and for being two of those precious blessings

Chapter 1

Devonshire, England
January 1818

"I will not marry him!"

Lady Aurora Huntley nearly toppled the study chair, leaping to her feet as if she'd been singed. With a look of utter incredulity, she stared across the desk at her brother, her chest tight with unspeakable fury. "My God, Slayde, have you lost your mind?"

"No." The Earl of Pembourne unfolded from his chair, his silver-gray eyes narrowed in warning. "I assure you, Aurora, I am quite sane. You, on the other hand, are bordering on irrational. Now, sit down."

"Irrational?" Aurora ignored the command, tilting back her head to gaze up at her tall, formidable brother. "You've just announced to me, as casually as one would announce the time of day, that in a matter of weeks you'll be marrying me off to an affable but uninspiring man who is no more than a chance acquaintance and for whom I feel nothing, and you find my anger irrational?"

"The Viscount Guillford is a fine man," Slayde refuted, hands clasped behind his back as if prepared to do battle. "He's honest and principled—I've done business with him for years and know that firsthand. He's also financially secure, well respected, even tempered, and generous, not to mention nice-looking and charming, as is evidenced by the number of women reputedly vying for his affections—and his name."

"I'm not most women."

A muscle flexed in Slayde's jaw. "I'm only too well aware of that. Nonetheless, the viscount is everything I just described and more. He's also—for some very fortunate and equally baffling reason—thoroughly smitten with you, even after a mere four or five meetings. In fact, according to him, he fell under your spell on his first visit to Pembourne. That was the time I was unavoidably detained for our business meeting and, to quote Guillford, you entertained him with your delightful company until I arrived."

"Entertained him? We chatted about White's and the finer points of whist. He made a gracious attempt to teach me to play. You were a quarter hour late. The moment you walked into the sitting room, I excused myself and left. That was the extent of the 'entertainment' I provided."

"Well, you must have made quite an impression. The viscount found you refreshing and lovely. Further, he's one of a select and rapidly diminishing few who remain unperturbed by the Huntley curse and by the scandal surrounding our age-old feud with the Bencrofts. When you consider the events of the past fortnight, that last factor could be the most significant of all Guillford's attributes. So, contrary to your protests, you are indeed going to marry him."

"But, Slayde . . ."

"No." Adamantly, Slayde sliced the air with his palm, silencing Aurora's oncoming plea. "My decision is final. The arrangements are under way. The subject is closed."

2

Aurora sucked in her breath, taken aback by the unyielding fervor of Slayde's decree. It had been months—last spring to be exact—since she'd seen that rigid, uncompromising expression on his face, felt that impenetrable wall of reserve loom up between them.

She'd thought the old Slayde gone forever—together with his obsessive hatred for the Bencrofts. That Slayde had vanished last May when he'd met and subsequently married Courtney Johnston who, with her quiet spirit and unwavering love, had permeated Slayde's heart, granting him peace with the past and hope for the future.

Until now, when all the wonder Courtney had effected was in danger of being shattered—and by the very man Slayde so loathed.

Lawrence Bencroft, the Duke of Morland.

Fury swelled inside Aurora as she contemplated the hell Morland had resurrected with his bloody investigation, his false accusations. Damn him for stirring up doubts that had, at long last, begun to subside. Damn him for casting aspersion on the Huntleys, then dying before he could be disproved.

Most of all, damn that bloody black diamond. Damn it *and* its heinous curse. For three generations it had haunted her family. Would they never escape its lethal grasp?

With a hard swallow, Aurora struggled to compose herself. "Slayde," she tried, reminding herself yet again that her brother's irrationality was founded in fear, not domination or cruelty. "I realize that the *ton's* focus has returned to the diamond with a vengeance since Morland's accusations and now his death. But . . ."

"The *ton?*" A predatory look flashed in Slayde's eyes. "Cease this nonsensical attempt to placate me, Aurora. You know bloody well I don't give a damn about the fashionable world or their gossip. What I *do* give a damn about are the three attempted burglaries, half-dozen extortion letters, and equally as many threats that have

3

besieged Pembourne over the past ten days. Evidently Morland's sudden demise, on the heels of commencing an investigation that—according to his *very* public announcement—would prove I was harboring the black diamond, has once again convinced numerous privateers and scoundrels, prompting them to act. Clearly they intend to ransack my home, threaten and browbeat me into producing the stone—a stone I've never seen and haven't the slightest clue where to find."

"But how can anyone invade Pembourne? You have guards posted everywhere."

Slayde scowled. "That offers reassurances, not guarantees. Aurora, I'm your guardian. I'm also your brother. That means I'm not only responsible for your safety, I'm committed to ensuring it. I won't see you harmed or vulnerable to attack."

"I'll take my chances."

"I won't." Slayde's tone was as uncompromising as his words. "I intend to see you safely wed, severed from the Huntley name for good."

Wincing, Aurora tried another tactic. "How does Courtney feel about your insistence that I marry the viscount?"

One dark brow rose. "I think you know the answer to that."

"She fought your decision."

"Like a tigress."

Despite her careening emotions, Aurora smiled. "Thank God."

"Don't bother. 'Tis a waste of time. You won't win this battle—not even with Courtney's help."

A knowing look. "Why not? She's not only my closest friend, she's your wife—*and* your greatest weakness. I have yet to see you refuse her anything."

"There's a first time for everything." Slayde inhaled sharply. "In any case, Courtney is not the issue here. You are."

"I beg to differ with you. Courtney *is* the issue here. As is your unborn child. How are you going to protect *them* from the curse?"

Pain flashed in Slayde's eyes. "With my life. I have no other means. I can't protect them, as I can you, by severing their ties to me. 'Tis too late for that. Courtney and I are bound in the most fundamental way possible— my babe is growing inside her. I cannot offer her freedom, a new life, even if I chose to. But with you—I can." Slowly he walked around his desk to face his sister. "There's no point in arguing, Aurora. I've already accepted Guillford's offer. You'll be married in a month." He paused, studying Aurora's clenched fists from beneath hooded lids. "I realize you're furious at me right now. I hope someday you'll understand. But whether or not you do, you're marrying Guillford. So I suggest you accustom yourself to the idea." Slayde's expression softened. "He adores you. He told me himself that he wants to give you the world. As for you, I know you enjoy his company. I've seen you smile, even laugh, in his presence."

"I behave similarly in the presence of Courtney's pup, Tyrant."

Another scowl. "You'll learn to love him."

Vehemently, Aurora shook her head. "No, Slayde, I won't."

She turned and marched out of the study.

"I spent all last night pleading your case."

Courtney Huntley, the very lovely, very pregnant Countess of Pembourne, sighed, shadows of fatigue etched beneath her sea green eyes. "He's adamant that this union take place."

"The whole idea is ludicrous." Aurora paced the length of her friend's bedchamber, her red-gold hair whipping about her shoulders. "Slayde of all people should realize that marriage must be founded on love, not reason. After all, that's why you two wed. My brother is so in love with you he can scarcely see straight. How can he want less for me?"

"He doesn't want less for you," Courtney defended at once. "I promise you, Aurora, if there were someone special in your life, someone you cared for, Slayde would refuse Lord Guillford's offer in a heartbeat."

"But since there isn't, I'm being forced to wed the most acceptable substitute?"

Courtney sighed. "I can't argue that Slayde's plan is a dreadful mistake. All I can do is explain that his worry for your welfare is eclipsing his reason. I've never seen him so distraught, not even when we first met. Since Morland died and speculation over the black diamond's whereabouts has escalated into a host of threats, it's as if he's been reliving years past. He's no more rational about me than he is about you. I'm not even permitted to stroll the gardens alone. Either he or one of the guards is perpetually glued to my side."

"Well, perhaps you're willing to accept it. I'm not."

A flicker of humor. "Willing? No. Resigned is a better choice of words." Tenderly, Courtney smoothed her palm over her swollen abdomen. "I'm a bit more unwieldy than I was a few months past—or hadn't you noticed? I suspect I wouldn't prove much of an adversary to the guards if I tried to outrun them."

Aurora didn't return her smile. "I can't marry Lord Guillford, Courtney," she whispered, coming to a halt. "I just can't."

Their gazes met.

"I'll talk to Slayde again," Courtney vowed. "Tonight. I'll think of something—Lord knows what, but I'll fight this betrothal with every emotional weapon I possess."

With a worried nod, Aurora looked away, contemplating her options.

Customarily Courtney's assurances would have been more than enough. But not this time.

Slayde had been too vehement, too single-minded, and there was too much at stake.

She'd have to ensure his cooperation on her own.

The manor was dark when Aurora slipped out the back door and through the trees. She'd mentally mapped out her route five times since the last of Pembourne's lamps had been doused, grateful she had a new escape route the guards had yet to discern.

That was because she'd only just discovered it.

She'd come upon the tiny path last week, by pure chance, while romping about with Tyrant. He'd raced off, thereby leading her to the small clearing. Curiously, she'd explored it, discovering with some surprise that the path wound its way to the southern tip of the estate. She'd stored that knowledge away by sheer force of habit, never expecting to use either the information or the route. Her perpetual attempts to escape the prison Pembourne represented had come to an end last spring, along with Courtney's arrival.

But today's decree called for drastic measures. And come hell or high water, she intended to take them.

Inching through the fine layer of snow that clung to the grass, Aurora made her way to the narrow section of trees behind the conservatory, then slipped through them, careful not to disturb the branches or make a sound. Although given the current circumstances she was sure none of the guards was concentrating on her whereabouts. First, because they were keeping vigil, looking out for intruders. And second, she thought with a grin, because her restlessness had so thoroughly vanished they'd become lax about keeping an eye on her. All the better.

Clearing the branches, Aurora's grin widened. The rear gates of Pembourne loomed just ahead. Beyond that, she knew, lay the dirt road which led to the village. Thus, the first part of her plan was complete.

She gathered up her skirts and sprinted forward.

Dawlish Tavern, as the pub's chipped sign identified it, was dark and smoky. Aurora's eyes watered the instant she entered, and she paused in the doorway, impatiently rubbing them as she tried to see.

Perfect, she thought a moment later. The occupants were definitely what her past governesses would have referred to as riffraff, clusters of ill-kempt men gathered about wooden tables laughing loudly as they tossed off tankards of ale and flung playing cards to the table.

The ideal spot to be ruined.

She didn't have much time. Already it was a quarter hour since she'd struck her deal with a local street urchin, having sent him on his way three pounds richer. First, as expected, he'd snatched up the one-pound note she'd offered in exchange for directions to the village's sole tavern. Then—also as anticipated—he'd pocketed the two additional pound notes, swiftly agreeing to deliver Aurora's missive to the Altec estate.

Aurora wasn't stupid. She was well aware the boy could simply bolt with her money, discarding her message before it had ever reached its destination and rendered its impact. She'd eliminated that possibility with her tantalizing promise of a five-pound note for the lad—*if* he returned to Dawlish Tavern with a written reply.

A chuckle rose in Aurora's throat, its sound drowned out by the tavern's raucous laughter. She could envision Lady Altec's face when the old biddy read the scandalous message from "a friend" revealing that Lady Aurora Huntley was consorting with sailors at a common pub. The elderly matron—Devonshire's biggest gossip— would probably jump into her phaeton and race down there posthaste, still clad in her nightrail, just to be an exclusive witness to the juicy scene.

Mentally, Aurora gauged her time. It would take the lad a solid half hour to travel to the dowager's estate, a few minutes to await a reply to the supposedly anonymous bearer of the tidings, then another half hour to return. That gave Aurora a little over an hour to find the right man to ruin her.

Abruptly she became aware that all activity in the room had stopped, and a dozen and a half pairs of eyes were fixed on her. She glanced down at herself and frowned. Despite her dust-covered gown and worn slippers, she still looked altogether too much like a lady. Well, her actions would soon disprove that notion.

"Wonderful—a full house," she pronounced, her tone shockingly familiar. "May I join you?" She gathered up her skirts and marched boldly over to a table.

The men stared from her to each other and back to her again.

"Lady, ye sure yer in the right place?" a stout, bald fellow inquired over the rim of his mug.

"That depends. If there's good ale and friendly company to be found here, then, yes, I'm in the right place."

More stares. Another gaping silence.

This wouldn't do at all, Aurora determined. How could she be ruined if no one would so much as speak to her?

"Would someone care to buy me a drink?" she asked, looking from one bristled face to another. "Never mind," she amended, realizing these men were undoubtedly poor, unable to squander funds on every woman who walked through the door. "I can pay my own way." So saying, she walked up to the counter, extracting a handful of shillings from her pocket and laying them on the counter. "Will this buy me a glass of ale?"

"A glass?" The tavern keeper cocked an amused brow. "Sweetheart, that'll keep your mug full till next week."

"I hope it doesn't take that long," Aurora muttered under her breath.

"What?"

"Nothing. May I have my drink now?"

"Sure." He filled a tankard and shoved it across the counter. "Let me or one of the girls know when you're ready for more. You've paid for dozens of rounds."

"Girls?" That was a problem Aurora hadn't anticipated. She turned, scanning the room again, this time noticing two or three barmaids making their way among the tables, trays in hand, broad smiles on their faces. Scowling, she noted the way the men were laughing and joking with them in a familiar manner they'd definitely not afforded her. A problem indeed. Still, there were only a few women as compared with a roomful of men. Surely one of those men wouldn't mind feigning a night of passion rather than pursuing a real one—especially if it meant earning money rather than parting with it?

That gave her an idea.

"Did you say I've paid for dozens of rounds?" she asked the tavern keeper.

"Um-hum. At least."

"Good. Then distribute them among the men."

Another startled look. "All right. Should I say who they're from?"

"Of course. Say they're a gift from . . ." A pause. ". . . The newcomer amongst them."

"Does this newcomer have a name?"

Not one she can provide, Aurora alerted herself silently. *At least not yet. Once these sailors learn I'm a Huntley, they'll run for their lives. And if that should happen before I convince one of them to stage my ruin, all my plans will have been for naught.*

"Rory," she supplied, reverting to the pet name her dearest friend, Mr. Scollard, had bestowed upon her years ago.

"Rory," the tavern keeper repeated. "All right, Rory. I'm George. And I'll fill the men in on your generosity."

"Thank you." With a brilliant smile, Aurora perched

on a nearby stool, openly surveying the pub and its occupants. Sailors and fishermen, she thought with great satisfaction. Just as she'd surmised. Ranging in age from young to old, and in stature from large to scrawny. Which of them would be the one to serve as her necessary cohort?

That spawned another concern.

"George—you do have rooms here, do you not?" she questioned anxiously.

His jaw dropped. "Yeah, I have rooms."

"Good." Sagging with relief, she took two enthusiastic swallows of ale . . . and shuddered. How could anything so golden and frothy taste so horrid? Steeling herself, she gulped down the remaining brew, suppressing her distaste to appear as nonchalant as possible. She *must* fit in if she wanted to elicit the assistance of one of these sailors.

"Fill everyone's mug," she heard George call to his barmaids. "Courtesy of . . ." A broad grin. ". . . Rory." He gestured toward Aurora, who raised her tankard in tribute.

A chorus of enthusiastic thanks ensued, and Aurora congratulated herself on her victory, dutifully guzzling down the second glass of ale George poured her. Actually, she mused, the brew didn't taste quite as bad as she'd originally thought. In fact, with enough patience the flavor rather grew on you.

"I'll have another," she informed George, holding out her mug. Blowing wisps of hair from her face, she shifted on the stool. "Is it warm in here?"

He chuckled, refilling her tankard. "Yeah, and it's gonna get a lot warmer if you don't slow down. Take it easy, Rory—this stuff's strong."

"I loathed the flavor at first," she confessed in a conspiratorial whisper. "But no longer. Now I'm enjoying it thoroughly."

"I can see that." George shook his head and resumed polishing the glasses. "What made you come in here?" he asked offhandedly.

"Oh, dear." Aurora rose, clutching her mug. "Thank you for reminding me. I have an end to achieve. And very little time to achieve it." Teetering a bit, she made her way over to the table of the nice bald fellow who'd addressed her earlier. He looked like the kindly sort. Perhaps he'd understand her dilemma—*and* her monetary offer—and agree to help her out.

She dropped into a seat beside him.

"'ey, Jackson," one of the sailors at the table prompted the bald fellow. "I think our new patron is waitin' for ye."

Jackson turned toward her and grinned. "Did ye want something . . . Rory?"

Self-consciously she chewed her lip. How could she blurt out her proposition in front of all these men, without any preliminaries?

She couldn't.

Her gaze fell to the cards in Jackson's hands. Whist, she concluded. They were playing whist. Now *that* was something she could chat about, thus breaking the ice enough for her to ease into her request.

Purposefully she gulped her ale, her stare fixed on Jackson's cards. "I have a bit of experience at this, you know," she announced. "Although, if I must be honest, I've only received instruction from one man, and only upon one occasion. However, I enjoyed it immensely and was a quick study. Given time, I'm sure I could be quite proficient."

Jackson's cards struck the table. "Brazen little thing, aren't ye?" he said, an odd light coming into his eyes. "Well, I've got lots of time. I can teach ye anything ye want to know."

"If ye don't fall asleep first," his whist partner retorted, slapping down his own cards. "If Rory wants instruction, *I'm* the one to give it. *If* 'er price ain't too high."

"Price?" Aurora questioned, lowering her tankard and wishing the room would stop spinning. *"You'd* be doing the teaching—why would I ask for a fee?" She shook her head to clear it. "Besides, I can't learn tonight. Tonight I need to . . ."

"Sure ye can!" a stocky man at the next table chimed in, striding over to her. "Yer a woman after me own 'eart, cravin' excitement, not shillings."

"What the hell would she want money for?" Jackson mocked. "She's got plenty. She paid for our drinks, didn't she? And 'er gown cost more than this whole bloody pub." He rose as well. "No, ye 'eard 'er, it's experience she's lookin' for." He glared at the others, his fingers closing about Aurora's arm. "And it's me she came to. C'mon, sweetheart. Let's go up."

Realization crashed down on Aurora with the force of a blow. These men thought she'd been alluding to her sexual proficiency, not her adeptness at whist. They were actually arguing over who was going to take her to bed.

Dear Lord, what had she gotten herself into?

"Please . . . wait," she began, determined to clarify her intentions *before* Jackson escorted her up to a liaison that was never going to occur. Yes, she wanted to go upstairs, but not for the purpose he had in mind.

"Mr. Jackson . . ." She struggled to speak coherently despite the fog shrouding her thoughts. "You don't understand."

"Oh, I understand, all right." He continued to drag her along. "And I'll make ye forget all about that clumsy man who had ye first."

"Let her go, Jackson."

The deep baritone permeated Aurora's disoriented state, simultaneously stopping Jackson dead in his tracks. An instant later a strong arm anchored her waist, dragging her away from Jackson and supporting her unsteady weight.

"C'mon, Merlin, don't ye 'ave enough women?" Jackson whined. "Leave this morsel for me."

"This 'morsel' isn't ready for the teaching you have in mind," the baritone shot back.

"She's sure as hell not ready for you."

"No, she's not. But at least I have the good sense to know it." He shifted, hauling Aurora against his side and heading away from the table.

"Merlin?" Aurora twisted about to assess her rescuer and ask about his unusual name. She was confronted by a broad chest and towering height, which she followed upward to hard masculine features set off by probing eyes the color of topaz, blazing through her like twin bolts of lightning.

Her own twisting motion spawned a surge of dizziness—one that made her stomach lurch with alarming intensity. "I don't feel very well."

"I'm sure you don't." Abandoning all attempts at subtlety, the man named Merlin swung her off her feet and into his arms. "Three rounds of ale—drunk in rapid succession—would make *me* a bit light-headed, and I suspect I'm a far more seasoned drinker than you are." His forward motion ceased, and Aurora squeezed her eyes shut in an attempt to stop the ceiling from shifting.

"George, which room's empty?" Merlin's voice rumbled against her ear.

"Take number four—second down on your left," the tavern keeper responded.

"Thanks. Send up coffee. A lot of it."

He was moving again, ascending a staircase, Aurora's unsettled stomach informed her.

Good-natured teasing followed in their wake.

"'ey, Merlin, let us know 'ow she is!"

"Yeah, and if she's as quick a study as she claims, we'll all 'elp teach 'er!"

The man carrying her swore quietly under his breath, shoving open a door and striding inside.

Aurora winced as the door slammed shut behind them. "Too loud," she muttered.

"Get used to it. Everything is going to sound loud until that coffee does its job. Do you need a chamber pot?"

"No. I'm never sick."

"Really? And how often are you foxed?" With that he deposited her on the bed.

"Never. I . . ." Startled, Aurora looked about, her retort dying on her lips as the significance of what she'd inadvertently accomplished registered in her cloudy mind. A room. Complete with a bed. And a man—one who seemed rational enough to listen rather than to immediately ravage her.

Instantly her stomach calmed.

"Perfect," she declared, congratulating herself for achieving precisely what she'd intended, when a moment earlier it had seemed as if her entire plan was about to explode in her face.

How much time did she have?

Squinting, she tried to focus on the clock on the mantel. "What time is it?"

"Half after ten. What the hell do you mean, 'perfect?' Perfect for what? What did you think you were doing down there just now?"

She sighed, lifting the cool pillow and pressing her cheek against it to still the throbbing in her head. "Staging my own ruin. At least what others would assume to be my ruin. Although, had you not come along, I fear my downfall would have been fact rather than fabrication. For which I'm extraordinarily grateful." She massaged her temples. "The situation was looking quite grim. Now, thanks to your intervention my scheme will succeed. Any moment now."

Aurora watched as Merlin pulled a chair alongside the bed and straddled it. He was sinfully handsome, she noted. *That* was an indisputable fact—foxed though she might be. True, his good looks weren't the classic kind Lord Guillford had, nor even the chiseled kind Slayde boasted. Rather, Merlin was handsome in a darkly alluring way that hinted at danger, open seas, freedom, and adventure—the kind of life she yearned for and couldn't begin to fathom. His powerful build, clad in an open-necked shirt and breeches, defied convention; his black hair, rumpled and longer than fashion dictated, swept his forehead in harsh, rebellious lines. His eyes, those fiery chips of topaz, were turbulent, alive, exciting. He looked like a pagan god—wicked, seductive—ideal for convincing the *ton* that she was in fact a fallen woman.

"Merlin," she murmured. "How unusual. Is it your given name or your surname?"

"Neither. 'Tis an acquired name."

"Ah. Then you're as brilliant as Arthur's advisor?"

"No. I'm as formidable as a falcon."

"The merlin?" Aurora inclined her head, puzzled. "But he's one of the smallest falcons. And 'small' is hardly a term I'd use to describe you."

"Agreed. But the merlin is also swift, unerring, and deceptively nonthreatening. All of which describe me perfectly." With that, Merlin leaned forward. "You said you were staging your own ruin. Or what others would assume to be your ruin. Why? Or should I say, for whom?"

"For the benefit of a kind, charming, and incredibly conventional man," she supplied. "However, that needn't concern you. All you need to do is sit there. Well, perhaps not just sit there." Frowning, Aurora tossed masses of tumbled hair from her face. "I suppose the two of us should look a bit more compromising than two friends sharing coffee. Perhaps an embrace? Not until the dowager arrives, of course. Until then we can just chat. In any case, I'll pay you handsomely for what will amount to no more than an hour's work."

One dark brow rose. "Pay me? For staging your ruin?"

"Exactly."

"How much?"

Aurora propped herself on one elbow, groping in her pocket. "A hundred pounds."

"A hundred pounds?" he repeated.

She heard the incredulous note in his voice and interpreted it as scoffing. Swiftly she reacted, reaching out and gripping his wrist to stay his flight. "Please don't go. I originally intended to offer two hundred pounds. But the remaining funds were in my brother's study. And I couldn't snatch them without being spied." She searched Merlin's face. "I'll owe you the other hundred pounds. I'm honest; I promise you that. We'll arrange a time and place to meet, at which time I'll pay you the rest. Only please—don't leave."

His gaze fell to her fingers, although he made no move to pry them from his wrist. "Two hundred pounds—a lavish sum. Tell me, Rory, who is this man for whom you want to be ruined?"

"My prospective husband. You see, I'm being forced to marry him. The only way I can free myself from the betrothal is to compromise myself."

Merlin's lips twitched. "I take it your conventional groom-to-be expects an untouched bride?"

"Absolutely."

"And I also assume that to complete this facade you've arranged for us to be discovered?" He awaited Aurora's nod. "By whom? Your father or the bridegroom himself?"

"Neither. By the biggest gossip in Devonshire. In fact . . ."

Aurora was interrupted by a knock.

"Is that she?" Merlin inquired, calmly remaining in his seat.

"No. 'Tis too soon."

"Then it's probably our coffee." He rose. "I'll get it. You're in no shape to stand up, much less walk." He crossed over and opened the door.

"Your refreshment," one of the barmaids announced, smiling at Merlin as she carried in a tray, placed it on the table. Seeing Aurora, she reached into her bodice and extracted a folded sheet. "There's an urchin downstairs who insists I give this message to the red-haired lady in the fancy gown. I assume he means you. If so, he says you owe him five pounds."

Unsteadily Aurora reached for the folded sheet. Smoothing it out, she forced her attention on the words.

Dear 'friend': it read. *Thank you for the tidbit. I'll look into it at once. Lady Altec.*

"Splendid!" Aurora nearly toppled from the bed. Resettling herself, she dug in her pocket and extracted two five-pound notes. "I'm grateful to you—and the lad. Please see that he gets one of these. The other is yours."

"Thank you." The barmaid's words were for Aurora, but her gaze was on Merlin. "Will there be anything else?"

"Not tonight, Bess," he replied.

"If you should think of something . . . ."

"I'll summon you at once," he assured her, holding open the door. "But for now, good night."

"Good night." With another wistful look, she was gone.

The instant the door closed behind her, Merlin turned back to Aurora. "Does the arrival of that note mean the 'biggest gossip in Devonshire' is on her way?"

A nod.

"Then the coffee can wait. First, we'd best discuss that compromising position you mentioned." He walked over, bypassing the chair and sinking down on the bed beside her.

A quiver—was it of warning or excitement?—ran up Aurora's spine. "Very well."

He leaned closer, studying her features as one would assess a fine painting prior to purchasing it. "You're a very beautiful woman."

How did one respond to so blatant a compliment? Aurora mused. Especially when one's dealings with men were as limited—as nonexistent—as hers?

Her silence spawned a flicker of curiosity in Merlin's eyes, tiny golden flames against burnished topaz. "Let me ask you something, Rory. Do you understand what was going to happen after Jackson whisked you upstairs?"

"What he *intended* to happen," Aurora corrected. "And of course I do. I might be foxed, but I'm not stupid."

Merlin's lips twitched. "I didn't mean to suggest that you were. I was merely trying to assess the degree of your naîveté."

"I'm not naive."

"No? Then how did you plan to extricate yourself from Jackson's *intentions?*"

A twinkle. "I'm a very resourceful woman, foxed or not. I'm also an expert at eluding those I choose to elude. *Should* Mr. Jackson have managed to drag me upstairs, and *should* he have been unwilling to listen to reason, I would have found the means to escape. I always do."

One dark brow shot up. "How intriguing. Are you often in situations where you need to elude men?"

"Constantly. Other than now."

"Why not now?"

She gave him a beatific smile. "Because I never attempt to elude my allies."

An answering smile tugged at his lips. "How do you

know I'm an ally? What if my motives are as untrustworthy as Jackson's? What if I decide to take advantage of your offer *and* our privacy by making your ruin an actuality rather than a performance?"

"You won't."

"What makes you so certain?"

"The fact that you want my two hundred pounds."

Merlin threw back his head and laughed. "Touché. It's rare that I'm bested, especially by a woman who's beside me in bed and too deep in her cups to walk away."

"Should I be flattered?"

Abruptly his laughter faded, supplanted by a quiet intensity that seemed to permeate the room. "I don't know," he replied, his gaze delving deep into hers. "You tell me." Even as he spoke, he shook his head, supplying the answer to his own question. "No. You shouldn't be. In fact, I'm beginning to think I'm the one who should be flattered. This arrangement of ours grows more appealing by the minute."

Heated silence.

"I think the effects of the ale are wearing off," Aurora noted aloud.

Merlin's knuckles grazed her cheek. "Good."

With a shiver of anticipation, Aurora realized she was in over her head. Merlin's presence was too overpowering, the atmosphere about them too intimate. She felt vulnerable in a way she hadn't until now—not even when Jackson was dragging her upstairs. And she hadn't a clue how to extricate herself, not when Merlin's warm fingers were drifting over her face.

"I didn't see you in the tavern prior to your rescuing me," she murmured.

"I was in the rear watching your performance." He traced the bridge of her nose. "It was fascinating."

"I felt like a fool," she confessed. "But I'd do anything to stop this betrothal from happening."

His fingers paused. "Is this prospective husband so untenable, then?"

"No. Quite the contrary. The viscount is a fine man. But he's just not . . . not . . ."

"Not exciting? Not challenging? Not the kind of man who would find your actions tonight amusing?"

"Exactly."

"The viscount, you said. Are you, too, of noble birth?"

Aurora hesitated. "Yes, but my family is not the kind to call people out—in fact, they'd do just about anything to keep our name free of public scrutiny. So don't be deterred."

"A family after my own heart." Merlin's palm slid beneath her heavy mane, savoring its silken texture. "And it would take far more than the peerage to deter me." He sifted red-gold strands between his fingers. "Your hair is exquisite. Like a flaming waterfall."

"I . . . thank you."

Shrewdly he assessed her. "You have no experience at all with men—except, of course, for eluding them—have you?"

"Will you bolt if I say no? Because if so, I'll try to lie. Although I must confess, I'm not very good at it." She awaited his reply, wishing her wits had returned along with her sobriety.

"No, I won't bolt, and no, you needn't lie. I suspected you were an innocent the moment you began your charade. And I assure you, you'll go home as untouched as when you arrived." A hint of a pause. "Well, nearly."

"Is the two hundred pounds acceptable, then?"

"Um-hum." He lowered his head, brushed his lips across each of her cheekbones. "Is this what you had in mind when you referred to a compromising position?" he murmured.

"I think so, yes." Aurora's breath suspended in her throat, and the warm glow of the ale melded into a hotter, more compelling heat. "Are you a sailor?" she whispered.

"Only during those times when I'm en route to my destination."

"Which is where?"

His mouth traced the curve of her jaw, nibbled lightly at her chin. "Many places. The world is vast, filled with opportunities. I simply wait—then seize them."

"You've traveled?" Aurora's eyes drifted shut and she clutched the bedding as the swimming in her head intensified.

"For years." He framed her face between his palms, and she could feel the warmth of his breath against her lips. "Do you think a kiss would be compromising enough?"

"I imagine it would be ideal." Was that the lingering effect of the ale talking?

"Shall we find out? Because if we're unable to be convincing, we'd best discover that fact now—before the dowager arrives."

"I suspect you're right." No, that was *she* talking.

Aurora was still reeling over her own audacity when Merlin's mouth closed over hers.

God help her, was this a kiss?

Shards of pleasure screamed through her in hot, jagged streaks, the simple joining of their lips igniting sparks too erotic to bear, too exquisite to abandon. Merlin felt it, too, for she heard his indrawn breath, felt him stiffen with reaction, shudder as the unexpected current of excitement ran between them. Then he angled her face closer, kissed her again—this time more deeply—and Aurora was dragged into an explosive inferno of sensation, one she'd never imagined, much less experienced. Flames leapt from Merlin's lips to hers and back again, and the kiss took on a life of its own, their mouths meeting, parting, only to meet again.

His tongue delved inside, finding and claiming hers, then taking it in deep, heated strokes that made everything inside Aurora melt, slide down to her toes.

She responded on instinct, immersing herself in the magic, her hands gliding up to his shoulders, clutching the warmth of his shirt. He raised her arms, twined them about his neck, and lifted her against him, sealing their lips in a bottomless, drugging, intimate kiss, penetrating her mouth again and again until the very room seemed to vanish, until nothing existed but the torrent of sensation blazing between them.

Neither of them heard the commotion below. Nor were they aware of the sound of pounding footsteps ascending the stairs. Thus, when the door to their room burst open and an unexpected audience swelled on the threshold, they both started, pulling apart to stare dazedly at the intrusion.

A gasp rose in Aurora's throat as Slayde strode into the room, nearly shoving George, a half-dozen sailors, and a sputtering Lady Altec from his path.

"Aurora, what in the name of . . ." His words died on his lips as he spied Merlin, and Aurora would never forget the look of naked pain, of stark disbelief on her brother's face. "You?" he bit out. "Of all the men on earth, *you?*" Stalking over, Slayde dragged Merlin from the bed, his rage a palpable entity Aurora could feel. "You filthy bastard, not even your father would have stooped this low." His fist shot out, connecting with Merlin's jaw. "Did it give you pleasure to ruin an innocent young woman? To destroy her life simply because she's a Huntley?"

On the verge of striking back, Merlin stopped dead, outrage supplanted by shock. "Huntley?" His stunned gaze shifted to Aurora, raking her from head to toe as if seeing her for the first time. "You're Aurora Huntley?"

An ominous knot formed in Aurora's stomach. "Should I know you?"

With a harsh laugh, Slayde reached over, yanking Aurora to her feet. "Didn't he introduce himself before he took you to bed? No? Then allow me. Aurora, meet the man you nearly forfeited your innocence to: Julian Bencroft, the newly ascended Duke of Morland."

Chapter 2

Six long years.

Julian stood in the center of Morland's expansive library, hands clasped behind his back as he surveyed the formidable room. He saw beyond the oriental rug and mahogany bookshelves, beyond the high walls and gilded ceiling. What he saw were memories: ugly, indelible memories.

He'd nearly forgotten how much he despised this estate.

How many bitter arguments had he and his father engaged in within these very library walls? How many accusations had been fired between them before Julian had stormed off for good?

More than he could count, still more than he chose to remember.

Wearily Julian massaged his temples, then walked over to pour himself a drink.

His father had loathed the very sight of him.

That was fact, not supposition. Heaven only knew how many times Lawrence had bellowed his outrage, his shame, his censure . . . his remorse that it had been Hugh, not Julian, who'd been taken from him.

The last alone had hurt. Not because Julian gave a damn at being the object of his father's hatred, but because any mention of Hugh brought with it an acute sense of pain and loss. Julian had cared deeply for his kind, gentle older brother, an affection Hugh had reciprocated despite the fact that although separated in age by merely a year, their interests, aspirations—their very natures—had been as different as day and night. So far as Julian was concerned, Hugh had been his only family. When he'd died of a fever during his first term at Oxford, Julian's roots had died with him.

Still, Hugh had been the one thing Julian and his father agreed upon: more specifically, Hugh's suitability as the heir apparent. He would have made a fine duke, fine in a way that Lawrence, with his unprincipled, uncompromising values, couldn't begin to fathom. Hugh's qualities—compassion, decency, fair-mindedness—were the *true* foundations of nobility.

Julian's goblet struck the sideboard with a thud. What the hell was he reminiscing about? Further, why had he come back—not only to Devonshire, but to Morland?

The answer was laughable.

He'd come back to pay his final respects to a man who'd denounced him and was probably rolling over in his grave at the fact that Julian was the last remaining Bencroft *and* the sole heir to his precious title. A man who regarded Julian as lower than dirt and little better than a Huntley.

A Huntley.

As a result of last night's disaster, that name conjured up an entirely new image—or rather, an entirely new Huntley. An image that included a swarm of curious onlookers exploding into his room at Dawlish's as he received an unexpected blow from the Earl of Pembourne . . . and a beautiful, candid, and incredibly exciting woman who'd set his blood on fire and then turned out to be none other than Aurora Huntley.

What had begun as an enchanting diversion had disintegrated into a nightmare worth forgetting.

Except that Julian couldn't shake the memory of Aurora's shocked, pained expression when her brother had revealed the identity of the man in whose arms she'd been caught. Nor the way she'd turned to look at him— not with hatred, nor with accusation, but with bewilderment, as if she couldn't fathom how all this had happened. Her vivid turquoise eyes had searched his face, lingering on his mouth, and Julian had read the conflict in that transparent gaze as clearly as if she'd spoken it aloud: Why hadn't she somehow known who he was? How had a plan she'd devised simply to extricate herself from an unwanted betrothal turned out to be the biggest scandal of her life, hurting not only herself but her entire family? Worst of all, how could she have reveled in the moments she'd just spent in Julian Bencroft's arms?

There wasn't a damned thing he could do about it. No apology could undo the damage that had been done, nor could a thousand avowals that nothing had happened, that they'd each been unaware of the other's identity, restore all Aurora had lost. Not that her brother would have listened anyway. After delivering his solitary blow to Julian's jaw, Pembourne had grabbed Aurora's arm and whisked her out of the tavern in less than a minute. Julian had followed shortly thereafter, having no intentions of fueling the fire by answering any of the aged dowager's rapidly fired questions or the sailors' bawdy comments.

Still, he felt guilty. Aurora had come to Dawlish's to free herself of a betrothal, ready to sacrifice her reputation in the process. Well, she'd certainly succeeded. Doubtless the intended bridegroom—whoever this oh-so-proper viscount might be—would cry off the instant he learned of his future wife's scandalous behavior. At which point Aurora would have what she sought.

But at what price?

"Forgive me, sir." Thayer, the longstanding Morland butler, knocked on the library door, interrupting Julian's thoughts. "You told me to advise you when Mr. Camden arrived. He's here and waiting. Shall I show him in?"

Slowly Julian turned, wondering—as he had so many times in the past—if Thayer ever changed expressions or lowered his nose even a fraction. "Yes, Thayer. Show him in."

"Very good, sir." Thayer disappeared, returning shortly with a tall elderly man who clutched a thick, official-looking portfolio. "Can I get either of you gentlemen anything?" the butler inquired.

"No. That will be all for now, Thayer."

"Very good, sir." He withdrew, shutting the door behind him.

The older man inclined his gray head, studying Julian with equal measures of deliberation and concern. "Hello, Julian," he said at last. "I'm relieved to see you've returned. Not only to England, but to Morland. It's been years since I've seen you standing within these walls."

Julian shot a pointed look at the family solicitor. "Don't become too accustomed to it, Henry. I don't intend to stay. After we complete today's business, we'll resume our routine practice of meeting in your office."

"When you're in England," Camden clarified.

"When I'm in England," Julian agreed, gesturing toward the sofa. "Have a seat. What can I offer you?"

"Whatever you're having would be fine." Camden lowered himself to the sofa and watched Julian pour a second healthy ration of brandy. "You arrived in Devonshire yesterday?"

"Yes. I left Malta within an hour of receiving your missive. Thank you for notifying me so quickly."

"Had I been certain of your whereabouts, I might have reached you sooner, giving you ample time to arrive home for the funeral. As it was, I could only guess based upon your last correspondence."

Stiffly Julian handed Camden his drink. "It wasn't essential that I attend the funeral. As for finding me, I never know where I'll be from one moment to the next. Trust me, Henry, you're more closely apprised than anyone of my whereabouts. Including myself, half the time."

"You're looking well," the solicitor noted.

"As are you. I trust your business is thriving as always?"

"Thankfully, yes. I can't complain. And you? How have your recent . . . adventures been?"

A corner of Julian's mouth lifted. "I'm not a pirate, Henry. All my business dealings are completely legal, if not orthodox. In any case, you needn't be afraid to mention them. And, to answer your question, my adventures have been quite lucrative."

"Good. I'll expect my ledgers to reflect that fact, then."

"And so they shall."

Self-consciously the elderly solicitor cleared his throat, obviously wrestling with his next choice of words. "Getting back to the reason you've returned to Morland, I'd feel remiss if I didn't offer you my condolences on your father's death—inappropriate as that might sound, given that I, better than most, know the differences that divided the two of you. Still, Lawrence was your father. Therefore, for whatever it's worth, my prayers are with you."

Julian traced the rim of his goblet. "You always were an incredibly gracious man, Henry—not to mention decent and honest. Why in the name of heaven you chose to work for my father, I'll never understand. Nevertheless I thank you for your kind words."

"My family has served yours for nearly seventy-five years, Julian, beginning with my grandfather and then my father before me. There was never a question as to whether I would continue in that tradition. Still, I won't deny there were subjects upon which your father and I strongly disagreed, most particularly those pertaining to the Huntleys and Lawrence's obsession with vengeance. Nonetheless I remained committed to serving him as honorably as I could. However," Camden added with a meaningful look, "that didn't include compromising my principles to accommodate him—even if asked."

"I understand," Julian replied, feeling a surge of admiration for Camden's integrity and candor. "What's more, I commend you." With that, he leaned forward. "Now, can we get to the purpose of this visit? I asked you to meet me here because I'd like to discuss the best way to go about selling this estate and putting the past where it belongs—behind us."

Camden frowned, opening his cumbersome portfolio and reaching in to extract a sealed document. "Before we do that, there's another matter we must see to first."

"Which is?"

"The reading of your father's will. Now that you've returned from abroad, 'tis time to address it. 'Tis also possible that hearing Lawrence's provisos could alter your plans."

"Really?" Julian felt more amused than worried. "Why? Did he decide to leave Morland Manor to some local urchins rather than to me?"

"Of course not. The estate, its furnishings, and whatever funds your father amassed are yours."

All humor vanished. "I don't want his money."

"Julian, please." The solicitor unsealed and unfolded the document. "I'm asking only for a few minutes of your time."

"I apologize, Henry. Go ahead."

"The majority of the will is standard, enumerating

precisely what I've just said. Thus, I'll skip down to the final clause. 'Julian,' it reads, 'unless, unbeknownst to me, your adventures have included the siring of heirs, you are now the last remaining Bencroft. This brings me no comfort. Like your great-grandfather before you, your hunger for parts unknown has induced you to forsake your responsibilities. Doubtless, within months of my death, the estate will be disposed of, the title gone, and the Bencroft name resting solely on your unreliable shoulders. For the title and estate, I realize you feel only disdain. But for the family name, the name that belonged to your brother Hubert and to the great-grandfather you so closely emulate, I allow myself to speculate otherwise. If I'm wrong, if you care not a whit if the Bencroft name remains sullied, disregard sentiment and view my forthcoming request as a challenge—the one thing other than money that propels a heedless mercenary like yourself. Either way, my request is as follows: Find and return the black diamond. End the curse. Clear the Bencroft name. Not for me. Not even for you. For Hubert. For his memory. Surely that is but a paltry task for a seasoned adventurer like yourself? Prove yourself, Julian. *That* is my request—no, my legacy—to you.'" Camden looked up. "The will was properly executed and witnessed in my office last spring."

With a muffled curse Julian rose, walking over to gaze out the window. For long moments he said nothing, merely clutched his goblet and grappled with his father's words, with their ultimate impact. At last he turned. "Is that it?"

The solicitor lowered the pages to the table. "With respect to your father, yes. Other than to inform you that he began another comprehensive search for the black diamond during the final months of his life."

"Did he keep records on this search?"

"He did."

"Then I'll need to see them."

Slowly Camden nodded. "You'll find them in his study. In the top drawer of his desk. That's where Lawrence kept all his important papers." He extracted a key. "This will open it."

Julian stared at the key as if it were a loathsome insect. "Fine. Leave it on the table."

"You're not obligated to fulfill your father's request," Camden reminded him, placing the key on the small end table beside him.

"'Request'?" Julian tossed off his brandy. "That wasn't a request, Henry, it was blackmail."

"Then why are you complying? Certainly not to unearth the stone—you've always expressed utter disdain for the diamond and all who seek it."

"I'm complying for Hugh. I'm complying because everything my father enumerated in that clause is true—about my priorities, about the ramifications of my being the last living Bencroft, about the debt I owe my ancestors." A bitter laugh. "My father might have been a coldhearted bastard but he wasn't stupid. He knew precisely where to find my Achilles' heel. And find it he did." Julian frowned, glancing restlessly about. "Clearly I'll need access to this mausoleum in order to amass his papers. Therefore, we'll have to defer our discussion about selling it—for a few months—until I've fulfilled the terms of my father's so-called legacy."

"You're confident you'll find the stone."

"I don't fail."

"Dozens of others have."

"I'm not others."

The elderly solicitor's lips twitched. "I would agree. In fact, when I compare my understanding of you with the stories passed down to me about your great-grandfather, I'd venture to say the two of you are a great deal alike. According to my family's reports, Geoffrey Bencroft was quite a colorful character."

"So I've heard."

"He never could resist a challenge. Can you?"

Julian arched a sardonic brow. "Evidently not."

"That's precisely what I wanted to hear—more than enough to ensure a decision I made long years ago." So saying, Camden extracted another sealed document from his portfolio, together with a small ornate chest— plainly the cause for the portfolio's weighted bulk—and a corresponding key.

"What is that?" Julian asked, his curiosity instantly roused.

"A strongbox. One whose contents have until now remained a mystery, even to me."

"I don't understand."

"You will." Camden tore open the envelope and extracted a single sheet of paper. "This document, witnessed by my father, was carefully locked in our office safe, together with the strongbox, sixty years ago. In order to properly carry out the terms specified herein, I was verbally apprised of what they were, although the document itself has remained unopened until this very day. Once I've read it to you, you'll understand why that is."

"I'm thoroughly intrigued," Julian murmured, his expression intent. "What does this mysterious document say?"

"It reads as follows. 'If you're hearing these words, then George Camden—or whichever of his descendants is currently handling the Bencroft legal matters—has deemed you worthy. I granted the Camdens the right to make this determination because I trust them, and because I realize I will no longer be alive to personally select the right man to inherit my most valuable asset: my heritage. My only son, Chilton, is thoroughly unacceptable. He has no heart, no insight, and no exceptional talents other than ruthlessness. If this document is being read aloud, then my prayers have been answered and the

Bencrofts can at long last boast a duke whose adventurous spirit and unwavering commitment—albeit to rules of his own making—match my own. But spirit and commitment are not enough. You must also possess instinct and cunning, both of which are as inborn as spirit. Therefore, I put to you this test. Before you lies a chest whose contents are known only to me. They are the link to your past—worthless to most, not so to one such as yourself. Camden will give you the key. 'Tis your task to open the box. Do so and the gates to your ancestry will open. Fail and they'll remain closed, lying in wait for an adventurer and a duke yet to be.'" Camden paused. "The document is signed Geoffrey Bencroft, 6th August, 1758."

"Fascinating." With each passing moment Julian had grown more absorbed. Now, he leaned forward, his gaze fixed on the chest. "Why would opening the box prove difficult?"

"Perhaps because there's no visible keyhole." Camden offered Julian both the box and the requisite key. "I studied the chest throughout my entire carriage ride to Morland. If there's a slot to be found, I certainly can't see it."

"Which leaves one of two possibilities. Either whoever crafted the chest chose to keep the slot concealed or the chest must be opened by some means other than a key." Julian examined the heavy box, exploring the domed lid, flat base, and gold plating that embellished the front and sides. "Iron," he deduced, rapping his knuckles along the surface. "Many layers thick." He glanced at the key, eyes narrowed in thought. "The key and the chest match perfectly, right down to their gilded trim. I doubt anyone would go to the trouble of constructing the two together just to render the key useless, especially since, according to my great-grandfather, the contents of this box would be valueless to most. So I'll abandon my latter theory in favor of the former, and assume the key does in fact open the chest. Now for the key. It's short and its notches are slender. The only way it could penetrate the box is if the spot concealing the keyhole were constructed of a thinner iron than that which comprises the remainder of the chest. And since I can't find any discernable thinning of the metal . . ." He frowned, running his fingers around the edges of the ornate trim.

"Yes?" Camden prompted.

"Then the means by which to open this chest is hidden beneath this decorative plate somewhere, doubtless under a particularly thick section that could hide the thinner iron beneath it." Again Julian assessed the box, his gaze lingering over each segment of trim. "Look at this," he noted aloud. "There are four engraved knobs, one on each corner of the chest. The lower two are definitely more substantial than the uppers. Let's try those." So saying, he gripped first the left then the right knob, exerting gentle pressure on each.

The left knob yielded no results.

The right one, however, seemed to give the tiniest bit, easing ever so slightly to one side.

It was enough to convince Julian he'd found what he sought.

Intensifying the pressure, he urged the knob over, sliding it away until the spot it had concealed was visible.

A slim keyhole met his gaze.

"Splendid," Camden breathed, shaking his head in wonder.

"Not yet," Julian corrected. "Not until we're sure of our success." He fitted the key into its slot and turned, waiting until he heard a click. Then he attempted to lift the strongbox lid.

It rose without protest.

"Now we're sure," Julian proclaimed, anticipation swelling inside him like a great untamed wave.

Abruptly Camden came to his feet.

"Henry?" Julian's head shot up. "Where are you going?"

"Home. Geoffrey's instructions were that the recipient of this box review the contents privately." Another amazed shake of the head. "You are astounding, Julian. Everything your great-grandfather hoped for and more."

Julian stood, his stare still fixed on the strongbox. "I'll contact you soon."

"No hurry." Camden gathered up the portfolio, keeping his gaze carefully averted from the strongbox. "I'll show myself out. Good luck, Julian."

Alone in the library, Julian locked the door, then returned to his seat . . . and the chest.

There were two items within: a gleaming dagger that boasted an ornately carved handle with the likeness of a fox upon it, and an old worn journal. With but a cursory glance at the dagger, Julian took up the journal and began to read.

An hour later, he lowered the book to the table, his mind racing with all he'd just learned. With newfound respect, he picked up the dagger, examining it at close range, marveling at what it represented.

The implications were staggering.

And they involved more than just the Bencrofts.

Leaning his head back against the sofa, Julian considered his options.

The solution came to him in a stunning jolt.

And a slow smile spread across his face.

"Was that Lord Guillford who just left?" Aurora asked as Courtney entered the bedchamber.

Her friend nodded, her face clouded with worry. "Yes."

"Need I ask why he'd come to Pembourne?"

"No."

"Did he say anything . . . unexpected?"

Courtney met the question head-on. "Only that you'd shocked and shamed him, and that it was probably best you remained unmarried—to anyone—given the circumstances."

"In other words, I've not only been labeled a harlot, but an unfeeling bitch who would blatantly scorn her own brother." With a frustrated sigh, Aurora rose from her rocking chair, wishing she could undo every moment since she'd left Pembourne last night. "Courtney, what can I say to make this easier for Slayde? How can I make him believe I hadn't an inkling the man I asked to ruin me was a Bencroft?"

"He does believe you," Courtney replied. "As for making it easier, I doubt that's possible. He was worried sick when he realized you were gone, especially after the guards found your tracks in the snow and realized you weren't taking an innocent stroll to the lighthouse to see Mr. Scollard, but were headed for the village. Then, reaching the village, running into Lady Altec, who delightedly informed him you were at Dawlish's—that gave Slayde an inkling of your motives."

"He must have been furious."

"Let's just say this is one confrontation I'm glad I missed. From what I could pry out of Slayde when he came home, I'd say he was totally overwrought by the time he burst into your arranged tête-à-tête. And then to find you with Julian Bencroft . . ." Courtney rolled her eyes. "Suffice it to say that this one, my impulsive friend, is not going to vanish overnight. You know how Slayde views the Bencrofts."

"The same way I do—as the enemy. Hell and damnation," Aurora exploded, "why couldn't that man in the tavern have been anyone but *him?*"

"I can't answer that. But, according to what you've told me, Lawrence Bencroft's son was as surprised to learn your identity as you were to learn his."

"He was. You should have seen the mortified look on

his face when he spoke my name. He uttered it as one would a vicious oath."

Courtney crossed over to the window, glancing shrewdly at her friend as she passed. "You sound disappointed about his reaction. What's more, you look disappointed." Pausing, Courtney turned, leaning back against the sill and folding her arms across her chest as she faced Aurora. "Would you care to tell me about Morland's new duke? I presume you did have a chance to exchange a few words before Lady Altec's arrival inspired you to fling yourself into his arms. Which reminds me, how is it that you heard the dowager's approaching footsteps but not Slayde's? I should think your brother's strides would be louder and far more familiar."

Aurora flushed.

"I repeat," Courtney said, "would you care to describe Julian Bencroft for me?"

"All right, yes, he's handsome," Aurora snapped. "And charming and exciting and worldly. He's also Lawrence Bencroft's son."

"And the embrace Slayde interrupted? Was that as staged as you professed?" Courtney waved away Aurora's stammering protest. "Aurora, this is me you're talking to. I *know* what a dreadful liar you are. Please— the truth."

Aurora stared at the carpet. "I feel so guilty, especially given how upset Slayde is. But, no, the kiss wasn't entirely feigned. Perhaps it wasn't feigned at all, now that I consider it. But at the time—I didn't think. I just acted. I don't know when the performance ended and the pleasure began. All I know is that I felt as if I were drowning and I had no desire to swim. I never imagined . . ." She broke off.

"I see." Turning to gaze out the window, Courtney lay her palm on her abdomen, unconsciously caressing her unborn child as she recalled precisely when she'd first experienced the feelings Aurora was describing. "And earlier on—what did the two of you discuss?"

"Adventures. Traveling abroad. Freedom."

"Really?" Courtney's eyes narrowed with interest as she spied the carriage rounding Pembourne's drive, halting before the entranceway steps. "Tell me, Aurora," she continued, watching the single occupant alight. "Is Julian Bencroft tall? Dark-haired? Unconventional in his attire—at least for a nobleman? Very lithe in his movements?"

"Have you met him?" Aurora asked incredulously.

"No." Courtney pivoted, throwing Aurora a speculative look. "But I'm about to."

"What?"

"A carriage bearing what I distinctly recall from our past encounters with the late duke as the Bencroft family crest just rounded the drive. From your description, I suspect the man on his way to our entranceway door is Julian Bencroft."

"My God." Aurora shot over to the window like a bullet, her heart slamming against her ribs as she saw the all-too-familiar build, the black windblown hair, the broad shoulders defined by a white linen shirt—unadorned by a cravat and unbuttoned at the neck. "It is he. Why on earth do you think he's here?"

"I haven't a clue." Courtney pursed her lips, considering the possible reasons for this inconceivable visit. "Let's give him time to state his business to Slayde. Then I'll go down and find out."

Chapter 3

Julian strolled the width of the marble entranceway, hands clasped behind his back as he awaited the return of the Pembourne butler. The servant had been blatantly rude, he reflected with a twinge of amusement. Oh, not at first. Not until Julian had announced himself. But once he'd heard the name Bencroft, the prim fellow had gone rigid, informing Julian that the earl was a very busy man and doubtless would be unable to see an unexpected guest. Then with a frosty glare, he'd stalked off to announce Julian's arrival.

The question was, was the butler's flagrant disapproval based on what he'd doubtless overheard about last night's scandal with Aurora or did it stem from the mere fact that Julian was a Bencroft? More to the point, how heavily steeped in age-old hatred was Pembourne's staff and, most particularly, was its master?

Pensively Julian contemplated that thought. He scarcely knew Slayde Huntley. They'd crossed paths at

Oxford and more recently at White's, on those rare occasions when Julian's sporadic journeys back to English soil corresponded with Slayde's equally infrequent trips home. It seemed the two of them were both wanderers, loners plagued by the past's grim echoes.

Echoes that incited them, whether out of an innate sense of unease or a desire to escape all reminders of an unrelenting past, to avoid each other, never sharing more than a cursory nod or a fleeting word.

Except when Hugh died.

Julian could still recall the genuine sorrow on Slayde's face when he'd approached Julian at the university, offered his sympathy—despite, and in full view of, the stunned, prying stares of their fellow classmates, many of whom half believed in the existence of the black diamond's ancient curse and thus entertained the possibility that the Huntleys were responsible for Hugh's death.

Slayde's act had been a courageous one. One that showed character and decency, as well as compassion.

One that Julian would never forget.

But thirteen years had passed since Hugh's death—years laced with unspeakable tragedy. How much had that tragedy transformed Slayde and his outlook?

The answer to that question would dictate the tenor of this meeting, one Julian was becoming increasingly eager to hold.

Veering about, he inclined his head in the direction Pembourne's butler had taken, half-tempted to abandon protocol and simply strike off on his own to search the corridor until he found whichever room Slayde was occupying. But no—he'd wait. For while he was determined to accomplish his goal, that goal would be far easier to attain if he were granted an audience rather than compelled to force his way in.

On the heels of that decision, the butler's returning

footsteps sounded, and an instant later the disapproving servant reappeared. "His Lordship will see you."

It sounded more like a death sentence than an invitation, Julian noted, smiling wryly to himself. "Lead the way."

He followed the manservant down a long corridor and into a mahogany-furnished study.

Slayde Huntley rose slowly from behind his desk. He looked coiled, ready to strike—yet beneath his eyes were shadows of fatigue, and lines of worry tightened his mouth. "I thought Siebert was mistaken when he announced the name of my visitor," he began. "I see I was wrong."

"Thank you for seeing me, Pembourne," Julian replied. "Graciously or not."

"The question is, why am I seeing you? I must be insane."

"Or perhaps only curious."

Siebert interrupted with a haughty sniff. "As no refreshment is required, I'll return to my post, sir," he declared, tossing Julian another icy stare before retracing his steps from the study.

A corner of Julian's mouth lifted. "Your staff is loyal."

"They have reason to be."

"I'm curious about your butler—Siebert, did you say his name was?—about Siebert's animosity. Does it stem from outrage over last night's indiscretion or a fundamental hatred for the Bencrofts?"

"Perhaps some of both." Slayde gripped the edge of his desk. "Why are you here, Morland?"

Without the slightest show of discomfort, Julian crossed over to the sideboard and poured himself a glass of Madeira. "Would you like one?"

"No."

Taking a healthy swallow, Julian leaned back against the sideboard, watching Slayde and gauging his reaction. "Before I begin, let me state my position on a less than pleasant topic—one we've always carefully avoided, as we've avoided each other. I've never subscribed to this timeless war between our families. I never intend to. I'm not sure where you stand on the issue. I know you despised my grandfather and, to a lesser extent, my father. But am I correct in assuming that prior to what happened last night, you had nothing against me personally?"

Slayde's brooding stare darkened. "I'm not certain how to answer that. No, I had nothing against you personally—until last night. However, that doesn't mean I ever forgot you were Lawrence Bencroft's son."

Julian had expected nothing less. "Regardless of that fact, I'd appreciate you putting aside your hostility long enough to hear me out."

A muscle worked in Slayde's jaw. "You ask a great deal, Morland. Your father's lying accusations have once again thrown my life into chaos and my family into danger. I'm fighting to keep them safe. And just when I'd ensured Aurora's future, she ran off to stage her own ruin. Her defiler? The last remaining Bencroft, the very man whose family has sought to destroy mine for nearly a century. So you'll forgive me if I'm a bit less than hospitable. As for hearing you out, I'll do so only because Aurora tells me you didn't realize her identity any more than she did yours. Nevertheless, be aware that after you've had your say, I intend to call you out. *Not* because you're a Bencroft, but because you're an immoral blackguard."

"Fair enough." With an unruffled nod, Julian tossed off his Madeira. "You do realize, however, that you'd be providing gossips such as Lady Altec with precisely the ammunition they seek."

"I doubt they could hurt Aurora any more than she's already hurt herself."

"I suppose that's true. Still, a duel won't be necessary."

43

"I disagree. Now, name the time and place."

"The time? As soon as possible. The place? Any church will suffice. Even Pembourne's chapel, if you prefer."

"You want to duel in a chapel?" Slayde asked incredulously.

"No, I want to marry your sister in a chapel."

Slayde's breath expelled in a rush. "What did you say?"

"I think I made myself clear. I've come to offer for Aurora. Is that so surprising? I am, after all, the man who ruined her for the Viscount . . . ?" Julian inclined his head quizzically. "Who was she to marry, anyway?"

"Guillford," Slayde supplied automatically, his expression a picture of stunned disbelief.

"Guillford?" Julian gave a derisive snort, shaking his head and prowling restlessly about the room. "No wonder Aurora was so eager to free herself. Guillford is a pleasant enough fellow—I've shared many a game of whist with him—but he's about as exciting as an unpainted canvas. Surely you realize how wrong he is for your sister."

"Morland, have you lost your bloody mind?" Slayde seemed to recover himself all at once. "Or is this your idea of some cruel and vicious joke?"

"I don't joke about my life, Pembourne." Julian stalked over to the desk, leaning forward to confront Slayde head-on. "Neither do I forsake my responsibilities—at least those I deem worth shouldering. Surprised? Don't be. The truth is, you don't know a bloody thing about me or about my principles. All you know is whatever you've convinced yourself are 'Bencroft' traits. Now let's get to Aurora. You're concerned over her future, and with good reason. Most of the *ton*'s suitable gentlemen are either married or terrified by the very name of Huntley. And once Lady Altec has spread her news—as I hear she does remarkably well—the final few potential suitors will vanish like the mist. Which reminds me, has the oh-so-proper Viscount Guillford cried off yet? If not, I'm sure he will the very instant his driver can rush him to Pembourne Manor. Now, let's see. Aurora is how old—nearly one and twenty? I fear her marital prospects look bleak."

Anger slashed Slayde's features. "So you're here to sacrifice yourself? How noble. And how unbelievable. What do you really want—to taunt me?"

"No. I want Aurora. I wanted her the minute I saw her. *Before* I knew she was a Huntley. Before I even knew what the hell she was doing in Dawlish's. She's a beautiful, captivating woman. One whom, for the record, I had no intentions of bedding last night. Nor, by the way, did she ask me to. On the contrary, she made her innocence a well-known fact from the start. All she wanted was to disentangle herself from an unwanted betrothal."

Slayde's color had returned and he was watching Julian with a guarded expression. "You really mean this, don't you?"

"Yes. Now the question is, are you going to forbid the marriage because I'm a Bencroft? If so, you're a fool. I'm *not* my father, nor am I my grandfather. I walked out of that house six years ago for a reason. I never intended to return. But circumstances altered that decision. So I'm here—for now."

"For now. How comforting. After which you'll be off again, roaming the globe, I presume."

"In time, yes."

"And what will Aurora do? Be imprisoned at Morland? She's miserable enough doing that here, and Pembourne is her home."

An unexpected grin tugged at Julian's lips. "If my suspicions about Aurora are correct, she'll be dashing about the world at my side."

"Don't look so damned smug. Aurora would accompany the devil himself in order to experience a life of adventure."

Julian's eyes glinted. "I'm sure you're right. Fortunately I'm not the devil. Moreover, at the risk of sounding arrogant, I don't think Aurora's accompanying me would be inspired solely by her desire for adventure. Your sister was as intrigued by me as I was by her. And if you're about to ask how I know that—don't. You won't like the answer."

Slayde's hands balled into fists. "You bastard."

"Unfortunately not. I'm a Bencroft. But that's already been too well established." Julian's goblet struck the desk with a purposeful thud. "Look, Pembourne. I'll give you a wealth of reasons why you should consider my offer. First, I happen to be the man Aurora approached—the man who eventually helped ruin her. Second, better than anyone, I know the ramifications of the black diamond's ludicrous curse. Hordes of scoundrels are hell-bent on finding the stone—using whatever means they have to. You want Aurora gone from Pembourne, safely taken care of. She would be. To begin with, she'd no longer be a Huntley. Thus, she'd no longer be a target for thieves—or worse. Further, let me assure you that no one, I repeat *no one*, for whom I'm responsible is ever harmed. I vow to you that as my wife Aurora will be fully protected at all times—by me. Safety will cease to be an issue. On to financial security. My father squandered his money. I did not. I'm wealthy enough to offer Aurora any luxury she might want. I can also bestow upon her the elevated title of duchess—albeit accompanied by the name Morland." Julian arched a brow. "Think about what a delightful upheaval we'd cause. After all these years, merging our families. That alone would make it worthwhile, even if it weren't for the splendid reasons I just enumerated."

"What about Aurora's wishes?" Slayde demanded. "Where do those fit in?"

"They didn't seem to concern you when you arranged her betrothal to Guillford."

"This is different."

"Very. Aurora didn't want him. She does want me."

"You're so bloody sure?"

"Why don't we ask her?" Julian suggested with a grand sweep of his arm. "Summon her to your study. Tell her of my offer. Then give me a half hour to talk with her. Alone. After which I'll leave, give her time to consider her options." His lips twitched. "If I'm wrong, if she refuses me, then you can call me out and shoot me dead. Or at least you can try."

For a long silent moment, Slayde just stared. Then he nodded. "Very well, Morland. Let's play by your rules. I'll have Siebert summon Aurora."

Four minutes later, Aurora knocked tentatively and stepped into the study. "You wanted to see me?"

Slayde rose. "No, actually my visitor wanted to see you." He inclined his head toward the sideboard where Julian lounged, watching Aurora's entrance. "You remember the Duke of Morland?"

Twin spots of color stained her cheeks, but she met Julian's gaze without flinching. "Yes—I remember. Good afternoon, Your Grace."

Julian grinned at her formal acknowledgment. Straightening, he crossed over until he stood before her, close enough to make out all the vibrant hues of her red-gold hair. "Lady Aurora," he replied, capturing her hand, slowly raising her fingers to his lips. "How are you?"

She inclined her head, myriad emotions flashing across her face. "The same as I was when you last saw me," she managed. "One doesn't change overnight."

His lips brushed her skin. "Doesn't one?"

He could actually hear her breath catch.

"Aurora," Slayde announced without prelude, "the duke has come here to offer for you."

Turquoise eyes widened with astonishment. "Why?" she blurted.

Julian's grin widened. "I think that's obvious."

"No—it's not." Aurora tugged her hand away. "I'm not some pathetic waif that needs a home, Your Grace. Nor must I be rescued from the outcome of my reckless act. You weren't responsible for last night's . . . episode. I was. There's no need for you to make amends."

"Amends?" Seeing the golden sparks ignite Aurora's eyes, the proud tilt of her chin, Julian found himself wondering if this plan was going to yield even more than he himself had realized. "I assure you, making amends is the last term I would use to describe my intentions. That would imply a sense of regret, which I happen not to feel." He cut himself short, determined for this conversation to remain private—for many reasons.

Pointedly he turned to Slayde. "We agreed that I might speak with your sister alone."

"Yes, we did." Slayde glanced at Aurora. "Do you have any objections?"

She looked as if she wanted nothing better than to voice some. But in the end curiosity won out. "I have no objections."

"Very well." Slayde snapped open his timepiece, making note of the hour. "Thirty minutes." He headed for the door. "I'll be just down the hall."

Julian waited until the quiet click of the door handle signified they were alone. Then he turned his attention back to Aurora, who was openly studying him, a wary expression on her face. She was even lovelier than he remembered, Julian mused silently. Her features were alive, vibrant, her figure slight yet enticingly curved—as

the close-fitting bodice of her morning dress revealed—
her eyes as vivid as flawless gems, her hair a shimmering
cloud of golden red.

Marriage was beginning to look infinitely appealing.

"Why are you staring at me?" Aurora interrupted his
thoughts to demand.

A corner of Julian's mouth lifted. "I could ask you the
same question. In my case, I'm staring at you because
you're beautiful. And your reason?"

"I'm just . . . surprised to see you. I'm even more
surprised by your proposal. And I'm awaiting an explanation."

He chuckled. "You're not surprised to see me. You
watched my arrival from your bedchamber window."

Aurora's jaw dropped—as clear an admission as if
she'd spoken it aloud. "Are you *sure* the name Merlin is
derived from the falcon and not the prophet? There
seems to be nothing you don't know."

"I'm sure." Julian recaptured her fingers, pressing her
palm to his lips. "Speaking of falcons, how is it you
know of the merlin?"

"My great-grandfather raised falcons. Our library is
filled with books about them. I never leave Pembourne,
so I have endless hours to read. Why do you want to
marry me?"

Her forthrightness was almost as bewitching as her
beauty.

And her revelation supplied yet another piece of an
ever-growing puzzle—one Julian was determined to
solve.

"Why do I want to marry you?" he murmured truthfully. "Many reasons. This is one." He kissed the pulse
at her wrist.

"Stop." She jerked her hand from his, clutching the
folds of her lilac morning dress and tilting her head back
to meet his gaze. "Your Grace . . ."

"Julian," he corrected.

"Julian. From what I know of you, you're a very independent man who spends his life sailing the world on one adventure or another. In addition, judging from that barmaid's reaction to you last night, I doubt you're ever at a loss for willing female companionship."

"I notice you haven't yet mentioned that I'm a Bencroft."

"I was getting to that. Your name—and mine—are the best reasons for us to stay as far apart as possible. So why are you here asking for my hand?"

Her spirit, her candor—she was the most innocently arousing woman he'd ever met, Julian decided. He captured a strand of her hair, rubbed its silky texture between his fingers, consciously aware of the fact that he couldn't seem to stop touching her. "Aside from the minor detail that we were discovered at the village tavern, in a private room, on a bed, and in each other's arms? Very well, Rory." Another grin. "Let's explore my reasons by employing that extraordinary honesty of yours. Can you tell me you didn't feel what I felt when we kissed?"

"Can you tell me you've never experienced that feeling before?"

"Yes. I can tell you I've never experienced that feeling before." Even as he uttered the words, Julian knew they were true.

Aurora searched his face, as if trying to assess his sincerity *and* his motives.

"Shall I be more specific?" Julian probed huskily. "Very well. I scarcely tasted your mouth and I burst into flames. I couldn't get enough of you—your taste, your scent, the feel of you in my arms. I lost all sense of reality to the point where the world ceased to exist other than you. I never even heard your brother's approach."

"Nor did I," Aurora confessed softly, her voice filled with wonder rather than embarrassment. "I felt everything you just described, and more. But, Your Gr . . . Julian, that's hardly a basis for a marriage."

"No, but it's a damned good start—especially since that kiss resulted in a scandal far more extensive than even you imagined when you walked into Dawlish's."

She sighed. "Yes—that. I'm too impulsive. 'Tis my worst fault—well, one of my worst faults."

"I'm looking forward to discovering the others." Julian's palm slid around to caress her nape. "Aurora, you're not a coward. Don't run from me. I'll give you everything you want—freedom, adventure, excitement . . ." He lowered his head, brushed her lips with his. ". . . Passion. I'll open the doors to a world you never knew existed. All you have to do is say yes."

Aurora drew back, clearly torn between desire and pragmatism. "We're virtual strangers."

"One word from you will change that."

She sucked in her breath. "Did Slayde actually agree to this? Scandal or not, the bitterness he feels for your family would preclude . . ." She broke free of Julian's touch, turned away.

"Go on," Julian urged, watching her spine stiffen, knowing at the same time that this was one issue that had to be addressed—for many reasons.

"'Tis nearly eleven years since my parents were murdered," Aurora stated. "I'm sure you know all the details—'twas hardly a secret. Slayde found them lying amid pools of blood in Pembourne's hallway. They'd been driven through by a sword. And for what? For possession of a diamond they'd never even seen, much less stashed away. A jewel the Bencrofts insisted we had." Her voice quavered, then strengthened again. "My poor implacable brother. He was already so intense, so damned autonomous. From that day on, those qualities magnified threefold as did his restlessness. He assumed the role of my guardian with a fervor that bordered on obsessive, sequestering me here at Pembourne amid a swarm of guards paid to ensure I never left the estate, while Slayde traveled the world, returning to Pembourne as seldom as possible."

"That must have been very painful for you," Julian said quietly, visualizing a frightened little girl who'd just lost both her parents and had to mourn them all alone, without the comfort of a brother who had none to offer. "Very painful and very difficult."

"It was—all of it. Not just my parents' deaths, but the terror of knowing their murderer was still out there, as were others who would kill to unearth the black diamond. Worst of all was the loneliness. Oh, I understood Slayde's motivation, but that made my isolation no less bearable. Without Mr. Scollard, I think I would have lost my mind."

"Who is Mr. Scollard?"

"The Windmouth lighthouse keeper—and my dearest friend. Other than Courtney, that is." Warmth flooded Aurora's tone. "Courtney's arrival in our lives changed everything. For Slayde *and* for me. She brought us love, constancy—she made us a family. She also effected a lull in the danger, publicly declaring that the black diamond was no longer in Huntley possession. Because of that brilliant tactic—added to the miracle of her love and now the child she's carrying—Slayde changed, softened, and finally relaxed his obsessive need to envelope me in a cocoon of safety." Aurora's hands balled into fists at her sides. "Until now, when his obsession was rekindled by your father's ravings, his blind accusations. It's all begun anew . . . the ransom notes, the threats, the attempted burglaries . . ."

Julian caught her shoulders, brought her gently around. "Aurora, we can put an end to all that."

"How?"

"Before I answer your question, let me say this. I know that for years Slayde believed my grandfather killed your parents. But as we now know, he was wrong. The murderer has been caught and punished."

"That can't undo a decade of torment. Chilton might not have committed the murders, but he and Lawrence stopped just shy of doing so. They spewed their venom in every way they could—in business, in public. Even in private, directly to my father's face the very month he died, swearing vengeance, vowing to make him pay for every setback your family had endured—setbacks Papa had no more caused than he'd caused your brother's death, although heaven knows, Lawrence proclaimed that to be a Huntley act as well. Nothing stopped the Bencrofts. Chilton and Lawrence dedicated their lives to undermining us. Worst of all, they invented and perpetuated the fallacy that we were hoarding the black diamond. And I've just described to you the results of that flagrant lie. So, no, Slayde will never forgive them. Neither will I."

"He'll never forgive *them,*" Julian repeated, cupping Aurora's chin and raising it until she met his gaze. "Perhaps that's the answer to your question about why Slayde would permit you to marry me. Perhaps your very astute brother recognizes that I'm not my father or my grandfather. I'm very much my own person." A weighted pause. "I can't undo the past, Aurora. But I sure as hell can change the future. We both can. Whether we do is up to you."

Conflicting emotions again darted across her beautiful face.

"Marry me," Julian urged softly.

"Has Slayde already given his approval?"

"He's left the decision to you."

"And if I refuse?"

"Then he intends to call me out and shoot me."

That elicited an impish grin. "It would seem 'tis *I* who am rescuing *you,* Your Grace."

"Does that mean yes?"

Amusement faded, eclipsed by a contemplative look. "You alluded to the fact that we can alter things, amend the future. The 'many reasons' you have for wanting this marriage—honor and physical attraction notwithstanding—what are they?"

This was the moment of truth, the moment Julian had anticipated with equal measures of excitement and apprehension.

He hadn't a clue how Aurora would react.

But he was about to find out.

"Let's sit down." Julian guided Aurora into a chair, then perched across from her on the edge of the desk. "I'm taking a risk sharing this information with you," he stated bluntly. "As of now, I'm the only one who's privy to it. But I'm willing to take that risk because I believe you'll be as intrigued by the truth as I am . . . and equally eager to act upon it."

Aurora's slender brows arched. "What truth?"

"First, you must promise not to repeat this to anyone."

"Julian—" She sounded amazed. "We met only last night. Why would you have faith in my promise?"

"Instinct."

"Have you forgotten I'm a Huntley?"

"Not for a moment."

"Nor can I forget you're a Bencroft."

"I'm counting on that."

Now she looked totally baffled. "I don't understand."

"Will you give me your word not to share what I tell you? It was meant for my knowledge alone—and now yours. If the details are revealed to the wrong person, if this situation is handled incorrectly, the future could become even bleaker than the past. But if it's approached the right way, we can undo so much damage, lift a sixty-year malediction from our shoulders . . . and transform rogues into heroes."

Aurora tensed. "This concerns the black diamond, doesn't it?"

"Your promise, Aurora."

"You have it." She leaned toward him, her eyes round as saucers. "Do you know where the diamond is?"

"Not yet. But I will. And before you ask, this has nothing to do with my father's investigation. This is an entity unto itself."

"Tell me."

"Have you ever heard of the Fox and the Falcon?"

Aurora's whole face lit up. "Of course! Some of Mr. Scollard's most wondrous legends center around them and all their daring exploits. Mr. Scollard is a visionary of sorts. He has the most extraordinary abilities, like bursts of insight into the past or future. Anyway, he's been sharing magical stories with me since I was a tot. And the mysterious Fox and the Falcon were among my favorites. The Fox—cunning, brilliant. The Falcon—precise, lethal. The fearless way they embraced danger, immersed themselves in exciting adventures. Such as the time they recaptured that enormous English brig from bloodthirsty pirates—calculating the ship's probable course, stealing aboard by night, overtaking the stunned blackguards before daybreak. Oh, and the time they embarked on that quest for the chest of jewels that had been smuggled from China to . . ." Aurora's brow furrowed.

"Ceylon," Julian supplied.

"Ceylon," Aurora breathed, staring at Julian in growing wonder. "So those stories *are* true. That's what you're saying, isn't it?" She scarcely paused, much less awaited an answer. "Of course they're true. Who better than you to know? You're an adventurer, just as they were. You've traveled the world, heard dozens of incredible tales—and you know the authentic ones from the fabrications. I told Slayde he was wrong; Mr. Scollard's yarns are far more than mere fairy tales. They are, aren't they?" This time she stopped, gazing at Julian like a hopeful puppy.

She wouldn't be disappointed. What he was about to divulge would send even Aurora's imagination soaring.

"Yes, Aurora, Mr. Scollard's yarns about the Fox and the Falcon are much more than fairy tales." Julian seized her hands in his, his fervent grip conveying the importance of his upcoming revelation. "His stories are accurate but incomplete. The Fox and the Falcon were indeed adventurers, but the purpose behind their various quests delved far deeper than a thirst for excitement. They were special agents retained by King George II from the year Seventeen Thirty-nine through the year Seventeen Fifty-eight to handle various delicate missions. They traveled abroad, restoring stolen treasures, rescuing English ships—the stories are limitless. They worked swiftly, brilliantly, and—as one would expect—anonymously, which is why no one ever learned the details of their dazzling exploits until now."

"Until now . . . and until you." Aurora's wonder was tempered by puzzlement. "How is it you discovered all these undisclosed facts? And, fascinated though I am, what have the Fox and the Falcon to do with the black diamond?"

"I'm getting to that. In Seventeen Fifty-eight the King ordered the Fox and the Falcon to go in search of the black diamond. Their objective was not to turn the stone over to the Russian prince who was offering a reward for its recovery, but to restore it to its rightful place in the sacred temple of India from which it was stolen centuries ago."

"That's very benevolent. But why would King George involve them in such a mission? The diamond's disappearance didn't impact England."

"Ah, but it did. Consider what was happening in India at the time. A year earlier, Britain had reestablished its supremacy in Bengal at the Battle of Plassey. Conflict was rampant. Rumors had sprung up among the natives that it was the English who had stolen the gem all those years ago and that until the diamond was restored, blood and death would rule Bengal."

"I see." Aurora nodded pensively. "Then for all our sakes, I wish the Fox and the Falcon hadn't failed in their mission."

"They didn't fail," Julian refuted, watching Aurora's forehead wrinkle in confusion. "At least not in finding what they sought. What they failed in was completing their assignment."

"I'm lost," Aurora pronounced. "I thought it was our great-grandfathers who found the black diamond."

"It was."

A heartbeat of silence.

Realization struck, sending Aurora bolting to her feet. "Julian, are you telling me . . ."

"I'm telling you that Geoffrey Bencroft and James Huntley were the Fox and the Falcon."

Chapter 4

With a shaken expression, Aurora sank back into her chair. "I think it's time you told me how—where—you uncovered this information."

"I fully intend to." Julian leaned forward, brushing a strand of burnished hair from her cheek. "As of today, I inherited my great-grandfather's journal, which explains everything I just told you—and more."

"But there were two generations of Bencrofts between you and Geoffrey! Why weren't your father or grandfather aware of the intrigue?"

"Because my great-grandfather didn't choose for them to be aware of it." Julian proceeded to explain the letter and the chest he'd been left, as well as what each contained.

"My God." Aurora shook her head, trying to assimilate all she'd just learned. "Then all these years . . . the hatred between our families, the bitterness, the accusations . . ."

"Could have been avoided," Julian finished. "The deception and animosity that we all thought destroyed our great-grandfathers' friendship never existed. Quite the opposite, in fact. Geoffrey and James were partners in the truest sense, bound by allegiance to each other and to England. Betrayal was out of the question."

"But then what went wrong?" Aurora demanded. "When they found the black diamond, why did my great-grandfather abandon yours and flee for England?"

"He didn't." Julian frowned, contemplating what he'd read in Geoffrey's final journal entry. "Before they left on their last mission, our great-grandfathers calculated the diamond's location to be high in the mountains of Tibet, where it had been hidden by a thief who never lived to reclaim it. Assuming that the specifics outlined in the journal unfolded as planned, the Fox and the Falcon sailed from England, adopting their customary roles as mercenaries in pursuit of great wealth and adventure. No one realized who they were, or that they were on the verge of finding and restoring the black diamond. Unfortunately they weren't the only ones combing the Himalayas. There were several other privateers headed there, too, equally intent on unearthing the stone and hell-bent on reaping the reward. According to the journal, the Fox and the Falcon had planned to swiftly uncover the stone, then throw the others off course by feigning failure. James was to take the diamond and head back to England—allegedly disgusted with his lack of success, actually intent on concealing the diamond until Geoffrey's return. Geoffrey, in the meantime, was to stay behind for a fortnight, pretending to search. But in reality, he was to assess the privateers—waiting until he convinced them that the stone had yet to be found before hastening home to England—at which time he and James would deliver the stone to King George."

"Geoffrey's cunning, James's precise tactics," Aurora

murmured. "Remarkable—in more ways than one. Not only did their separate departures convince the others that the diamond had yet to be found, it also increased the Fox and the Falcon's chances for a successful escape. Anyone pursuing them would be forced to divide up and go after each man individually. After all, who had the stone—Geoffrey or James? Their plan was brilliant."

"As were they," Julian concurred.

"So my great-grandfather hid the stone, then fell to his death, dashed on the rocks at the foot of Dartmouth Cliffs." Aurora inclined her head. "Was he pushed?"

"That question will probably remained unanswered. Eventually word leaked out that James had absconded with the stone, brought it to Devonshire. But did someone kill him to get it?" A shrug. "We'll never know for sure."

"But we do know that Geoffrey died of a fever en route to England—and that with him died the last vestiges of the Fox and the Falcon." Aurora's expression grew quizzical. "Why didn't King George reveal the truth at that time, at least to our families? That would have explained so much, and avoided even more."

"First of all, I doubt that the King knew the diamond—or James—were even in England. If he did, he would have tracked James down and demanded he turn over the stone. But remember, the agreement between our great-grandfathers was that they go to the King *together*. So, I'm willing to bet that James told very few people he'd returned, and no one about the location of the black diamond. Less than a week later, he died. As for why the King didn't reveal the truth about the Fox and the Falcon after both had perished, my guess is that he was afraid to take the risk. Remember, the Fox and the Falcon hadn't managed to restore the gem, only to find it. If word of their mission were to have seeped out, it would have appeared to some as if England intended to keep the jewel—and the fortune it generated—for itself. Moreover, the King himself died less than two years later, precluding any possible change of heart time might have wrought."

"So the Fox and the Falcon became only a legend . . . until today."

"Exactly."

Aurora sat back, her expression more exhilarated than dazed. "This is all so incredible."

"The rest of the tales are equally incredible. Each and every one of the quests my great-grandfather described is a dazzling adventure unto itself. When you read that journal . . ."

"May I?" Aurora jumped in eagerly. "May I read the journal?"

Julian had been awaiting that particular request. "Hmm," he replied, taking his time, presumably entertaining the notion. "I don't know what to say. The journal was, after all, meant for my eyes and my eyes alone. To show it to a—what was the term you used? Ah—to a virtual stranger, would be a blatant violation of my great-grandfather's wishes." One brow arched in undisguised challenge. "On the other hand, if my *wife* were to come upon the journal by chance, if her curiosity were to overcome her self-restraint, compelling her to read the entries—then, that would be an accident of fate, would it not?"

Despite herself, Aurora began to laugh. "You, Julian, are a shameless rogue. Tell me, is there ever a time you don't get what you want?"

"Until now, no." Julian raised Aurora's chin with a determined forefinger, reminding himself why he was here and what he intended to accomplish. "In this instance only you can decide whether I get what I want. My unblemished record, Rory, is in your hands."

"Somehow I suspect your record is the only unblemished thing about you."

"You're evading my question."

"Actually I'm preparing to ask my own. Everything you just revealed to me about the Fox and the Falcon—how does it factor into your proposal? How will my becoming your wife ensure the success of whatever goal you hope to attain?"

"By reestablishing a partnership that was thwarted sixty years ago, and by seeing it through to fruition." Julian's tone grew fervent, all humor vanishing beneath the conviction that pulsed through his veins. "Think about it, Rory. By combining all the Huntley and Bencroft resources, including individual fragments of information left to each of us, we can fulfill our great-grandfathers' mission. As a result, we can restore dignity to their names, justify their cause, and end a sixty-year period of ostracism and hatred that should never have been."

"You intend to hunt for the black diamond."

"I intend to *find* it. Find it and restore it to its rightful place in India."

Aurora raised her chin a notch higher, studying Julian with uncanny insight. "This means a great deal to you, far more than another exciting adventure, and far more than honor. After all, you didn't even know your great-grandfather, and according to you, you had no use for either your father or your grandfather. Monetary gain certainly isn't a factor, not if you mean to turn over the stone without reaping a reward. So what is this ardent resolution of yours based on?"

Julian sucked in his breath, taken aback by her perception. "I'm not sure which stuns me more, your audacity or your insight."

"My audacity, most likely," she supplied. "Slayde tells me it's uncommon and intolerable. Although at this particular moment, I believe it's my insight that is functioning more acutely. It tells me you're avoiding my question."

"Perhaps I am," Julian replied, memories of his

father's taunting dare melding into images of Hugh— images that still had the power to make his chest constrict with the painful sense of loss. "There are some things I simply choose not to discuss. I assure you, however, my reasons aren't sinister, only personal."

"Very well, I'll ask a less personal question, then. Aren't you intimidated by the black diamond's curse?"

Keeping up with this woman, much less staying one step ahead of her, was going to be the challenge of a lifetime. "No," Julian replied. "I'm not intimidated— not by this curse or any other. Why? Because I don't believe in curses, only in people who perpetuate them."

"You sound just like Slayde."

"Then your brother is a wise and sensible man." Julian paused. "I presume you do believe in the curse?"

"Absolutely. Just because we don't see things doesn't mean they don't exist. Mr. Scollard taught me that. In this case, I think the tragedies that have befallen our families speak for themselves. The curse is real." A mutinous spark lit her eyes. "And don't try to dissuade me. Slayde's attempted it. So has Courtney. I'm unyielding in my conviction."

"That doesn't surprise me." Julian grinned. "You're unyielding about everything. Tell me, did your parents name you Aurora because like the dawn you're relentless until you've awakened everyone to your presence?"

To Julian's surprise, a wave of sadness crossed Aurora's face. "Actually, that's one memory I do have of my parents," she murmured with none of Julian's reticence to discuss that which was close in heart. "I must have been about four years old. I remember asking Mama why she chose to name me Aurora. She said that she and Papa decided on that name because the day I was born the sun rose in their hearts, and because I filled every subsequent day of their lives with sunlight."

Julian framed Aurora's face between his palms. "That's lovely," he said gently. "And accurate. You are like sunlight, a brilliant source of warmth and joy. Forgive me for extinguishing your light, *soleil*—even for a moment."

She gave him a small smile. "You're forgiven."

That fleeting glimpse of the vulnerability which hovered just beneath Aurora's fiery exterior elicited a rush of guilt—and a tremendous sense of responsibility—within Julian. In sharp contrast to his reckless existence and despite her own adventurous spirit, Aurora was naive and protected, cushioned by her brother's imposed isolation. True, as a Huntley she was susceptible to danger—accentuated danger thanks to Lawrence's unfounded accusations that the black diamond was secreted at Pembourne. That susceptibility, however, would vanish when she relinquished her family name and took on Julian's. The question was, vanish in exchange for what? Aurora hadn't any idea what lay ahead as his wife, the transformation he was proposing along with marriage—a transformation that extended far beyond the imminent quest for the black diamond, traversed the entirety of his life, *Merlin's* life.

Julian frowned. He had to think beyond the immediate crusade, consider the future that would follow. Aurora wanted no part of refuge and seclusion, and he wasn't fool enough to believe she'd remain home while he ventured forth to take on the world. No, his prospective bride would doubtless expect to be right at his side, brimming with enthusiasm as they sailed away to embrace whatever challenges lay ahead. And her expectations would be justified. After all, hadn't he just offered her passion, freedom, adventure? Indeed he had. And he could offer her all of them in abundance. The problem was that along with freedom and adventure came perils. Had Aurora any idea what those perils might be, how many powerful enemies could be acquired in this type of work?

How many he himself had already acquired?

No. She hadn't. And it was up to him to apprise her.

"Aurora," he said abruptly. "Before we continue, you need to understand a few things, not only about the black diamond, but about me."

"Very well." She settled herself, folding her hands in her lap. "I'm listening."

"I'll begin with the stone. There are dangers associated with hunting it down, just as there were when our great-grandfathers went after it. Why else do you think Geoffrey, after two decades of serving the King, suddenly made provisions with his solicitor to keep the Fox's journal and dagger, something he hadn't done prior to any of his previous missions? He obviously realized the dangers were far greater than usual, that there were hordes of bloodthirsty privateers out there who would gladly slit his throat to gain possession of the jewel."

"I surmised as much," Aurora put in as calmly as if she were discussing a change in the weather.

"Aurora." Julian's palms dropped to her shoulders, gripped them tightly. "I vowed to your brother mere minutes ago that I would make certain you remained safe. I mean to keep that vow. But I need your cooperation. This isn't a game. Privateers don't adhere to rules, nor do they operate by a code of honor. If you and I strike an agreement, it will be I—not you—who incur the risks. Is that clear?"

Exhilaration splashed across Aurora's face. *"That's* why you're so adamant about this marriage taking place. You not only believe that by joining forces we can expedite the search for the black diamond, you believe my help is required to unearth it. What is it I must do? Where is it we must travel to gather our clues? India? Tibet? China?"

This was worse than Julian had feared. "Did you hear a word I just said?" he demanded.

"I heard you." She sat forward eagerly. "Tell me where we must voyage to ensure that it is we and not those odious privateers of whom you spoke who find the stone."

"If I'm right—nowhere."

Her shoulders slumped. "Nowhere?"

"Other than Pembourne and Morland Manor," Julian amended, finding it difficult not to smile at her crestfallen expression. "Consider the facts. Our great-grandfathers were partners. Mine left the legacy of the Fox to his first deserving heir. It stands to reason that the Falcon might very well have done the same. 'Tis up to us to find that legacy, in whatever form James left it. By reading Geoffrey's journal, I peeled back one layer of the past. 'Tis time we peeled back the second: namely, learning more about James. The logical place to do that is right here at Pembourne. Your great-grandfather's past might not be as concisely arranged as Geoffrey's, but he's bound to have left clues. Clues which when added to those we already possess, together with those I have yet to uncover at Morland, will shed light on the Fox and the Falcon—their lives, their treasures . . . and most of all, the place in which they concealed those treasures. A place that can only be uncovered by the Huntleys and the Bencrofts when working together—as partners."

"You believe the black diamond is hidden in one of our homes?"

"No. I believe your great-grandfather returned to England and secreted the stone in the customary hiding spot he and Geoffrey used to conceal their wares prior to delivering them to King George. 'Twas the only way James could be certain that should anything happen to him, Geoffrey would know just where to go to retrieve the stone and fulfill the mission. However, I also believe the clues leading to that location are in not one, but both our homes. And that with a direct and concentrated effort, we can amass them, find that hiding place . . . and consequently, the black diamond."

"Which is right here in England." Aurora gave a

resigned sigh. "Your theory makes sense. If all the clues are hidden at Pembourne and Morland, 'twould explain why none of the privateers who have combed the globe in search of the stone was successful in finding it." A quizzical look. "But if we're not going abroad, what new dangers would be threatening us?"

"To begin with, you'd no longer be within your brother's fortress, protected by his guards," Julian pointed out. "You'd be coming and going with your husband, placing your life, your well-being, in his hands—*my* hands." Julian's thumb caressed her cheek. "And that, *soleil*, requires trust."

Aurora never averted her gaze. "I realize that."

"Trust," he added meaningfully, "is a gift that must be earned over time—which we don't have."

"I disagree. Not about the fact that we haven't the luxury of time, but about the fact that time is a requirement for trust. Trust comes from within and is ofttimes instinctive rather than earned. I trusted you without even knowing your name, from the moment you scooped me up in Dawlish's and rescued me from my own stupidity. I trusted you then. I trust you now."

"I'm humbled." Julian felt oddly moved by the heartfelt candor of her words. "Further, I promise to do everything in my power to live up to that trust. Including being honest with you, even if it means your refusing my proposal."

"Which brings us to whatever it is you were alluding to when you said there were a few things I needed to understand about you."

"Exactly." Julian drew a slow, contemplative breath. "The search for the black diamond notwithstanding, do you realize what I do? Who I am? Are you truly aware of the kind of life I lead?"

"By experience, no. By definition, yes. You're a mercenary, a man who seeks wealth and excitement by traveling the world, taking on ventures that yield huge monetary rewards and equally huge doses of exhilaration and triumph."

A corner of Julian's mouth lifted. "Accurate enough. But you failed to mention the darker aspects: the dangers, the risks, the consequences of restoring one man's possession by wresting it from another. In short, I've learned to sleep lightly, with one eye open, and never to be caught with my back turned. If I did, let's just say there are many who for various reasons and in various parts of the world would be delighted to plunge a knife into it."

Aurora's brows drew together, not so much with worry as with speculation. "In other words, you have quite a few enemies."

"Enough."

"Can you tell me about them? Or about your exploits, for that matter?"

"Perhaps someday," Julian hedged. "For now, you need only know the facts. My life is turbulent. Turbulent and dangerous."

"I suspected as much."

"You're not intimidated?"

A smile curved Aurora's lips. "Why should I be? You vowed to Slayde that you'd keep me safe."

"So I did." Julian was claimed by an odd surge of relief—one that had nothing to do with his determination to find the black diamond. "And so I shall." His gaze fell to her lips, sparking a nearly uncontrollable urge to drag her into his arms, rekindle the fire they'd ignited last night. "Once we've restored the black diamond, you're welcome to stay behind, forego the rigors of my existence," he offered, knowing damned well he didn't mean a word of it. The more intimate aspects of this marriage, the erotic fantasy of Aurora as his wife, necessitated having her with him—under him, surrounding him—every possible moment.

Evidently Aurora sensed the direction his thoughts

had taken, because her awareness of him seemed to intensify, her breath coming a bit faster, her lips parting beneath his heated gaze. "Stay behind?" she managed.

"Um-hum." Giving in to his craving to touch her more fully, Julian slid his hand beneath her hair, caressing her nape in slow, heated strokes. "I own a great deal of property, including a manor in Cornwall that overlooks the water." He angled her head, pressed his lips to the pulse at her throat, fully aware he was using seduction to influence her decision and feeling not a shred of guilt for doing so. "When I'm in England, I spend most of my time there. I think you'd like it. You could make it your home during my absence." His mouth slid around, tasted the delicate line of her jaw. "I employ a small staff of servants there. They could look after you while I'm abroad. I'd be away several months at a time. . . ."

"No." Aurora was trembling but her words were utterly coherent, her hands balling into fists at her sides. "I've had more than enough tranquility and confinement to last a lifetime. If we marry, I want to accompany you on your adventures."

"I think that could be arranged," Julian murmured, teasing the corner of her mouth with his. "Most of the time," he clarified, his hands gripping her shoulders, urging her closer. "If there's excessive risk involved, I reserve the right to insist that you stay in England, safe."

"So long as that isn't too often," she qualified breathlessly. "I'm not afraid of risk."

"Only curses," he modified in a husky whisper.

"Only curses."

"Agreed, then. On most excursions you'll accompany me."

"After all, you did promise me passion." Her cheeks were flushed, her eyes drowsy with awakening sensation. "And passion, as I understand it, requires proximity, does it not?"

"Indeed it does. *Close* proximity." Aroused beyond

bearing, Julian stood, dragging Aurora to her feet and into his arms. "I think we've negotiated enough, don't you, *soleil?*"

"Oh, definitely." Unashamedly Aurora reached up, twined her arms about Julian's neck. "From the tenor of our conversation, I was beginning to fear you wanted strictly a marriage of convenience."

"You have no worries on that score." His fingers slid down the length of her arms to her shoulders, threaded through her hair. "No worries at all."

With that his mouth seized hers, capturing it for a scorching, melding, bottomless kiss that eclipsed the memory of last night beneath its molten flames.

Blood pounded through Julian's head, hammered at his loins, as the same dark wave that had claimed him at Dawlish's engulfed him, dragging him into a hot sea of sensation. Aurora's taste was heaven, her scent and feel more intoxicating than brandy—even through the confines of their clothes. He couldn't get enough of her, parting her lips, possessing her with deep, hungry strokes of his tongue. He hauled her closer, lifted her into him.

And felt the exhilaration of her response.

With an inarticulate sound of pleasure, Aurora threw herself into the kiss, holding him fiercely, meeting the tantalizing strokes of his tongue with her own.

The fire blazed higher.

Anchoring her with one arm, Julian's other hand slid around to cup her breast, his thumb finding her already hardened nipple and rubbing it—back and forth, back and forth—groaning aloud at the sheer agonizing pleasure, drinking in Aurora's tiny whimpers of arousal. He tore his mouth from hers, lowering his head to capture the hardened peak between his lips, tugging at the wet silk until Aurora cried out, clutched his shirtfront in tight, shivering fists.

He was actually on the verge of lowering her to the

oriental rug when the grandfather clock in the hall began to chime, penetrating Julian's passion-dazed mind and reminding him of where they were, how brief a time remained before Slayde returned.

With a herculean effort, he raised his head, staring into Aurora's astonished turquoise eyes as he slowly lowered her to her feet. "Are you all right?"

A quavering nod. "I think so."

"Then you're faring better than I." Dragging air into his lungs, Julian tried to remember when he'd ever felt so disoriented, so out of control . . . so frustrated. "I'm half-tempted to whisk you off to Gretna Green right now and damn the formalities to hell."

"I'm half-tempted to let you," Aurora returned candidly, adjusting her bodice with unsteady fingers.

Julian watched her, wanting nothing more than to tear the gown from her body and bury himself inside her. "Aurora—marry me."

She tilted her head back, an impish grin curving her lips. "You're a very convincing man, Your Grace. Further, if what just happened wasn't an acceptance of your marriage proposal, I don't know what would be."

"What just happened was only the beginning." He framed her hot cheeks between his palms, raised her gaze to meet his. "Remember one thing, Aurora. I want that stone. But I also want you."

Her fingertips traced his lower lip. "How fortunate. Soon you'll have both."

"Is that a yes?"

"That's a yes."

"I'll get a special license." He drew her fingers into his mouth one by one, nibbling lightly. "How much time do you need?"

"How much do you intend to provide?"

"A fortnight. No more. Less if possible."

"I think a fortnight would be ideal. It would give me

enough time to prepare and Courtney enough time to convince my brother he's doing the right thing by handing me over to you."

Julian chuckled. "I presume the latter will take a full two weeks."

"Maybe not. Slayde must already be amenable to the idea or he wouldn't have allowed us this time alone. But even if he doesn't require much convincing . . ." She broke off, a wistful look crossing her face.

"What is it?"

"Would you think I were foolish if I told you I'd always dreamed of a church wedding? Not a big church—heaven knows, the Huntleys haven't enough friends to fill even a small one, given how isolated I've been and how terrified people are of us. But a church nonetheless, one that makes me feel like a real bride, dressed in a traditional wedding dress of silver and white, and a lace veil topped by a coronet of wildflowers." She gave a rueful sigh. "I suppose the whole notion is absurd given the scandal I caused yesterday. We should simply have the clergyman conduct a simple, expedient ceremony and have done with it. 'Tis just something I always dreamed of."

"Then consider your dream a reality." Rather than amusement Julian felt strangely touched by the details of her dream.

"You don't mind?"

"On the contrary, I can hardly wait to see what a vision my traditional bride will be."

"The bridegroom will have to be a vision as well," she reminded him.

A twinkle. "Am I to understand my betrothed finds me lacking in physical appeal?"

"I think you're aware of just how appealing you are— to your betrothed *and* to heaven knows how many other females. What I meant was . . ."

Julian pressed his forefinger to her lips. "I think I can

manage to don conventional attire for one day—so long as you promise to help remove it that night."

"Julian." Aurora began to laugh. "You're incorrigible."

"Then we're evenly matched." He kissed her palm before releasing it. "We have but one thing more to discuss before Slayde reappears and we announce our betrothal."

"Which is?"

"A reminder of the promise you gave me not to discuss with anyone anything I revealed to you."

"I haven't forgotten. And I intend to keep my vow. Further, I understand why you secured it. Your father's ludicrous announcement that Slayde harbored the stone at Pembourne recaptured the interest of too many bloodthirsty thieves and privateers. If news of the Fox and the Falcon were to venture beyond our families, everyone would be doubly convinced that Lawrence spoke the truth. Criminals would descend on Pembourne like vultures, endangering Slayde, Courtney, and their unborn child. No, Julian, I would never divulge the truth to anyone. Other than Slayde and Courtney, of course."

"No." Julian shook his head. "When I said no one, I meant no one."

Aurora's jaw dropped. "Including Courtney and Slayde?"

"Including Courtney and Slayde."

"Absolutely not. I could never agree to that."

"You already did," Julian reminded her. "Not twenty minutes ago."

Flustered anger colored her cheeks. "But why? The truth behind the Fox and the Falcon affects Slayde as much as it does me—maybe more. He's suffered longer and in some ways more profoundly than I have; he's spent eleven years heading and protecting a family that's feared, condemned, and constantly in danger. Not to mention Courtney, who nearly lost her life as a result of the black diamond. No, Julian. I insist that you release me from that aspect of my vow. Lord knows, Courtney and Slayde have the right to know."

"Indeed they do. And we'll tell them—in a fortnight. The instant my ring is on your finger."

Aurora looked totally at sea. "I don't understand."

"Then I'll explain." Julian pressed on, determined to surmount this crucial obstacle. "Aurora, you trust me. You believe everything I've expressed to you is the truth. Unfortunately I don't think Slayde would see it that way. And I'm just not willing to take that risk."

"You think he'd doubt the existence of the journal?"

"I wish it were that simple. If the existence of the journal were all Slayde doubted, I could allay his reservations by producing it. No, I don't think he'd doubt the journal, I think he'd doubt my honorable intentions. Namely, to restore the diamond and walk away—without any compensation or reward."

"Oh." Aurora inclined her head quizzically. "You're concerned Slayde would believe you mean to keep the stone or sell it to the highest bidder."

"Exactly. Reaping a fortune. *After* I seduced his sister into marriage for the sole purpose of gaining entry to Pembourne—and whatever clues it contains. All of which he'd presume I would do just to expedite my hunt for the very diamond that would eventually make me a very rich man—and my wife a very disheartened woman." Julian's arm made a wide berth. "Hell, I wouldn't blame Slayde for his suspicions. The timing, the myriad coincidences, the sharp divergence from my solitary life—if you were my sister, I'd suspect the worst."

Aurora tucked a wisp of hair behind her ear, contemplating Julian's logic. "You're right," she agreed at last. "That's precisely the conclusion Slayde would draw. But a fortnight won't alter his opinion. He'll be equally as skeptical of your motives then as he is now."

"I agree. A fortnight won't alter his opinion. But

there's one thing it will alter: your marital status. By then, you'll be Mrs. Julian Bencroft, legally bound to me in a way Slayde can no longer undo, skepticism or not."

Surprise widened Aurora's eyes. "That's the risk you were referring to? You want to keep the facts from Slayde and Courtney simply to ensure that my brother doesn't refuse his permission for us to wed?"

"No, I want to keep the facts from them simply to ensure that you have the wedding you've always dreamed of, and to have those you love by your side." Julian's jaw set. "I intend to marry you, Aurora. Now that you've given me your consent, nothing—not even your brother—will stand in my way. For my part, we can leap into my carriage and ride off to Gretna Green this very minute, after which you're welcome to tell Courtney and Slayde everything. However, I don't think that's what you want. It would preclude your having the traditional wedding you just described *and* prevent your brother and sister-in-law from taking part in your wedding. Which would shatter your dream." He shot her a questioning look. "If I'm wrong, tell me. My carriage is in your drive. We can leave posthaste, be married in days."

"No. You're right. That's not what I want." Aurora looked touched and puzzled all at once. "For a man who's been a loner all his life, you're remarkably compassionate."

"At times."

"Then thank you for making this one of those times." She cleared her throat. "Julian, I can't help but wonder—when you asked Slayde for my hand, you obviously omitted quite a bit of what prompted your proposal. What reasons *did* you give for offering for me?"

"Honest ones. The same ones I gave you, other than the issue we just touched upon . . ." A wicked grin. ". . . and an elaborate explanation of what happens

75

when you're in my arms. Somehow, I didn't think he'd appreciate that."

"No, I don't think he would." The mischief was back in her eyes. "Very well. The truth remains our secret—but only until our wedding day. Then we tell Courtney and Slayde everything. Not merely tell them, but elicit their help. Remember, my brother knows a great deal more than I about the Huntley family history." She looked knowingly at Julian. "And you needn't worry that Slayde will insert himself in our search. Imminent fatherhood keeps him chained to Courtney's side. Dashing from estate to estate would not appeal to him at this particular time. So rest assured, information and advice is all we'll receive from my brother."

"I'll take your word for it. In fact, I'll agree to everything you just said—with one modification. We'll tell Courtney and Slayde everything the day *after* our wedding. I have plans for that evening and night—exciting, prolonged, tantalizing plans. And they include neither visitors nor conversation."

"I see." An anticipatory flush stained Aurora's cheeks. "In that case, I suppose the revelation can wait one extra day."

"I'm glad you feel that way." With mock sobriety, Julian extended his hand to her, palm up. "We're in agreement, then?"

Aurora smiled, placing her fingers in his. "We are."

"Good." Julian pressed a chaste kiss to her knuckles, his head snapping up as approaching footsteps reached his ears. "And clearly not a moment too soon."

On cue the door swung open and Slayde reentered the study, accompanied by a fine-boned young woman who was classically beautiful and extremely with child—a young woman who could be none other than the Countess of Pembourne.

"Your half hour has passed," Slayde announced,

glancing from Julian to Aurora to their still-joined hands.

"So it has," Julian concurred.

"Courtney, this is Julian Bencroft—" Slayde wrapped a protective arm about his wife, as if trying to stave off the ugly memories evoked by the name he was about to utter. "—the Duke of Morland. Morland, my wife Courtney, the Countess of Pembourne . . ." A pause. ". . . *and* Aurora's closest friend."

"I'm delighted, my lady." Julian stepped forward, kissed Courtney's hand.

"Your Grace." The countess's sea green gaze was more curious than distressed.

"Please, call me Julian. After all, we're about to become family." He tossed Slayde a cheerful look. "Speaking of which, I'm happy to report that you needn't load your pistol. A duel will not be necessary. A wedding, however, will be."

Slayde sucked in his breath, his eyes narrowed on his sister's face. "Aurora, is this truly what you want?"

"Surprisingly, yes." The glow emanating from Aurora couldn't be mistaken for anything short of genuine pleasure. "This is truly what I want."

A taut moment ticked by.

"Bloody hell," Slayde muttered. "I don't know what to do."

Julian watched Courtney and Aurora exchange a long meaningful look, after which Courtney nodded. "Slayde," she murmured, touching her husband's arm. "It's all right."

He gazed down at her, seeking and finding what he sought. "Very well," he conceded, his stare shifting to Julian. "But be good to her, Morland. Else you'll answer to me."

"You have my word," Julian drawled, giving Aurora's fingers a provocative squeeze. "I'll be extraordinarily good to her. In fact, you have my word—your sister will never want for anything." He nearly grinned as he felt Aurora's skin grow hot.

"When did you want this wedding to take place?" Slayde demanded.

"I opted for this afternoon," Julian answered frankly. "Unfortunately Aurora needs a bit more time, as does the obtaining of a special license. So we agreed upon a fortnight."

"Fine. We'll contact Vicar Rawlins. He can ride out to Pembourne, conduct the wedding in the estate's chapel—swiftly and with minimum notice from the outside world. The whole ceremony will be over in a matter of minutes, after which you can whisk Aurora away from Pembourne and from whatever dangers lurk at its gates."

"Pembourne?" Aurora broke in, with an adamant shake of her head. "Absolutely not! Slayde, I'm a prisoner to this estate. I will not get married here as well."

"Slayde," Courtney interrupted in her soothing, gentle tone. "I understand how adamant you are about ensuring Aurora's safety. But every woman wants to be a bride, to have a real wedding day. I treasured ours; I still do. Let Aurora have hers. We'll make arrangements with Vicar Rawlins, travel quietly to his church—the one where you and I were joined. Mr. Scollard can attend, as can anyone else Aurora or Julian wishes. Then we'll have a small celebration here at Pembourne, where the entire staff can attend and help us see the newly married couple off. Surely a few hours can't make much difference." A bright smile lit her face. "Besides, those hours will loudly proclaim Aurora's farewell to the name Huntley . . . and her welcome to, of all things, the name Bencroft. Would you truly want to deny Lady Altec, who will mysteriously receive word of the upcoming event a mere hour before it takes place, the opportunity to embellish upon a juicy tidbit that will—why, the very next morning—

surge beyond Devonshire, sweep through the ranks of the *ton* like a summer storm?"

"I see your point," Slayde conceded. "What good does Aurora's new status do her if nobody knows of it." His eyes narrowed suspiciously on his wife's angelic expression. "Mysteriously receive word of the upcoming event? Surge beyond Devonshire the very next morning? Why do I sense one of your schemes in the making?"

"No schemes. Simply a discreet missive delivered to Lady Altec an hour before the ceremony takes place— enough time to race off to tell her friends, not enough time for anyone to intrude upon the event. Also a few tasteful announcements of what will then be an accomplished fact to appear in the *Morning Post,* the *Gazette,* and the *Times* on the morning following the wedding— timing that will thereby preclude any unsavory types from using Aurora's wedding day as an opportunity to descend upon any of us or upon Pembourne in search of the black diamond. By the time the newspapers—or Lady Altec, whoever travels more swiftly—reach the eyes and ears of the *ton,* Aurora will be away from Pembourne and the curse."

Julian's jaw dropped, although he noted no one else in the room seemed to share his surprise. Clearly the countess's serene facade was a deceptive cloak for a character as strong and resourceful as Aurora's—the sole difference being that Courtney's fire simmered while Aurora's flared.

Abruptly Julian understood how these two women had become such close friends.

"How does that sound to you, Julian?" Courtney inquired.

"It sounds brilliant," Julian heard himself reply. "However, I must say that the true congratulations here belong to your husband. Living with one tempest is enough. But two?"

For the first time, a semblance of a smile tugged at

Slayde's lips. "I appreciate your commendation—a well-deserved one, I might add."

Aurora groaned.

Courtney tossed Julian a challenging look. "One thing more. If we hold the ceremony away from Pembourne, it will give you the opportunity to accustom yourself to the responsibility that—according to my husband's mutterings over the past half hour—you vowed to assume: that of keeping Aurora safe."

"A test, my lady?" Julian suggested boldly.

Courtney's gaze shifted from Julian to Aurora and back, her eyes twinkling with pleasure. "I think not. An onset, Your Grace."

Julian chuckled, welcoming Courtney's spunk. "In that case, I'd be delighted to shoulder my new role as Aurora's protector the very instant she becomes my wife."

"Good." Courtney turned to her husband. "Slayde?"

Still, Slayde hesitated. "The ride to the village might be too much for you and the babe."

"Our child isn't due to make an appearance for more than a month beyond Aurora's chosen wedding day," Courtney reminded him gently. "As for the ride, it's scarcely a mile from Pembourne to the village. Both the babe and I will fare wonderfully, my love. I promise."

"Fine." At last, Slayde seemed to be convinced. "A wedding it is. At the village church. With a party to follow, here at Pembourne. Would that please you, Aurora?"

"Oh, yes," Aurora breathed. "Very much." She grinned at Courtney. "Thank you."

"You're more than welcome," her friend answered in that tranquil way of hers.

"Julian." Slayde's tone and expression had lost all traces of lightheartedness. "There's one last issue we must discuss, that being the reality of your father's grand proclamation prior to his death. I realize there was no affinity between the two of you; however, I need to know your intentions with regard to his investigation. Do you mean to continue it, to support his ludicrous claim that I'm harboring the black diamond here at Pembourne? If so, you'd best tell me now before you whisk away my sister, then insert her between us."

Julian felt Aurora's pointed gaze—a gaze not furrowed in worry over where his allegiance might lie, he noted thankfully, but one that was bright with curiosity over how he proposed to address Slayde's query—one Julian himself had been anticipating.

"The answer, Slayde, is no," he returned smoothly. "I don't intend to pursue my father's so-called investigation. And not because I won't come between Aurora and her family—although I respect her feelings for you and Courtney—but because I've already perused my father's papers thoroughly, and they're no more than an empty and grasping crusade conducted by a mean-spirited man. His entire investigation consists of a notebook filled with empty accusations and rambling avenues that have turned up nothing. There isn't one shred of tangible evidence there, nor even a concrete path worthy of pursuit. Certainly nothing to compel me to further his course. In fact, I'd all but decided to dispose of his notes when it occurred to me you might want to see them, to assure yourself that I speak the truth." Julian gestured toward the window. "The papers are in my carriage. My footman will fetch them before I leave. Read them at your leisure. Then do with them what you will. In the interim, I'll make a public statement retracting my father's accusations. I might not be able to undo all the damage he caused, but perhaps I'll shake some reason into people, succeed in deterring a few prospective thieves from invading Pembourne. Does that satisfactorily address your concerns?"

Slayde gave an audible sigh of relief. "It does."

"Have we covered all your objections, then?"

"To my amazement, yes."

"Good." Julian's fingers tightened about Aurora's. "Then 'tis time to embrace the future." He turned to his bride-to-be, gave her a conspiratorial wink that spoke volumes. "The future—and all it entails."

Chapter 5

"Ah, Rory. Excellent. It's five minutes past six. You're just in time for tea and sunrise. A half hour for the former, a quarter hour for the latter."

Mr. Scollard brushed a shock of white hair from his forehead and gestured toward the tray of refreshment laid out in the Windmouth Lighthouse's small sitting room. "Come. Sit by the fire. It will warm the winter chill away. As will the tea."

"Fortifying tea, I hope," Aurora replied, slipping out of her mantle and crossing over to accept the proffered cup of steaming brew. She had long since given up being surprised by Mr. Scollard's foreknowledge of all her visits—a knowledge based not on firsthand scrutiny of her approach, but on some innate awareness that only Mr. Scollard possessed. One simply accepted Mr. Scollard's visionary abilities as a given, part of what made him the remarkable man he was.

"Very fortifying. Stronger than usual." He indicated a platter piled high with iced cakes, three of which he placed on a plate for his guest. "I made more of your favorite cakes, too. After all, this is a celebration of sorts. Even if the path leading to this all-important threshold was strewn with your customary impatience and impulsiveness." He arched a pointed brow at Aurora, then settled himself on the settee. "I don't know what I'm going to do about that reckless nature of yours," he declared, kindling the fire to a higher blaze. "'Tis a good thing I soon won't have to contend with it alone."

"Mr. Scollard." Taking his cue, Aurora plopped down in an armchair, leaning forward and staring earnestly into his face. "Have I done the right thing? Am I making a mistake? Have I totally lost my mind? I never truly imagined I'd marry at all, much less wed Julian Bencroft. What should I do?"

"My suggestion? Drink your tea. It won't stay hot forever."

"Really?" Aurora shot him an I-know-better look. "I rather suspect it might. 'Tis your tea, after all." Dutifully she drank down the whole cup, feeling that extraordinary surge of energy Mr. Scollard's tea always produced. She then proceeded to gobble up one of the cakes she so relished. "Um. Delicious," she proclaimed between bites. "But three of them? Even *I* have never managed to devour more than two." Gratefully she accepted the refilled cup Mr. Scollard handed her, then bit into her second cake. "Although I am hungrier than usual this morning. Perhaps I can indulge myself just this once. Not a crumb more than three, however. I've already been measured for my wedding dress—late yesterday afternoon, in fact. The modiste will have my head if all those exquisite yards of silk and lace don't fit."

"Wedding dress?" Mr. Scollard's forehead wrinkled in concentration. "Oh, yes. That delicate silver and white gown you've envisioned since you were five; a gown you obviously never imagined wearing, given the fact that—what was it you just said?—ah, given the fact that you never truly imagined you'd marry at all."

Aurora's lashes swept her cheeks as her friend's message found its mark. "Very well, so I daydreamed a bit as a child. Oh, all right," she amended, feeling Mr. Scollard's penetrating gaze. "So I *still* daydream now and again. That doesn't mean I ever thought I'd actually realize my dream."

"Of course not. Because you couldn't conceive of a man interesting enough to spend your life with. A man as vital and alive as you. A man with a thirst for life and a hunger for adventure. A man like Julian Bencroft."

Silence, but for the crackling flames of the fire.

"Or is it not the idea of marriage itself that's rendered you so off balance," Mr. Scollard pressed gently, "but the idea of marriage to this man in particular?"

"Everything about Julian Bencroft renders me off balance. I don't think I've righted myself since we met."

"And that disturbs you? Odd, I thought it was tedium you found disconcerting."

"I did. I do." Aurora gave a dazed shake of her head. "Listen to me. I don't know what I'm saying, much less what I'm feeling. Please, Mr. Scollard, help me."

His vivid blue eyes shone with equally vivid memories. "Your expression . . . your plea . . . you sound much as another did not too long ago. Another whom you love very much."

A sage nod. "You're speaking of Courtney."

"Surely you recall how she grappled with her feelings for Slayde?"

"Yes, but that was different."

"Was it?"

"Definitely. Courtney and Slayde fell in love. They shared their thoughts; they understood each other . . . why, Courtney transformed my brother into an entirely different man."

"After being thrust unexpectedly into his life—yes, she did. As Slayde did for her. My point exactly." Mr. Scollard took a thoughtful sip of tea. "Love is an astonishing force. Stronger than all other forces combined. Except perhaps fate. Fate, much like you, is not only fervent, she has a definite mind of her own. It appears she's decided to insert herself in your life."

"For good or for ill?"

"Your instincts say for good." A glimmer of humor. "Evidently so does your balance. Else it would have found a way to right itself by now. Two days have passed since you met the duke, and one sleepless night has elapsed since his proposal—and his revelation. Surely that's enough time to regain your sensibilities."

Aurora sat bolt upright, having scarcely heard Mr. Scollard's final sentence. "So you *do* know."

He shrugged. "There's much I know, still more I don't."

"Exactly what is the *much* to which you refer?" Aurora asked cautiously, guarding her words in a way she'd never anticipated doing with her oldest friend.

A smile touched Mr. Scollard's lips. "Your honor is as fierce as your spirit. I'm proud of you, Rory. The duke requested secrecy, and secrecy you have granted. Despite the tragedies you've faced, the limitations that have so thwarted your need to fly, your character has flourished. You'll make an exemplary wife, at least for one as uncommon as you." With that, Mr. Scollard set down his cup. "Now, to address your question about the *much* to which I refer. I refer to Geoffrey Bencroft and James Huntley. Fine men, both. Loyal to their country. Brave and intelligent—with an insatiable thirst for adventure. Much as the great-grandchildren they begot. The ones who have inherited their legacy and are soon to be joined in a partnership as profound as that of the Fox and the Falcon—a partnership that is identical in some ways, splendidly different in others." Mr. Scollard's eyes twinkled. "I needn't elaborate on the differences. In any case, Geoffrey's mind was keen, perceptive, cunning as that of a fox. James's tactics were flawless, unfailing, lethal as those of a falcon. 'Tis wrong for their memories to remain tarnished. Just as it's wrong for the black diamond to remain unrestored to the sacred temple from which it was taken. But none existed who could right those wrongs. None until now."

Aurora sucked in her breath. "If you were aware of all this, why didn't you tell me?"

"The legacy wasn't mine to share; therefore, I saw only smoky fragments, wisps of truth—until yesterday when the duke opened that chest. Suddenly the haze lifted and my vision cleared."

"Then tell me, is it Julian's and my fate to fulfill our great-grandfathers' quest?"

"You have much to fulfill, equally as much to be fulfilled. Both those tasks pose daunting challenges."

A sigh. "And of course, it's too soon for you to predict whether we'll meet those challenges."

"Meet them you shall. Surmount them?" A resigned shrug. "I see only that which is offered for my sight."

Aurora propped her chin on her hand. "Tell me about Julian."

"What is it you wish to hear?"

"Anything. I need your guidance."

An insightful look. "Do you?"

"Of course—yes." Aurora felt utterly exasperated. "I'm marrying a total stranger, a man as transient as a gypsy, as fleeting as the tide, and as overwhelming as the forces of nature."

"I concur wholeheartedly." Mr. Scollard placed a fourth cake on Aurora's plate. "All the more reason to gather your strength. Excitement can be quite taxing. As can freedom, adventure, and, of course, passion."

That brought her up short. Aurora cast a swift sidelong glance at her friend, wondering how to interpret his comment. Oh, she hadn't a doubt that he'd deliberately chosen the very words Julian had used to describe her future as his wife. But by passion did Mr. Scollard refer to a vast ecumenical passion for life? Or did he refer to something far more intimate? Could he actually perceive the wild explosion that stormed her senses each time Julian took her in his arms?

Her perusal provided no answers. The lighthouse keeper's expression was nondescript as he calmly stirred sugar into his tea. "Your betrothed is not totally dissimilar from your brother, Rory," he asserted. "Remember, autonomy is often a result, not a choice."

Aurora's speculations vanished, her mind racing off in this new and significant direction. "Especially in Julian's case; his father was a horrid, vengeful man."

"Indeed."

"What do you know of his mother?"

"Only that she was a quiet, docile woman whose health was as weak as her will. She died twenty years ago. Julian and his brother Hubert were lads at the time. Sadly, Hubert inherited his mother's frail constitution."

"Hubert was the same age as Slayde."

"Yes, senior to Julian by a year. Hubert and Slayde entered Oxford simultaneously. Unfortunately Hubert fell ill and died during that first term."

"I recall Slayde being terribly distressed when that happened," Aurora murmured. "As were my parents when Slayde told them the news. Obviously my family thought highly of Hubert."

"He was a good man, honorable of purpose, generous of nature. Quite different from his father and grandfather."

Aurora frowned. "And from Julian?"

"Not in principles, but in fact. Very different."

"Were they close?"

"In heart, yes."

"In heart," Aurora repeated. "Does that mean they cared about similar things or about each other?"

"Feelings are best expressed by those who experience them," Mr. Scollard replied.

A discouraged sigh. "If that's an answer, its meaning eludes me."

"That's because the answer you seek is not mine to convey. You will hear it from another, to whom the answer and the feelings belong. At which time, the meaning to which you refer will become abundantly clear—to both of you."

"If that *another* is Julian, I'll have to assume he talks in his sleep. As you yourself just pointed out, my betrothed is a very autonomous man, not one to expose his feelings—to anyone, much less a wife."

"The merlin is deceptive."

"Not *this* merlin," Aurora countered. "Certainly not like his namesake, the merlin falcon, who appears to be small and nonthreatening. No, Mr. Scollard, Julian is anything but deceptive. He's overwhelming in every way—stature, presence; he looks every bit as threatening as he is."

"But is he every bit as threatening as he looks? Or is that a deception unto itself; one of which even the duke himself isn't aware?"

Aurora blinked, thoroughly confused. "I don't understand what you mean."

"You will." Mr. Scollard patted her cheek and rose. "Soon. Now come. 'Tis time to climb to the tower and watch the onset of the new day. Then I must get on with my chores and you must get on with your daydreams." Another twinkle of those omniscient blue eyes. "By the way, fret not. Your wedding dress will fit perfectly. Four cakes or not."

* * *

As always, Mr. Scollard was right.

Thirteen days later, the dress *did* fit perfectly. Although, Aurora mused as she pirouetted before the looking glass, was the impeccable fit the result of Mr. Scollard's prophecy alone or had it something to do with her own inexhaustible bursts of energy—the bubbling anticipation that had made settling down for meals virtually impossible?

She'd probably never know for sure. All she *did* know was that ever since Mr. Scollard's prediction, she'd scarcely managed to stand still, much less sit, a fact that had thoroughly exasperated the poor maids who'd required her overseeing to pack her bags, and infuriated her already peevish modiste who had insisted on measuring *mademoiselle* for a wardrobe of new suitable gowns. Suitable for what? Aurora had wanted to scream. The next months would doubtless be consumed not with attending lavish house parties, but with searching for the black diamond. Madame Gerard, however, didn't know that. Further, the woman was unyielding, claiming that a married woman—and a duchess no less—required an entire line of new dresses, one for every occasion. Rather than argue, Aurora had steeled herself for what turned out to be prolonged hours of taking measurements, choosing colors, and selecting fabrics.

The sole diversions that had gotten her through the endless fortnight were her daily romps about the grounds with Tyrant—prompting a host of frustrated guards to follow in their wake—and her recurrent visits to the lighthouse. Three or four times each day, she'd raced down and burst into Mr. Scollard's domain, interrupting his work to pace about, babble incessantly, then become restless and rush back to the manor. The lighthouse keeper, extraordinary man that he was, had never complained, only listened patiently and silently, an odd smile playing about his lips.

During several sleepless nights, Aurora had contemplated slipping out of the manor and making her way to the far grounds of Pembourne where her great-grandfather's falcon cages stood. No one had disturbed them in years, so they'd be just as James had left them, other than the fact that they were now empty. Or perhaps not empty, perhaps holding a clue that would help her and Julian find the black diamond.

No. She'd dared not give in to that temptation lest the guards report her actions to Slayde, necessitating an explanation she'd promised Julian she would not give—yet.

Julian.

Apart from Aurora's speculations over the black diamond, Julian had been the major source of her sleeplessness. Maddeningly, she'd seen him but once during that interminable waiting period, four days prior to the nuptials when he'd come to flourish their newly acquired marriage license and to tell her privately—during the two minutes he managed to get her alone—that he'd uncovered nothing of consequence at Morland.

He'd also managed during those same two minutes to kiss her senseless—deep, drugging kisses that had left Aurora trembling long after he released her, long after his carriage disappeared around Pembourne's drive.

Between her preoccupation with the mystery hovering at their doorstep and the escalating fire Julian had kindled inside her, Aurora was ready to explode into a million scalding pieces.

The arrival of today, her wedding day, had indeed been a welcome relief.

For the first time since Julian's proposal, Aurora had applauded the deluge of activity that awaited her. From the instant the sun rose, excited servants had darted in and out of her chambers, preparing her bath, fussing over the selection of her undergarments, crooning over her gown.

At last, there she stood, gazing at her own reflection, nearly giddy with anticipation. Reverently she caressed the delicate silver and white creation that billowed at her feet, wondering if the flame-haired apparition staring back through awed turquoise eyes could in fact be she.

"You look beautiful." Courtney hovered in the doorway, a vision in lilac silk, lovely and glowing with impending motherhood and sisterly pride. She beamed her approval as two maids feathered Aurora's filmy lace veil about her shoulders in a shimmering white cascade. "Your bridegroom is going to swoon the instant you enter the chapel."

With a wry grin, Aurora reached up, touched the coronet of wildflowers that crowned her head. *"That* I doubt. Somehow I think there has yet to be a sight overwhelming enough to cause Julian to swoon."

"You underestimate yourself—*and* your effect on the man you're about to wed." Courtney walked over, nodding warmly from one maid to the other. "You've done a splendid job. Thank you both. I'll take over from here."

A minute later, Courtney and Aurora were alone.

Aurora cast a speculative glance at her friend. "Is something amiss? You're not feeling ill, are you?"

"Everything is fine. I feel wonderful." Courtney smiled, laying a caressing palm atop her abdomen. "The babe and I both do," she added. "The reason I asked the maids to leave is so you and I could talk—alone. This is the last chance we'll have to do so, at least the last chance before you leave Pembourne as Julian's wife."

Even as Courtney spoke, the sound of horses' hooves reached their ears, confirmation that the Huntley carriage had been brought around front and was now being readied for its drive to the chapel.

"Our last chance to talk alone?" Aurora murmured with her first glimmer of trepidation. "That sounds so—

final. Courtney, our friendship . . . our times together . . ." She chewed her lip, tried again. "You, better than anyone, know Pembourne has been more of a prison to me than a home. Slayde spent most of my life abroad, sequestering me here amid a host of guards. I realize he was only doing it to protect me. Nevertheless, my devotion to the servants notwithstanding, I have no affinity for this estate. But you—that's another matter entirely." Aurora's voice quavered a bit. "I feel as if we're sisters, and I don't mean only through wedlock. You mean the world to me, and marriage or not, I don't want things to change between us."

"Between us?" Courtney shook her head fiercely, seizing her friend's hands and squeezing them tightly. "That's never going to happen. Nor did I mean to imply that it might. As far as you and I are concerned, the only thing that will change is your residence. We'll still see each other constantly, confide our thoughts and our feelings, share our exploits. No, what I wanted to discuss was a different relationship, one you're first entering into; one that definitely *will* change your life." A pause. "Aurora, you're embarking on a whole new path. Along with a whole new set of experiences, different from any you've ever known. Beginning tonight."

Aurora didn't pretend to misunderstand. "You're referring to my wedding night."

"Yes. I am." Courtney's gaze probed Aurora's, her sea green eyes alight with concern rather than embarrassment. "You and I have conversed about everything under the sun—except this. So let me begin by asking, do you know what to expect?"

"Yes—and no," Aurora replied truthfully. "I've read every book in Pembourne's library, some of which become quite detailed on the subject of coupling. I've also been to the barn enough times to see animals mate. So yes, I know what to expect. Or rather, I thought I did.

But when Julian holds me, kisses me . . ." She shook her head in bewilderment. "I feel things I don't understand at all. So do I know what to expect? I think not."

"That's because what you understand are the mechanics," Courtney returned softly. "Unfortunately those are the easiest, perhaps the only, aspects of lovemaking one can truly explain. The rest you have to experience yourself. And you will. The pull between you and Julian is strong, so strong it's palpable. Let that pull guide you, and I suspect that tonight will be the most extraordinary night of your life, followed by countless others in its wake."

Aurora blinked in amazement. "Somehow I know you're right. *How* I know that is beyond my comprehension, given that Julian and I are virtual strangers. Courtney, I've been alone with the man but twice. Yet, both times I became someone else, behaved like a total wanton. I never imagined feeling so . . . acting so . . ."

"You needn't explain. Further, you're *not* a wanton. You're a warm, vibrant woman who's only just discovering what it's like to be attracted to an equally vibrant man." Courtney's expression turned impish. "I shall try to restrain myself from reminding you that 'twas I who predicted this very situation would someday occur. Further, I shall avoid mentioning that your response to my prediction was to insist you were never going to marry, never going to find a man interesting enough to spend your life with. Well, it appears I was right, doesn't it?"

"You didn't do a very good job of restraining yourself," Aurora commented, her lips twitching. "Nevertheless, yes, you were right. Tell me, how did you become so clever?"

"Simple. I met your brother. You, better than anyone, know how I feel about Slayde."

"And how he feels about you. Slayde makes you come alive in a way I'm only now beginning to understand."

"Yes. He does. And I have a nagging suspicion that Julian will do the same for you."

"I share that nagging suspicion." Aurora made a helpless gesture. "And to think I'm saying such a thing after sampling no more than the most cursory taste—a taste that nearly made me swoon."

Laughter bubbled up in Courtney's throat. "Then if I were you, I'd prepare to succumb, for the entire feast lies just ahead."

The trip to the chapel was uneventful, the guards having followed closely behind to ensure that nothing and no one disrupted the morning nuptials. Messengers had been dispatched to London days earlier with strict orders to deliver the wedding announcement in time for tomorrow's newspapers, then to travel to Lady Altec's estate and deliver Courtney's missive just before the ceremony commenced.

Thus the chapel was quiet and peaceful at half after eleven when Slayde escorted Aurora down the aisle to begin her new life.

Aurora's heart was pounding so wildly she could scarcely breathe, her gaze darting about the small pillared chapel, from Mr. Scollard's proud expression to Courtney's loving smile to Vicar Rawlins who stood ready to perform the ceremony.

Coming to rest upon the sinfully handsome man to whom she would soon be joined.

Clad in a formal dark cutaway coat and breeches, Julian turned toward her, his topaz eyes glittering more brilliantly than all the room's candles combined. As promised, he was the essence of protocol, his snow white cravat starched and crisply tied, his double-breasted waistcoat cut just so. Even his black hair had been trimmed, although it still hung longer at the nape than was fashionable, just brushing the collar of his frilled white shirt. Conventionally dressed or not, he still looked dangerous, formidable, like a reckless pirate in gentleman's attire.

He was devastating.

His bold stare met Aurora's, then swept her from head to toe, thorough, possessive, blazing with unmistakable approval and undisguised hunger.

She and Slayde stopped before him, and Aurora felt her brother hesitate, clearly questioning what he was about to do.

Julian sensed it, too, although the only overt sign he gave was the slight tensing of his body, the ever-so-subtle narrowing of his gaze. He stepped forward and held out his hand, addressing Slayde even as he waited for Aurora to place her fingers in his. "She belongs with me, Slayde."

From the corner of her eye, Aurora saw Slayde glance at Courtney, saw her friend's reassuring nod.

Slayde released his sister, stood by as she placed her hand in Julian's. "Be good to her," Slayde commanded quietly. "Make her happy."

"I intend to."

The very words, the fierce promise they contained, made Aurora's mouth go dry. She moved to stand beside her bridegroom, walked the remaining distance with him to the altar, wondering if her nerves—*and* her knees—would hold out to the ceremony's end.

"You're breathtaking, *soleil*," Julian murmured, a whisper of sound that flooded her body with heat. She didn't dare reply, didn't dare so much as look at him. If she did, whatever semblance of control she had left would shatter.

The vicar began speaking the timeless words, asking the age-old questions that would forever transform Aurora's life.

As if in a dream, she heard Julian speak his vows,

heard herself utter her own. Julian turned to her, his hand steady as he slid the delicate gold band upon her trembling finger, the metal cool against her overheated skin.

The ring reached its destination and Julian lingered, his thumb caressing her palm in a motion that both soothed and inflamed.

". . . I now pronounce you man and wife."

The finality of the proclamation, suspended in the air, permeated the chapel with its significance. The unthinkable had just occurred. After four generations of relentless hatred, the Huntleys and the Bencrofts had been irrevocably joined.

With a gentleness that surprised her, Julian tipped Aurora's chin up, brushed her lips with his. "Hold on a little longer," he urged in a husky, teasing voice. "At least until there's a secluded spot for me to carry you to. *Then* you can collapse."

Despite the swooning sensation induced by his vow, Aurora smiled. "That's quite an incentive, Your Grace," she whispered back. "Why, I'm feeling steadier on my feet already."

Julian sucked in his breath, golden sparks igniting his eyes. "Careful, *soleil*. Else we'll miss the party you wanted so badly." With that he straightened, gripping Aurora's elbow and guiding her to the congratulations that awaited them.

The midday breakfast at Pembourne was perfect. Laid out in the spacious green salon, it boasted a buffet of delicacies ranging from potted salmon and lobster to turkey and ham in jelly, to pastry sandwiches with all different types of jams and marmalade, to a magnificent brides-cake adorned with a rainbow of wildflowers. Most of all, it encompassed all the people Aurora loved, from Courtney and Slayde to Mr. Scollard, to the servants who had raised her.

It was everything a bride could dream of.

Still, throughout the entire splendid event Aurora was acutely attuned to Julian's presence beside her—a fact that he was not only aware of, but hell-bent on intensifying. His glances were frequent, seductive, his movements orchestrated to ensure as much physical contact with his bride as possible—his fingers brushing her, his breath ruffling her hair, his arm anchoring her waist. By mid-afternoon, Aurora's head was swimming, the tension inside her having escalated to the point where she felt as if she were dangling at the edge of a tantalizing precipice.

She wondered how much more she could endure.

"Shall we?"

She was standing at the window clutching her wine-glass and watching the sun shift to the west when Julian's deep voice resounded behind her, asking the long-awaited question.

Nearly dropping the glass, she whirled about to face him. "Shall we what?" she blurted, sounding like a bloody ninny.

A corner of his mouth lifted. "And here I thought you were eager for tonight to begin."

"I am." She drew a calming breath. "Does this mean you're ready to leave?"

"I was ready before the party began. I simply tried to give you as much time as you needed to fulfill your dream. Have I?"

"Yes." There was no point in lying. She wanted to be alone with Julian as much as he wanted to be alone with her.

"Good." His smile applauded her candor. "Then go up and change. After that, you can say your good-byes and we'll be gone."

Aurora blinked as a sudden thought occurred to her. "Are we going to Morland?"

"No," he stated flatly. "Morland is not my home. We'll attend to business soon enough. For tonight, we're traveling to my manor in Polperro."

"Polperro! Is that where your Cornish manor is located? Mr. Scollard has told me so many legends that revolve around Polperro."

"I'm sure he has. And yes, that's the home of which I spoke. 'Tis a quiet manor nestled beneath the cliffs, right along the Channel. I think you'll find it infinitely more appealing than Morland's dreary walls. I know I do."

"I'm sure I will." Aurora fingered the lacy folds of her gown. "Since I'll see Courtney and Slayde tomorrow, I won't need to make any lengthy good-byes."

"Splendid. I'll have my carriage brought around. Your bags have already been placed inside. But I'll make sure everything is in order."

Aurora's brows rose. "You're very resourceful."

"You have no idea how resourceful—yet. But you will soon." With a provocative wink, Julian strolled off.

Her heart drumming, Aurora slipped from the room and sprinted up the stairs. Without assistance she unpinned her headpiece, then reached behind her, working free enough buttons of her wedding dress so she could squirm out of it. She lay both gown and headpiece on the bed, pausing to caress the gown's diaphanous lace, touch the rainbow-hued flowers that had crowned her veil.

Yes, her wedding day had indeed fulfilled all her dreams.

But she had a distinct feeling that her wedding night would surpass them.

With that in mind, she scooted about the bedchamber, readying herself for the trip to Polperro.

A quarter hour later, clad in a soft pearl-colored carriage dress, Aurora descended the stairs and made her way back to the salon. Standing at the threshold, she motioned to Courtney, who spied her friend at once.

Acknowledging Aurora's signal, she turned to Slayde, touching his arm to alert him to the situation.

Together they walked out and joined Aurora in the hallway.

"I thought I saw you disappear," Courtney said with a twinkle. "I assume you needed no assistance donning your gown?"

"No. I managed just fine. Besides, I didn't want to disturb the servants. They're all having such a lovely time."

"You're leaving, I presume," Slayde inserted.

"Yes." Aurora's heart accelerated yet another beat. "We're going to Julian's house in Polperro."

"Very well." Slayde didn't question the choice.

"Have your bags been loaded?" Courtney asked.

"Yes. Julian took care of everything. He's gone to summon his carriage, after which we can be off."

"Here he is." Slayde gestured toward the entranceway where Julian had just reentered the manor.

Courtney gave Aurora a fierce hug. "Remember what I said," she whispered.

"I will." Aurora returned the hug, then leaned up to kiss her brother's cheek. "Thank you for this day," she said solemnly. "It was all I hoped for, and given the circumstances, more than I deserved."

"You *deserve* to be happy," Courtney countered. "And I believe your new husband is just the man to manage that." She cleared her throat as Julian approached, raising her voice to a normal tone. "When will we next see you?"

"Tomorrow," Aurora answered.

"Or the day after." Julian's expression was the picture of innocence. "After all, the ride to Polperro will take several hours; longer, since much of it will be under cover of darkness. Aurora will be exhausted by the time we arrive. She needs a chance to rest and settle in. So don't worry if our visit to Pembourne is delayed a day or two." So saying, he captured his bride's arm, drawing her gently—but determinedly—toward the door. "The day was memorable," he added, his gaze locked with Slayde's. "Thank you. And don't worry. Aurora is in the very best of hands."

Chapter 6

Pembourne's iron gates disappeared in the distance, the
sun an orange glow on the horizon.

"At last," Aurora sighed, leaning back against the
carriage seat. "Freedom."

Julian chuckled, crossing one long leg over the other.
"An ironic proclamation. Most people would refer to
marriage as confinement, not freedom."

"Are you one of those people?" Aurora inquired,
feeling not the least bit threatened.

"I was once. Now? I think not." One dark brow rose in
amusement. "Given your smug expression, I suspect you
already knew what my answer would be."

"I did. Not because I'm smug, but because you're
hardly a man who would commit himself to a life he
expected to be confining."

"True. Nor are you a woman who would agree to
marry such a man."

"Also true." Aurora smiled. "I suppose we both crave the same things."

"We do. What's more, we will. I'm counting on it."

There was no mistaking the suggestive gleam in Julian's eye, the husky note in his voice.

Aurora found herself wishing the journey ahead were not quite so long. Or, given that it was, that the message Julian was issuing were not quite so explicit or quite so effective.

Silence hovered—thick, charged.

Excruciating.

"Lady Altec must be racing about Devonshire with her news by now," Aurora blurted at last, unable to withstand the escalating tension.

"You're nervous," Julian stated in that same unbearably seductive tone.

"No, I'm searching for a topic of conversation."

"Don't." Julian yanked the carriage curtains shut, then swung across to sit beside his bride.

"Don't what?" Aurora managed. "Don't be nervous? Or don't search for a topic of conversation?"

"Either." He tipped her chin up, wrapping one red-gold tress about his forefinger. "We've waited an interminable fortnight—not to mention an unending day—for this." He brought the tress to his lips, savored its texture with his mouth. "Finally, finally, the wait is over."

"Not yet," Aurora reminded him, staring at the tanned column of his throat, her heart slamming against her ribs. "Polperro is still hours away."

"Exactly." Julian lowered his head, kissed her neck, the curve of her shoulder, the hollow behind her ear. "And I intend to make the most of every heated moonlit hour."

Aurora's eyes widened. "You're not suggesting . . . ?"

"Indeed I am." He feathered kisses across her cheekbones, the delicate bridge of her nose, nibbled lightly at her lower lip. "Did you really expect me to wait hours longer? Never, *soleil*. I've been on fire for you from the instant we met, burning to be inside you. Now my ring is on your finger. And nothing is going to stop me from making you mine."

"But, Julian . . ." Aurora struggled for sanity. "In a carriage?"

"Um-hum." His tongue traced her lip. "Shockingly unconventional, wouldn't you say? A closed carriage, a cramped seat. Nothing but you, me, and the ecstasy of our joined bodies becoming one." He kissed her deeply.

"What if the driver should . . ."

"He won't." Julian was tugging pins from her hair, tossing them haphazardly to the carriage floor. "No one will." His molten gaze bore into hers, lush with promise. "No one will see how abandoned I make you. No one will hear your cries of pleasure. No one but me." He tunneled his fingers through her hair. "Adventure. Excitement. Passion. Everything I promised you. Say yes."

Aurora shivered, excitement flaring deep inside her.

"Tell me you want this," Julian breathed into her lips. "Tell me you've dreamed about having me inside you, filling you to bursting, moving until you shatter in my arms. Tell me, Aurora."

"I have," she whispered, her head swimming from the impact of his words, the graphic images they invoked. "Constantly."

"Then let's throw ourselves into the fire—douse it, reignite it. We have hours. Let me make you my wife. Here. Now. Then let me take you to bed and start all over again, make love to you until you beg me to stop."

Aurora's palms slid up his coat to his shoulders. "Somehow I doubt that will happen."

"Good. Then we'll make love until we die." Julian's arms closed around her, no longer coaxing but insistent. "Say yes."

She could barely speak. "Yes."

His mouth crushed down on hers—hot, hard—blazing with an unrelenting possessiveness that said there would be no turning back, no stopping until their passion was spent.

Aurora never wanted to stop.

With a soft cry of pleasure, she twined her arms about Julian's neck, submerging herself in the kiss, tilting back her head and parting her lips to his seeking tongue.

A hard shudder wracked Julian's body, and he took what she offered, dragging her onto his lap as his mouth ate at hers, devouring her in a kiss of absolute, utter possession. He raised her arms higher about his neck, crushing her against him as their tongues mated, stroked, melded, their breath coming in tight, harsh rasps.

Aurora was lost. The power of Julian's body, the fervor of his touch, the unyielding pressure of his lips as they claimed hers—the sensations were almost too much to bear. Liquid heat surged through her, rendering her breasts heavy and her muscles weak. Shaking with reaction, she pressed closer, her fingers gliding through the longer hair at his nape, sliding beneath the cool strip of his cravat.

Julian's entire body went taut.

Abruptly he responded, his hand shifting to unfasten her gown, to find the smooth skin of her back and awaken it with his hungry caresses. The gown slid down baring her shoulders, the upper slope of her breasts. He tore his mouth from hers, his gaze a topaz inferno as he stared down at her. Then he lowered his head, burning a series of hot open mouthed kisses across her newly bared skin.

Desire coiled tight in Aurora's abdomen, licked fire through her loins. She shifted restlessly on Julian's lap, cradling his head in her hands as she silently begged him to continue.

Her wordless plea was answered. Julian shifted lower, capturing her nipple through her chemise, drawing the aching tip into his mouth, and surrounding it in liquid heat. He repeated the caress—once, twice, then again and again as his need intensified.

A muffled whimper escaped Aurora's mouth.

Suddenly Julian raised his head, scrutinized Aurora's face, and then satisfied with what he saw, yanked at the ribbons of her chemise, pushing it away from her body.

Her breasts spilled out, rising toward him, the tight nipples begging for his touch.

"You're so bloody beautiful," he muttered, reaching out to cup her warm flesh, smooth his palm over the sensitized peak.

"Julian . . . please." Aurora was trembling, her whole body exploding at his caress. "Please."

Again he lowered his dark head, running his open mouth across her breast until waiting was no longer feasible. Then he captured her naked nipple between his lips, drew it into his mouth—not softly, gently, but urgently, fully, his tongue lashing across the hardened peak.

Streaks of jagged heat rushed through Aurora, and she cried out, grateful that the noise of the carriage drowned out her ragged pleas.

"More of you," Julian muttered thickly, "God, I need more of you." He shifted to her other breast, his hands and mouth taking her simultaneously this time, as if he couldn't bear to deny himself one shred of the ecstasy derived from possessing her.

Dizziness surged through Aurora's head and her eyes slid closed, all sensation concentrated beneath Julian's caresses. Just when she thought she'd die, his mouth left her breast and reclaimed her lips, his tongue beginning a rhythm of thrust and retreat that was a prelude of what was to be. His arm slid beneath her, arched her closer to him, his thumb moving provocatively across her damp nipple as his mouth ravaged hers.

The earth shifted and the soft cloth of the carriage seat pressed against Aurora's back. Somewhere in the dim outskirts of her mind, she realized she was in a prone position. An instant later Julian followed her down, covering her half-naked body with his fully clothed one.

Aurora's lashes lifted and she stared into Julian's blazing eyes, his handsome face taut with desire. She reached up, tugged at the knot of his cravat until it came free, then tossed the strip of cloth to the floor. His buttons came next—his shirt and waistcoat—and despite their trembling, Aurora's fingers managed to complete their task. She spread open the sides of his shirt, marveling at his strength, the corded muscles rippling beneath his skin. Awed by his overwhelming presence, she smoothed her palms over his hair-roughened chest, the powerful breadth of his shoulders. Julian lay poised, utterly still, the fine sheen of perspiration covering his skin the only indication of the effect she was having on him.

Until her thumbs found his nipples. Shuddering beneath her teasing caress, Julian growled her name, lowered his full weight on her, crushing her into the seat, melding his body to hers.

"Julian." It was a whimper of unbearable pleasure and incredible discovery. Aurora arched, rubbing her breasts against him, gliding her palms beneath his open shirt to explore the solid planes of his back.

With a muttered oath, Julian threaded his fingers through her hair, discarding the remaining pins he encountered along the way. "God, you feel so good," he rasped, nudging her thighs apart and settling himself between them. "So damned good." He pushed against her, and Aurora gasped, feeling the rigid evidence of his hunger as it pressed against her yearning core. Even separated by his breeches and her gown, the sensation was overpowering, so acute she couldn't breathe.

"Do that again," Aurora managed.

A muscle working in his jaw, Julian repeated the motion, pushing deep into her warmth, circling his hips so she could get the full impact of the caress.

"I'm going to die," Aurora gasped, parting her legs further, beckoning him deeper. "Don't . . . stop . . ."

Her plea ended on a moan as he thrust forward again, grinding his hips against hers and groaning her name.

Cool air swept over her as Julian rose up, lifting her and tugging her gown and chemise down and away, dragging her stockings along with them.

She was naked.

Rather than embarrassed, Aurora felt only a wondrous sense of relief. She cracked open her eyes and watched Julian's expression as he drank in her nudity.

"Exquisite." His fingers followed his gaze, rounding the curve of her waist and hips, smoothing over the flat of her stomach, descending lower to find the haven he most sought.

His hand was shaking violently as he brushed the auburn cloud between her thighs, shifted lower to open her, touch her where she so desperately needed him to be.

A hoarse growl escaped his lips as he encountered her wetness, the heated warmth that beckoned him into her. His finger slipped inside, parted the tender folds, and eased deeper, touching, stroking, awakening.

Aurora's hips lifted of their own accord, her eyes widening at the realization of her body's reflexive, clamoring response. The feel of him inside her was rapture—and yet at the same time it wasn't enough. She whimpered as he aroused her, his finger withdrawing only to glide forward again, repeating the caress over and over until Aurora begged for more, knowing that without it she would die.

Julian gave it to her. He added a second finger, stretching her as he penetrated, giving her a dizzying sense of fullness that made Aurora moan, toss her head to and fro. Still it wasn't enough—and he knew it—for abruptly his rhythm intensified, his caresses delving deeper, moving faster, matching the undulations of her hips.

When his thumb found the bud of her desire, Aurora nearly came up off the seat. Her breath lodged in her throat, shock waves of sensation shooting through her like cannon fire.

"Julian . . . my God . . ." She yearned to say more, to plead with him to continue, but she couldn't speak, could scarcely recapture her breath. All she could do was gaze wildly up at him, praying he'd read the urgency in her eyes.

Julian's forehead was dotted with sweat, his own eyes blazing with a fierce hot light. "I know, Rory," he muttered in a guttural tone. "I know. I need that, too."

With that his thumb glided over her again, then again, his fingers continuing their excruciating assault as his thumb worked its magic.

With a sharp inarticulate cry, Aurora reached a pinnacle of sensation. Everything inside her converged then shattered, her body unraveling in a series of contractions that spiraled out from her core, quaked through her limbs.

Julian made a harsh, triumphant sound, his teeth clenching as he pressed deeper, letting her climax wash over him, grip his fingers in completion.

Collapsing onto the seat, Aurora went limp, her muscles weak, her body boneless in the exquisite aftermath. Eyes shut, she drifted dazed and replete, yet thoroughly aware of Julian's caresses within her, soothing her as he withdrew.

She cracked open her eyes. "That was glorious."

Despite his fierce arousal, the unabated tension permeating his body, Julian grinned at her straightforward understatement. "I'm glad."

"But there's more." She reached up, tugged at the top button of his breeches. "For both of us."

Julian's hand stilled hers, all humor having vanished. "Aurora, listen to me. This is your first time. No matter how gentle I am, I'm going to hurt you. I swear, I'll do everything in my power to minimize that pain. But my control is about to snap, that's how close to the edge I am. If you touch me, I'll . . ." His breath expelled in a hiss as, totally disregarding her husband's warning, Aurora wriggled her fingers free, worked them into the opening of his breeches, and did precisely what Julian had cautioned her against.

"You're so hot," she whispered, freeing two buttons to ease her way. "So powerful. I can actually feel you pulsing against my hand." She dispensed with the remaining buttons and watched in fascination as his rigid manhood sprang free. "Julian, you're magnificent." She traced a line to the straining tip.

Julian went wild. Growling her name, he tore off his clothing, flinging it about the carriage even as he came down over his bride, tugging apart her thighs and settling himself between them. "Dammit, Aurora," he rasped. "I'm going to . . ."

"I want that," she breathed, awed by his expression, the near-violent motions of his body. His hips were thrusting even before he penetrated her, his taut manhood desperately seeking the heated entrance it craved.

With unerring skill he found her.

Renewed pleasure shimmered through Aurora in rippling waves as Julian crowded into her tight hot passage. His earlier caresses had left her damp, pliant, and she opened to him eagerly, readily, gasping as she discovered this new extravagant sense of fullness. He pushed deeper, stretching her more, demanding that she take all of him.

"God." He ground out the word. "You feel so . . . damned . . . good."

"So do you," Aurora whispered. And she meant it. Nothing could describe this exquisite sensation of being possessed; nothing could lessen its wonder. Not even when the fullness transformed to pressure, threatened to become pain.

Biting her lip, Aurora wrapped her arms around Julian, caressing his feverish skin, feeling the sweat-drenched planes of his back shuddering beneath her touch. Her palms shifted to his shoulders, savoring the rigid muscles that—despite his earlier claim—trembled as they fought to slow his frenzied entry. "Don't," she whispered. "Don't hold back."

He shook his head, hard. "I'm hurting you."

"I don't care."

"Feel . . . with me," Julian rasped, his breathing harsh, labored. "Feel . . . beyond the pain . . ." He broke off, shifting his weight to his elbows, his hand sliding between their bodies, his fingers finding her.

A jolt of pleasure shot through Aurora, making her arch, drawing Julian deeper inside her. Pain became a reality—a reality that was eclipsed by the escalating sensations Julian's touch rekindled. He lowered his head, kissed her, his mouth hot and slow, his tongue gliding over hers even as his fingers glided over her most sensitive spot. Again, again—until everything went spinning away in a tidal wave of sensation and Aurora's nails dug into Julian's back, tugging him closer, needing him more, more.

When she was beyond rational thought, Julian acted.

With one purposeful lunge of his hips, he thrust past the thin veil of her innocence, burying himself to the hilt in her clinging warmth. Aurora tensed, her body registering a fleeting protest.

That protest died as quickly as it had begun.

Ever so slightly Julian rocked against her, his fingers

continuing their erotic assault, refusing to allow her pleasure to recede. She melted around him in a rush, lifting against his palm, and by her very action, forcing him so deep inside her, she gasped.

Julian's reaction was savage. Throwing back his head, he emitted a feral roar, the veins in his neck standing out with the force of his need. He dragged his hand free, grasping Aurora's thighs and lifting them high around his waist. Clutching her bottom, he hauled her against him, opening her fully and crushing her loins to his.

This time it was Aurora who screamed.

Drowning pleasure coursed through her, throbbing through her body, drenching her yearning core. She shook her head vehemently when Julian withdrew, only to cry out her rapture as he drove forward again, filling her to bursting and grinding their hips together. His thrusts intensified—faster, harder—melding their loins over and over as he moved on her, in her. Reality vanished, time ceased to exist, and the world disintegrated into nothing but Julian . . . Julian . . . Julian . . .

They went over the edge together. Aurora sobbed as the contractions claimed her, washed over her in great untamable waves. From a distance she heard Julian emit a guttural shout, grip her to him as if to bind them forever. Then he was pounding into her, pulsing surges of release flooding from his body to hers in spasms Aurora could actually feel.

Drenched in sweat, they collapsed on the carriage seat, Julian's body blanketing Aurora's completely. She was acutely aware of the tremors rippling through him, the final surges of his seed spilling into her. Rather than cumbersome, his weight felt wonderfully comforting, and Aurora's eyelids drooped, too weary to remain open another instant. She was more exhausted than she'd ever dreamed possible, her body too numb to ache, too sated to move.

She must have slept.

A bumpy, jostling motion awakened her, and her eyes fluttered open. Frowning, she tried to recall where she was, why it was so dark, and why the room was moving.

The powerful body atop hers jogged her memory.

Shifting a bit, Aurora became abruptly aware of how battered she felt, how cramped the carriage seat really was. Still she was reluctant to stir. She touched strands of Julian's damp hair, stroked his head as it rested in the crook of her neck, his body relaxed and devoid of tension.

And inside hers still.

"You're awake." Julian's observation was deep, husky, murmured just beside her ear.

Aurora smiled. "You sound disappointed."

"Only because you feel so bloody good." He raised his head, his expression half teasing, half sober. "And now I'll have to move."

"Don't." Her arms tightened around him.

"Sweetheart, I've all but crushed you." He cast a rueful glance at the seat. "For the first time I regret our whereabouts. Were this a bed, I'd manage to ease over enough to free you of my weight while staying deep inside you. As it is . . ." He brushed her lips with his, then—with great reluctance—withdrew, kneeling on the seat and helping Aurora to a sitting position. "Are you all right?" he asked quietly, concern knitting his brows.

Aurora leaned her head back, studying her husband with drowsy, sated eyes. "Oh, I think I'm a good deal better than 'all right.'" She stretched, unbothered by her nudity, her sigh the epitome of contentment. "Passion, excitement, and adventure all within hours of exchanging our vows. I'm duly impressed, Your Grace."

Julian chuckled, brushing tendrils of hair from Aurora's flushed cheeks. "As am I, *soleil*—even if you did completely ignore my warning."

"Is that a complaint?"

"On the contrary. Even I never anticipated quite how high our fire would burn."

Scrambling to the edge of the seat, Aurora reached down and groped through their discarded clothing until she found Julian's waistcoat, extracted his timepiece.

"We've only been traveling two hours," she announced. "That gives us more than enough time to rebuild the fire—several times, in fact."

Laughter rumbled from Julian's chest. "Are you going to be insatiable, my beautiful bride?"

"Would you mind?"

"I'll adjust—somehow." Julian tugged her into the circle of his arms. "Of course, we'll have to save our more inventive explorations for my bed, where I'll have room enough to fully enjoy you—in every way." He kissed her hair, traced the delicate column of her spine. "But I think we can find enough to keep us occupied. At least for the duration of our journey."

They arrived at Julian's Polperro manor in an utterly disheveled state—if the flustered expressions of the driver and footmen who saw them alight were any indication. Thankfully, the remaining servants were all abed, partly because the hour was late and partly because they'd been advised to make themselves scarce. Thus, no one else witnessed the newly married couple's less than conventional entrance.

Julian ushered Aurora straight to his bedchamber, along with the tantalizing promise that she could explore the manor to her heart's content—after *he'd* finished exploring *her* to his.

Aurora was more than happy to delay her explorations indefinitely.

Kicking off her slippers, she crawled onto the bed, eagerly awaiting their next foray into the exhilarating world of passion. As if on cue, her body registered a protest, the discomfort between her legs intensifying, the muscles in her limbs throbbing a dissent. Hell and damnation, she admonished herself, watching Julian cross over to the fireplace, stoke the flames a bit higher. A long, enticing night awaited—a night she refused to forego because of her own understandable but intolerable physical limitations.

Julian turned, his gaze sweeping over her, probing, astute. "Rest for a minute," he commanded gently. "I'll be right back."

Relieved for this opportunity to recoup her strength, Aurora complied, curling onto her side and wriggling about until she found a comfortable position.

She half-dozed. From a distance, she heard sounds, but their meaning didn't register until she felt Julian undress her, swing her into his arms. Then she blinked, glancing about, and realized with surprise that while she'd rested, he'd produced a large copper tub and filled it with pots of steaming water.

"In you go," Julian murmured, lowering her into the bath.

Aurora sighed with pleasure as the hot water washed over her, relaxing her cramped muscles and magically easing the soreness between her thighs.

"Better?" he asked.

"Heaven. How did you know?"

One dark brow rose. "How did I know? I'm the cause of those aches, remember? The man who just spent long hours ravaging his virgin bride in a cramped carriage."

A smug smile curved her lips. "I remember. I also remember doing my share of the ravaging."

"So you did." With a wicked grin, Julian began stripping off his clothes. "Nonetheless, the time has come to restore your poor battered body." So saying, he seized a bar of soap and stepped into the tub. "Of course you'll require a lady's maid to help you wash."

A giggle escaped Aurora's lips. "You're a very formidable lady's maid."

"Ah, but a very good one," he attested. "I'll make certain you're well scrubbed and thoroughly relaxed."

"Well scrubbed, perhaps. But thoroughly relaxed? That I doubt."

"Such a skeptic." Julian eased behind his wife, settling her between his legs, his back against the side of the tub, hers resting against his chest. "How's that?"

She sank against him. "Perfect. I apologize for doubting your abilities to soothe."

"Apology accepted. Now lie still." He massaged her shoulders, kneading the tension away in blissful, gradual increments.

Aurora made a soft appreciative sound, her eyes sliding shut as Julian worked his magic. Her body felt light, buoyant, all the stiffness and discomfort dwindling slowly away.

Long, languorous minutes passed, interrupted only by the sounds of rippling water.

Gradually Julian altered his approach, addressing the duties he'd vowed to perform. He lathered his hands, smoothing them up and down Aurora's arms. "Time to act the part of lady's maid. I'll begin with your arms."

A frisson of pleasure accompanied his every caress. "Mmm," Aurora murmured.

"I agree. Your skin is flawless." Julian's fingers interlaced with hers, his palms warm and soapy, unbearably erotic as they rubbed lazy circles against hers. "Tell me, where shall I wash next?"

That incredibly seductive voice made her heart pound, caused her slumberous state to lift like the morning fog.

Abruptly she was wide awake.

"Where would you *like* to wash next?" she inquired, her loins dissolving with that now familiar yearning.

Julian sensed her reaction instantly. She could tell from the way his fingers tightened over hers—ever so slightly—the way his lips nudged aside her heavy mane of hair, kissed the back of her neck. "Don't ask that question unless you're prepared for the answer. And let me warn you: I respond in actions, not words."

"Another warning, Your Grace?" Aurora could scarcely speak past the drumming of her heart. "Didn't you realize from our earlier encounter how undaunted I am by your warnings?"

"Ah. I'd forgotten." His hands freed themselves, only to slide under her legs, lifting them as he eased them apart. "Very well then. I'll rely upon my instincts to select the proper areas to wash." So saying, he draped each of her thighs over the powerful columns of his.

Aurora moaned as warm water cascaded between her legs, swirled about her tender flesh, no longer soothing but arousing. Behind her, the hard ridge of Julian's shaft pulsed to life, throbbing against her back. "Julian . . ."

"Yes, *soleil.*" Keeping his own desire carefully leashed, Julian ran his soapy fingers up her calves, her knees, the trembling muscles of her inner thighs—washing her limbs and easing closer and closer to her aching core. "I'll continue with your legs. After all, they've been cramped for hours. Surely they require some tender ministrations." Shifting higher, he massaged her soft skin, his thumbs circling just shy of where she wanted them.

"Julian . . ." She half-sobbed the protest, struggling to shove her body downward, to seek out his touch.

"Is that not to your liking? Is this then?" One hand left her thigh and swept over the smooth skin of her abdomen, coasting upward until it brushed the underside of her breasts.

Her nipples hardened painfully, her breasts swelling in urgent arousal. "I can't bear it."

"You needn't bear it, *soleil,*" he murmured, burning a trail of hot kisses from her shoulder to her neck. "Just tell me what you want and it's yours."

"Touch me," Aurora managed. "Please, touch me."

Swiftly one palm covered her breast and grazed her nipple, while the other palm completed its journey, cupping her intimately. Before she could catch her breath, Julian's fingers slid inside her, glided into her hot slippery passage.

"Julian!" She arched, sensation slamming through her with renewed fervor. Blindly she groped behind her, determined not to touch heaven alone. She found and grasped her husband's engorged manhood, stroking him from base to tip and back again.

Julian reacted like a wild man. Growling deep in his chest, he abandoned his caresses, gripping Aurora's waist and whipping her about to face him. Wedging her thighs apart, he brought her down to straddle him, not stopping until his straining flesh found its goal, pressed into the wet velvety folds. "Can you take me again?" he rasped, the question moot, given that he was already pushing deeper, groaning as she melted around him.

Aurora answered it anyway. "Yes—oh, yes." She pressed downward, the pleasure far too acute to allow pain to intrude. "Tell me what to do."

"Move. Like this." He cupped her hips, raising and lowering her until Aurora's eyes widened, her hands clutching his shoulders as she took over the motion.

Julian urged her on. His grip became bruising as his thrusts quickened, turned savage. His powerful hands worked her, dragged her down, impaling her on his full length. His eyes blazed topaz fire, his teeth clenched as he battled against the climax escalating inside him.

Abruptly he lost the battle.

With a feral shout, Julian went rigid, disbelief flashing in his eyes as he swelled—and exploded. Crushing his wife's loins to his, he plummeted over the edge, the corded muscles in his neck standing out as he lurched upward again and again, pounding into Aurora with the full force of his climax. "Aurora . . ." he gasped. "Come with me. Come . . . with . . . me. . . ." His eyes slid shut as wild hot bursts of completion jetted from his body into hers.

Julian's plea, the feeling of his seed spurting into her, propelled Aurora into her own release. Grasping his forearms, she followed him into the sun, crying out his name, shuddering as gripping spasms claimed her, clenched about her husband's pulsing flesh.

She went limp, sagging against him like a rag doll, grateful for the solid strength of his arms as they held her. She pressed her head to his chest, hearing his heart thunder against her ear, the harsh, uneven sound of his breathing.

"God," he managed. "That was . . . unbelievable."

With the greatest of efforts, Aurora nodded, not even bothering to raise her head. "It grows more shattering each time," she whispered raggedly, her limbs still quivering with reaction.

Something about her response caused Julian to tense anew—this time not in passion. "Aurora." He tugged back her head, silently commanding her to look at him. "You can barely speak. And you're trembling like a leaf. Did I hurt you?"

Aurora's lashes lifted. "Oh, no," she refuted at once. "On the contrary, I never imagined so splended a bath. Nor so splendid a lady's maid."

Julian looked visibly relieved, if not amused. "Nevertheless, this bath was meant to ease your discomfort, not worsen it." He shook his head, uttering a stunned admission evidently meant more for himself than for her. "The problem is, I can't keep my hands off you."

"What an exhilarating confession," Aurora replied, giving her husband an impish look. "Too exhilarating to question. And so opportune. After all, I have yet to be washed—a serious dilemma, given that the water has grown cold. So please put your preoccupation to good use; scrub me as quickly as those incomparably skilled hands can manage, then transport me to your bed." She shifted her hips a tantalizing fraction. "After which, I invite you to indulge your craving—and your hands— yet again."

Julian's body leapt to life, his fleeting moments of temperance forgotten. "Again and again, *soleil*," he muttered thickly, reaching for the soap. "So many times, in fact, that it might be days before we return to Pembourne."

Aurora tended to agree.

The night was everything she'd dreamed of and more, endless hours drenched in a sensuality more exquisite than she'd ever imagined possible. Julian was tireless, his stamina far surpassing hers, his inhibitions nil, his desire for her unquenchable.

Finally, just before dawn, they rested, Aurora's head nestled in the curve of her husband's shoulder.

"Have I overtaxed you?" Julian murmured, sifting strands of Aurora's red-gold hair through his fingers.

Aurora smiled. "I was about to ask the same question of you."

A chuckle. "Fear not. I'm exceptionally resilient when it comes to you. Whatever limits are to be set must be yours to determine."

"Mine? Oh, dear. I guess we really won't be returning to Pembourne anytime soon."

"Does that disturb you?"

"Given the cause of our detainment—no. The Fox and the Falcon have waited this long. They'll wait a bit longer."

"Indeed they will." Julian traced the delicate curve of his wife's spine. "I haven't forgotten my promise, you know."

"Which promise is that?"

"To show you the world. The moment the black

diamond is restored to its rightful home, you and I will go on an extended wedding trip."

Aurora's face lit up. "That sounds perfect." An inquisitive pucker formed between her brows. "Don't you ordinarily travel alone?"

"Always."

"I thought so, given your line of work."

"A wedding trip with you can hardly be described as work, *soleil*," he said huskily.

"I realize that. Still . . ." A thoughtful pause. "Julian, you invited no one to our wedding. Surely there must be someone you're bound to—a friend, a colleague?"

"Not particularly."

She sighed. "You're as autonomous as Slayde used to be."

"You sound amazed."

"Puzzled is a better choice of words. Having been alone a great deal of my life, I can't imagine anyone choosing a life of loneliness."

"Choosing to be alone doesn't necessarily imply that one is lonely. It simply implies that one elects when he'll have company and who that company will be."

"Women, you mean?"

"Why do you assume that?"

"Because I saw the expression on that barmaid's face when we were at Dawlish's. She looked like a mare snuggling up to a stallion."

"A stallion?" Julian's grin was seductive. "I rather like that analogy."

"I don't."

"Meaning?"

"Meaning I don't think I can abide infidelity." Aurora felt a wave of surprise at the fervor of her own declaration. "Odd, I never considered that fact before—probably because I never truly expected to marry. But now that I have, albeit under a highly unconventional set of circumstances, I find the whole idea of faithlessness unacceptable." She inclined her head, gave her husband another quizzical look. "Is that going to present a problem?"

Julian's forefinger traced her kiss-swollen mouth. *"Soleil,* the only problem I foresee is my insatiable craving for you. With you in my bed, I have little interest—or remaining stamina—for other women."

Aurora's turquoise eyes twinkled. "And when you're away from me?"

"I'll work on regaining my strength. You'd best do the same." His knuckles brushed her cheek. "Because when I return, you won't be leaving this bed for a week."

"Now *that* particular warning I like." Aurora bent, kissed the hard planes of Julian's chest. "So long as you don't travel without me too often."

"You have my word, *soleil.*" He rolled her onto her back, his eyes burning with that now-familiar fire. "I can hardly wait to introduce you to the world."

"Among other things," Aurora replied with a tantalizing smile.

"Oh, yes. Most definitely among other things."

The sun continued to make its ascent, drizzling daylight over Cornwall and all of England. Throughout the shires people began opening their morning newspapers, astonished to read that the Huntleys and the Bencrofts had forged their families, that the Earl of Pembourne had bestowed his sister's hand in marriage upon none other than the newly ascended Duke of Morland.

In his quiet Devonshire manor, Viscount Guillford sighed, rereading the announcement for the second time then folding the paper and laying it on his end table. So Morland had married Aurora. 'Twas a noble gesture— the *only* gesture—he supposed. Still, he was surprised Pembourne had permitted the union, given his feelings for the Bencrofts. Ah well. Once again, life had taken an unexpected turn, one to which he'd have to resign himself. After all, he couldn't very well marry a woman who'd been discovered in another man's bed, no matter how appealing she might be.

Wearily Guillford rubbed his eyes. 'Twas time to reassess his options and redirect his future.

Miles away in a seedy Cornish pub, a stout and bristled man was reading the same wedding announcement—but experiencing a far more violent reaction.

Downing his ale, he stared at the newspaper, his black eyes boring into the words.

Once again, that bastard plans to seize what he wants, he seethed, rage pounding through his skull. *Well, he'd best think again. This fortuitous union of his won't go unchallenged. He'll pay. On my brother's grave, he'll pay.*

Chapter 7

Merlin was back.

That was Aurora's first thought—her only thought—as she sat beside her husband in Pembourne's sitting room, listening to him provide Slayde and Courtney with a direct, precise explanation of the truth behind the Fox and the Falcon. Undaunted by either Slayde's terse interruptions or Courtney's white-faced stare, Julian pressed on, offering the facts and evidence with a master's skill and an investigator's objectivity. Gone was the provocative, unhurried lover of the past few nights, in his place an intense, commanding man as single-purposed as he was imposing.

Realization dawned, blatant and sobering.

Aurora might know her husband in the biblical sense, but in every other way Julian Bencroft remained an enigma.

"This is incomprehensible," Slayde muttered when at last Julian fell silent. Reaching out, he took the fox-handled dagger from the strongbox Julian gave him, examining it briefly before turning his attention to Geoffrey's journal, skimming the pages one by one. "All these years. All that hatred."

"Senseless hatred," Julian amended. "Hatred steeped in nothing but lies. Lies that drove our families apart, and precluded us from finding the very thing we all sought—the black diamond. Well, that will all change. As of now."

Slayde's head snapped up, his eyes narrowed in suspicion. "Is that why you married my sister? To expedite your search for the stone?"

Julian never so much as blinked. "To some extent, yes."

"Dammit." Slayde's fist slammed to the table. "I should have followed my instincts, kept you as far away from Aurora as possible. You might not be a vicious blackguard like your father, but your motives are equally selfish."

"Slayde, stop," Aurora demanded, gripping the arms of her chair.

Her brother shook his head. "He's a bloody mercenary, Aurora, driven solely by a thirst for wealth. He means to use you to find that stone so he can sell it to the highest bidder . . ."

"Slayde . . . wait." It was Courtney who spoke, laying a gentle restraining hand on her husband's shoulder. "I have the distinct feeling there's more to this than we've heard." Her discerning gaze shifted to Aurora. "All the facts Julian is now revealing to us, you were privy to them already, weren't you?" she asked quietly. "And I don't mean since your wedding day; I mean from a fortnight ago."

"Yes," Aurora acknowledged, grateful as always for Courtney's innate understanding of her. "Julian filled me in on everything the day he came to Pembourne to offer for me."

Slayde sucked in his breath. "Then why didn't you tell us immediately?"

Aurora shot him a pointed look. "Julian was concerned that you'd misunderstand his intentions and forbid us to marry—a circumstance neither of us was willing to tolerate. Thus, he gave me my choice: ride to Gretna Green and wed posthaste, after which I was welcome to tell you the truth, or enjoy the wedding day I so badly wanted—with both you and Courtney present—but keep my silence until after the vows were exchanged. Either way was fine with him, so long as the end result was achieved. The choice was mine. And I made it."

Courtney's lips curved. "In other words, Julian, you wanted to prevent Slayde from drawing precisely the conclusion he just drew."

"Yes," Julian replied. "A conclusion that in all fairness to Slayde, I, too, would have drawn were Aurora my sister." He leaned forward, all power and presence. "However, now that I've disclosed the truth, let there be no misunderstandings between us. I intend to find that stone. I'd like your help, but it's not essential that I receive it. Any more, incidentally, than it was essential that Aurora become my wife in order to accomplish my goal. Helpful, yes, but not essential. As I explained to you a fortnight ago, I sought Aurora's hand for a multitude of reasons. Most of which I shared with you. *All* of which I shared with Aurora. And many of which had little or nothing to do with the black diamond." A flicker of a smile. "Although, I must admit to being delighted—if unsurprised—by Aurora's reaction to the truth behind the Fox and the Falcon. I had hoped she'd react in precisely that way, and she didn't disappoint me. She was as intrigued by my great-grandfather's revelations as I—*and* as eager to complete their mission and put the past to rest. That prospect factored heavily into her decision to accept my proposal. So, while I'm delighted for Aurora's cooperation—after all, I can't deny it will expedite my search—I did not trick your sister into becoming my wife."

"Fine," Slayde stated flatly. "You've convinced me. Now go on."

"Go on?"

"Yes. I've heard that you intend to find the black diamond. I've heard that you had numerous and honorable reasons for marrying Aurora. What I have yet to hear is what you intend to do with the stone once you find it."

"Ah. You want to know whether your skepticism is warranted, whether my greed will eclipse all else from view."

"Exactly. I'm not going to help you make your fortune at my family's expense."

"*Our* families' expense," Julian corrected stiffly. "Remember, the Bencrofts have suffered the same injustices, if not the same number of tragedies, as the Huntleys."

"And you intend to right those injustices? Your sense of honor will compel you to relinquish the hundreds of thousands of pounds you'd reap by selling the diamond—and all to restore the reputation of a family you claim to despise?"

Tiny flames ignited Julian's eyes. "I'll repeat what I said to you the day I sought Aurora's hand. You know very little about me, and even less about my values, priorities, and motivations. 'Tis time to shatter your misconceptions. Mercenary or not, I'm not driven by wealth. Oh, I enjoy the handsome compensations I earn, but my way of life offers me so much more than just money; namely, excitement, challenge, a sense of adventure—and, yes, sometimes the opportunity to see justice served. Especially this time, when that justice is of so personal a nature—personal and meaningful, despite the animosity I felt for my father and grandfather.

By finding the jewel, I can pay tribute to two very deserving men, one of whom happens to be my great-grandfather, end an animosity that should never have begun, and silence a curse that—whether I deem it ludicrous or not—has labeled us pariahs of society."

"You don't believe in the curse?"

"No more than you do," Julian shot back. "But what you and I do or do not believe has little bearing on the way the world views us. Not that I give a damn about being ostracized. Nor, I suspect, do you."

"I didn't . . ." Slayde refuted quietly. ". . . until now." His gaze flickered to Courtney, shifted lower to settle on her very swollen abdomen. "'Tis no longer only my life that's at stake. If I can protect my family, my child, from enduring the scars of the past, the fear and the isolation, I will." A hard swallow. "I must."

"Then trust me," Julian urged, his expression intense. "Accept that I don't plan to keep or sell the stone. I plan to turn it over to the Crown as our great-grandfathers intended, and to see it restored to the temple from which it was seized."

With one final glance at the journal, Slayde gave a terse nod. "Very well. Although I'm still reeling from all I've just learned . . . the ramifications."

"We all are, Slayde," Aurora put in. "I only just read the journal last night, then again on the carriage ride this morning. What James and Geoffrey did, the men they truly were—it's inspiring. I feel so proud and so determined to untarnish their names."

"How can Slayde and I help you?" Courtney interrupted. "Do you suspect the diamond truly is hidden at Pembourne after all?"

"No." Julian shook his head. "The Fox and the Falcon were far too clever to store their recovered treasures in one of their homes. I'm convinced they had a secret hiding place, one that has yet to be unearthed."

"Hundreds of privateers have hunted for the black

diamond," Slayde reminded him. "Why hasn't one of them come upon this hiding place?"

"Because they hadn't the necessary clues to do so."

"And we have?"

"Yes. We need only uncover them."

Slayde frowned. "You've lost me, Julian."

"I said I didn't think the diamond was hidden at Pembourne or Morland. That doesn't mean the clues leading to it aren't."

"Of course." Slayde's palm struck the table with a bang. "What better way to ensure that only the Huntleys and the Bencrofts—together—find the gems recovered by the Fox and the Falcon than to bury clues in both our homes."

"Exactly," Julian confirmed. "I've dealt with enough stolen treasures myself to know that there are an infinite number of sites where one can conceal them—inside caves, behind stone boulders, beneath grassy tracts—the possibilities are limitless. Any of those sites would take either detailed instructions or a map to find. My great-grandfather obviously believed that the same heir who would be worthy of his legacy would also be shrewd enough to amass the clues he and James left, then use the combined information as a guide to their specific hiding place."

"So where do we begin searching for these clues?" Courtney demanded, a spark of excitement in her eyes. "At least those concealed here at Pembourne?"

"We begin by reviewing whatever knowledge Slayde has of James Huntley: his habits, interests, which rooms at Pembourne he customarily occupied. We also pore over any documents or personal effects of James's that might still exist, any of which might help determine our path."

"Personal effects?" Frowning, Slayde rose. "I don't recall James leaving anything of consequence—certainly nothing as dramatic as a dagger or a journal. As for documents, I'll go through every shred of paper at Pembourne looking for a clue of some kind. Personal habits are another issue entirely. According to my father, James had few ties to the estate . . . or to anything else in England, for that matter. As you well know, he spent most of his time abroad. He seldom returned to Pembourne for more than a few weeks at a time."

"But when he did, he could usually be found on the far grounds with his falcons," Aurora inserted. "They were his greatest fascination—significant enough, obviously, to spawn his alias."

"That's true." Even as he spoke, Slayde arched a surprised brow at his sister. "I didn't realize you knew so much about our great-grandfather. I was aware of James's affinity for falcons because Father referred to it several times during our discussions on the Huntley family history—discussions meant to prepare me for the title I would someday inherit. But you were no more than a babe then. How is it you recall those conversations?"

"I don't. Nor do I need to. Mr. Scollard told me all about Great-grandfather's preoccupation with his falcons." Aurora pursed her lips. "Now that I think of it, perhaps I should have paid more attention to Mr. Scollard's stories. I always assumed he was just imparting interesting tidbits of my past. Knowing him as I do, I should have guessed he was revealing something of great value. In any case, that's how I learned of James and his falcons. Moreover, I picked up scraps of information from Siebert on the day I first discovered the empty falcon cages. I was fifteen at the time, and insane with boredom. I accosted Siebert the moment I returned to the manor; after all, he'd been at Pembourne forever, so it stood to reason he'd heard tell of James's pastime. And of course he had, however minimally. After grappling with the countless questions I fired at him, our poor butler suggested I peruse the library where James kept dozens of volumes on the subject of falcons."

"And did you?"

"With pleasure. It provided me with a much-needed diversion." Aurora shot Slayde a pointed look. "Need I remind you that I was confined to this estate for over a decade?"

"Need *I* remind *you* that you spent most of that decade trying to escape, giving my guards a merry chase?"

Aurora grinned, feeling not a shred of remorse. "Very well, then. During those few occasions when I wasn't eluding your guards or visiting Mr. Scollard, I was reading. I'm familiar with every book in our library. A good portion of them are about the art of falconing, with James's notes and dates jotted in the margins. You'd be surprised at how much I gleaned about the different types of falcons and their characteristics. Which brings me to my first suggestion: I think we should pore over every one of James's books *and* search the falcon cages—which I've been dying to do since Julian's first visit—to see if there might be some clue concealed within them."

"They've been untouched for years," Slayde reminded her. "I doubt there's anything in them but cobwebs and dust."

"Still, it's worth a try."

"I agree," Julian interrupted, coming to his feet. "So let's stop talking and begin searching. James must have left something of himself behind, just as Geoffrey did. In addition, if I'm right, if the clues leading to the black diamond are hidden at Pembourne and Morland, 'tis up to us to find them, combine them, and complete our great-grandfathers' mission."

"I'll begin in the library," Courtney offered. "First I'll collect all James's falcon books. Then I'll scrutinize them one by one." Seeing Aurora's stunned expression, she grinned, patting her abdomen. "No, Aurora, I haven't lost my adventurous spirit, only my agility. My attempts to cross the grounds would only slow you down and worry Slayde silly. 'Tis best that I remain here and take on a more sedentary job."

"Without question," Slayde concurred instantly. "Aurora, you accompany Courtney to the library. And don't let her do anything foolish. *You* climb the ladder and hand down the books. The two of you can read through them together. I, in the meantime, will go through and inspect every personal article Father bequeathed me when he died—just in the event James passed something down, something we inadvertently overlooked, given that we hadn't a notion of his true identity. Julian, before I get started I'll instruct Siebert to show you to the falcon cages. You're welcome to scour every inch of them for clues. Agreed?"

"Agreed." Julian nodded his assent.

Aurora bit her lip, torn between flagrant refusal and allegiance to Courtney. Hell and damnation, she didn't answer to Slayde anymore. Further, he knew bloody well she was itching to inspect those falcon cages—and equally averse to being cooped up in this blasted manor again. On the other hand, she understood the basis for her brother's command. Courtney would never be content being idle. Left alone she would scramble up the ladder to reach every one of those texts, jeopardizing her well-being even as she convinced herself that she and the babe would remain unharmed.

In the end there was no choice to make.

"Come, Courtney." Aurora gestured to her friend. "Let's get started."

Julian caught Aurora's arm as she passed. "I'll personally rush straight to the library and deliver any clues I might find," he vowed quietly.

Aurora's head came up. *He understands,* she realized

in astonishment, seeing the approval—together with some profound, unnamed memory—flicker in his eyes. *He admires my decision.*

It was that unnamed memory that captured her interest.

Studying Julian's enigmatic expression, Aurora had the oddest feeling that her husband's admiration stemmed from something personal, some firsthand experience . . . or relationship . . . that elicited the kind of loyalty he evidently respected. Could it also be responsible for the honor he so fervently pursued? And if so, who or what had inspired it?

Lord, she had so much to learn about this man, so much she *intended* to learn if they were going to have a real marriage. That notion almost made her smile, given that—by her own claim—she'd never expected to marry at all.

Mr. Scollard had been right all along—as usual.

"Soleil?" Evidently Julian thought her silence implied skepticism. "I *will* let you know if I discover anything in the cages."

"Thank you," she said aloud. "I'll try to be patient. But waiting is something I'm not very good at."

"Ah, now *that* I know from firsthand experience," he stunned Aurora by muttering, his tone low and wicked, clearly meant for her ears alone. "And I promise, *soleil*—I'll try never to keep you waiting."

Before Aurora could respond—or even recover, for that matter—the teasing look on Julian's face had vanished and he was heading toward the door. "Let's find Siebert," he instructed Slayde.

Watching her husband's departure, Aurora pondered the astonishing transformation he seemed able to make so effortlessly. It was as if a flash of Julian emerged from the confines of Merlin's formidable presence, only to disappear as quickly as it had come.

Well, she relished a challenge as much as he did. And she'd just encountered the greatest challenge of all: Julian himself.

"You're disappointed," Courtney pronounced as Slayde followed Julian out the sitting-room door. "You were obviously yearning to explore those falcon cages. Aurora, I'm not a child. Go with Julian. I can collect books on my own."

"Absolutely not." Aurora gave an adamant shake of her head. "I have no intentions of letting you climb ladders or overtax your strength. Besides, that's not disappointment you're seeing; it's contemplation."

"Contemplation," Courtney repeated. "Over what—Julian?"

"Yes." A sigh. "My new husband is a very complex man."

"So I noticed." Courtney cleared her throat, her gaze fixed on Aurora. "Despite your craving for adventure, I know how terrified you are of the black diamond, how certain you are of its curse. I also realize Julian won't rest until he finds it, which places you right at the heart of this search—a reality that's doubtless as frightening as it is exhilarating. Yet, despite all this upheaval, you look radiant. May I assume the past few days yielded all I predicted they would?"

Aurora shot her friend a grin. "You may."

"You're happy then?"

"Ecstatic—at least when I'm in Julian's arms. Now, if only I could unlock his thoughts as easily as I unlock his passions . . ." She frowned. "Somehow I think that's going to be a significantly more difficult task."

"I'm sure it will be." Courtney's lips twitched. "Especially given that unlocking his passions probably required no more than a moment or two alone in his bedchamber."

"Bedchamber? We scarcely lasted beyond Pembourne's gates." Aurora flushed as she recalled her first moments of wedded bliss. "We consummated our marriage in Julian's carriage," she confessed in a confidential whisper. "Are you shocked?"

Laughter bubbled up in Courtney's throat. "By the Fox and the Falcon, yes. By you? Never." She squeezed Aurora's hands. "I can hardly wait to hear more. Unfortunately I'll have to exercise some patience. Dozens of books beckon us."

"Yes," Aurora agreed, staring off in the direction of the library. "As does the black diamond."

A half hour later, a stack of texts were strewn across the library's oriental rug and Aurora was sifting through the top and final shelf of books.

"Nothing," Courtney muttered from the settee. Readjusting the cushion behind her back, she tossed another book to the floor. "Other than some interesting margin notes on the differences between the peregrine and the merlin. I can't find a single item either within the text or penned by James that even remotely resembles a hidden message."

"I'll climb down and help you," Aurora replied, extracting two more thick volumes, cradling them against her as she descended the wooden ladder.

She'd scarcely righted herself when Julian strode through the doorway, anticipation rippling through his powerful frame.

"Julian—what is it?" Aurora demanded.

"This." Julian held out a somewhat rusted but visibly ornate key for her inspection. "I found it lying alongside the falcon cages."

"Is that significant?" Aurora examined the worn scrap of metal intently. "I assume it was once used to keep the falcons locked in their cages."

"It was. I tried the key. It fit the locks perfectly."

"Then . . . ?"

"This key looks exactly like the one my solicitor presented to me, the one that opened Geoffrey's strongbox. It has the same short shaft, slender notches, and gilded trim. I'm on my way to Slayde's study to see just how identical the two keys are."

"You're thinking that Geoffrey made James a key so he could gain entry to the strongbox?" Courtney questioned.

"That, of course, is the logical assumption." Julian frowned, turning the key over in his palm. "But I've got an excellent memory for detail. And although the similarities are stark and unmistakable, I don't recall the original key's notches being quite so close together."

"There is another possibility," Aurora proposed, the notion exploding inside her like fireworks. "Perhaps James commissioned a matching strongbox of his own—*and* a key that presumably unlocked not only his falcon cages, but that opened his strongbox as well. If so, perhaps that strongbox contains information as vital as that which Geoffrey bequeathed Julian."

Julian's head shot up, his astonished gaze fixed on his wife. "My theory precisely."

"Don't look so astounded, Julian," Courtney advised him cheerfully. "Aurora has the quickest and most inventive mind I've ever encountered in a man *or* a woman. You'd best accustom yourself to that fact."

"It would seem so." Julian eyed his wife, looking not the least bit threatened by Courtney's pronouncement. "Do you know, Rory, with your daring and intelligence, 'tis a pity you've been confined to Pembourne all these years."

"For the world's sake, perhaps, but not for Merlin's," Aurora quipped back, her grin impish. "I'd make an extraordinary mercenary—and a formidable adversary. So feel relieved that marriage has rendered me an ally."

Julian laughed, a rich, husky sound that permeated the room like warm honey. "I do, *soleil*. Very relieved." His gaze fell on the key and his laughter faded. "Time to test our theory."

"I'm going with you," Aurora declared instantly.

"As am I." Slowly Courtney eased to her feet. "Although I'm a bit dubious about your suspicions. Had James possessed such a strongbox, Slayde would have known of its existence."

"*If* the box were among James's personal effects." Julian was halfway to the door. "If not, it could still exist—hidden. In which case it's up to us to determine its whereabouts."

Only three steps behind her husband, Aurora paused and cast a swift glance at Courtney. "Do you mind if I run on ahead?"

"Of course not." Courtney waved for her to do just that. "Oh, one question: who is Merlin? Other than a falcon, that is."

"A most extraordinary mercenary—the one I offered myself to at Dawlish's a fortnight ago," Aurora called over her shoulder. "I'll explain later. I don't want to miss anything."

With that she darted after Julian.

Slayde was already trying the key, Julian looming over him, when she burst into the study. "It doesn't fit," Slayde announced, extracting the key and holding it up beside the original. "You're right. The notches are different. As far as this second key fitting anything other than the falcon cages—more specifically, some hidden strongbox—wouldn't James have told someone if he had commissioned such a box? How else could he ensure that it fell into the right hands? He certainly couldn't assume someone would pass by our falcon cages and suspect the key used to unlock them would also unlock some unknown strongbox."

"Not unless the person passing by had already seen the key to Geoffrey's box and noticed the resemblance." Julian clasped his hands behind his back, his body taut with concentration. "Your solicitor," he asked abruptly. "Is it Henry Camden?"

Slowly Slayde lowered the keys to his desk. "Yes. It is."

"I thought as much. He's mine as well, and has been for years. In fact, his father George was retained by my great-grandfather—*and* yours, I suspect, given the nature of Geoffrey and James's partnership."

"That makes sense. And, yes, the Camdens have served us for generations. Both Henry and his father before him were outstanding solicitors—consistently trustworthy and competent."

"Very competent." A glint of speculation lit Julian's eyes. "And very trustworthy. Maybe trustworthy enough to endow with not one, but two strongboxes for safe-keeping—Geoffrey's *and* James's."

"'Tis possible," Slayde murmured. "Henry would never have mentioned James's strongbox to you—not without specific instructions to do so. He's far too principled. He'd wait until James's descendent approached him."

"You," Julian qualified.

"Yes—I."

"Then we'd best be off now." Julian plucked the second key from the desk, glancing out the study window as he did. "There are but a few hours of daylight left. We'll ride until dark, then stay at an inn and be waiting for Henry first thing in the morning when he opens his office."

"No." Slayde gave an adamant shake of his head.

"No?" Julian started.

"You heard me, no." Slayde folded his arms across his chest, his eyes a steely gray. "I won't leave Pembourne, not with the dangers hovering at its gates." He held up his palm, silencing Julian's objections. "Don't waste my time with senseless arguments. My family name means a great deal to me, but not as much as my wife and child. I'll tear this manor apart piece by piece, scrutinize every object and document I find for hidden clues. But until that black diamond is found and restored, until the invasions of my home cease to occur and the threatening notes stop arriving, I will not leave this estate. Period."

Julian sucked in his breath. "Fine. We'll send for Henry, then; ask him to ride to Pembourne at once. It will delay our answers a day or two, but if that's the only way . . ."

"It's not."

Both men jerked about to stare at Aurora, who shot them an exasperated look.

"Have you forgotten that Slayde is not the only living Huntley?" she demanded. "Married or not, I'm still James's great-granddaughter. Slayde, pen a letter of permission for me to take to Mr. Camden. Then you remain here with Courtney, and I'll ride to Somerset with Julian. We'll forfeit not an instant of time, and if Henry is indeed in possession of a Huntley strongbox, he can present it to me."

Triumph flashed in Julian's eyes. "You're absolutely right—he can. An excellent idea, *soleil.*"

"I think so, too." Aurora gave him a beatific smile, gathered up her skirts, and headed for the door. "I'll have your carriage brought around at once."

Darkness had fallen when Julian unlocked the room the innkeeper had provided them and guided Aurora inside. Frowning, he hesitated in the doorway, glancing up and down the semidarkened corridor of the quiet Somerset inn. Distant clinking sounds reached his ears from the floor below as the inn's coffeehouse patrons enjoyed their dinner and port. Other than that, all was still, the corridor housing the sleeping quarters as deserted as the stairway leading to it.

Julian's gaze swept the hall one last time before he stepped into the room, shutting and bolting the door.

"Julian, what is it?" Aurora demanded, her turquoise eyes bright with curiosity. "That's the second time you've checked behind us since we arrived, not to mention the long intervals you spent staring out our carriage window during the journey. Is someone following us?"

"It appears not." Julian crossed over, moving aside the drapes and peering down to the ground below. "Although I can't shake the feeling . . ." He shrugged, turning to his wife, his smile restored. "Forgive me, *soleil*. I didn't mean to distress you."

Aurora arched a brow as if deciding whether to question him further.

"If there's something to be concerned about, you'll be the first to know," Julian assured her, consciously forcing himself to relax. Until he had proof that they were indeed being followed, there was no point in alarming his wife.

"I wasn't feeling distressed or alarmed," Aurora clarified, stunning Julian yet again with her unique blend of audacity and candor. "I was feeling neglected." Slowly she unfastened her mantle and tossed it to the chair. "I'm relieved to hear there was a reason for your decided lack of interest during this carriage ride, much unlike our previous ones. I'd rather learn that your actions were a show of caution rather than disinterest."

"Disinterest?" Julian would have laughed at the irony of his wife's statement had his body not been screaming its own immediate blatant contradiction. Just her words, her provocative tone, ignited his blood, set him on fire. "No, *soleil,* I assure you, disinterest is one reaction I never have around you."

"I'm glad." With a siren's smile, Aurora tugged the pins from her hair, shaking it out in a luxuriant crimson waterfall. "Then perhaps you'd like to make up for your earlier lack of attention—right now, in this lovely cozy inn."

"With pleasure." Julian stalked across the room, capturing Aurora and hauling her into his arms. "I'm suddenly grateful Henry's office isn't closer to Devonshire," he muttered, his fingers deftly unfastening the buttons of his wife's gown in rapid succession. "Very grateful." Greedily he covered her mouth with his.

"So am I," Aurora breathed, unbuttoning Julian's shirt and tugging it free. Her palms slid inside, glided up the warm, hair-roughened skin of his chest.

Her thumbs brushed his nipples and the filaments of Julian's control snapped.

In seconds he had Aurora naked; a heartbeat later his own clothing was in a pile on the floor. Kicking it aside, he swept his wife to the bed, pausing only to yank back the bedcovers before he tumbled her to the sheets and lowered his full weight upon her.

"You make me insane," Julian said huskily, tangling his hands in her hair. "How many times have I had you these past few days—a dozen? More?" He kissed her—a deep, bone-melting kiss that sent blood pounding through his brain, desire hammering at his loins. "It's a wonder you can still walk—that either of us can breathe. And the most amazing part is, it's not enough. The fire between us just keeps blazing hotter, higher. I want you so much, I'm consumed with it." Tugging back her head, he buried his lips in hers.

Aurora responded instantly, wrapping her arms fiercely about Julian's back, arching up to increase the exquisite friction of their naked skin. "I want you the same way," she managed, shivering in the way that made live flames lick through his veins.

His knee wedged her thighs apart, his manhood hard and straining, already desperate for release.

Staring into Aurora's passion-glazed eyes, Julian

abruptly stopped, his hands balling into fists on either side of her head.

Dammit. He wanted more than this, more than a swift, fevered coupling. He wanted to awaken his wife to yet another level of passion, to share the wonder of her discovery as he took her to new heights, to feel her come apart in his arms.

To satisfy another fantasy that had clawed at him since the moment he'd spied her at Dawlish's.

Vehemently he gritted his teeth, clamped down on his reckless need for completion.

"Julian?" Aurora sounded confused, her hands tugging at his shoulders, urging him down to her. "Why are you stopping?"

"Because I want to savor this—to savor you." He nipped lightly at her lower lip, trying to ignore the tantalizing motions of her body as she moved restlessly beneath him. "Soon," he promised huskily, kissing the scented hollow at her throat.

"No . . . now."

He shifted lower, teased one nipple with his tongue. "Not yet."

"Julian—please . . ."

Her plea burned through him like a brushfire, the urgent arching of her body more than he could bear. "All right, *soleil*—now."

Abandoning his intentions to prolong the moment, Julian shoved himself downward, gripping Aurora's thighs and lifting them high over his shoulders.

He felt her start of surprise, but he didn't wait, lowering his head and taking her in the most intimate of caresses. His lips opened her, his tongue gliding over her sweetness, possessing her in a hot, wild caress that nearly brought him to his knees. He heard her sharp cry of pleasure, felt her fingers clench in his hair, but all he knew was the unbearable ecstasy of her taste, her velvety softness, the tiny inner rippling of her flesh. He repeated the caress, taking her more fully, a hard shudder wracking his body as she sobbed his name, begged him to continue.

He couldn't stop if his very life depended on it.

Anchoring her legs, Julian gave her what they both needed, penetrating her with deep, heated strokes of his tongue, his heart slamming against his ribs as he brought his wife closer and closer to climax.

Abruptly she arched, a high thin cry escaping her as she plunged over the edge, her body dissolving into exquisite spasms of completion.

Julian couldn't withstand another moment.

Raising up, he surged into her in one blind, inexorable thrust, his hands gripping her bottom, pulling her harder, more fully against him, forcing him as deep inside her as he could go. His eyes slid shut and he shuddered, her contractions pulsing around his rigid shaft—once, twice—igniting the climax already clamoring at his loins.

With a feral shout he surrendered, crushing her hips to his, pouring his seed into her in great explosive bursts of release.

Drenched in sweat, Julian collapsed, Aurora's body damp and shivering under his. He could scarcely breathe, much less speak, so he simply buried his face in the fragrant cloud of his wife's hair, his thumbs gently stroking her hips.

It took long minutes for the dark haze of passion to lift.

"Did I hurt you?" he managed at last, his voice sounding hoarse, shattered to his own ears.

Aurora shook her head against his shoulder.

"But I'm hurting you now." Julian attempted to lift himself away, only to feel Aurora's arms clamp more tightly about his back.

"No," she whispered fiercely.

Unsteadily, Julian rose up, propping himself on his elbows and studying his wife's beautiful, flushed face from beneath hooded lids. "No?"

"No." She wriggled a bit, her inner muscles tightening, drawing him into an exquisite pool of liquid heat. "Stay with me."

Julian bit back a groan, his body surging to life with astounding speed. "I'm here, *soleil,*" he replied softly, pushing deeper into her velvety warmth. "Better?"

"Ummm . . . no—not better, wonderful."

A chuckle rumbled from Julian's chest. "Do you know," he murmured, stroking damp strands of hair from her face, "for a woman who tells me she adores my lovemaking, you say 'no' with appalling frequency?"

Aurora's lips curved. "Only when you attempt to leave me or make me wait. Although I must say, tonight's delay was magnificent—worth every exquisite moment."

"I've imagined doing that to you since that first night in Dawlish's," Julian confessed, tracing her soft kiss-swollen mouth with his forefinger.

Her flush intensified. "Then what took you so long?"

"I was busy realizing my other fantasies."

"I see." Aurora raised her legs to hug his flanks. "Does that mean all those fantasies have now been exhausted?"

"Exhausted?" Julian shook his head, rolling over and settling Aurora astride him. "Somehow, *soleil,* I doubt that word will ever apply to us." He brought her mouth down to his, deepening his presence in her body and unleashing the inferno that seemed never to subside.

And the fire raged on.

Aurora was lost in slumber, her body curved softly against Julian's, when he heard the creak from the hallway.

It was a fleeting sound, gone as quickly as it had come. But it was enough.

The hair on the back of his neck stood up, every one of his muscles tensing with awareness. Cautiously he eased away from his wife, simultaneously reaching to the floor and groping for his clothes—never taking his eyes off the bolted door. He found his breeches, jerking them on in a few purposeful tugs, then snatched up his coat, rifling through it until he extracted the pistol he'd concealed within. Slowly, pistol cocked, he prowled toward the thin shaft of light emanating from beneath the closed doorway.

Another creak—only this time closer—right outside the room.

Someone was definitely out there. The question was, who?

Eyes narrowed, Julian reached his destination, his fingers noiselessly slipping the bolt free, then closing around the handle.

In one lightning motion he yanked open the door, grabbing by the throat the dark figure hunched outside. Without pause he slammed down the barrel of his pistol, striking the intruder's wrist and knocking his weapon to the floor.

A muffled cry escaped the man's lips as Julian dragged him into the room.

"All right, you found me," Julian muttered, shoving his victim against the wall. "Now, who are you and what do you want?"

"M-M-Merlin . . . it's . . . me," came the choked reply.

Julian's grip loosened and he angled the man's face toward the sliver of light drifting in from the hallway. "Stone?"

A pained nod.

"Well, what do you know." Julian released him,

watching in mild amusement as the stout square-faced man struggled to regain his balance. "That was quite a performance. Very different from your customary arrivals. Since when have you resorted to such dramatic entrances?"

"Christ, Julian, I think ye broke somethin'," Stone wheezed, gingerly turning his head from side to side. "Like my neck."

"If I'd broken your neck, we wouldn't be having this conversation," Julian said with light reassurance. Leaning into the hallway, he retrieved Stone's weapon, then eased the door shut as he handed Stone the pistol, barrel down. "Now, would you care to tell me why you're hovering outside my door, coiled to strike like some deranged murderer? Or, for that matter, why you followed my carriage from Devonshire to Somerset—I am correct in assuming that was you?"

"Ye saw me?"

"No. If I had, I would have asked you these questions then, rather than with my hand at your throat. I simply sensed I was being watched."

"Yeah, right—don't ye always." With an acquiescent nod, Stone tucked away his pistol, glancing past Julian into the quiet darkness of the room. "I had to be sure this was yer room. I thought so, but I didn't want any surprises on the other side of the door. I needed to see ye right away. I went straight to Polperro, but ye weren't there. I tracked ye to Devonshire and followed ye from there. I would've stopped yer carriage, but I didn't know how much ye'd told yer . . ." A pause. ". . . wife. I didn't want to say more than I should, so I waited until ye stopped for the night. I've been in that hall for hours, waitin' until I couldn't hear yer voices anymore, so I'd know yer bride was asleep."

"Well, his bride is now awake," Aurora announced,

marching across the room in a swirl of bedsheets. "As for how much he's told her, the answer is less than nothing. But all that's about to change." Jaw set, she gazed up at Julian, an expectant look in her eyes. "Julian—pardon me, Merlin—I'd appreciate it if you'd introduce me to your friend."

Chapter 8

Julian's lips twitched. "Very well, *soleil*—as you wish."
He made a grand sweep with his arm. "Aurora, meet
Stone. Stone, meet my less than traditional bride. And
forgive her rather scanty attire," he added, drawing the
sheets more firmly about Aurora's shoulders. "We
weren't expecting company."

"Mr. Stone," Aurora acknowledged, a thousand questions darting across her face. "Are you and my husband
well acquainted?"

Stone's gaping expression was almost comical. "Are
we . . . ?" He tossed Julian a helpless look. "I . . . that
is . . ."

"Stone and I go back many years," Julian supplied.
"We're business associates. In fact, he's supplied me
with any number of crucial business tidbits, which have
aided me in determining my best course of action."

"In other words, he's your informant," Aurora replied

calmly. "He warns you when it would be ill advised to turn your back."

This time Julian couldn't stifle his grin. "Something like that."

"I see." Aurora turned back to Stone. "And is this one of those times, Mr. Stone?"

Stone continued to gape.

"You can close your mouth, Stone," Julian suggested. "And feel free to answer Aurora's question. She won't relent until you do."

"Right." Stone complied, dragging a sleeve across his forehead and studying Aurora as if she were a foreign object. "Yeah, this is one of those times." With that he glanced at Julian. "Maybe we should talk alone."

Julian's amusement faded. He knew that particular tone. Stone didn't use it often or without cause. Whatever had prompted this nocturnal visit was serious. "Aurora, give us a minute."

"But . . ."

"Aurora." His head snapped about and he regarded her with stony resolve. "Go back to bed. Now."

He saw the way his wife's eyes widened at the harshness of his command, and a twinge of regret shot through him. But the twinge vanished in a heartbeat, supplanted by a wealth of pragmatism. There were some boundaries he would not permit to be crossed, not even by his spirited bride. He had in fact anticipated this very quandary, been fully aware that Aurora viewed his existence as a grand ongoing adventure—rife with excitement, lacking in drawbacks. And he'd known it would be up to him to set her straight, not only to preserve his valued independence but to safeguard Aurora's life. There was, as he'd told her, a difference between adventure and danger. The former was an exhilarating gift, the latter a dark reality. The ability to distinguish between the two was crucial.

So was the notion of setting limits to Aurora's place in his life.

"Rory." Julian gripped her shoulders, met her bold turquoise gaze. "I need to speak with Stone—in private."

"Very well." Unexpectedly his wife complied, gathering up the trailing bedsheets that enveloped her and heading off to the bed.

Julian frowned, watching Aurora's retreat and wondering what had caused her sudden—and totally uncharacteristic—acquiescence.

"That's some bride ye have," Stone muttered, following Julian's gaze. "Beautiful as hell, but is she always so . . . so . . ."

"Yes," Julian finished abruptly, jerking about to face his friend. "But you didn't come all this way to discuss Aurora. What's the problem?"

"Macall."

"Macall?" Julian sucked in his breath. "What about him?"

"He's here—in England. He knows about ye marriage, and about *who* ye married. He's sworn to exact his long sought-after revenge—only now he means not only to kill ye but to steal the black diamond he's now sure ye have. It's no secret he wants yer blood, Merlin. He has for almost a year. And now that he knows where ye are, he won't rest until he finds ye."

"Dammit." Julian's fist sliced the air. "This is one complication I don't need right now. What the hell brought Macall to England? Last I heard, he was combing Malta for me. I kept my departure from there too quiet for him to have learned I was gone."

"He ran out of money, came to Cornwall lookin' for work. Unfortunately yer wedding announcement ran in every bloody newspaper in England. It didn't take long for him to find out ye'd married a Huntley."

"So naturally he assumes I've got my hands on the black diamond."

"Exactly. He hated ye before. Now? Imaginin' ye've come upon the fortune of a lifetime? He's a madman. Nothing would make him happier than stealin' that stone out from under ye—bringing ye to yer knees, then driving a sword through yer belly as he taunts ye with his stolen prize. He's crazy, Merlin. Ye'd best be careful. Damned careful."

"Indeed." Julian raked a hand through his hair. "Where is he now?"

"Not on my tail, that's for sure. I checked behind me a dozen times. Besides, he might know yer in England, but he doesn't know I am." Stone massaged his neck. "Then again, I haven't got myself written up in all the newspapers."

"Very funny. Where was he when last you heard?"

"In Cornwall. Goin' from pub to pub. Gettin' closer to Polperro. My guess is he's hidin' out near yer manor, waitin' for ye to return."

"Probably." A terse nod. "Now I'll be ready for him."

Once again, Stone's glance slid past Julian. "Ye've given Macall more ammunition than he had before," he muttered, gesturing in the direction of the bed.

"I can handle it." Julian yanked open the door. "Thanks for finding me. I'll be in touch."

"Or *I'll* find *ye* if need be. In the meantime, keep yer eyes open." Stone moved to go.

"Good night, Mr. Stone," Aurora called across the room. "Doubtless we'll meet again."

Stone blinked. "Yeah. Sure. Good night." He slipped out the door and disappeared.

Julian eased the bolt back into place, keenly aware of Aurora's watchful gaze. He didn't need to look to know his wife was steeling herself for either an altercation or an inquisition. Curiously that notion elicited as much excitement as it did stubborn resolve. Odder still that, despite all his planning, he hadn't anticipated quite how difficult it would be for him to establish plausible boundaries for his marriage. He was an extraordinarily thorough man, one who conquered the odds by carefully determining them, then finding a way to stack them in his favor, thus minimizing the risk of failure. He'd done precisely that in procuring Aurora's hand. Oh, he'd known damned well their marriage would pose complications to his way of life. Still, he'd expected to find a tolerable compromise, one that satisfied Aurora's craving for freedom—and his craving for her—without thoroughly upending his existence and endangering her life.

What he hadn't expected was the staggering power of their attraction for each other, the insatiable hunger his wife seemed perpetually to ignite within him. It was damned disconcerting, casting him into unchartered waters in which he had no intention of navigating.

It was time to haul himself ashore.

Squaring his shoulders, Julian turned, crossing over and perching on the edge of the bed—intentionally waiting for Aurora to set the tenor of the conversation.

"Your friend seems a most interesting man," she began, drawing up her knees and propping her chin atop them. "Quick, effectual, and loyal."

"He is."

"You're not going to tell me anything." The blunt assessment was issued as calmly as if she were commenting on the weather.

Julian frowned, taken aback by his wife's unexpectedly calm demeanor. He'd expected anger, defiance, maybe even resentment. But not this tranquil appraisal of the obvious.

What the hell was she up to?

"No, I'm not," he responded, using the same straightforward delivery as she.

"Why not?"

"Because this is one of those situations I alluded to when I warned you there'd be exploits you were prohibited from taking part in. Exploits that involved danger— danger I intend to protect you from."

"On the contrary," Aurora countered, tucking a stray curl behind her ear. "When you spoke of the exploits you intended to protect me from, you said I'd be excluded only when leaving me behind would keep me safe. Obviously such is not the case this time. 'Twould be impossible to leave me behind; Mr. Camden wouldn't turn over anything belonging to my great-grandfather to anyone but a Huntley. Further, there's been no real journey involved—we've traveled but one shire away. Yet, although we're still in England you're plainly at risk. Which, as I've learned from my own past experience, puts me at risk, too, simply by virtue of the fact that I share your name as well as your proximity to the danger. Thus, this is nothing like the situations you described when you offered for me. Therefore, you have no choice but to keep your promise to protect me by telling me what—or who—is threatening us. Because in this instance, whether you like the idea or not, the status of your future directly affects mine."

For a long moment Julian simply stared. Then he began to laugh.

"Is that your way of saying you still refuse to tell me anything?" Aurora demanded.

"No. This is my way of saying your logic is infallible. In fact, had Napoleon been lucky enough to have had you for an advisor, I shudder to think what England's fate might have been."

Aurora's whole face lit up and she leaned forward, excitement dancing in her eyes. "I'm bursting with curiosity. Who is Macall? Why is he after you? Why is he so hell-bent on exacting vengeance?"

Julian's laughter intensified. "Eavesdropping, were we?"

"I'm quite good at it."

"You're quite good at many things."

"Yes I know."

Abruptly Julian's laughter vanished. The flush on Aurora's cheeks, the sparkle in her eyes—damn. There was that bloody uncontrollable urge to drag her to the sheets and make love to her again.

Aurora perceived the direction his thoughts had taken. He saw the realization on her face, heard it in the slight catching of her breath. Teasingly, she leaned closer, giving him a siren's smile. "Soon," she promised, echoing the vow he'd made earlier. "First, tell me about Macall."

"Blackmail, *soleil?*"

"Incentive, Merlin."

"Fair enough." Julian captured her fingers in his, sobering as he contemplated what he was about to say. "Gerald Macall and his brother Brady were lowlife privateers. They made their money stealing goods and smuggling them to whoever paid the most."

"Were?" Aurora asked, brows raised.

"Yes. Brady is dead. I killed him."

"Why?"

"Ten months ago the two of them seized a painting— one that would have brought them a huge sum. I intercepted it and returned it to its rightful owner. The Macalls came after me. Brady drew his sword, tried to run me through. My pistol was quicker and far more lethal. The bullet pierced his heart, killed him instantly. Gerald swore then and there that I'd never live out my days—he'd see to that. Evidently he's chosen now to realize his threats."

"To whom did the painting belong?"

"To a very gracious Italian count who, unfortunately, had become a touch feebleminded in his old age. Unbeknownst to him, his butler was a disreputable cur who stole the painting—never thinking the count would notice its disappearance—and sold it to privateers for a handsome sum. The count turned out to be less feeble than his unsavory butler had thought. He not only figured out that his painting had been stolen, he also deduced the identity of the thief. His butler was thrown in prison and a huge reward was offered by the count for the painting's return. It evidently had sentimental as well as material value—his deceased wife had presented it to him upon the birth of their first grandchild. It was the pride of his collection, not to mention being worth a small fortune. The Macalls were hired by some dishonest bastard here in England; I have no idea who. From what I later learned, he promised to double the reward if they found the painting and brought it to him, rather than returning it to the count. Whether he intended to do that or whether he was just falsely enticing two greedy scoundrels is something we'll never know."

"Where did they find the painting?"

"In the storeroom of a French gallery. It had been disguised—hidden beneath the canvas of a rather bland oil painting. I'd traced it there two days earlier."

"Two days earlier! Then why didn't you seize it?"

Julian rubbed a silky tendril of Aurora's hair between his fingers. "Because, my impatient wife, one doesn't just march into a gallery and make off with a painting."

"You could have bought it."

"It wasn't for sale. My guess is the owner knew bloody well what lay beneath that canvas's ordinary veneer. For all I know, he was the one who had concealed it there. I couldn't take that chance. So I waited until I'd had ample time to map out the best way to break into the storeroom at night and make off with the painting undetected. I was poised to do just that when I got word the Macalls were about to strike. That necessitated a change in plans. It wouldn't do to have the three of us trip over each other in our attempts to snatch the painting. Hence, knowing what proficient thieves they were, I simply sat back and let them do the ugly deed. They seized the painting . . . after which, I seized them."

"I see." Aurora averted her gaze, a troubled expression clouding her face.

"There's a disagreeable side to adventure, *soleil*," Julian reminded her quietly. "I tried to tell you that."

"I didn't care about you then."

That pronouncement caught Julian completely off guard. "Pardon me?"

"You think I'm upset because you killed a man. Well, you're wrong. You also think I'm a sheltered child, but, as *I've* tried to tell *you*, I'm not. The day you stood in Slayde's study, described to me what you do, I understood fully that some of your encounters were not . . . tranquil. So if you think my reaction is one of horror, you're a fool. On the contrary, I'm proud you acted so honorably, restored a treasure to its rightful owner." Aurora swallowed, her fingers tensing in Julian's. "But I'm worried."

"Aurora." He caught her face between his palms, brought her gaze around to meet his. "I won't let anyone hurt you."

" 'Tis not me I'm concerned about," she replied, vulnerability and confusion reflected in her eyes. " 'Tis you."

Julian felt a constriction in his chest.

"Before, you were a stranger," she explained simply. "Now you're my husband. I'm as surprised to hear myself saying this as you are. But these past few days . . . I never expected . . ." She hesitated, as if trying to make sense of her puzzling sentiments. "The important thing is, I don't want you hurt. And suddenly I realize you might be."

"Don't worry, *soleil*." Julian eased the sheets off her shoulders, unnerved by her emotional stirrings—or perhaps by his own reaction to them—silencing both in the only way he knew how. "I won't be hurt." He pressed his lips to her throat, cupping her breasts as he dropped the sheets to the bed. "I have a remarkable incentive to stay well."

Aurora moaned softly, pleasure rippling through her in tiny shivers. "Julian," she whispered. "Make love to me."

Her words were silenced by his mouth.

"Good morning, Your Grace. Have you an appointment with Mr. Camden?" The young clerk frowned, rifling through his book as he searched for a nonexistent notation.

"No, Tolladay, we don't," Julian returned, looking impatiently about the meticulous walnut-furnished office. "But my wife and I need to see Mr. Camden on a matter of some urgency. We've driven a long way. I'm certain he'll make himself available."

Tolladay consulted his watch, then glanced at the closed inner office door. "He had an early morning appointment, sir. They should be finishing up any minute now."

"We'll wait," Julian assured him.

As if on cue the door opened, and Henry Camden's voice drifted out to them. "I'll see to it straightaway, Guillford."

"Oh no," Aurora muttered under her breath.

"Relax." Julian squeezed her elbow. "It was inevitable that we run into him sometime. It might as well be now."

"Julian." Camden spotted his guests and halted in surprise. "I had no idea you were here. Was I expecting you and your bride this morning . . . ?" He broke off, realizing the awkwardness of the situation.

"No, Mr. Camden," Aurora inserted quickly. "And we apologize for arriving unannounced. I hope it doesn't present a problem." Her gaze flickered to the viscount. "Hello, Lord Guillford."

Guillford was staring at them, shifting uneasily from one foot to the other. "Aurora," he acknowledged in a strained tone. "Camden and I have concluded our meeting, so your arrival presents no problem for me." He cleared his throat, plainly striving to regain his composure. "Before I take my leave, let me extend my sincere congratulations on your recent marriage."

"Thank you, Guillford," Julian said, his stance as casual as the viscount's was stiff. "My wife and I both appreciate your good wishes."

"Yes, well, I'd best be on my way." Guillford turned to Henry. "Please contact me when you have those figures." With that he left the office, shutting the door quietly behind him.

Aurora's breath expelled in a rush. "Mr. Camden, I'm sorry. I had no idea."

"Nonsense." Henry waved her protest away, a hint of a smile playing about his lips. "A little scandal is good once in a while. It keeps one on one's toes." He gestured toward his inner office. "Won't you both come in?"

"Thank you for being so gracious," Aurora said when they were seated.

"Not gracious, my dear—adaptable." His kindly eyes twinkled. "You've been wed to this gentleman for but a few days. I've worked with him for years. I've learned to expect the unexpected. Speaking of which, before we address the reason for your visit, I, too, would like to extend my best wishes. May you enjoy a long and happy life together."

"We intend to, Henry," Julian replied. "Long, happy, and—if the past few days are any indication—rife with excitement."

"Which brings us to the purpose of your visit?" Camden prompted.

"Yes." Julian leaned forward. "Henry, this meeting concerns Geoffrey's strongbox."

"I see." The solicitor glanced uneasily at Aurora.

"My wife knows everything." A corner of Julian's mouth lifted. "Actually, a good deal more than you do, given your timely exit from Morland Manor the day you presented me with the chest." He held up his palm, anticipating Henry's protest. "I realize your decision to leave when you did was rooted in your customary integrity."

"I won't deny I was curious about Geoffrey's legacy," Henry clarified. "But curiosity is not the quality upon which my family built our reputation. As I explained to you at Morland Manor, Geoffrey's instructions were that you view the contents of the chest alone."

"And I better than anyone understand why—else I'd be sharing my findings with you now."

"I understand."

"But I have shared them with Aurora. So don't worry about speaking freely."

"Very well." A puzzled expression crossed Camden's face. "But I don't understand. Given your information and my lack thereof, what can I do for you?"

"You can tell us if my great-grandfather entrusted you with a similar chest," Aurora inserted.

The solicitor frowned. "I don't understand."

Aurora chewed her lip, carefully measuring her words. "Based upon a discovery we made at Pembourne, we have reason to believe that James Huntley might have bequeathed a twin chest to his heirs. Did he?"

"Not to my knowledge."

"Mr. Camden, I'm a Huntley," Aurora reminded him. "I understand you'd feel more comfortable if Slayde were here issuing this request, but with Courtney about to deliver their first child, that just wasn't possible. I did bring a note in Slayde's hand, should you require it, asking that you release to me anything of James's that you might have in your possession . . ."

"That wouldn't be necessary," Camden interrupted. "I've known you since you were a babe, Aurora. If I had what you were seeking, I'd be perfectly willing to turn it over to either you or Slayde. The fact is, I don't. Whatever you discovered that led you to believe James possessed a similar strongbox—at least one he entrusted to my family's care—was misleading. I simply don't have it."

"Dammit." Julian came to his feet. "It's got to be somewhere. I *know* it exists. Every instinct tells me so."

Slowly Henry rose from behind his desk. "If my curiosity were aroused before, it's clamoring now."

"I know, Henry. And soon, I hope, we'll be able to supply the answers to all your questions. But for now—" Julian gripped Aurora's elbow, guiding her to her feet. "We'd best be going."

"Very well. I wish you luck." Henry studied them both, an ironic gleam in his eye. "'Tis hard to believe there might at long last be peace between the Huntleys and the Bencrofts. I'd begun to think of that as an impossibility. But if anyone can accomplish the impossible, Julian, you can. Especially with this particular young lady by your side." He crossed over and opened the door for them to pass. "I'm certain you'll find precisely what you seek."

By the next day, Aurora had her doubts.

Having left Somerset posthaste, they'd driven to Pembourne at a breakneck pace, hoping that in their absence Courtney and Slayde had uncovered something of consequence.

The results were as disheartening as their own. Despite hours of poring over books and scrutinizing papers, neither Courtney nor Slayde had turned up one shred of pertinent information on either James Huntley or his falcons.

"What's next?" Slayde demanded, lounging dejectedly on the library settee.

"Morland." Julian spat out the word as if it were poison. "It's time to tear my father's home apart, bit by bit. Since the key was concealed at Pembourne, perhaps the strongbox—or at least a hint of its whereabouts—is hidden at Morland. 'Twould be just like our great-grandfathers to divide the clues between the two estates. It would ensure that both families were needed to locate the chest."

"But you've already searched Morland several times over," Aurora protested. "Surely you of all people would have spotted a strongbox that looks identical to your great-grandfather's."

"If it were visible, yes. But it's possible I overlooked Geoffrey's hiding place. Certainly I might have over-looked a clue, if that's what's concealed at Morland rather than the box itself. Remember, Rory, at the time I explored the estate, I wasn't looking for anything specific. Now I am."

"Julian," Courtney suggested from her propped position in an armchair, "isn't it possible your line of thinking is leading you in the wrong direction?"

"How so?"

"Let's presume the strongbox exists, and that the key to James's falcon cages unlocks it. It's still possible that no clue of the chest's whereabouts can be found at either Pembourne or Morland—and for a very good reason. Has it occurred to you that James used the chest not to house a clue, but to house the black diamond when he hid it?"

Julian raked a hand through his hair. "I considered that possibility. However, given the nature of James and Geoffrey's partnership, I think not. If Geoffrey used his strongbox to convey a piece of this puzzle, I'm willing to bet James did the same. What's more, I don't believe James would ever have taken the risk of hanging a key that would unlock something as valuable as the black diamond out in the open for all to see—even if the chances were slim that someone would realize its dual purpose."

"Even if someone suspected that the key fit a strong-box as well as a cage, they wouldn't know where to find that strongbox," Slayde pointed out. "Which is the very dilemma we now face—*and* the reason I agree with Julian. Why would our great-grandfathers provide us with the key to their greatest treasures without also providing us with the means to find those treasures? They wouldn't. Thus, if another strongbox exists, I believe it exists to convey additional information to make our search a plausible one."

"Oh, it exists," Julian stated flatly. "I know it. Clearly James and Geoffrey wanted us to realize that, which is why they made the two keys look so similar. The question is, where is the strongbox? In my opinion, the avenue leading to its discovery lies either here or at Morland."

"Then let's go." Aurora bolted to her feet, snatching Julian's hand and heading toward the door. "We're wasting time. It's only an hour's drive to Morland. Courtney and Slayde can continue exploring Pem-bourne. You and I will tear through Morland, stone by stone."

An hour and a quarter later, Aurora and Julian's carriage passed through Morland's iron gates and rounded the drive to the manor. Aurora felt a chill encase her heart as she caught sight of the cold, austere dwelling, ugly memories crowding her mind as the house loomed closer.

"Aurora?" Feeling his wife tense beside him, Julian frowned, watching her obvious fervent reaction. "Are you all right?"

"I'd forgotten how morose this estate looks." A shiver. "It hasn't changed a bit."

Julian's brows arched. "You've been here?"

"Only on the grounds. And only once. With Courtney. Before she and Slayde were married. She came to confront your father. She was hoping to bring Slayde some semblance of peace. I accompanied her, waited in the carriage while she spoke with Lawrence."

"My father would sooner have sold his soul to the devil than have granted peace to a Huntley."

"Yes, I know."

Julian's knuckles brushed her cheek. "You don't have to go in—not if it upsets you."

"Of course I do!" Aurora sat bolt upright. "I'm as determined to find that strongbox as you are—certainly determined enough to overcome a trace of uneasiness."

"Spoken like a true adventurer." Julian winked, glancing about as the carriage came to a halt. "Given your abundance of spirit, do you feel brave enough to strike out on your own? Because we'll make the most effective use of our time if we divide up. And since neither of us wants to stay here a moment longer than necessary, my goal is to find what we're seeking and be gone as quickly as possible."

"An excellent plan. Where shall I begin?"

"I'll search the first floor, go through each sitting room, salon, and anteroom. You go to the upstairs level and scrutinize each bedchamber—desks, nightstands, wardrobes—then check out the sitting rooms. I suspect you'll find most of the furniture bare, since no one other than my father and his servants have lived here for years."

Aurora nodded, accepting Julian's assistance in alighting. Then, head held high, she accompanied him to the entranceway door.

"Your Grace. I wasn't expecting you." A haughty-looking butler received them, and Aurora immediately recognized him as the man who'd admitted Courtney on their one and only visit to Morland.

"Thayer." Julian looped an arm about Aurora's waist.

"This is my wife, the Duchess of Morland." He pronounced the title with purposeful intensity, as if daring Thayer to treat Aurora with disrespect.

"Your Grace." Thayer's lips pursed but he bowed, greeting Aurora with all the dignity her new title commanded. "Welcome to Morland."

"Thank you."

"Her Grace will be exploring her new estate," Julian informed Thayer. "Please provide her with whatever she needs—including privacy, should she prefer it."

"Of course, sir." Thayer bowed again.

"I'd like to see the sleeping quarters," Aurora suggested, trying hard to sound like an eager bride.

"Shall I accompany you, Madam?" Thayer inquired.

"No, thank you, Thayer. As my husband guessed, I'd truly prefer exploring on my own."

"Of course, Your Grace."

"I'll be on my way then." She met Julian's purposeful gaze. "If you gentlemen will excuse me?"

"You know where to find me," her husband replied quietly.

"Indeed I do." Warmed by Julian's reassurance, Aurora gathered up her skirts and headed for the staircase.

She abandoned protocol the instant she was out of sight.

Darting around the second floor landing, she surveyed the vast deserted hallway, itching to begin her scrutiny. *There must be dozens of bedchambers here,* she mused. *I certainly have my work cut out for me.*

With that she began, marching into each chamber, going through it inch by inch before moving on to the next. As Julian had predicted, the rooms were all but naked, the desks empty, the wardrobes bare—almost as if no one had ever lived here, not even the late duke whose bedchamber had already been cleared of personal belongings. It was downright eerie, she thought with a shiver. Room after room was the same, filled only with pristine oriental rugs, stark mahogany furniture, and a cold barrenness that permeated every chamber like an icy wind.

Morland Manor was as much a mausoleum on the inside as it was on the outside.

Two hours later, Aurora rounded the hall to the next section of sleeping quarters, letting herself into what appeared to be yet another impersonal room.

Tucking a strand of hair behind her ear, she went to work, inspecting the empty wardrobe and nightstand, digging under the four-poster bed before settling herself behind the desk.

No wonder Julian loathed this place.

The thought popped into her mind as she tugged open the desk drawer, and she found herself trying to imagine what it must have been like for him to grow up here. His mother had died when he was still a boy, and his father had been an unfeeling tyrant who'd all but driven him away. How lonely he must have felt. True, she, too, had lost her parents when she was young. But not before they'd given her a foundation of love, a home in which she belonged, and a grown brother who, independent though he was, devoted much of his energies to her well-being.

Julian had once had a brother, too, she reminded herself. A brother he'd lost just as they'd both become men. Had that affected him deeply? Had he and Hubert been close in more ways than years?

Reflectively Aurora pondered the brief conversation she and Mr. Scollard had had regarding Julian's older brother.

"He was a good man, Rory. Honorable of purpose, generous of nature. Quite different from his father and grandfather."

"And from Julian?"

"Not in principles, but in fact. Very different."

"Were they close?"

"In heart, yes."

"In heart. Does that mean they cared about similar things or about each other?"

Mr. Scollard had never truly answered her question, other than to say she'd have to find her answers elsewhere, presumably from Julian.

An unlikely prospect, she thought ruefully. Julian was reluctant to disclose even the factual details of his life, much less the personal ones. She'd all but dragged information from him about his feud with the Macall brothers—and *that* he considered merely an unfortunate consequence of his occupation. The idea of his divulging emotional details of his past was inconceivable.

Still, she had no intention of abandoning her attempts to amend that fact.

Aurora was about to shut the drawer when a flat pad in the far right corner caught her eye. She extracted it, noting it was a sketchbook and wondering whose drawings it contained. Flipping it open, she was confronted with one of the loveliest pencil sketches of a waterfall she'd ever seen. Enchanted, she turned the pages one by one, discovering a whole pad of exceptionally well-delineated sketches depicting scene after scene of natural beauty—a grove of trees overlooking a pond, the first snow blanketing a winter landscape, a sunset over the English Channel. Whoever had penciled these drawings was incredibly talented.

Too curious to wait, Aurora tucked the sketchpad beneath her arm and went downstairs, peeking into the first sitting room she encountered.

"May I help you, Your Grace?"

Aurora jumped, whirling about to face the Morland butler. "Oh, Thayer. You startled me. Yes. I was looking for my husband."

"He's in his late father's study," was the haughty reply.

"Which is . . . ?"

"Down the hall, fourth door on your left."

"Thank you." Aurora hastened off, still unnerved by Thayer, the manor . . . everything that reminded her of Lawrence Bencroft.

The slam of a drawer greeted her as she stepped into the study.

"Julian?" she asked tentatively, watching him rifle through the desk.

He was on his feet instantly. "Did you find something?"

"I don't think so—at least nothing significant. 'Tis just that all the bedrooms I went through were utterly bare with the exception of the last. I found this—" She held out the pad. "—in the desk."

Julian walked around and took the sketchbook, flipping it open to the first scene. An odd expression crossed his face and he scrutinized the picture, drinking in every stroke, almost as if he'd been reunited with a long-lost friend and wanted to absorb every detail he'd missed during the time they'd been apart. Swallowing hard, he sifted through the pages, pausing now and again to study a particular scene or part thereof.

"They're exceptional," Aurora offered softly, feeling as if she was intruding upon an intimate reunion—and as if a vast chasm had suddenly sprung up and was now separating her from her husband.

"Yes. They are. He was incredibly talented. I'd almost forgotten." Julian turned away, his tone strained, his shoulders stiff. Wordlessly he placed the pad atop the desk.

"Did Hubert draw those sketches?" Aurora tried.

A prolonged pause. "Yes. And if you don't mind, I'd prefer not to discuss my brother."

"Why not? He obviously meant a great deal to you."

"He did. But he's been gone over thirteen years."

"My parents have been gone nearly eleven. That doesn't mean I've stopped missing them."

Slowly Julian turned to face her, his stance less rigid, his expression veiled. "I know, *soleil*. And I'm sorry for all you've endured, both then and now. However, my situation is entirely different. Any unresolved issues I have regarding Hugh involve much more than a sense of loss or grief. So while I appreciate your concern, please—don't deem me some broken toy that needs fixing."

Frustration annihilated discretion. "A broken toy?" Aurora blurted. "Hardly. What I deem you is a stubborn man who needs friendship. Or who needs anyone, for that matter. You're so bloody self-contained, so determined to preserve your damned autonomy. You infuriate me!"

To Aurora's amazement, a corner of Julian's mouth lifted. "And you're going to reform me?"

"I'm going to try," Aurora retorted. "If you'll let me."

For a long moment, Julian said nothing. Then, he leaned back against the desk, regarding her from beneath hooded lids. "What would you like to know?"

"About your brother. Tell me about Hugh."

"Why?"

"Because he was an important person in your life. Because you obviously cared a great deal about him. And because I have the strangest feeling he's indirectly responsible for our marriage."

That brought a flicker of interest. "Do you?"

"Yes. If you recall, on the day you proposed I said I believed there was some reason—or person—that was compelling you to right the past, to find the black diamond in order to untarnish the Bencroft name. Someone other than your father or your grandfather. You chose not to answer me then. Perhaps you'll answer me now. Was that person your brother?"

"Ever the intuitive one," Julian murmured, folding his arms across his chest. "Very well, *soleil*, yes, it was."

"Then I'd like to hear about him."

"Hugh was the finest man I'd ever known—principled, compassionate, wise beyond his years, even as a child."

"Were the two of you close?"

"We were as different as day and night. Hugh was even-tempered, composed. I was opinionated, wild. He was as stable and traditional as the heir apparent he would have become; I, on the other hand, was restless, impatient—disinterested in the estate, the businesses, and a title that meant as little to me as the unsavory man who held it. Hugh chose to overlook—no, I suppose a better choice of words would be that he chose to accept, though never share—our father's utter lack of scruples. I didn't, couldn't. Nor could I understand Hugh's tolerance. He himself was such a decent, moral man. But he believed in loyalty to one's family; that was one of his most fervent principles. Now that I think of it, I suppose the only traits my brother and I truly had in common were our commitment to our respective principles and our devotion to each other." Julian lowered his gaze, stared at the floor. "I wish we'd also shared my good health and strong constitution. But we didn't. Hugh was as frail as I was hardy. I scarcely recall a time when he wasn't either ill or recovering from an illness. I used to lie awake at night listening to his coughs and wishing I could share some of my vigor with him. Unfortunately it wasn't possible. When he died . . ." A shrug. ". . . the last filament connecting me with Morland Manor was severed."

A lump formed in Aurora's throat. "I remember the year he died," she said quietly. "I was young, but I vividly recall Slayde relaying the news to my parents when he returned from Oxford on holiday. He was terribly upset, family differences or not. Clearly he thought very highly of your brother."

"Slayde was decent as hell when Hugh died, despite the hatred that existed between our families. I've never forgotten him for that. I never will."

"As I said, you and Slayde are alike in many ways."

"Including our commitment to our families—at least those members of our families who need and deserve that commitment. Slayde would give his life to protect yours. I didn't have that option; I couldn't save Hugh no matter how hard I prayed, how desperately I tried. But I'll be damned if I'll let his name be tarnished—either by my father and grandfather's evil or by a theft that was never committed. So, yes—I intend to restore Hugh's honor. I only wish to God I could restore his life."

Aurora couldn't help it. She went to Julian, her palms caressing his forearms. "Hugh's honor is as intact as your feelings for him. Neither need be restored. Why would you believe otherwise?"

"Because as my father cleverly pointed out, Hugh's honor is no longer his to demonstrate but mine to reestablish."

"Why would Lawrence say that?"

"To get me to do his bidding. And the damned thing about it is, the bastard's reasoning was sound. Every wretched word of it."

"He conveyed all this to you after Hugh's death?"

"No—after his own."

Aurora sucked in her breath. "I don't understand."

"Let me fill in the missing pieces, then." Now that Julian had begun talking, he seemed unable to stop. "My great-grandfather isn't the only one who bequeathed me a formidable challenge the day I asked Slayde for your hand. When Henry delivered Geoffrey's strongbox to Morland Manor, I also had the dubious privilege of hearing my father's will read. He, too, left me something—only in his case it was hardly a gift." Aurora felt Julian's arms tense. "He bequeathed me the curse of the black diamond, dared me to find the stone and undo the curse. And he accomplished precisely what he sought: my cooperation. How? By reminding me that it was not only my name and his that were sullied, it was my brother Hugh's as well. That until the stone's theft was resolved, Hugh's name would always be associated with a tarnished past. And that as the last remaining Bencroft, I was the only one who could right this heinous wrong—not for him, but for Hugh. He was right. As were you when you guessed I had another motivation for wanting to find that bloody diamond. I do. And that motivation is my brother."

"Lawrence blackmailed you into finding the stone?" Aurora repeated, stunned that even a scoundrel such as Lawrence would stoop so low. "He actually taunted you into feeling it was your responsibility to clear Hugh's name?"

"I'm immune to my father's barbs, Aurora. At least those aimed at me and those without basis. But consider it. As the last living Bencroft—and a man who cares not for his own reputation but for his brother's—whose responsibility is it to protect Hugh's memory if not mine?"

As livid as Aurora was, she couldn't argue with Julian's logic. Whether or not the burden he now carried was undeserved, it was his nonetheless. "No wonder you were hell-bent on convincing me to marry you," she murmured.

"That wasn't my only reason."

"I know," she assured him quickly. "I didn't mean to imply that it was. Nor am I surprised by your motives. As I said, I knew something personal was driving you. I simply didn't know what. Now I do." Her small jaw set. "But if I hated Lawrence Bencroft before, I could kill him now."

"Because of me?"

"Weren't you the one who just spoke of protecting one's family?" Aurora demanded. "Well, you're my husband. Doesn't it stand to reason that I'd want to protect you, too?"

A tiny flame warmed Julian's eyes. "Yes, *soleil,* I suppose it does." He drew her against him, pressed her head to his waistcoat. "Thank you."

"You're welcome." She smiled, elated that she'd actually made some progress in her attempts to penetrate Julian's stubborn emotional wall. "See? Sharing your feelings is a great deal like making love. It only hurts the first time, and only for an instant. After that it's sheer pleasure."

Julian's laughter rumbled against her ear. "I'll take your word for it, *soleil.*"

"See that you do." Aurora's gaze fell on the sketchbook. "Hugh was a very talented artist."

"Yes, he was." Julian released her, bending to scoop up the pad. "He had an incredible flair for detail. In that way, 'twas he, not I, who took after Geoffrey."

"Your great-grandfather sketched?"

"Not in the true sense of the word, no. Still, I'd say he was quite good. Wouldn't you?" Julian pointed at the wall, where a detailed sketch of Morland's grounds hung.

"Geoffrey drew that?" Surprised, Aurora walked over, closely examining the diagram, which appeared to be a vast expanse of land strewn with large sections of hedges, delineated by two paths leading south to the manor below—one from the stables, the other from the gardens—and a third path winding about from the tenants' quarters north to the far grounds of the estate.

"He did indeed. If you look closely, you'll see his signature and the date. I should know. I spent over an hour scrutinizing the bloody sketch in the hopes that it would provide us with a clue. Unfortunately it's precise but unrevealing."

"Precise," Aurora muttered. "Like a falcon. Ironic, given that Geoffrey was the Fox. Then again, equally ironic that you're the Merlin. Almost as if fate wanted to ensure that Geoffrey and James's partnership prevailed—as they themselves did with the equal division of their legacy." She studied the diagram, marveling at the time it had taken to capture such detail. "You're right. Hugh did inherit his great-grandfather's skill. It's astonishing how vivid these paths look, almost as if they're all rushing purposefully toward specific destinations." She traced the two converging lines with her forefinger. "These two are surging toward the hedges surrounding the manor, first separately, then as one. And this one—" She pointed to the rambling path leading from the tenants' quarters. "This one's veering north, to disappear completely." A fascinated smile touched her lips. "Do you know, this whole drawing reminds me of a legend Mr. Scollard likes to tell—he's shared it with me many times, probably because it's been a favorite of mine since I was eight."

"And which legend is that?" Julian asked with an indulgent grin.

"The legend of the Tamar River. Do you know it?"

"All I know of the Tamar is what I discovered navigating it. It's incredibly picturesque, winding through hills and valleys, flanked by villages and limestone peaks as it divides Cornwall from Devon and flows down to Plymouth. That whole region breeds the sort of lyricism poets write about. So while I'm not familiar with any particular legend regarding the Tamar, I'm not surprised one exists."

"Would you like to hear it?"

A chuckle. "I'd be delighted."

"The legend explains how the Tamar got its name." Aurora gazed at the drawing, lost in her story. "The river was named after a beautiful sea nymph—Tamara—who in ancient times lived in a cave far beneath the earth and wanted desperately to see the magnificent colorful world she knew existed above. So despite her father's warnings that giants tread the grounds of Dartmoor directly above, she found her way to the surface only to discover her father's warnings had indeed been true. Two giants—Tavy and Torridge—saw her and fell in love with her, each determined to have her for his own. They pursued her across the moors to the North Cornish coast, where they captured her and demanded she choose between them. Her father, furious that she'd disobeyed him but unable to convince her to return, used his magic to cast the giants into a deep sleep and to transform Tamara into a silver flowing stream. When Tavy awakened, he sought his own father, who used his enchantment to convert his son into a stream that rushed across the moors and wound its way through the woodland in pursuit of Tamara. Tavy found her at last, and they joined together, flowing slowly into the Hamoaze. As for Torridge, he, too, managed to be transformed into a stream, but became confused and ran about in the wrong direction, heading north through the hills where he spilled into the Atlantic Ocean." Aurora touched the line that in Geoffrey's drawing was the path leading from the tenants' quarters northward. "This would be Torridge, rushing north through the woods to disappear into the ocean. And these—" She traced the two lines on the diagram that headed south, converging in the front section of the hedges that enveloped Morland Manor. "—these would be Tamara and Tavy, meeting in Dartmoor, near Tavistock, and flowing together to the sea."

"Meeting in . . ." Julian's expression sharpened, his eyes narrowed on the sketch. "Did you say that legend is well known?"

"Why, yes, I suppose so. Mr. Scollard has recounted it often enough."

Abruptly Julian shot to his feet, crossing over to Aurora in four long strides. "Repeat that final part—about the two rivers meeting."

Aurora shot him a puzzled look. "I never suspected

you to be such a romantic. Very well. These paths here resemble the course Tamara and Tavy took as they merged in Tavistock and flowed toward the Hamoaze."

"That's it."

"What's it?"

"You just gave us our answer." Julian pointed to the area on the sketch depicting the manor, the section where the two paths merged and wound their way downward. "The strongbox is somewhere in this vicinity."

"Julian, what in the name of heaven are you talking about?"

"Think, Rory. I suspected the strongbox was at Morland, yet it was nowhere to be found. So I decided it wasn't the box itself James and Geoffrey had concealed here, but a clue leading to its recovery. As it turns out, it was both. The clue is right here, staring us in the face. And the box? Figuratively it's in Morland Manor, just as the sketch depicts. Actually it's somewhere beyond the moors of Devonshire, between Tavistock and Calstock."

Aurora's eyes widened. "You're saying Geoffrey drew this sketch as some sort of secret map?"

"Exactly. Look closely and think of your legend. If these two paths represent the two rivers, and Morland Manor represents the place where they meet, then these smaller hedges in front of the manor are the hills of Tavistock and the tall hedges behind the manor are the limestone cliffs that lead to the ocean. See the different shapes? That's precisely the way the cliffs look, at times split by crevices, at times soaring into towering summits that pierce the sky."

"Yes—it makes sense." Aurora's heart began slamming against her ribs, her gaze poring over the entire section of the sketch that defined Morland Manor. "No wonder Mr. Scollard kept reiterating that particular legend to me. When will I learn that everything he says means more than it seems, even if I don't realize it at the time? He obviously knew I would someday need that information to . . ."

She broke off as with a rush of exhilaration she located what she sought.

"Julian, look." Her hand shook as she pointed to the base of the first rear hedge—a blurry section that was nearly lost beneath the majestic peak that rose from its foundation. "There's a heavy pencil mark here—rather like a filled-in circle—that doesn't seem to belong. Do you suppose . . . ?"

"Indeed I do." Julian studied the spot, his eyes gleaming with triumph. "What better place to conceal the strongbox than in a crevice at the base of a lone cliff? 'Tis ideal, brilliant. And so are you." He pulled Aurora into his arms, kissing her fiercely then releasing her. "Let's go."

"Go?" Her breath caught, and not only from the impact of Julian's kiss, but from the implication of his words. "To the cliffs?"

"Absolutely." Julian's expression reflected her own wild exhilaration. He reached into his pocket, extracting the key he'd found at James's falcon cages. "Come, my beautiful adventurer. 'Tis time to explore Mr. Scollard's legend, to see where your nymph Tamara and her giant Tavy take us."

Aurora's enraptured gaze lifted from the key to her husband. "Lead on, Merlin. To our next adventure— and to the recovery of James's strongbox."

Chapter 9

The cliffs were even more breathtaking than Aurora had imagined.

Traveling from Morland by carriage, she and Julian spent the night in Plymouth, then left by ketch at dawn, heading north from where the river Tamar rushed into the sea, and passing the majestic expanse of limestone cliffs until they reached its northernmost peak.

"I'm grateful James chose a crevice and not a summit in which to hide the strongbox," Aurora commented, gazing up at the towering cliffs. "Those are a bit too intimidating a challenge, even for me."

"They're dangerous as hell," Julian concurred, glancing down at Geoffrey's diagram. "We're also fortunate he chose this first peak rather than the ones beyond as his hiding place. Not only will that preclude our doing much climbing, it will also lessen the time it takes to recover the strongbox. Just beyond this point, the Tamar narrows from a swell to a stream. That's where we reverse our direction and head south. Geoffrey's diagram was explicitly drawn facing south—most likely to hide the crevice from view of those traveling north by sea. But as it is—" Julian gestured toward the green canopy appearing ahead. "—we're almost there."

Minutes later, Julian skillfully veered the ketch about, steering past the wooded area which, although devoid of blossoms during the winter months, were lush with evergreens filtered with sunshine. The stream curved closer to the cliffs, which rose up from the water like a crashing wave.

"There's the crevice on Geoffrey's drawing," Aurora exclaimed, gathering up her skirts and rushing to the ship's bow.

Julian followed her gaze, staring at the rift in limestone that corresponded with Geoffrey's heavy pencil mark on the diagram. "It is indeed." Swiftly he lowered the sail, easing the ketch closer, then tying it to the trunk of an old oak tree that jutted out from the base of the cliff. "Let's go." He gathered up his tools and leapt off the ship, turning to assist Aurora only to find that she'd already scrambled onto land and was making her way up the steep incline.

He chuckled, following her lead and arriving at the crevice just behind his wife.

"Julian—hurry!" Aurora was virtually jumping up and down.

"Sorry to detain you, *soleil,*" he teased. "I stopped to gather our tools. I thought they might prove useful. Or did you intend to claw your way through layers of stone?"

Aurora flashed him a rueful smile. "I'm sorry. However, I did tell you that patience was not one of my virtues."

"So you did." Grinning, Julian squatted, feeling about the area with his hand, reaching deeper until he encountered a loose section of stone. Purposefully he tugged at it, twisting and flinging aside small pieces of rock until he'd worked the larger section of stone free.

With a harsh sound of triumph, he lifted it away.

"Is it there?" Aurora demanded, kneeling beside him.

Julian frowned. "I don't know. I'll have to pound and chisel a bit. My hand won't fit in the crevice."

"Mine will. Let me explore the hollow, see if I can feel the strongbox. At least that will determine whether we should continue tearing this section of rocks apart or turn our attentions to an adjoining spot." Aurora leaned forward, sliding her palm into the designated area, working her hand deeper until her fingers struck a hard, smooth object. "Julian," she said excitedly. "I think I found it."

"Good." Julian's tone was even. "'Tis time to employ a cardinal rule of adventurers. Nothing is yours until you're certain that what you've found is indeed what you seek. And even then it's not yours. Not until you're holding it in your hands and you've eliminated any potential obstacles that might stand in your way. Now, stay as you are. I'm going to work a few more of the surrounding stones free. Once I have, I want you to move your hand about, feel along the surface of the box. Do you recall any of the details on Geoffrey's strongbox?"

"Yes. There was gilded trim all the way around. And knobs—two smaller, two larger, one of which hid the keyhole."

"Excellent." Julian was already digging, working the stones around Aurora's wrist away one by one. "Let your fingers be your eyes. Search for the very details you just described to me."

"All right." Aurora shifted impatiently, willing away the stones Julian was slowly urging free.

"Patience, *soleil,*" Julian murmured, reading her mind. "Haste often breeds disaster." A grunt as he hauled aside a huge section of rock. "How's that?"

"Better." Aurora's palm flattened atop the hard surface, moving about as she explored their find. "It's the strongbox," she proclaimed. "I'm sure of it. I can feel the gilding, the knobs, even all four sides adjacent to the top. We've found it, Julian."

"Then it's time to seize our prize." With single-minded intensity, Julian tugged Aurora's hand free, peering into the crevice and nodding purposefully. "From what I can make out, it looks intact. Let's maneuver it up."

For a half hour they chipped and pounded at stones. At last their efforts were rewarded.

Tossing the tools aside, Julian bent forward over the newly formed chasm, lifting the chest from its rocky bed. With a harsh grating sound, the chest eased free.

"Oh, Julian, it really is James's strongbox." Aurora wiped a dirty sleeve across her forehead, oblivious to the fact that her face was now muddied, her gown and mantle ruined beyond repair. "Let's open it."

"Not yet. Not until we're in the ketch, safely on our way."

Something about Julian's tone made her look about. "Do you think we were followed?" she asked, scrutinizing the vast acres of woods, the tiny village beyond. "And if so, by whom? Your man Stone? That scoundrel Macall? Or one of the thieves that's been prowling about Pembourne in search of the black diamond?"

"The latter is unlikely," Julian replied, sitting back on his haunches. "Those thieves have lost interest since I retracted all the ludicrous accusations my father spouted."

"You're right. The threatening notes and attempted burglaries have all but ceased. So, if it's not privateers . . ." Aurora scanned the area again. "Stone would have no reason to conceal himself, especially now that he and I have officially met. Do you think it's

Macall? Do you think he discovered your whereabouts and tracked us here?"

"No." Julian shook his head. "Macall's determined enough to hunt me down, but not shrewd enough to follow me undetected from a distance—especially by water. If he were out there, I'd have spied him hours ago. No, actually I don't think we were followed—this time. However . . ."

"I know," Aurora interrupted, her eyes twinkling. "The cardinal rule of adventurers. Eliminate any potential obstacles." She rose to her feet, brushing clumps of dirt from her gown. "Tell me, Merlin—is hurrying permitted? Or is that too conspicuous? Must we walk unobtrusively so as not to arouse suspicion?"

Julian chuckled and stood up, the strongbox and tools tucked beneath his arm. "Hurrying is not only permitted but advisable. Come."

They scrambled down the cliffs, Aurora's gown catching and ripping several times along the way. At last they reached the ketch, at which time she bounded by Julian, leaping aboard and fidgeting restlessly as her husband lowered the strongbox and tools to the deck, then swung down beside her. "Now," she urged. "Quickly. Open it."

Julian extracted the key, then paused, offering it to Aurora while he untied the rope that bound their ketch to land. "Why don't you?"

"I?" Aurora stared. "Really?"

"James was your great-grandfather. Technically the strongbox belongs to you." A teasing grin as he raised the sail. "Besides, you deserve a reward. You've proved to be quite a splendid—and successful—adventurer." He folded her fingers around the key, then resumed his place at the helm. "You open. I'll steer. It's all yours, Rory."

Trembling with excitement, Aurora knelt beside the strongbox, locating the knob that corresponded to the one beneath which Geoffrey had concealed his keyhole.

She grasped it firmly and eased it aside until the slot was revealed. Then she fit the key into the slot, exerting pressure—a little at a time—until the lock gave, opening with a telltale click.

Aurora's gaze met Julian's.

"Bravo, *soleil*," he praised. "Now let's see what James left us."

Wetting her lips, Aurora raised the lid, baring the chest's contents for them both to see.

A dagger adorned with the head of a falcon greeted their eyes. Beneath the dagger lay a single sheet of paper covered with text, discolored with age.

Aurora lifted both articles from the strongbox and turned her attention first to the dagger, which she held out for Julian's inspection. "It's identical to Geoffrey's."

"Indeed it is," he concurred. "Clearly this is James's way of ensuring us that what we've found is genuine— left to us by the Falcon." Julian veered the ketch on its course, casting a quick look at the paper in Aurora's hand. "One edge of the page is jagged. And the words are printed, not penned. What do they say?"

"The page must have been torn from a book." Aurora frowned, turning the paper back to front, scanning the contents. "There's printing on both sides. The content describes the hunting habits of the falcon—more specifically, the merlin and the kestrel."

"The two smallest falcons," Julian noted aloud. "Interesting. We'll have to read the text more closely, see what particular wording James wants us to distinguish. Are there any marks penned on the page?"

"No marks, no underlined or circled words, not even a notation in the margin—not on either side." Aurora fingered the page's uneven edge. "The good news is that none of the contents were cut off when the page was torn free." A pause. "I wonder what book James took it from."

"That might be equally as significant as what's printed

on the page itself," Julian mused aloud. "I suggest we leave Plymouth immediately, ride directly to Pembourne to show our findings to Slayde and Courtney. After all, we have no immediate reason to return to Morland now that we've found the strongbox. And your brother and sister-in-law deserve to know our findings."

Aurora shot him a knowing look. "Not to mention that Pembourne contains James's library—and all his falcon books—which you're eager to get your hands on, given that one of them is doubtless the book we seek."

Julian chuckled. "You're becoming increasingly more insightful."

"Perhaps my insight is strengthening only with regard to you," Aurora suggested pointedly, studying her husband's profile to gauge his reaction. "Careful, Merlin. I'm beginning to understand the way you think."

An amused sideways glance. "Should I feel threatened?"

"Only if you insist on retaining those wretched walls of yours." Her smile was beatific. "If not, I'm quite harmless."

"I'm glad to hear that, *soleil*. I've started to see for myself just how formidable an adversary you would be."

Julian's tone was teasing, which irritated Aurora more than the wariness she'd been expecting. Teasing meant he was intentionally evading the subject, skillfully thwarting any inroads she hoped to make. *Damn you, Julian*, she fumed silently. *You can't shut me out forever. I won't let you.*

The fervor of her own resolve gave her pause. Yes, Julian was a challenge—one she'd vowed to rise to. But the intensity of her determination to break down his emotional walls far exceeded anything she'd ever experienced in the mere facing of a challenge. What exactly was troubling her so much? Julian was giving her all the things he'd promised when he offered for her: adventure, excitement, passion. He'd vowed to share the exhilaration of his life, the wealth of his experience. He'd said nothing about relaying his innermost thoughts, sharing his feelings.

Opening his heart.

So why was it so bloody important to her that she secure those things? Why couldn't she just accept the wonders she'd already been offered—exploring the world, seeking out the black diamond, fueling the fires of passion? Why were those enticements no longer enough?

The answer was as startling as it was obvious.

She was falling in love with her husband.

Aurora nearly groaned aloud. *How could this be happening?* she pondered in astonishment. A month ago she hadn't even known Julian Bencroft. 'Twas impossible for him to have captured her heart in a matter of days.

And yet she'd trusted him in a matter of minutes.

She'd told him so herself on the day he proposed, argued that time was not a requirement for trust, that trust came from within and was ofttimes instinctive rather than earned. And how could she refute that statement when she knew in her heart it was true? She *had* trusted Julian from the onset, had believed in his noble intentions, his decency, his honor. She'd placed her life and her future in his hands, knowing somehow he would give her everything she craved.

What she hadn't realized was just how much she craved.

But love? Unlike trust, love took time, familiarity, cultivation. Didn't it?

It hadn't with Slayde and Courtney.

Aurora squeezed her eyes shut, the full impact of her realization sinking in. *I'm a fool,* she berated herself inwardly, contemplating the overwhelming sensations she experienced each time she and Julian made love— sensations too profound to stem merely from lust, incited by a fervor that intensified more with each joining. *A stupid, bloody fool. What did I think Mr. Scollard was trying to tell me when he compared me with Courtney, reminded me of the days when she grappled with her feelings for Slayde after being thrust unexpectedly into his life? Mr. Scollard was as much as telling me I'd soon experience something similar with Julian. Only I was too dim-witted to hear.*

Well, I hear you now, Mr. Scollard, she acknowledged ruefully. *The question is, what am I going to do about it? For now—nothing.*

The decision erupted in her mind with the same conviction as had the realization of her feelings. And while she was still reeling from the knowledge that she was falling in love with Julian, she was sensible enough to know that she couldn't act upon her newfound discovery—not now. Not with the black diamond still unrecovered, the echoes of the past still haunting their lives. There was too much closure yet to be had, too many hurdles to be contemplated and surmounted.

And unearthing the black diamond was only the first. After that came she herself.

Aurora drew a slow, steadying breath, grasping the open strongbox in her hands as if it were an anchor. She'd never truly imagined falling in love, and now that she had—well, she needed time to understand these new startling feelings that had stormed her senses, taken her completely by surprise.

Then came the third—and perhaps the most difficult—hurdle of all: Julian.

How could she convey these feelings to him? What could she say, and when? How severe would his reaction be?

That he'd be irked was a certainty. Aurora was too honest to delude herself into thinking otherwise. She, better than anyone, knew the way her husband regarded her: as an exciting and delightful diversion, a tempting indulgence to be savored at will, even a kindred spirit and worthy companion. But love? Love was not part of

Julian's plan any more than were the constraints spawned by emotional bonds. Julian was an adventurer. He would not welcome the potential limitations love would impose on his way of life. He was also a loner— one who'd already divulged more of himself than he liked and who would be reluctant to permit further intrusions into his private thoughts and feelings.

Lord help her, what impasse had she backed herself into this time?

"Aurora?" Julian's voice was questioning, his gaze curious. "Why are you staring into that strongbox as if it contains another secret we have yet to unearth?"

"Because it does." Jolting back to reality, Aurora fingered the frayed page that lay within the box. "We still have to determine why James chose this particular page to tear out and hide. It's obviously a crucial clue that he meant for us to find."

"Then you agree we should go to Pembourne?"

Pembourne. The prospect sent waves of relief flooding through Aurora—for reasons that had little to do with James's library. "Yes, definitely," she concurred, thinking that traveling to her old home meant receiving precisely what she needed: the wondrous balm of Courtney's counsel. "I suggest we leave Plymouth at once and ride directly to Pembourne."

It was late at night when they arrived, and Aurora glanced anxiously at the manor, experiencing another surge of relief when she saw that the lamps on the first level were still lit.

"They're awake," she murmured, nearly leaping from the phaeton. She bounded up the steps, knocking loudly and repeatedly until Siebert opened the door.

"Good evening, Siebert. It is I," Aurora announced.

"I never doubted that for a moment, my lady," the butler returned dryly. "Who else would be breaking down the door at this hour of night?" He stepped aside to admit the two of them, nodding politely—if aloofly—at Julian. "The earl and countess are in the sitting room."

"Thank you, Siebert."

Aurora exploded into the sitting room like a cannon. "We found the . . ."

"My God, what happened to you?" Slayde demanded, bolting to his feet and staring at his sister. "Were you in an accident?"

"What?" Confused, Aurora followed Slayde's gaze, realizing for the first time what a sorry state she was in. "Oh. I must have torn my gown."

"Torn your gown?" Slayde was still gaping. "Aurora, you're covered with dirt, your gown and mantle are shredded, and you have scratches all over your arms. What in the hell went on at Morland?"

"Your ingenious sister figured out the location of this—that's what went on," Julian supplied, flourishing the strongbox as he entered the room.

"It was at Morland Manor?" Courtney exclaimed, sitting upright on the sofa.

"In a matter of speaking." Julian proceeded to fill them in, concluding by showing them the strongbox and its contents.

"Well," Courtney murmured, shaking her head in amazement, "it appears we're going to have to pore over James's library yet again."

"*I'll* begin tonight," Julian qualified at once. "Slayde, you're welcome to join me. But our wives are going to bed."

Aurora's head shot up. "Not I," she protested. "Courtney needs her rest. But . . ."

"Aurora—" Julian held up his palm, silencing her protest, his tone as unyielding as it had been in the inn when he'd demanded she let him speak with Stone in private. "You haven't eaten since breakfast. You're pale, covered in scratches, and swaying on your feet. In short, you're exhausted. There are hundreds of books in that library. It's doubtful Slayde and I will discover anything over the next few hours. If we do, I'll awaken you. I'm accustomed to this pace. You're not. So don't argue with me. Eat something, take a hot bath, and go to sleep."

"Very well." Normally Aurora would have fought like a tigress. But if there was anything she wanted equally as much as she wanted to tear through those books, it was the chance to talk to Courtney. Further, Julian was right. She felt unusually weak and her head was pounding painfully—almost as if the effects of the day were descending upon her all at once. "I'll rest—for a while."

She retired to her old room, where she ate two helpings of supper, soaked in a hot tub, then slipped into her nightrail and wrapper and padded down the hall to Courtney's bedchamber.

Tentatively she knocked.

"Come in."

Aurora opened the door and poked her head inside. "'Tis only I."

"I know. I've been expecting you." Courtney placed her brush on her dressing table, waving Aurora into the room. "Are you feeling better?"

"Much. I guess I was hungrier than I realized."

"And dirtier." Courtney grinned. "Have a seat."

Aurora closed the door behind her, glancing about the chamber. "Are you expecting Slayde?"

"Eventually. After he spends half the night in the library poring over books with Julian. In truth, I think he welcomed the opportunity. These days my poor husband prowls about quite a bit before bedtime, coming to my chambers only when he's very, very sleepy."

A new understanding lit Aurora's eyes. "I would imagine this is a difficult time—for both of you."

"Difficult, but worth it." Courtney lay her palm on her abdomen. "Besides, it will only be a few more weeks before our babe arrives. After which I intend to heal as quickly as I can—if for no other reason than to end Slayde's nighttime strolls."

The two women laughed.

"A month ago you would have scoffed at what I just said," Courtney noted aloud.

"A month ago I was a child," Aurora replied, dropping into a chair. "A child and a fool. Courtney, I'm in a terrible predicament. I don't know what to do."

"Is this about Julian?"

"Yes, heaven help me."

Courtney's delicate brows drew together. "He's not causing you unhappiness, is he?"

"No. Well, yes. But not in the way you mean."

Slowly Courtney sank onto the bed, regarding her friend with keen insight. "You're falling in love with him, aren't you?"

To Aurora's horror, tears welled up in her eyes. "Yes," she managed. "And I can't seem to stop it from happening."

"Why would you want to?"

"Because it changes everything. Because adventure and excitement—even passion—are diversions, while love is profound, real. Because my emotions are in turmoil. I can't control them nor do I fully understand them." A pause. "And because Julian would hate the idea."

"Ah. So that's what this is all about." Courtney skipped over the bulk of her friend's tirade and focused on her final statement. "You're worried about Julian's reaction when you declare your love."

"You can't imagine how vehemently he's going to resist the whole idea."

"Oh, can't I?" Courtney's eyes sparkled. "You, my dear friend, have a very short memory. Last spring, 'twas you who were counseling me about this very thing."

"That was entirely different."

"Really? How so?"

"Because I knew Slayde was in love with you. So, for that matter, did he. He was just too much of a dolt to accept your love in return."

"And Julian?"

"Julian is a stubborn, self-contained loner who refuses to share his thoughts *or* his feelings, much less his heart."

"That sounds remarkably like a description of Slayde when I met him." Courtney leaned forward and took Aurora's hands in hers. "I realize the two men are not exactly alike, nor are the circumstances that defined their lives. But they do share quite a few similarities— strong ones. Surely you've noticed."

A morose nod. "I've noticed. Unfortunately all the traits they share are negative ones. They're like two immovable rocks. Only Julian, unlike Slayde, has no desire—or reason—to budge."

"I'm sure Lawrence and Chilton had a lot to do with that fact." Courtney's expression grew thoughtful. "Remember, Slayde never had to endure the ostracism and rejection Julian did. I can't imagine that was easy."

"It's more than Lawrence's renunciation that shaped Julian's outlook," Aurora replied quietly, giving voice to the conclusion she'd drawn after listening to Julian fervently, albeit reluctantly, discuss his brother. "Hubert's death had a lot to do with Julian's remoteness— perhaps more than Julian himself realizes. He and his brother were very close."

"Hubert died quite young," Courtney murmured. "If I recall correctly, Slayde told me it happened his first year at Oxford. Are you saying that as a result of Julian's loss and the pain it incited, he cut himself off emotionally?"

"Yes. But I think it goes far deeper than that." Aurora frowned. "Courtney, Hubert was sickly all his life. Julian spent much of his childhood coming to grips with the fact that there was nothing he could do to change the reality of his brother's frailty, that no matter how hard he prayed, he couldn't transfer his own vigor to Hugh. He felt helpless and guilty. I think there's a part of my husband that feels responsible for Hubert's death—not for causing it, but for being unable to prevent it. He's never been the same since Hubert died. I believe the reason for that is because, upon Hugh's death, Julian lost not only the sole person who mattered to him, but a piece of himself as well."

"Poor Julian." Courtney's eyes softened with compassion. "No wonder he chose the path of an adventurer. 'Tis far easier to remain detached when you never stay still long enough to face others . . . or yourself."

"Exactly. And he's managed to accomplish precisely that—up until now, that is. Coincident with Julian's homecoming, everything changed. He's been plunged into the heart of his past and his pain."

"By whom?"

"His father."

"Lawrence?" Courtney gasped. "What impact could that monster possibly have on Julian's life now? He's dead!"

"But his cruelty is very much alive. He's blackmailing Julian into doing his bidding, using Julian's feelings for Hubert as bait." Aurora proceeded to explain the terms of Lawrence's will and their effect on her husband. "Julian is driven. He's fighting to redeem himself in a way that has nothing to do with his father's rejection and everything to do with his own sense of guilt and loss."

"No wonder Julian is so consumed with finding that diamond," Courtney realized aloud.

"And why, once he has, he'll resume his life as it was," Aurora added bleakly.

"With one exception: now he has a wife. A wife he elected—no, fought—to marry, one with whom he'll doubtless prefer to roam the globe."

"So long as all she demands of him is to share his adventures and his bed."

"But not his love."

"Exactly. You yourself just said he'll never stand still long enough to put down roots or—heaven help him—fall in love."

"All the more reason why it's up to you to *make* him stand still long enough for that to happen."

"What?" Aurora's head came up.

"You heard me," Courtney stated flatly. "Aurora, you, better than anyone, know that winning Slayde over was a monumental challenge. He was determined for the Huntley name, along with that detestable curse, to die with him. To that end he swore off marriage and children. I was desperately in love with him and miserable at the prospect of our never having a life together. *You're* the one who told me to go after my future, because ultimately it was Slayde's future as well."

"I did say that, didn't I?"

"Um-hum. But advice, my friend, is easy to give. Carrying it out, especially when it means battling 'an immovable rock,' is hard. Damned hard. I have no doubt you're up for the challenge. The question is, do you love Julian enough to seize it, to hang on until you conquer it?"

"You ask arduous questions." Aurora massaged her temples. "But Lord help me, I think the answer is yes."

"So do I." Courtney's lips curved. "Let's explore these emotions of yours. You once asked me what it felt like to be in love. Now 'tis my turn to ask you. Tell me how Julian makes you feel."

"How Julian makes me feel?" Aurora sucked in her breath. "Like a storm-tossed sea. Like the branches on an oak when the wind sweeps through them. Like a waterfall plunging over the edge of a cliff and crashing to a swirling pool below. Like . . ."

"All right, all right," Courtney interrupted, laughing. "I should have expected that."

"It's nothing like the description you gave me."

"Perhaps that's because love is different for each of us. For me it meant a sense of peace, belonging. For you it means exhilaration, adventure. Aurora, we both know you'd never be content with a serene and quiet life."

"Nor do I seem destined to have one. Certainly not once I've conveyed my feelings to Julian."

"You're so convinced he'll react badly?"

"Aren't you?"

"No. I think you're underestimating how much he cares for you. Oh, I don't expect he'll admit it; allowing himself the vulnerability of needing someone will doubtless seem an untenable prospect."

"Untenable? He'll never permit it."

"We don't always have control over our emotions."

"Courtney, this is preposterous." Aurora sprang to her feet, pacing restlessly about the bedchamber. "Julian and I have been married less than a week. Prior to that we scarcely knew each other." She halted, pivoting about to face her friend. "How long did it take you to realize you were in love with Slayde?"

"Less time than it's taken you to perceive your feelings for Julian. And remember, Slayde and I were truly strangers—in every way. You and Julian are married; you share an intimacy Slayde and I didn't experience right away."

"That's passion, not love."

"In your case it's passion coupled with the same emotional affinity Slayde and I shared. In truth, I can't imagine a more powerful combination. So time is not the issue here."

"Perhaps not. But, Courtney, I'm not as selfless as you. I can't bear loving a man who can't—won't—return my love."

"You won't have to," Courtney replied softly. "Trust me, Aurora. Julian is half in love with you already. I see it in his eyes when he gazes at you, in his voice when he boasts of your skill as an adventurer. Even in the protective way he looks out for your well-being. And his desire for you—well, that's self-evident. All the seeds are there. 'Tis up to you to make them grow. After that, both your lives will be transformed."

Aurora was on the verge of disagreeing when Courtney's final statement sank in. "Odd," she commented aloud. "Mr. Scollard said almost those exact words when he spoke of my future with Julian."

"Really?" Courtney jumped on her friend's revelation. "When was this?"

"Right after Julian offered for me. I raced straight to the lighthouse to see Mr. Scollard. He, too, said that Julian and I would transform each other's lives—at the same time, incidentally, that he revealed the true story of the Fox and the Falcon—*before* I told it to him."

"None of that should surprise you, knowing Mr. Scollard." Courtney dismissed Aurora's disclosure with a wave of her hand. "What else did Mr. Scollard say about you and Julian?"

"He cautioned me that the merlin was deceptive, sometimes in ways even he himself doesn't comprehend. And he heralded love as the strongest and most wondrous of forces, with the exception of fate."

"Excellent! As always, Mr. Scollard is a genius," Courtney exclaimed. "Further, I concur with his opinion exactly. It gives me all the more confidence in the advice I'm about to dispense."

"Which is?"

"Don't wait to tell Julian you love him. When the next opportunity arises, tell him."

"Immediately?" Aurora's jaw dropped.

"Yes. For many reasons. First, you're far too forthright to restrain yourself. Second, despite your concern to the contrary, Julian is far too arrogant to reject your declaration. He might even savor it. Either way he'll need time to adjust, to face his own feelings and come to grips with the inevitable. Believe me, it will be far easier for him to lower his walls if he's certain your love awaits on the other side."

"And how do I convince him of that?"

"That, my dear friend, is something only you can decide and only you can accomplish. But somehow I think you'll manage quite well."

"You're serious." Aurora's heart was pounding like a drum.

"Absolutely."

"Courtney, what if he . . . ?"

"He won't."

"I have to think about this." Aurora resumed pacing. "I never imagined a man could have so much power over me. Ironic, isn't it? I just secured my freedom and now I'm bound in a more fundamental way than I was before."

"But this time it's by choice."

"Or by fate," Aurora amended, considering Mr. Scollard's words.

"Yes, fate." Courtney leaned contentedly back against the pillow, regarding her friend with a smug grin. "I suspect fate has wondrous plans for you."

"If you say so."

"Do you doubt Mr. Scollard and me?"

Aurora rolled her eyes. "All right," she decided. "I'll tell him. Heaven help me, I'll tell him."

Chapter 10

Dawn's pale rays awakened her.

Rolling onto her back, Aurora blinked, opening her eyes to stare up at the familiar ceiling, wondering why she felt so out of sorts awakening in her own bedchamber.

The answer spilled forth like the sunlight.

Julian wasn't beside her.

Propping herself on her elbows, Aurora scanned the room, confirming that her husband indeed was not there. She'd waited up half the night for him until her aching body and heavy eyelids won out and sleep had claimed her.

Perhaps that had been for the best.

She was still reeling from her conversation with Courtney, or rather, from its outcome. She'd expected many things from her friend: compassion, understanding, profound discussion. All of which she'd gotten in abundance. What she hadn't expected was the sheer impulsiveness of Courtney's response. It was she who was the reckless one, the one who rushed impetuously into situations. Courtney was calmer, more rational, capable of weighing all the ramifications before acting. And yet, just when Aurora was facing the most overwhelming of challenges, when she'd somehow found the sensibility to restrain herself from blurting out her feelings to Julian, Courtney had urged her to do precisely that.

What's more, she'd agreed.

Had she agreed because it suited her nature to do so, or because she truly believed telling Julian was the right thing to do? Swiftly she reevaluated the reasons she'd originally conjured up for deferring her revelation: the compelling search for the black diamond, her own reticence, and, most significantly, Julian's.

Courtney's reasoning annihilated them all. If what her friend suggested was true, Julian might be taken aback, even unnerved by her declaration of love; but ultimately he would need that love, rely upon it as his foundation while he sought not only the missing stone, but an internal peace both he and his past had wrested away.

Groaning, Aurora swung her legs over the side of the bed and tossed back her thick mane of hair.

Hell and damnation, Courtney was right.

With that woeful admission she rose, an ironic smile curving her lips. Love obviously did change a person. For the first time, deferral had seemed infinitely more appealing than candor.

Crossing over to the wardrobe, Aurora pulled out one of the few gowns she'd left behind for those times she visited Pembourne—a welcome fact, given that the dress she'd worn yesterday was torn beyond repair. She washed and dressed hastily, her thoughts now veering in a completely new direction.

Julian had never come to bed. That could mean but one thing: that he and Slayde were still in the library, poring over James's books in the hopes of finding the one from which the hidden page had been torn.

And she wanted to be there when they found it.

Running a brush through her hair, she glanced briefly at her reflection in the looking glass, then dashed out the door, through the hallway, and down the stairs.

She burst into the library.

"What have you found . . . ?" Breaking off, she stared about in amazement. The library shelves were three-quarters bare, the floor piled high with volume after volume of discarded texts. Amid the debris sat Slayde and Julian—Slayde slouched in an armchair, Julian sprawled on the settee. Each of them had an open book spread across his lap, and each of them looked up red eyed when she entered.

"Nothing." Julian snapped shut the book he held, raking a frustrated hand through his hair. "Not one damned thing, that's what we've found. Countless books on falcons, dozens that specifically pertained to the merlin and the kestrel—not one that was missing a page."

"You both look like death." Aurora crossed over, plucking the book from her husband's hands. "Did you get any sleep at all?"

"No." Slayde's tone was equally curt, his stare glazed and disoriented. "What time is it anyway?"

"Morning. Or hadn't you noticed the sunlight peeping through the windows?"

"I'm not in a lighthearted mood, Aurora." Her brother flung down the volume he'd been reading, rising unsteadily to his feet. "So don't try to be amusing."

"I'm not." Aurora turned on her heel and walked out.

Returning a few minutes later with a steaming tray, she announced, "Cook is preparing an early breakfast and two more pots of coffee—one for you and one for the staff. I pleaded your case to everyone in the kitchen.

Once the servants heard the sorry state you were in from working all night, they insisted you take the first pot of the day." She lowered the tray to a sideboard, pouring two full cups. "Here." She handed a cup to each of them. "This will soothe your foul tempers and make you far easier to live with."

"I doubt that," Slayde muttered, taking an appreciative gulp. "But thank you."

"You're welcome." She turned to Julian and watched him down the entire cup. "Better?"

"Much. Thank you, *soleil.*" He set down the saucer, rubbed the back of his neck. "We've covered almost the entire library. We also searched the study and several of the salons, just in case James stored the book elsewhere. It's nowhere to be found."

"Nowhere you've yet looked," Aurora corrected. "James didn't go to all the trouble of concealing that page in a buried strongbox for nothing. We just haven't stumbled on the right location yet. We will. Or rather, *I* will." She folded her arms across her breasts. "Julian, neither you nor Slayde is in any condition to continue. You can scarcely see, much less concentrate. I, on the other hand, have had a hot bath—which you sorely need after our digging expedition—two plates of food, and several good hours of sleep. I want you both to follow suit: eat the breakfast Cook is preparing, soak in the tubs I'll have sent up, and go to sleep. Not for the entire day," she added hastily, seeing her husband's oncoming protest. "Just for a few hours, until your body has recouped enough strength to push on." She touched his unshaven jaw. "Julian—please."

An odd look crossed Julian's face, and he nodded slowly. "Very well—but only for a short time."

Aurora flashed him an impish grin. "I promise to awaken you if I discover anything significant," she teased, parroting his vow of last night.

Julian's lips curved. "That puts my mind at ease." His lips brushed her palm before he turned away. "Come, Slayde. We've received our orders."

Slayde hesitated, glancing restlessly toward the bookshelves.

"Don't even consider it, my love." It was Courtney's voice, her tone adamant as she entered the room. "If Aurora hasn't convinced you, then allow me. Should you decide to push yourself further, without food or sleep, I shall be forced to romp about the grounds with Tyrant, stroll to the lighthouse and visit with Mr. Scollard, and prune the flowers in the conservatory—all of which I'm perfectly capable of doing, albeit at a slower pace, but have foregone over the past month due to your incessant worry." She gave him a beatific smile. "Shall I tell Siebert I'll be exercising Tyrant this morning?"

"You made your point." Slayde shot her a warning look. "You stay put. Julian and I are on our way to the dining room."

"I'm glad to hear that."

Courtney and Aurora waited until the men had stalked off before they dissolved into laughter.

"Slayde turned sheet white when you suggested dashing about with Tyrant," Aurora commended. "I think he would have agreed to anything to keep you and the babe in the manor."

"Probably." Courtney's laughter faded, a knowing glint coming into her eyes. "Did you see the expression on Julian's face when you begged him to rest?"

"He looked . . . off balance."

"He looked like a man in love," Courtney corrected.

A surge of hope. "Do you really think so?"

"I really think so."

Aurora's eyes sparkled. "I suddenly have energy enough to take on the rest of the library on my own."

"I suggest you let me help," Courtney proposed, smiling. "That way you can save a bit of energy for your husband. I believe you have something to tell him when he awakens."

"Yes, I believe I do."

As it turned out, Aurora's announcement was deferred yet again.

When Julian and Slayde returned to the library at noon, it was to find their tired, discouraged wives sitting amid an even denser array of discarded books.

"I don't understand it," Aurora puzzled, scooting down the ladder. "The book *has* to be here."

"It has to," Julian muttered. "But so far, it isn't."

"Pardon me, my lord." Siebert stood in the library doorway, gaping at the wild disorder looming before him. "The Viscount Guillford is here to see you."

"Guillford?" Aurora's head snapped around.

"Damn," Slayde muttered. "I completely forgot. Guillford and I have an appointment to discuss a business investment." He frowned. "I'll have Siebert show him directly to my study. In that way he won't see the chaotic state the library is in, nor will you need to face him."

"I agree about the library," Julian interjected. "Were Guillford to come in here, it would pose a lot of questions we'd prefer not to answer. But I disagree that Aurora should hide from him. To begin with, I'm sure he knows she and I are at Pembourne; my carriage is in your drive. Besides, it's time to put to rest the ludicrous scandal surrounding our marriage. We've already run into Guillford once, in Camden's office. We're bound to see him again, just as we're bound to cross paths with Lady Altec and her gossiping friends—plus all the other prying members of the *ton*. 'Tis time to show them just how well suited my bride and I are. The sooner we do, the less uncomfortable it will be—not for me, since I don't give a damn what they think of me—but for Aurora." His expression softened. "My wife has waited a long time for some semblance of a coming-out. I suggest we help make her experience, however limited, a pleasant one."

"I agree," Courtney put in. "After all, we've extended our apologies to Lord Guillford. We have no need to make further amends. Moreover, 'tis not as if he and Aurora were deeply in love. His pride was wounded, yes, but his heart was hardly shattered. From what I hear, there are at least a dozen women eager to help him heal—especially if it means acquiring his name, his title, and his wealth. Honestly, Slayde, I think Julian's right. Let's stop treating this marriage as if it's anything less than what we truly wanted for Aurora."

"Your points are well taken." Slayde nodded. "Very well. Let's all greet the viscount together. It will ease the scandal—if not the shock—surrounding this marriage."

"Once we've made our appearance, Julian, Aurora, and I will continue in the library while you have your meeting with the viscount," Courtney added.

"A very brief meeting," Slayde murmured. *"Very* brief. I want to find that book. Siebert, show Lord Guillford to the anteroom. I'll be out to greet him in a moment."

"Very good, sir." Siebert paused, clearing his throat. "Shall I summon some footmen to reassemble the library?"

"Not yet, Siebert. Later—but not yet."

Lord Guillford rose, hands clasped behind his back, when the two Huntleys and the two Bencrofts entered the anteroom. His expression was composed, but he looked visibly surprised to see them all standing before him.

"Guillford—good day." Slayde greeted his guest politely. "Forgive the delay; my wife and I were just visiting with Aurora and Julian."

"Of course. I understand." The viscount bowed in

their general direction. "Countess. Morland. Aurora. 'Tis good to see you all." A quick glance at Slayde. "If you'd rather reschedule our appointment . . ."

"Not for our sake," Julian inserted smoothly. "Courtney was just helping Aurora and me gather the remainder of her things. We stopped merely to say hello to you. You and Slayde are perfectly welcome to conduct your meeting as planned."

"Are you about to embark on a wedding trip?" Guillford inquired.

"Not just yet. I have a few business matters to conclude before I can leave England."

"Ah. Your father's estate."

"Among other things," Julian replied vaguely.

"It must be very difficult for you," Guillford added, glancing from Julian to Aurora. "Having to contend with so much at one time: your father's death, an unexpected marriage—and an unlikely one at that—plus these other business matters you just mentioned."

"Not at all." Julian's eyes narrowed. "I'm accustomed to handling a number of ventures at one time. As for my father's death, that was more an inconvenience than anything else. However, being summoned to attend to his estate had its compensations. Had I not been in Devonshire, I would never have had the opportunity to meet my bride. That was a fortunate day indeed. I'd lost hope of ever meeting a woman daring enough, unique enough, exciting enough, to share my life. As luck would have it, Aurora is all that and more." Julian wrapped a possessive arm about Aurora's waist. "Unlikely? Quite the opposite. If anyone is destined to end the age-old feud between our families, it's Aurora and I. We thrive on challenge. What's more, we always win."

"How delightful for you." A flush crept up Guillford's neck.

"Well, we've taken up enough of your time," Aurora piped up, torn between amusement and pity. Even armed with jealousy and resentment, the viscount was no match for Julian. "Courtney, let's collect the rest of my belongings. Then Julian and I can be on our way."

"Of course." Courtney's smile was bright. "Good day, Lord Guillford."

"Good day."

"You're brutal," Aurora hissed at Julian once they were all safely outside the door. The laughter in her eyes banked. "Thank you," she said simply.

"For what? I merely stated the truth."

"Then thank you for stating the truth. It greatly eased my discomfort."

"You have nothing to feel uncomfortable about," Courtney declared loyally, leading them back into the library. "The viscount is going to have to recover from his infatuation with you."

Aurora nodded. "I know. Still, having all your support means the world to me."

"We're family. That's what family is for." Courtney glanced about. "Time to resume our tedious project. We have only two shelves left to explore. Let's get busy."

Julian climbed up and handed books down to Aurora, who in turn passed them to Courtney to begin perusing. Within an hour they were finished, as only a quarter of the remaining books dealt with the subject of falcons.

"Now what?" Aurora demanded.

"Now we consider other possibilities," Julian replied. "James wants us to find that book. That means we're not thinking along the lines he intends us to. So let's think along another. Where else would he store a book?"

"Do you think it's hidden?"

"No. The strongbox was hidden because it was outside our estates' protective walls. If we follow our original premise—that all clues, other than the locked strongboxes, were placed in our respective homes—then the book is situated somewhere at Pembourne. In which case, James would have no reason to hide it. Only the Huntleys would have occasion to find it.'"

"What about the servants? Visitors?" Courtney asked. "What if someone other than a Huntley happened upon the book?"

"Like the key to the falcon cages, the book wouldn't mean anything to someone unless he had the missing page and was specifically searching for the book it had been torn from," Julian responded. "No, my instincts still tell me the answer is right in front of us."

"I think not," Aurora exclaimed abruptly.

Julian's head whipped around. "You've thought of something."

"Actually, *you* have. You just didn't see it through to its obvious conclusion. Consider the order of events our great-grandfathers orchestrated: Geoffrey's strongbox delivered to you at Morland by Mr. Camden. James's strongbox key, hanging alongside the falcon cages at Pembourne. Geoffrey's map, sketched and hung at Morland. And now the page and the dagger found in James's strongbox, clearly possessions that originated at Pembourne." Aurora stared at her husband, exhilaration pumping through her blood. "If we follow the one-for-one partnership method to which our great-grandfathers clearly subscribed, it would mean the next clue should either originate from or be awaiting us at Morland."

"Of course!" That wild excitement exploded across Julian's face, his topaz eyes blazing sparks of fire. "You're absolutely right. Morland, Pembourne, Morland, Pembourne—now Morland. Why the hell didn't I see it?" He slammed his fist on the side table. "Dammit—a whole day wasted. Never mind; we'll make up for it." He sprang into motion. "We'll leave for Morland at once."

"I'll have Siebert bring your carriage around," Courtney offered, wincing a bit as she rose to cross the room.

"No." Julian stayed her with his hand. "You've already overtaxed yourself far too much."

"I'm not an invalid, Julian."

One black brow arched. "No, but *I* will be if Slayde thinks I've pushed you too hard. Please, for my sake stay here and rest. Besides, this way you can fill Slayde in after he concludes his meeting with Guillford. Tell him where we are and what we're doing." A grin. "Also, tell him his sister is a genius." He caught Aurora's hand. "Come. We have a book to find."

Aurora's exhilaration gave way to keen awareness just after their carriage turned onto the main road.

Abruptly Julian became a different man—wary, rigid—slowing the phaeton three times to scan behind them. The fourth time he pulled off the road entirely, reining the horses and swinging down from his seat to prowl about.

"We're being followed," Aurora determined.

"Yes. This time we are." Julian strolled around in front of the phaeton, pretending to check the horses' tack, his gaze darting about the clusters of trees surrounding them. "And whoever is doing the following is not far behind." He frowned thoughtfully. "I'd investigate this on foot, but I won't leave you."

"I'll go with you." Aurora began to climb down.

"No," Julian commanded. "Stay put. If whoever's following us sees me lurking about with you alongside, he'll realize we've spotted him. I think we should continue on to Morland. Our pursuer evidently thinks we're heading someplace far more interesting, else he wouldn't be following."

"How do you know that?"

"Because the route that leads inland to Newton Abbot is a fairly well-traveled one. No common highwayman follows people from their homes and assaults them in broad daylight."

"Except you don't believe our pursuer is a common highwayman," Aurora reminded him.

"True, I don't. I think our pursuer knows precisely whom he's tracking and why. Which is all the more reason he'll hold off. No one who's familiar with my ability to defend myself would dare attack me under these conditions—not if he wanted to live. Further, I think the point is a moot one. Once our unwanted visitor figures out our destination, his interest in us will vanish, at least for the time being. Remember, Morland Manor is—in most people's minds—my home. Taking my bride there would seem anything but suspicious; 'twould seem the most natural thing in the world."

"As opposed to the more fascinating, inexplicable route you'd be taking if you were going off in search of— or to collect—the black diamond."

Julian flashed her a smile as he swung back into his seat. "Exactly." He guided the horses onto the road, continuing their journey as if nothing were amiss.

"That makes sense," Aurora concurred pensively. "So we simply go on our way and hope our pursuer loses interest."

"No, we go on our way, keeping up our guard lest our pursuer *not* lose interest." A quick glance at his wife. "Does this unnerve you?"

"Unnerve me? Not in the least. In truth, I find the whole situation rather exciting." Aurora sat up straighter, her entire face aglow. "I feel like an especially sly fox during the hunt, one who knows he's swifter and more cunning than either the dogs or the men who are stalking him."

Julian's eyes glittered, with humor and excitement. "I'm glad the thrill of the chase enthralls you so. Nevertheless, *soleil,* let me give you a small but essential warning: never become overconfident. Overconfidence breeds recklessness."

"And recklessness breeds failure?"

"In most cases." Julian brought Aurora's hand to his lips and pressed a hot, openmouthed kiss to her palm. "There is, however, one place where you can always unleash that enticing recklessness of yours—and be greeted with naught but success."

His husky tone, his pointed caress found their mark, and a surge of heat shot through her. "Really?" Her fingertips caressed his jaw, his mouth. "Odd, I seem to recall many places where you welcome my particular brand of recklessness."

Julian sucked in his breath, his expression a dizzying combination of raw hunger and stark amazement. "Only you could tempt me to forget everything—our current predicament, the book we're seeking—everything. We're in the midst of chaos, yet all I want to do right now is pull off the road and bury myself inside you until nothing exists but the staggering magic we make with our bodies."

Everything inside Aurora melted, slid down to her toes. "What if I were to entice you?"

"You'd succeed. So don't. It would endanger your life—something I've vowed never to do." With a quick hard kiss to her knuckles, Julian released her. "But once we're safely within those walls, once we've found that bloody book . . ."

"You offer a splendid incentive."

"An incentive—and a whole lot more." With a slap of the reins, Julian sped onward.

"Morland's library is a good deal more diverse than Pembourne's," Aurora noted. Seeing how few of the books reported on animals or nature, her shoulders sagged with relief. "But our task here should be far easier than it was at Pembourne. There we had to scrutinize an army of texts, lest one of the countless books that mentioned birds of prey be the one we sought. Whereas here—" She sighed, squatting down beside the lower section of shelves on the far wall. "—I'm relieved to see volumes on philosophy, history, religion, all of which we can eliminate as possibilities. That narrows things down significantly."

"Perhaps too significantly," Julian murmured, contemplating the room. "At first glance, I don't see a single book on falcons."

"We'll obviously have to delve more deeply."

"Agreed. Now, to determine a logical place to begin . . ."

"Don't determine. Search."

Julian tossed her a look. "So bloody impatient. Very well, Rory, this time we'll do it your way. But only because no harm can come of it."

"Yes, sir," she muttered.

"I'll start with the shelves on the opposite wall. Call out if you find anything significant."

"Don't worry. If I find that blasted book, Courtney and Slayde will probably hear me at Pembourne." So saying, Aurora began, skimming the titles from the bottom shelf up.

She was on the third section about an hour later when she gave a speculative frown. "I didn't know your family was interested in weapons."

"Weapons?" Julian glanced up from his task. "They weren't—at least not to my knowledge. Why?"

"Because this whole shelf is devoted solely to books on that subject: pistols, swords, cannons—an entire variety."

Slowly Julian descended the ladder, a puzzled expression on his face. "That's odd."

"Perhaps, but I doubt it means anything with regard to Geoffrey. These probably weren't even his selections for the library. After all, there were—subsequent to Geoffrey and prior to you—two other Dukes of Morland."

"One of whom was a tyrannical maniac consumed with nothing but regaining our fortune and rebuilding our businesses, the other of whom was a drunken weakling consumed only by his bottle and his vengeance."

Aurora turned, inclining her head quizzically. "You're saying no one has used this library since Geoffrey?"

"I'm saying that even if my grandfather or my father glanced at a book on occasion, they were hardly the types to designate which reading material should be stocked in the library. Neither of them would give a damn. My guess is that whatever books we're finding now have been here since Geoffrey's era." Julian crossed the room, his forehead wrinkled in thought. "Odd that he'd openly display books on weaponry, even if he was interested in the subject. Given his covert role as the Fox, I assume he'd avoid exhibiting an entire shelf of books on a topic that might arouse suspicions. Which weapons in particular are represented, did you say?"

"A multitude of them," Aurora murmured, tracing the titles with her forefinger. "There is one book on field guns, one on rifles, one on military muskets, two on flintlock pistols, one on gun shields. There are two books on cannons, three on swords, and one on . . ." Aurora frowned, tugging at the final book which was small, wedged tightly between the previous book and the wall. "One on . . ." She yanked it free. ". . . eighteenth-century daggers." Even as she said it, she jerked around to face Julian, who'd reached her side. "That would cover the time period in which the Fox and Falcon daggers were crafted."

"Indeed it would."

"Let's scrutinize this book cover to cover." Aurora was halfway to the settee.

"Don't bother. It isn't necessary." Julian crouched down where Aurora had made her find, peering into the now-vacant corner that had held the book on daggers. Abruptly he shifted his attentions one shelf lower.

"Here's what we're looking for." He straightened, flourishing a book entitled *England's Smallest Falcons.*

The volume Aurora had been holding struck the floor. "How did you know that was there?" she gasped.

"James told me. Or rather, his strongbox did. Think about the items he left us."

"His falcon dagger—and the page from his book."

"Arranged in what manner?"

Aurora's eyes widened. "The dagger was atop the page."

"Exactly. So I merely followed his lead. You found the dagger. I merely looked beneath it." Julian clutched the falcon volume tightly. *"This* is the book we have to scrutinize cover to cover."

"Let's begin by poring over the section directly before and after the page James tore out," Aurora suggested, dropping onto the settee and reaching eagerly for the book. "Maybe we'll find a clue there."

"Agreed." Julian sat beside her, flipping through until he found the appropriate spot. "You were right," he announced immediately, scanning the page just after the missing one. "It is a section on the hunting habits of the merlin and the kestrel. 'The merlin hunts low, rises up to drop like a stone onto its prey,'" Julian read aloud. "'It feeds on small mammals, insects, and mice. The kestrel makes a sudden drop from above onto its prey, reaps its prize, then carries on.'" A contemplative pause. "Nothing significant there. Wait." Julian's eyes narrowed, and he angled the book toward the light. "There are faint lines drawn beneath several of these words: 'feeds,' 'reaps,' and 'carries on.'" He scowled. "That's strange." With that he glanced back at the page immediately preceding the missing one. "This is the end of the previous section. It concludes by describing specific markings of both falcons: 'The merlin has a slight mustache and a bold black tail band. The kestrel has pointed wings and issues the eternal call of 'killy, killy,

killy.'" Again, Julian angled the book. "'Black' and 'eternal' are underscored. I'm beginning to doubt these notations are mere coincidence."

"They're not." Aurora gripped Julian's arm, her own hand icy cold. "Combine all those words, only arrange them in a different order: 'black' . . . 'reaps' . . . 'eternal' . . . 'carries on' . . . 'feeds'—don't they conjure up something in your mind?"

"The curse of the black diamond." Julian pored over the few pages once again. "Damn—all the underscored words are derived from that wretched curse."

Aurora shuddered, repeating the heinous phrase she'd committed to memory only too long ago. "'He with a black heart who touches the jewel will reap eternal wealth, while becoming the carrion upon whom, for all eternity, others will feed.'" She swallowed hard. "Is James warning us that the curse is real?"

Julian glanced at his wife, clearly aware of her rising apprehension. "I doubt it," he said, his voice deep, reassuring. "More likely he's warning us that others believe it is; that so long as the diamond remains unrestored, England is in danger. Remember, Rory, James had no idea of the dark events and scandal that would follow his death. He was worrying about his country, not his family."

"You're right." Aurora folded her hands in her lap, firmly mastering her trepidation. "I'm sorry; I become a bit irrational when it comes to that stone."

"I understand." Julian scowled. "The true bafflement here still remains. Not for a minute do I believe James went to all this trouble merely to warn us. His entire plan—his and Geoffrey's—all their precisely placed clues were designed to lead us to the diamond. Well, the underscored words we just read pertain only to the curse, not to its resolution. We still don't know where to look for the stone itself." Restlessly Julian skimmed the book, flipping through its yellowed pages.

The volume fell open to the inside cover—and the inscription that was scrawled upon it. "Aurora—look."

Aurora responded to the urgency in her husband's tone, peering eagerly over his shoulder.

Geoffrey, the inscription read, *Like the falcons depicted within, you are far greater than you appear—a rock of strength, a giant among men. As it is with the merlin and the kestrel, chart your path, then soar to the highest peak and the key to all life's treasures will be yours. Your friend, James.*

"So, James gave this book to Geoffrey as a gift," Aurora murmured, rereading her great-grandfather's words.

"Ostensibly."

Her head came up. "What do you mean, ostensibly?"

"I mean that James was the renowned breeder of falcons, not Geoffrey. 'Tis *his* library that's crammed full of books on birds of prey. Geoffrey has nary a one—except this."

"I see where your thoughts are headed." Aurora nodded vigorously. "If someone—the wrong someone—ever came upon this text and questioned its unlikely appearance at Morland, that someone had only to open the book and see the personal inscription, at which point he'd presume it was a gift and dismiss any reservations he might have." A puzzled frown as she reread the inscription. "I wonder why James chose these specific words. They *must* mean something."

"To begin with, they mention every one of the clues that led us to James's strongbox: 'Key,' 'chart,' 'giant,' referring to the giants from your Tamar legend. Clearly James is ensuring we've amassed all the necessary pieces—which we have."

"But pieces to what? To take us where? Back to the Tamar?"

Julian frowned. "I think not. Still, I don't know—yet. We'll have to reread everything we just uncovered, then study the entire book line by line, see what other specific references James left for us. Remember, thus far we've read only the page we found in his strongbox, two additional pages, and an inscription. Until we have more information I can't readily guess the right course to take to lead us to the diamond."

"Hell and damnation!" Aurora exploded, jumping to her feet. "We can't have come this far only to be thwarted."

"We aren't thwarted." Julian rose, placing the book on an end table. Reaching for Aurora, he captured her shoulders, rubbing them gently. "Rory, you wanted to be an adventurer. In order to do so, you *must* exercise a modicum of patience. No one, no matter how brilliant, unravels an entire mystery all at once. Puzzles—especially complex ones like this—take time to solve. I think we've done one hell of a job, given that we've only been working at it a few paltry days."

Aurora sighed, relaxing under her husband's massaging hands. "I suppose you're right. My head aches from thinking, and from the frenzied pace."

"Of course it does." His thumbs shifted, caressed the sides of her neck. "Ofttimes, you know, 'tis necessary to put some distance between yourself and your adventure. That distance affords you objectivity, perspective, all of which are essential to come to the right solution—and all of which are shattered when you're too close to a subject. Trust me—I've been involved in this type of work a lot longer than you have." He stroked her nape in slow, soothing caresses. "Remember the painting I told you about, the one I found in France? Well, as I said, I had to squelch my urgency, await the right moment to act—else all would have been lost. We have the same plight here. Not only with regard to our actions, but with regard to our thoughts. We've been consumed with this mystery for a fortnight, not to mention that its essence has dominated our lives forever." Julian paused, his voice dropping to a husky whisper. "What we need now is an effective diversion."

"Really?" Aurora's lips curved. "Have you one in mind?"

"Um-hum. It's perfect: exciting, inspiring, all-encompassing—it will command every drop of our energy, both mental *and* physical."

"It sounds fascinating . . . and taxing. What is it?"

A wicked grin was her response, and Julian released her only long enough to cross over and lock the library door. "The one you promised me on our carriage ride to Morland—or did you think I'd forgotten?"

Obviously he hadn't.

Neither, for that matter, had Aurora's body. It clamored to life along with Julian's pointed reminder. "No. I didn't think you'd forgotten." She gazed up at her husband, sobering as he returned to her side, wrapped his arms around her. "I just wasn't certain you'd want to indulge in that particular diversion here."

"I want to indulge in that particular diversion with you anywhere," Julian breathed, kissing her throat, her neck. "Libraries included."

"I wasn't referring to the library. I was referring to Morland." Aurora's eyes slid shut and she had to struggle to retain her thoughts, much less give voice to them. "Your memories of this manor are not very pleasant."

"True." Julian unfastened her gown, tugging it down along with her chemise. "Then, it's up to us to make new ones that *are* pleasant—no, not pleasant—spectacular." His lips found the hollow between her breasts, dipped lower. "Is that all right?"

With a moan Aurora gave in, grasping Julian's arms, arching to bring him closer. "Yes."

"Good." He bent to taste her breasts, drawing each tight aching nipple into his mouth, tugging until Aurora had to bite her lip to keep from screaming. "Don't cry out," her husband warned in a husky whisper. "We wouldn't want to bring Thayer running. I don't think he's equipped to handle what he'd find if he broke down that door." With that, Julian lowered his head, resumed his torture.

"Julian . . ." Aurora whimpered his name, clutched his elbows for support. It felt like a year, rather than a day, since they'd been together like this.

Julian swept her into his arms. "The rug or the settee?" he demanded hoarsely. "Both," he answered himself. He lowered her onto the settee, dragging off her clothes and leaving her utterly, gloriously naked. "You're breathtaking." He kneeled on the carpet, urging her to the edge of the sofa, wedging his shoulders between her thighs. "Remember—don't scream," he warned again.

Then, he lowered his head and buried his mouth in her sweetness.

Aurora grabbed a cushion, pressing it to her mouth to stifle her cries. Julian's fingers gripped her thighs, opened her more fully, his tongue lashing on her, in her, with thorough intensity, carrying her to instant unbearable heights. Her hips jutted forward, pressing her closer to the exquisite sensations and the man who was causing them.

Julian slid his hands beneath her, lifted her up and into him, his caresses abruptly intensifying, igniting her nerve endings until they frayed and snapped.

Without warning her climax slammed through her, shattering her into hundreds of pieces, making her arch and twist and hug the cushion she held with all her might.

Julian left her, and she floated, vaguely aware of him tearing at his clothes, flinging them randomly about. "Come here," he muttered thickly, gathering her into his arms, tossing the settee cushion aside. "Hold on to me instead."

He lowered her to the carpet, coming down over her and entering her in one ravenous thrust.

"Julian!" She couldn't remain silent, her own contractions beginning anew as her still-sensitized flesh reacted to the force of his entry.

"God." He ground out the word, his powerful hands anchoring her hips, dragging them up to meet the frenzied motion of his.

Aurora raised her legs, wrapped them around him, twining her arms about his neck. "Julian," she whispered, staring into the burning topaz flames in his eyes. Ardently she drew his mouth down to hers.

They kissed—deep, hungry kisses—again and again, Julian's powerful body moving in fast, urgent thrusts. He tangled his hands in her hair, devoured her mouth, taking her tongue, her breath, making them his.

"Come for me again," he commanded on a rasp. "Let me feel you—with me, all around me. Now, Aurora."

"Yes." Her nails dug into his back, the clawing tightness preceding her release already too excruciating to withstand. "Now . . ."

"Look at me." He waited only until she complied. Then, their gazes locked, he drove into her deeply, holding himself there, impaling her until she dissolved into wrenching spasms around him.

"Julian!" Aurora threw back her head, cried out his name as everything inside her converged and exploded.

"Yes . . . yes . . . *yes.*" He erupted, pouring into her like a man possessed, shouting her name again and again as he sought her womb, spilled his seed at its mouth.

They collapsed, drenched in sweat, gasping in air as if they'd been drowning. Neither moved or spoke. They just sank into each other's arms, their minds utterly dazed, their hearts thundering like cannon fire.

"Your Grace?" Thayer's crisp tone accompanied his knock and permeated their passion-drugged haze. "I heard a commotion. Is there something amiss?"

Julian's moan was a wisp of sound in Aurora's hair.

"Your Grace?" Thayer rattled the unyielding door handle. "Sir, I asked if something was amiss."

This time Julian gathered enough strength to reply. "No, Thayer," he called, propping himself—with enormous effort—on his elbows. "Everything is fine. The duchess and I were just . . ." He kissed the hollow at Aurora's throat. ". . . exploring the library."

Aurora bit her lip to control her mirth.

"Very good, sir." Sounding unconvinced and decidedly curious, Thayer retraced his steps.

Aurora's gaze met Julian's and she dissolved into laughter. "Thank goodness the door held. Thayer would have swooned. Maybe worse."

"Definitely worse," Julian concurred, lazily stroking strands of hair off his wife's face. "As it is, the man already thinks I'm a heathen."

"That's only because Lawrence let him believe that," Aurora demurred softly.

"Perhaps." Julian shrugged, flashing his heart-stopping smile. "On the other hand, my actions just now would support his claim. I did behave like a savage."

"Not a savage. More like a pagan god," Aurora amended, her fingers sifting through the longer hair at her husband's nape.

That assessment seemed to amuse him. "A pagan god?"

"Um-hum." Aurora was still floating on a pink-tipped cloud where nothing existed but the shimmering aftermath of their union. "That was how I first viewed you when we met at Dawlish's."

Julian arched a brow. "Did you? Why?"

"Oh, many reasons. Mostly because you were sinfully handsome in a dark and forbidden way that made everything inside me melt."

"Ah. Now that notion is even more appealing than the one in which you likened me to a stallion." His lips brushed her neck, swept over the sensitive hollow behind her ear.

"I thought it might be." A tiny shiver ran through her.

"And now?"

"Now . . . what?" Aurora's head was already swimming with sensation, everything inside her weak and trembling, reawakening to Julian's touch.

"You said you *viewed* me as a pagan god." His hips pressed forward, his body responding to her signal, swelling to fill her. "How do you view me now?"

"The same way," she admitted. Her breath broke as he withdrew, surged deeper. "You're powerful, unconventional, turbulent, seductive."

Julian caught her face between his palms. "And you're a fire in my blood." His thumbs caressed her cheeks. "One that nothing can extinguish." He held her gaze, keeping his rhythm slow and deep, watching her face as she arched to meet his thrusts. "God, you're beautiful," he ground out between clenched teeth. "So damned beautiful." His burning eyes bore into hers. "Do you feel it?" he murmured. "Do you?"

"Yes—oh, yes." The world was spinning away, and Aurora had no desire to recapture it.

"Tell me. Tell me what you're feeling."

Something profound and wonderful was unfolding inside her—something that had nothing to do with passion. "I love you," she whispered.

Julian went rigid.

The pink cloud disintegrated.

Oh God, how could she have blurted it out like that?

Aurora squeezed her eyes shut, willing the floor to swallow her whole. Damn her impulsive tongue. Damn her unmitigated candor. Damn her inability to think beyond Julian's touch. Damn, damn, damn.

"Aurora, look at me."

She complied reluctantly.

"Say that again."

She searched her husband's face, looking for a sign, any sign, of his reaction to her declaration. But all she could see was intentness, a wary anticipation as he awaited her reply. Well, it was too late to retract her words now. "I love you," she repeated. A pause. "Are you very angry?"

"Angry?" Julian caressed her face, tunneled his fingers through her hair. "Why in God's name would I be angry?" He lowered his mouth to hers, kissing her with a wealth of tenderness, a touch of awe—and a fine tension that hadn't been there before. "No one's ever given me those words before," he admitted quietly. "I'm humbled." He buried his lips in hers. "I'm honored." He slid his arms beneath her thighs, raised them to hug his flanks. "And I'm more profoundly touched than I can say."

"I'm . . . glad." Aurora desperately needed to think, to understand what Julian's words truly meant. But she couldn't, not when he was making love to her; transporting her to that extraordinary place she ascended to only in his arms.

"Let me show you," he was breathing into her lips. "My dazzling Aurora—let me show you."

In contrast to his earlier abandon, this time Julian was achingly tender, his body moving in exquisite strokes that seared through her body, delved straight to her soul.

Afterward, lying quietly in her husband's arms, Aurora's thoughts tumbled forth, tripping over each other in their desire to be heard.

Julian's reaction had been neither the anger she'd feared nor the arrogance Courtney had suspected. Instead, he'd felt honored, humbled, touched—emotions she'd never have attributed to Julian Bencroft.

But then, why not?

Hadn't she seen glimpses of his warmth, his ability to feel—not only in the way he treated her, but in the way he'd spoken of his brother? The answer to that was an unequivocal yes.

No one's ever given me those words before.

It was high time someone did.

Still, Aurora reminded herself, he *had* tensed when she'd first uttered her admission—out of shock, yes, but out of something more.

And that something was uneasiness; concern that being loved meant sacrificing his autonomy, relinquishing his freedom, altering his life.

Loving in return.

Julian might be half in love with her, but he was going to fight like hell to keep the other half to himself.

How unfortunate that he couldn't see how much he needed her.

How spectacular that she'd have to show him.

Chapter 11

"So this is your Windmouth lighthouse." Julian paused, tilting back his head to view the entire stone structure, nestled at the foot of the hills just south of Pembourne.

"Isn't it glorious?" Aurora darted about, assessing the fifty-seven-foot tower with as much pride as if she herself had constructed it.

"It is indeed."

"You'd never know it was over a hundred years old, not with the condition Mr. Scollard keeps it in. His magic is evident in every gleaming stone, every flicker of the lighthouse beam . . ."

"Every thrilling legend," Julian teased.

He saw the unexpected flash of hurt in her eyes—something he'd never seen before, much less put there—and instinctively he reached for her, drew her to him. *"Soleil,* I didn't mean . . ."

Aurora gazed up at him, that incomparable candor supplanting the hurt, compelling her to explain. "You're but the second person I've ever brought here. Somehow I knew Courtney would love both the lighthouse and Mr. Scollard. With you—I'm just not certain. You're more of an enigma, Julian; you have the mind of a realist and the soul of an adventurer. Frankly, I don't know what sort of reaction to expect from you. I know I shouldn't care— but I do. You're my husband, and I badly want you to understand, perhaps even to share, my faith in the lighthouse and Mr. Scollard." She paused, a sort of sad resignation crossing her face. "However, I suppose I, too, must be realistic. So if what I wish cannot be, if you find this whole experience dubious at best, all I ask is that you respect my feelings. This lighthouse has been my refuge all my life, the only place I could go to find peace, joy, and most of all, friendship. Mr. Scollard is as dear to me as if he were my own father. So if you find him—or the enchantment I feel over his legends—inane, please refrain from saying so. And please, don't ridicule me."

"Aurora." Struck by an unfamiliar surge of emotion, Julian framed his wife's face between his palms, damning himself for causing the light of her exuberance to be doused even for a moment. "I'd never ridicule you. Nor did I mean to diminish either Mr. Scollard's role in your life or the magnitude of your faith. On the contrary, I find everything you've shared with me about the Windmouth lighthouse *and* its keeper fascinating." Julian's thumbs caressed her cheekbones. "And if I haven't yet told you this, I'm telling you now: I find your enthusiasm, your zest for life, both exciting and infectious—one of your most alluring traits. Never explain nor excuse it. And never, never let it fade." He felt an odd constriction tighten his chest. "As for the lighthouse being your refuge, I'm glad you had such a place, such a man, to go to."

"Because you didn't," Aurora finished for him. She stood on tiptoe, brushing her lips to his. "But you're about to." With that, her melancholy vanished, and she tugged Julian toward the lighthouse door. "I know Mr. Scollard will help us solve our puzzle." She tapped Julian's coat pocket, within which the falcon book was carefully tucked. "He'll guide us as flawlessly as his lighthouse beam guides passing ships."

As if on cue the door swung open and a white-haired gentleman with brilliant blue eyes stepped out. "Rory— good. The tea is still hot." He wiped his hands on an apron, his keen gaze leveled on Julian. "'Tis a pleasure, sir." He paused. "I shan't address you by your title, not out of any disrespect, but because you loathe the memories it conjures up. All that will change, of course. Not my form of address, but your aversion. Actually, both. But the former won't be the result of the latter. No, I'm proud to say that by the time you've overcome your aversion, I'll be addressing you by your given name. Therefore, I'm not destined to refer to you as 'Your Grace.'" A decisive nod. "Won't you come in?"

Somehow Julian was more amused by the convoluted greeting than he was surprised. In fact, Mr. Scollard was precisely what he had expected. "'Tis a pleasure to meet the man of whom my wife speaks so highly."

"Ah, she speaks of me, but she dreams of you."

"Mr. Scollard!" Aurora's jaw dropped.

The lighthouse keeper chuckled as he led them inside. "I've no more embarrassed you than I've uttered a great revelation. Your openness precludes both."

Julian liked Mr. Scollard already.

Strolling into the cozy sitting room, he glanced about, noting the pot of tea and cakes—complete with three cups—that awaited them. The room was furnished with twin armchairs, a cushioned settee over which hung pastel watercolors, and a brick fireplace housing a roaring fire, and Julian found himself thinking that the decorating matched Mr. Scollard perfectly: warm, distinct, and attuned to the finest of details.

"Have a seat, sir." The lighthouse keeper gestured toward an armchair, hurrying over to pour the tea.

"Since you've already foreseen it, why not begin addressing me by my given name now?" Julian suggested, lowering himself to his seat and placing the book on the end table beside him. "I'm not terribly partial to 'sir.'"

"But you *are* partial to black tea laced with brandy." Mr. Scollard offered him a cup. "A preference you acquired in the Far East—a delectable melding of their tea and your fine French brandy. Julian," he added, blue eyes twinkling.

"Quite right." Julian grinned, taking an appreciative swallow. "It's good to know I can find that enjoyable combination right here in England. This tea is exceptional."

"I'm pleased you like it."

"*I* won't," Aurora announced, leaning forward on the settee and eyeing the untouched cup before her. "Must I drink it?"

"No," Mr. Scollard replied. "But you'll want to. Else how will you wash down your favorite cakes?"

"All right." Sighing, she took a tentative sip, her expression growing puzzled. "This is neither black nor laced with brandy."

"Of course not. Why would it be? It's the duke who likes his tea that way, not you." The lighthouse keeper settled himself in the other armchair, taking up his own cup. "Yours is lighter of strength and sweet, just as you prefer. And mine is my own favorite blend, imported from Java, with just a touch of cream."

"But you made only one pot . . . never mind." Aurora reached for a cake. "Why am I questioning you?" She took an enthusiastic bite. "Julian, try one of these. But I'm warning you—they're addicting. I very nearly didn't fit into my wedding dress, thanks to Mr. Scollard's cakes."

"By all means, help yourself," Scollard urged him. "You have long journeys ahead—journeys of the body, mind, and heart. You'll need your strength, more for some destinations than for others."

Julian chewed thoughtfully, ingesting far more than the delicious confection. "Do I?" He licked his forefinger. "Then I hope my journeys are equally as satisfying as these splendid cakes."

"Some fulfillments are more readily attained than others. However, flavors too swiftly savored ofttimes dissolve like confections on the tongue. 'Tis the arduous journeys, the ones whose goals are clouded, even unperceived, that yield the greatest rewards." A thoughtful pause. "Then again, some readily attained fulfillments, rather than transient, are pivotal representations of the greatest prize any adventurer could seek."

"Are we speaking of the black diamond or my own personal quests?" Julian stared intently at Mr. Scollard.

"I believe you just spoke of both."

A faint smile. "I suppose I did." Julian leaned forward, abandoning his refreshment and seizing the falcon book in his hands. "This is one quest I perceive only too well."

"'Only too well'—an interesting choice of words." Scollard glanced at the volume but made no move to touch it. "How may I help you?"

"Rory and I need to understand James's message. Would you please look at the inscription and the underscored words?"

"It isn't necessary. I've seen both."

Incredulity flashed in Julian's eyes. "Very well. Can you tell us which of the two are significant?"

"Both."

"Yet we're missing some crucial piece."

"Perhaps. On the other hand, perhaps you're still not ready to assimilate that which you've already been offered."

"What avenue must we pursue to become ready?"

Scollard's gaze never faltered. "One you must discover yourself."

"Can you tell me nothing else?"

Mr. Scollard placed his cup and saucer on the table. "On the contrary, I can tell you several things. First, that you're quite thorough. Your great-grandfather would indeed be proud—proud and confident that you will restore honor to a name long tarnished by injustice from without and bitterness from within."

Julian inclined his head. "Is that your belief or your prophecy?"

"'Tis fact, Julian. You've already acted more honorably than the two generations dividing you and Geoffrey, obscuring your nobility. Your inner strength matches his; your physical strength is far greater. And your assets exceed any he ever knew, for your partnership surpasses friendship."

That he understood. "You're speaking of Rory," Julian said, glancing tenderly at his wife. "And, if so, you and I are in complete agreement. My wife is an incomparable asset."

"And a journey unto herself."

Julian frowned. "You've lost me."

"No, you've just yet to reach where I stand. You will." Mr. Scollard refilled the cups. "Now, back to what I can tell you. The book—it bears many messages, some I see, others I don't. What I do see is a man, an old man with wisps of memory stored in his mind and a wealth of resolution hovering at his feet."

"An old man?" Aurora's saucer clattered to the table. "What old man? Where can we find him? What does he know? Can he help us find the diamond? Have we ever met him? Is he a pirate? Has he sailed with Julian?"

Scollard gave her an indulgent smile. "Ah, Rory, if I *am* a wizard, it's to keep up with your questions. No mere mortal could do so." He cast a sympathetic glance at Julian. "Stay sharp as you are. Else you'll fall by the wayside."

Julian chuckled. "I'll remember that."

"Mr. Scollard, tell us!" Aurora persisted.

"Very well." The lighthouse keeper pursed his lips. "The one who has firsthand knowledge. In a Cornish pub—I'm not certain which one. More than anyone else. That you'll have to discover for yourself. No, you haven't. No, he's not. And, no, he never has." A pleased nod. "I believe I've answered them all in order."

"I have no idea what you just said," Aurora replied, frustration lacing her tone.

"Really, Rory, if I can provide the answers, you can at least keep track of the questions."

"Perhaps if you combined all the answers into one," Julian suggested, biting back laughter despite his rampaging curiosity.

"Fine." Mr. Scollard gave a tolerant sigh. "The elderly fellow of whom I speak was a sailor, not a pirate. He's far too old to have sailed with you, Julian; he retired from his trade before you were born. He spends most of his time reminiscing with other onetime sailors at a small pub not too far from your manor in Polperro—" A pensive lapse. "I cannot see precisely where, but I do know you've never met. Whether or not he leads you to the black diamond, he's necessary for the completion of the journey, for he'll draw forth ghosts of the past that must be silenced forever, else the future will remain out of reach. And he knows more of the truth than anyone else to whom you might speak, for he's the last person yet alive who sailed with Geoffrey on his final voyage to England."

Julian nearly bolted from his chair. "You're saying he was actually on the ship where my great-grandfather died?"

"I am."

"Mr. Scollard," Aurora inserted, her eyes huge, "how old is this sailor?"

A shrug. "Some years past eighty. Fairly lucid, though. And his memories of sixty years ago are vivid."

"How can we find him?"

"That I will leave to your husband, who is far more adept at these matters than I." Mr. Scollard tensed a bit, alerting them to the magnitude of his next words. "Don't underestimate the dangers that await from sources expected and unknown. They lurk in numbers, and in numbers must be undone. Greed is a great propellant. Vengeance wields more power still. And desperation is the most menacing by far, for it offers reward with no risk. Take great care, for the path upon which you now embark is deep with shadows, dark with hatred. Go with vision, perception, wits, and purpose. Return with peace, safety—and by the grace of God." A surge of trepidation crossed Mr. Scollard's face. "My gifts are limited. I wish I had more with which to protect you. I have only flashes of insight, heartfelt prayers, and a profusion of faith. May they be enough." He stared off, his eyes veiled with concern. "The obstacles are vast, the treasures vaster still. But go you must. 'Tis necessary to attain resolution. May finding it not cost more than its worth." He blinked, returning from wherever he'd been. "Finish your tea, both of you. Then go. Share your insights with Courtney and Slayde. After which, do what you must. And most of all, return to tell me of your discovery."

Throughout Scollard's discourse, the color had drained from Aurora's cheeks. "Mr. Scollard, I've never heard you talk like this," she whispered. "Are we truly in such grave danger?" The tip of her tongue wet her lips. "Will we . . . prevail?"

Scollard rose, walked over to ruffle Aurora's hair. "I see only that which I've told you," he said quietly. "Hold fast to your strength and your husband." His solemn gaze met Julian's. "Take care of her. As she will of you."

"I don't like this." Slayde was pacing about the yellow salon. "Scollard never says such ominous things as the ones you've just relayed. Aurora, maybe Julian should seek out this sailor on his own."

"No." Aurora gave an adamant shake of her head. "That's out of the question—and not only because I'd be exploding with curiosity." She swallowed, staring at her lap. "I'd be sick with worry."

"Julian?" Slayde arched a questioning brow in his direction.

"I told you I'd take care of Aurora, and I will," Julian replied, studying his wife's bowed head. "But locking her away, squelching her spirit is not the answer. Like the falcon, she needs to soar; which, in this case, means accompanying me, seeking the same answers I do." He saw Aurora's head snap up, her expression a mixture of wonder and relief. "I haven't forgotten the vows I made when I asked for her hand," he added pointedly, addressing Slayde but speaking to Aurora. "Not to my wife or to you—" His jaw set, he met Slayde's gaze head-on. "Aurora will go with me. However, she will also be safe."

Slayde scowled.

"Slayde," Courtney interceded, "there was a time not long ago when I was in a similar position to Aurora, a time you let me accompany you to the seediest section of Dartmouth to resolve our pasts."

"I did that against my will."

A smile. "I know. And I suspect Julian is doing this against his. But don't try to deter him. Certainly don't try to deter Aurora. Lest you've forgotten, 'twould be easier to upend a dozen limestone cliffs."

"Fine." Slayde shot Julian a look. "You'd best keep your vows."

"I always do."

A nod. "It's late. Spend the night at Pembourne. You can start for Polperro at first light."

"I think that's a sound idea." Julian rose. "It's been a long, exhausting day."

"I agree." Aurora, too, came to her feet. "It feels like a year since we dashed out of here this morning."

"Which reminds me," Julian asked Slayde, "what was Guillford's reaction to our appearance? Did he say anything after we left?"

"About you and Aurora? No. Your names were glaringly absent from our conversation. He still feels insulted by what he considers to be a flagrant slap in the face; I can sense it. But there's not a damned thing I can do about it. The man is entitled to his feelings, and he's just too set in his ways to overcome them. I don't think you need worry that he'll ever cause a scene—that same adherence to the rules of proper protocol will prevent him from acting in an unseemly fashion. I suspect he'll continue to be civil whenever your paths cross, be that in business or social circumstances. But I wouldn't expect any invitations to his house parties."

"I'm crushed," Julian returned dryly.

"I'm sure. In any case, he's nearly as stiff with me as he is with you. He probably believes that since Aurora was my charge, I'm responsible for her appalling behavior. Not to mention that I placed him in an untenable position; after all, I'm the one who promised Aurora to him, eager and untouched."

"I was never eager. Even when I was untouched," Aurora muttered.

"Be that as it may, he has definitely cooled off toward me. His sole interest in coming here today was business. It seems he's found a splendid racehorse, one he's convinced will yield huge profits. Unfortunately his own funds are tied up in other investments, so he asked if I'd be willing to put up the money for purchasing and training the stallion, after which the initial profits reaped from the horse's winnings would be mine. Once I'd recouped my investment, we would split the profits fifty-fifty. The deal was sound. I agreed. Immediately thereafter, the viscount stood up, announced that Camden would handle the details of our transaction, and took his leave. The entire meeting took less than an hour. Your carriage had scarcely rounded the drive when Guillford's followed suit." Slayde inclined his head in question. "Why? Does the viscount's disapproval trouble you?"

"Not in the least," Julian returned. "Although I do think the man is being absurd about the matter. He has a flock of women to choose from—" A smug grin. "— even if they do pale in comparison to my wife. Still, I realize this is not about Guillford's severed betrothal, for he knows as well as I do that he and Aurora are about as right for each other as a fox and a hen. This is about his bloody propriety." A dismissive shrug. "Either he'll get over it or he won't. The choice is his. I have more pressing matters to contend with. Such as getting some rest so I can track down the old man Scollard spoke of *and* ensure my spirited wife's continued well-being."

"Of course—that's it," Aurora exclaimed.

"What's it?" Julian's head whipped around.

"Nothing . . . I just realized . . . that is, it finally dawned on me . . ." She broke off, clearly searching for a believable reply.

"It finally dawned on you . . . ?" Julian prompted, biting back a smile. Whatever great revelation had just erupted in his wife's mind, she obviously had no intentions of sharing it. Lord, she was the very worst of liars. "What is it that dawned on you?"

Instantly Aurora's expression brightened and she gave an exaggerated yawn. "The fact that I'm half-asleep." A swift side-glance at her sister-in-law. "What's more, I noticed that Courtney is looking extremely peaked."

"Am I?" Courtney inquired, her eyes twinkling.

"Yes. You are." Aurora shot her friend a meaningful look. "In fact, if you gentlemen don't mind, I think we should start up for bed."

"I agree." Julian played along, taking a step toward the door.

"No!" Aurora burst out. "That is . . . I meant Courtney and myself. You and Slayde stay here until your business is concluded."

"Our business is already concluded, Aurora," Slayde inserted dryly. "Yours, on the other hand, is apparently just beginning. You look like a rabbit about to bolt."

"Do I? I'm just tired." Her glance fell on the falcon book clutched in Julian's hand. "I think you two should stay in the salon a few minutes longer. Slayde, you should copy down the inscription and the underscored words in James's book, so you and Courtney can contemplate their meaning while Julian and I are in Cornwall."

"Aurora . . ." Slayde folded his arms across his chest. "I've seen that look on your face a hundred times before. What are you up to?"

"Nothing." Pausing only to nudge Courtney's elbow, Aurora began inching her way toward the door. "I promise you, Slayde, I'm going nowhere but upstairs. You and Julian can watch me make my ascent."

"So you can shimmy down the oak just outside your bedchamber and make your escape?"

Courtney began to laugh. "I don't think that's what Aurora has in mind, darling. Not if she means to include me in her plan." Courtney lay a gentle palm on her abdomen. "That poor oak would collapse beneath my weight."

"You're beautiful," Slayde countered instantly, his gaze softening with tenderness. "And so slight it's a wonder *you* haven't collapsed beneath the weight of my child. No, love—the oak would fare splendidly. Aurora,

233

on the other hand . . ." He glared at his sister. "She would not fare nearly as well if she made any attempt to drag you off . . ."

"Oh, for heaven's sake!" Aurora interrupted, rolling her eyes in frustration. "I'm not planning anything. Why would I? I have nothing to escape from. If you must know, I simply want to talk to Courtney alone."

"Go right ahead, *soleil.*" Julian gestured toward the door. "Go up and have your chat. Slayde and I will follow shortly."

Aurora eyed him uncertainly. "You believe me?"

"Indeed I do. For several reasons. One, because you're a deplorable liar. Two, because I trust my instincts. And three, because I'd track you down in a heartbeat, and you know it."

A tiny smile played about her lips. "Yes, I do." She turned and tugged Courtney's arm. "Come. I need to see you."

Courtney complied, her shoulders shaking with laughter. "Really? I never would have known."

They exited the salon.

"Are you sure you know what you're doing?" Slayde demanded, scowling as he watched the women's retreating backs.

"Positive." Julian grinned, following Slayde's gaze. "Evidently my wife has something quite pressing to share with yours."

Slayde's jaw tightened. "That's precisely what I'm afraid of."

"All right, Aurora." Still grinning, Courtney settled herself on a chair in Aurora's room. "We've completed our subtle exit. I've had ten seconds to catch my breath. Now, what's on your mind? I hope nothing you want kept secret—obviously our husbands are going to have a million questions about the hasty retreat we just bid."

"That's fine. Although I think they'll be terribly disappointed when they hear what it was I wanted to discuss with you." Aurora leaned back against the closed door, her eyes shining with excitement. "I've just come to a wonderful realization—one that has nothing to do with the diamond, or with danger, or with the fictitious escape Slayde is convinced I have planned."

"But one that has everything to do with Julian," Courtney guessed.

Aurora nodded. "I told him."

"You told him you love him?"

"Yes."

"How did he react?"

"Not in the way I'd imagined. Nor in the way you'd imagined, either." Aurora crossed over and perched on the edge of the bed. "Although you were right about one thing—I'm completely unable to keep things to myself. I blurted out my admission the instant the opportunity arose. Then again, I never can seem to think straight when I'm in Julian's arms."

"I take it you confessed your feelings during an intimate moment?"

Another nod.

"In that case, Julian was as vulnerable as you," Courtney pointed out.

"*Too* vulnerable, at least from my husband's perspective. Had he had his full wits about him, he'd have done a better job of cloaking his reaction—even if my declaration did come as a huge surprise."

"Which, I'm presuming, it did?"

"Absolutely. Julian looked stunned and decidedly tense."

"Did he say anything?"

"He *said* he was moved, humbled, and honored—and that no one had ever offered him those words before."

"That sounds promising."

"Yes, but it was what he *didn't* say that's plagued me all day. Immediately after I blurted out my feelings, he withdrew somehow—not physically, not even verbally; but then again, that's not Julian's style. His self-restraint isn't worn on the surface like Slayde's was. Outwardly my husband is charming and expressive. Openness comes easily to him—but only in bed and in conversation. Anything deeper is another matter entirely. Feelings, emotions—that's where his self-imposed boundaries are set. His *own* feelings and emotions." Aurora drew a slow, purposeful breath. "Courtney, I've had several hours to think about this, to analyze the conflict Julian is experiencing. And what I finally understand, perhaps what you already understood, is that *my* loving *Julian* presents little or no problem for him. He has only to accept my feelings while still retaining control over his. The real problem would be if he let himself love me in return. Now *that* would render him vulnerable, something he refuses to be—for all the reasons you and I have already discussed."

Courtney nodded. "But he's already falling in love with you. So he's already vulnerable, whether he chooses to admit it or not."

"I know that," Aurora said quietly, interlacing her fingers, pressing her palms tightly together. "And on some level, so does Julian. But he's not going to give in without a fight. Until now he's been safe, transient—no family, no home, and no possibility of loss. Loving me would change all that. 'Twould mean relinquishing his autonomy, entertaining a risk far greater than those incited by all his adventures combined." She paused. "And there's one thing more. Do you remember what I said about Julian feeling guilty for not being able to prevent Hubert's death?"

"I remember."

"I think that's a big part of this, too. Have you ever noticed how often and how vehemently my husband vows that he'll protect me, ensure my well-being?"

"You think that's because he couldn't do that for his brother?"

"To some extent, yes. All his life, Julian has been strong, self-sufficient, a man others looked to for solutions. He takes that role very seriously, even in his work. He feels a tremendous responsibility to set things right, to restore and protect. Well, one can't be omnipotent and vulnerable all at once, can one?"

"I suppose not." Courtney frowned. "If what you're saying is true—and it certainly makes sense that it is—how are you going to convince Julian to change?"

"That's where my realization of a few minutes ago comes in." Aurora leaned forward, her entire face aglow. "Mr. Scollard provided me with the answer earlier today, only I didn't hear it—truly hear it—until now." A twinkle. "That's because he didn't intend for me to. As always, his answer was painstakingly concealed so I'd be forced to go through this entire thought process to fully understand things before I arrived at my solution."

Courtney nodded, having experienced Mr. Scollard's brilliant guidance firsthand. "What did he say? And where did it lead you?"

"He told me to hold fast to my strength and to my husband. And he told Julian to take care of me—as I would of him." Aurora's lips curved. "After reviewing all I just told you, then hearing Julian declare for the dozenth time that he meant to ensure my well-being, it struck me in a flash. Mr. Scollard was paving my way with his counsel. What I derived from his words is this: if as my husband, Julian is hell-bent on protecting me—which we know he is—then as his wife, I shall be hell-bent on protecting him, too. Not out of guilt or duty, but out of love—which, as you and I both know, is Julian's true underlying reason for wanting to shelter me, even if he is too unnerved to admit it to me or himself. In any case, that's the whole point of my plan. Not only am I going to guard my husband like a lioness, I'm going to prove something to him in the process—that loving someone can make you strong, not weak."

Courtney shook her head in amazement. "I'm duly impressed. That was an extraordinary display of reasoning, even for you. However, you did omit one or two details, such as how you intend to accomplish this. More importantly, what is it Julian needs protection from? You're not alluding only to the search for the black diamond, are you?"

Silence.

"Aurora, answer me. How is it you plan to protect Julian—and from what—or rather, whom?"

"I can't answer those two questions, at least not yet. But Courtney, you were right, twice over, in fact. Julian *is* falling in love with me, and my love *will* be there to cushion his fall when he does."

"I never doubted either of those things." Courtney's expression remained troubled. "Aurora, you're not going to do anything dangerous, are you?"

"Only if it's necessary," Aurora replied honestly. Her back straightened and her chin came up. "But no matter what it takes, I'm going to protect my husband—*and* open his stubborn eyes in the process."

Chapter 12

"I noticed you never told Slayde and Courtney your suspicions that we were being followed when we left for Morland yesterday," Aurora commented as their carriage sped through the gates of Pembourne, en route to Polperro.

Julian shrugged. "There was no reason to. Nothing actually happened—'twas only an instinct. An accurate one, I'm certain, but an instinct nonetheless. Besides, your brother is already frantic in his worry over Courtney's safety. If I told him this, it would only add to that apprehension. Further, whoever was pursuing us was after me, not the Huntleys."

"You're sure?"

"I'm sure." A pause. "Speaking of issues left undiscussed, what was it you were so eager to divulge to Courtney last night? You never did tell me."

Aurora shot him an impish grin. "You never asked. In

fact, you said very little when you came to bed. You seemed to have other matters on your mind."

"I did." Julian tugged her closer, rubbing his chin across her satiny tresses. "The same matters that are always on my mind when it comes to you." His hands slid up to cup her breasts. "It's inconceivable what you do to me."

With a tiny shiver, Aurora shifted about to face him, reaching up to unfasten his shirt. "We have hours and hours," she reminded him seductively. "A long, tedious carriage ride with nothing to do." Leaning past her husband, she drew the carriage curtains as he had on their wedding day.

Julian caught her arm, stilled its motion. "Is this because you don't want to answer my question?"

"No." Aurora gazed directly into his eyes, thinking about her plan and the steps she'd taken to ensure it. "This is because I want you as much as you want me. As for your question, I'd be more than happy to answer it. The reason I was so eager to talk to Courtney was because I wanted her to know that I'd followed her advice and told you I love you."

Julian drew a swift breath. "I see."

"Now will you make love to me?" Aurora whispered, pushing open the sides of his shirt, searching his face as her palms swept over the hard hair-roughened planes of his chest.

With a ragged sound of need, Julian dragged her mouth to his. "Until the fire consumes us," he breathed fiercely.

The fire prevailed throughout their journey to Polperro.

So did the carriage that trailed unobtrusively behind them.

Julian's property was every bit as wonderful as Aurora's cursory inspection had promised. Then again, this was the first time she was able to view her new home in the daylight. The grounds were modest, with but a small garden and several acres of manicured lawn surrounding the stone manor. But the view was spectacular even from the drive: the cliffs towering in the background, the waters of the Channel stretching below as far as the eye could see.

"Can we walk a bit before we go in?" Aurora demanded, her eyes sparkling as the carriage came to a halt.

"Of course."

The words were scarcely out of Julian's mouth when Aurora flung open the carriage door and leapt out, nearly knocking down one stunned footman in the process.

Chuckling, Julian joined her, issuing a few instructions to his driver and footmen before capturing Aurora's arm, guiding her precisely where she wanted to go: down the tiny winding path that led to the water.

When they reached the sandy strip along the shore, Aurora rushed forward, nearly giddy with excitement. "It's everything you said and more," she declared, strolling to the water's edge where the waves of the Channel broke gracefully, drenching her slippers and the hem of her gown with their foam. "The cliffs above us, the water below—it's a legend-seeker's dream."

"I thought you'd like it." Julian grinned, clearly enjoying her exuberant reception.

"Like it? I love it!" Impatiently Aurora raised her skirts and wrung out the wet muslin.

"I don't think that will help. The gown is ruined."

Aurora laughed, letting the soggy material droop to the sand. "True. Then again, it was ruined hours ago—by you."

"Is that a complaint?" Julian shot her a thoroughly smug look.

"No, you arrogant man, that was a sated assessment." She spun about, shading her eyes so she could study the manor, its ivy-covered walls angling sharply into a second wing that sloped backward toward the shelter of the cliffs. "The house is larger than I originally thought."

"Too large?" Julian wrapped his arms about her from behind.

"No. Perfect."

"Good. Then, would you like to go inside and meet the staff?" He nuzzled her neck. "Or shall I impede this tour as I did the last—by carrying you up to bed?"

"Not this time." Aurora laughed, stepping out of his embrace. "As it is, your servants have doubtless labeled me a wanton. What would they think of a repeat performance of last time—and in broad daylight, no less?"

"I don't care what they'd think. Do you?"

Aurora sobered. "You know I don't. But I would like to finish our tour." Pausing, she rubbed the folds of her damp gown between her fingers, trying to explain something that was as foreign to her as it was to her husband, and hoping that by doing so she wouldn't further unnerve him. Then again, her bloody candor would allow nothing shy of the truth. So she might as well plunge right in and take her chances. "Julian, in many ways this is my first real home. Pembourne was more like a prison for me, at least until Courtney arrived. Even then, my affinity was for her and Slayde, not the house. I know I claimed not to require roots—but perhaps I was mistaken. Perhaps I just required a different kind of roots, the kind I never knew existed—until now. Is that notion totally unfathomable? Or, if not unfathomable, then untenable?"

Julian's gaze narrowed, tiny flames darting through the topaz depths. "No. That notion is neither unfathomable nor untenable." He threaded his fingers through her hair. "I'd be delighted to acquaint you with your new home—but only if you vow not to become too attached to it. Because what *is* both unfathomable and untenable is the thought of doing without you for months on end. I can scarcely take my hands off you long enough to show you around. So don't change your mind about traveling abroad with me."

Aurora's throat tightened at what was as close to an admission of need as Julian had allowed himself thus far. "I won't. I couldn't." She lay her palm against her husband's jaw. "I'd be as empty as you would."

He turned his lips into her palm, then caught her fingers in his. "Come, *soleil*. Meet your staff."

Julian's staff was as unconventional as he—from Daniels, the stout ununiformed butler, to Hadrigin, Julian's bearded and brawny valet, who was not only not uniformed but was addressed by the other servants as 'Gin'—a name Aurora suspected had little to do with the abbreviated form of his surname. Then there were the other two dozen or so informally dressed men and women who greeted her not with customary bows, but with broad grins and unaffected—though no less warm and respectful—hellos.

"Well?" Julian asked, eyes twinkling, when they'd made their way through the rustic house and were alone in his bedchamber. "What do you think of the residents of Merlin Manor?"

Aurora's brows arched. " 'Merlin Manor'?"

"Of course." Julian's teeth gleamed. "Aren't all noblemen and their estates known by the same name?"

"Indeed they are." Aurora couldn't control her laughter. "Tell me, is it my imagination, or are all your servants just a bit unconventional? And while we're on the subject, just how did Gin get his name?"

"They're as unconventional as I—well, maybe a bit more so," Julian conceded. "As for Gin, not only can he tie a wicked cravat, he can toss off five measures of his namesake beforehand—*and* still complete his task with steady fingers."

"That's quite a feat." Aurora wiped tears of laughter from her eyes. "Did his references state as such? Or did you simply ask his previous employer?"

"Neither." Julian's smile vanished, his offhanded tone ringing with a fine underlying tension. "I met him during my travels. His employer was a filthy pirate who was about to run Gin through for releasing a tavern maid rather than dragging her back to the ship for mutual enjoyment. I convinced the murderous bastard he could do without both the girl and Gin."

"Is the tavern maid here as well?"

"She's Emma, the girl I introduced you to in the sitting room. The one who stared at you with those worshipful eyes."

Aurora blanched recalling the slight, fair-haired maid she'd encountered dusting the side table, her blue eyes widening with awe as she'd dropped curtsy after awkward curtsy. "Julian, she can't be more than sixteen years old."

"Fifteen," he corrected. "Thirteen when the incident I just described took place." He caressed Aurora's cheek. "Don't look so horrified. She's fine and thoroughly intact, thanks to Gin's interference. Now I have two outstanding servants and they each have a home." Julian's thumb traced Aurora's lips, then stroked the distressed pucker between her brows. "Think how dreadful it was for me until then," he joked, trying to make her smile. "I not only had to make up my own bed, I had to tie my own cravats."

"You never wear cravats anyway," Aurora replied absently, her thoughts racing ahead, then coming to a screeching halt. "Julian—your servants, all the men and women who work here, they're all like Gin and Emma, aren't they? All victims you rescued from dire circumstances?"

"Don't make it sound like I'm such a hero, *soleil.* Yes, I helped them escape disagreeable situations, offered them jobs and a place to live. But my servants work damned hard for their wages." A corner of Julian's mouth lifted. "You might not believe this, but I'm not an easy man to live with. I'm also demanding as hell to work for, whether I'm here or abroad. My staff's duties are extensive and varied, including the ability to handle all types of unsavory guests who might drop in uninvited during my absence."

"That doesn't lessen the magnitude of your actions." Pride and respect surged in Aurora's chest. "You, Julian Bencroft, are a wonderful man. You might live by your own rules, but those rules are far more exemplary than all the *ton*'s combined. Your nobility transcends a mere title." Her small jaw set, resentment flashing in her eyes. "This only proves that your father, besides being a scoundrel and a liar, was a stupid, bloody fool. I'd like to thrash him for denouncing you."

Tenderness softened Julian's features and he drew her to him, tilting back her head for a kiss. "You're arousing as hell when you're angry."

Aurora found herself smiling again. "Let's see . . . when I'm angry, when I'm secretive, when I'm adventurous, when I'm bold, when I'm eager, when I'm . . ."

"All the time, then." He silenced her with his mouth.

"'Ey, Merlin . . . that's gonna 'ave to wait." Gin strode in, looking not the least bit perturbed by the heated embrace he'd interrupted.

Neither was Julian, who made no move to release his wife. "Good-bye, Gin. By the way, it's time you learned to knock."

"Next time. Right now, Stone's 'ere to see ye."

This time, Julian did lift his head. "Stone? Now?"

A nod. " 'E says 'e's got news."

"Good. I intended to send for him; this saves me the trouble. Tell him I'm on my way."

"No." Aurora gripped his arms. "Tell him *we're* on *our* way." She didn't back down, not even when Julian's eyes narrowed, his mouth forming the word "no." "The matter you want to see Stone about concerns me as well." She stopped without further elaboration, given that Gin was still present—not merely present, but standing practically atop them, gaping. "Besides—" She focused her attention on Julian, tossing him a teasing grin. "—Mr. Stone and I are old friends. Why, he's seen me in the most shocking state of undress . . ."

"Stop." Julian chuckled, pressing his forefinger to her lips. "You're impossible. Fine. Come with me."

"I'm right beside you." Aurora glanced innocently at Gin as she passed. "Is something wrong?"

"Hmm?" The valet shook his head, his mouth snapping shut. "No, ma'am. Everything's right—and gettin' righter by the minute. In fact, I think this job's about to become so interestin', I might just have to stay sober to enjoy it."

"What's your news, Stone?" Julian stalked into the sitting room, Aurora by his side, shutting the door in their wake. "You remember my wife," he added, touching Aurora's elbow.

Stone's pupils dilated, but he merely nodded. "Yeah, good to see ye, Lady . . . Lady . . ."

". . . Aurora," she supplied. Her lips twitched. "Or Mrs. Merlin will do. Whichever you feel more comfortable using."

"Oh . . ." He swallowed. "I guess I'll think about it and—"

"Stone." Julian recalled his colleague's attention to where it belonged. "Have you seen Macall? Is that why you're here?"

"Yeah, that's why I'm here, and no, I haven't seen him—not firsthand. I can't take the chance he'll recognize me. But I've got my ear to the ground. And from what I'm hearing, he's in a bad way, Merlin—drunk at night, roughin' people up in the streets, yellin' about how he's gonna make you pay. He disappears for hours at a time each day, probably combin' the streets lookin' for ye. And now that yer home . . ."

"We're going to have to finish this, Macall and I," Julian pronounced in a steely voice. "Unfortunately his timing is rotten. But that can't be helped. If he's determined to come after me now, so be it. I'm ready; I have been since you told me he was in England."

"You haven't spotted him yet, have you?"

"No. But someone's been following me these past few days. My guess is, it's Macall."

"There's somethin' else you should know. Macall's got himself a new sword, a rare bronze one he stole in Malta. I hear the sword's hilt is covered with jewels, and its blade is deadly enough to slash a man in two. Word is he's saved it especially for you, brandishes it every day and claims he's gonna drive it straight through your heart, then step over your dead body and make off with the black diamond."

"My, my. The scoundrel is obsessed, isn't he?" Julian leaned against the wall, looking thoroughly unconcerned.

Aurora felt her insides knot.

"Anything else?" Julian inquired.

"Not until Macall stops waitin' and does somethin'. And if he does, I think ye'll know about it before I do."

"I think you're right. Well, enough about Macall. I have another matter to discuss with you. What do you know of an old sailor, one who's retired from the sea and now spends his time reminiscing at a local pub?"

Stone blinked. "Hell, Merlin, that could describe thirty men."

"No. It couldn't. When I say *old*, I mean *extremely* old, not fifty or sixty. More like eighty, even a few years past, but with a quick mind and a great memory—one that's filled with stories of the sea."

"That old, huh?" A thoughtful frown. "Now that ye mention it, there was this fellow—I think his name's Barnes. He was in a couple of the pubs I checked out in Fowey—the Brine and the Cove—drinkin' and chortlin' about his days at sea. I didn't give him a second thought, not until ye just said what you did. To tell ye the truth, I was too busy findin' out if anyone had seen Macall to pay attention to much else. But this Barnes fellow was *real* old, like the age ye're describin'. And real friendly to everyone, like he's a regular customer there." Stone frowned. "I don't think he's trouble, if that's why yer lookin' for him."

"It's not." Julian straightened, his gaze fixed on Stone's face. "Describe him."

"Like I said, I wasn't watchin' him too close. Let's see. Gray hair—what was left of it anyway. Stooped shoulders—hell, he was old as the hills. Whiskers. A scratchy voice. That's all I remember."

"It's enough." Julian rubbed his chin thoughtfully. "Fowey—one port west of here. That would explain why I've never met him. I know the two pubs you're referring to, although I've never frequented either one. The Brine is on the wharf, and the Cove is about a mile farther along the riverbank."

"Yeah. And *ye* might not go in 'em, but Macall does—him *and* his sword. He's been in each of those places three or four times, gettin' drunk and askin' about ye. So stay the hell away from there, Merlin. Ye'd be lookin' for trouble."

"No, I'll be looking for Barnes. Macall's the one who's looking for trouble." Julian glanced over at Aurora who had gone sheet white, and scowled. "You'll have to excuse us, Stone," he said abruptly. "My wife looks tired from our journey. I think I'll escort her upstairs. Besides, our business is concluded—for now."

"Sure." Stone appeared distinctly unconvinced, but said nothing further. "I'll be on my way. No need for Daniels to show me out." He hesitated, glancing quickly at Aurora. "Remember what I said, Merlin. Macall's after ye—and he's got more ammunition now. Don't let him use it." With that, Stone took his leave.

"Aurora?" Julian walked over, tipped up her chin. "Are you all right?"

"I thought I'd be fine," she managed. "But the idea of that animal hurting you . . ." She inhaled sharply. "Am I the ammunition Stone was referring to?"

"That's immaterial. None of this should worry you. I'll be fine, and so will you. I'll see to it."

"You're a man, Julian, not a god. How can you be so sure?"

"Because I am." A corner of his mouth lifted. "What do you mean, I'm not a god? I thought you'd likened me to a pagan god."

"Damn you, Julian." Aurora's hand balled into a fist, struck her husband's shoulder. "Stop being so glib, so arrogant. We're talking about your life, not a game."

"I know." Julian sobered, bringing Aurora's fist to his lips. "I've been trying to tell you that from the onset. You weren't listening."

"It didn't seem real."

"So we are." His breath brushed her knuckles. "But it is. Still, there's no need to dwell on the unlikely. I've survived for years. I intend to keep doing so. As for you, you need never worry. I vowed to keep you safe—and I shall."

"Who are you reassuring, me or yourself?" Aurora demanded, an emotional dam bursting inside her. "You've made that same vow repeatedly since the day you asked for my hand—almost as if you need to convince yourself of its validity. Why? I never doubted your word, nor have you ever fallen short in your efforts to keep me safe. Or is it not me you're thinking of, not my situation that's prompting your self-doubt? Is it someone else, someone you believe you failed adequately to protect? If so, I can only assume that someone is Hubert." Aurora felt Julian tense, but she pressed on nonetheless, her fingers caressing his clenched jaw. "Julian, you *didn't* forsake your brother. You *did* keep him safe, in all the ways you conceivably could. You offered him the shelter of your friendship, your respect, and your decency—in a family where only greed and self-serving hatred existed. You'd have gladly offered him your life if it was within your power to do so. But it wasn't. Some forces are simply too great to surmount even for an infallible protector such as yourself. Frailty of the body is one of those forces, tragically, the one that determined Hugh's fate. He was sick, Julian, too sick and weak to persevere. That was an indisputable fact, one that was not within your power to change. So you must stop blaming yourself. Whatever and whoever *is* in your power to safeguard, you do—me, your servants, the treasures you've recovered, and the victims you've saved. And, yes, Hugh, as well—his principles, his compassion, his spirit. True, there will always be some objectives too great to realize, even for you, some elements of fate that are out of your hands. But Julian, that doesn't make you weak, it makes you human."

A muscle worked at Julian's throat.

"As for you," Aurora continued, *"your* future, *your* fate—I won't let you walk into danger as if your life doesn't matter. It does—to me." To her astonishment, hot tears sprang to her eyes, trickled down her cheeks. "Julian, I love you." She swallowed. "And I need you."

"I need you, too—now." Emotion flickered wildly in

Julian's eyes, turned his voice to gravel. Abruptly he turned, kicking the door shut and throwing the bolt before sweeping Aurora into his arms, carrying her to the sofa.

"This is not the kind of need I meant," Aurora protested, shaking her head.

"I know." Julian grasped handfuls of her gown, dragging them up in hard, purposeful motions. "But this is the kind I can silence along with all your fears, your doubts, your worries. This is the way I can combat your pain, fill all your emptiness."

"And yours?" Aurora asked softly, searching his face.

"Yes," he admitted hoarsely. "And mine." He lowered her to the cushions, crumpling her gown about her waist, his fingers lingering briefly on her naked thighs before shifting to tear at the buttons of his breeches. "Don't turn me away."

"I couldn't," Aurora whispered, her heart in her eyes.

Julian drew a harsh breath—then expelled it. "I don't think I can wait."

"Then don't." She opened her arms to him.

He made love to her like a wild man, driving himself into her with a hammering need and a frenzied hunger he could neither curb nor fathom. He shouted her name when he climaxed, flooding her with his seed even as he absorbed her exquisite spasms of completion.

Afterward he lay on her, in her, more overcome by what had just happened than he'd been by all his enemies combined. The melding of their passion with the emotional words that had preceded it was more than he could bear.

He took slow, steadying breaths, his heart racing— and not only from the unimaginable intensity of his climax.

Long minutes passed.

Aurora's slow, even breathing told Julian she was

asleep. Slowly he eased himself to his elbows, gazing into her beautiful face, her damp lashes fanning her cheeks like spikes of red-gold flame.

God help him, he was in over his head.

What had begun as an exciting adventure—passion and purpose necessitating an enticing, crucial union—had in a matter of days escalated into something much greater, something he'd never fathomed in his wildest dreams.

His wife was in love with him.

Just reflecting on Aurora's declaration made Julian's chest tighten, made a shambles of all the ludicrous denials he'd silently issued with regard to his own detachment. It was absurd to pretend nothing was changed, that Aurora's profession—while heartfelt and moving—altered nothing, deepened nothing, ignited nothing.

He'd be a liar and a fool.

Slowly Julian's hand came up, his knuckles caressing the smooth contour of his wife's cheek. The truth was, he wanted those words—and the emotion that spawned them. He relished the fact that Aurora had given him her heart, reveled in hearing her speak the words aloud. Even his body reacted fiercely, erupting more powerfully each time she gave voice to her feelings.

So much for his rationalization that the dynamic sexual pull between them was rooted in something purely physical—that Aurora's fiery spirit and beauty alone were responsible for arousing this unprecedented and insatiable craving inside him.

Clearly it was much more.

Sexual desire, no matter how intense, couldn't explain the tenderness he felt as he watched her discover the world, taste her first adventure, her first triumph, her first passion. Nor could it explain his own growing need to share her life and to have her share his, to keep her beside him every second—including instances when he'd *never* before allowed his domain to be invaded, much less invited someone to invade it: meetings with Stone, expeditions to uncover his prizes, gleanings into his past.

Lord help him, he'd even discussed Hugh with her, something he'd never felt compelled to do with anyone, partly because it hurt too bloody much and partly because he'd never found anyone to whom he wanted to divulge something so personal. Physical intimacy was one thing, emotional intimacy another.

Although with Aurora both were beyond comprehension.

She'd even made walking into Morland Manor bearable. From this point on, whenever he reflected on the mausoleum in which he'd grown up, the house that until now had signified naught but emptiness and pain, he would envision not the angry battles with his father, but the enthralling moments in Aurora's arms.

Moments during which she'd told him she loved him.

He didn't doubt that it was true. Especially after what had just transpired in this room—not their lovemaking, but the fervent discourse Aurora had delivered just prior to it. The poignant way she'd confronted his self-censure, urging him to accept Hugh's death, to let go of a past he couldn't change—and all because she wanted him to attain a peace that had until now eluded him. Her insight into his thoughts, his motivations, was staggering—even he himself had never realized just how deeply Hugh's death had impacted his outlook, the choices he'd made, the intensity of his commitment to those for whom he felt responsible.

She wanted him safe . . . no, she'd ordered him to be safe, in the way only Aurora had of doing. And she'd made no effort to conceal why. It was because she loved him, needed him. She'd admitted it without the slightest hesitation, offered him the kind of emotional openness he'd never believed possible.

But then, this was Aurora—utterly and refreshingly forthright, vibrant, impetuous. And so bloody passionate she scalded him down to his soul.

In over his head? Hell, he was drowning.

Julian's hand fell away from Aurora's cheek, his mind racing with the implications of all he'd just contemplated.

It was time to stop running, to stop dismissing his feelings for Aurora as the natural consequence of an ever-burgeoning passion, to stop fearing the ramifications of what already was.

The truth was staring him straight in the face.

He'd fallen in love with his wife.

The realization was startling, even though on some peripheral level he'd known it—battled it—for days. He who needed no one, relied upon no one, shared his life with no one, had lost his heart to his bride.

More startling still was the fact that as he now confronted the reality of his feelings, he found himself accepting them with astonishing ease—at least with regard to the relinquishing of his emotional freedom. Probably because when it came to Aurora, what he'd be relinquishing paled in comparison to what he'd be gaining. His breathtaking bride had totally reshaped and redefined his views of passion and marriage, offering him a union that was exquisitely unconventional and far superior to anything he'd ever anticipated, much less witnessed in others. Love with her would doubtless be the same. Having Aurora by his side would renew his excitement, his sense of adventure. For, as they traveled the world together, he'd be seeing it all for the first time—through his bride's exuberant eyes.

Yes, loving Aurora would give him a real reason to sail off on new ventures. But more significant, for the first time in his life it would give him a real reason to come home.

A muscle worked in Julian's jaw. The whole idea of

being in love with his wife would be downright captivating were it not for the more sobering aspect, the one Aurora herself had touched on during her impassioned speech—and the one that had compelled him to battle his feelings for her.

Safeguarding lives was something he took very seriously. That task was difficult enough when those involved were emotional strangers. But when they were his brother, and now his wife, it became infinitely more critical, his sense of responsibility intensifying to vast proportions.

He'd been fully aware of all that the day he asked Slayde for Aurora's hand; and he'd accepted his new obligations the day he slipped a wedding ring on her finger. She'd become his that day, and he would protect her life with his own.

Then it had been critical.

Now it was essential.

Because now he was in love with her, transforming his task from a fierce responsibility to an emotional necessity. And *that* rendered him susceptible, vulnerable, giving his enemies—and Aurora's—a sharp edge.

So be it, Julian thought, determination pulsing through his veins. He'd sharpen his wits, heighten his resolve to shield Aurora from harm. And he *would* shield her from harm, come hell or high water. But he wouldn't—*couldn't*—stop loving her. What's more, he didn't want to. Loving her felt more right than all his triumphant adventures combined.

He had to tell her.

Tenderly he brushed a strand of hair from her forehead, lowered his mouth to hers. He would awaken her, make love to her, whisper his newly discovered feelings as she shattered in his arms . . .

The grandfather clock in the hall chimed six.

Julian frowned, jolted back to a less-pleasant but all too crucial reality. The night was upon them. He glanced toward the window, noting that the winter sky was already dark. They'd have to hurry if they wanted to reach Fowey, check out both taverns Stone had mentioned, and still hope to find Barnes. Given the sailor's advanced age, he would probably leave his fellow seamen and go home to bed at a reasonable hour.

Finding him was vital.

Just as vital was getting Aurora in and out of those seedy pubs as quickly as possible. The later the hour became, the greater was their chance of running into trouble.

And of running into Macall.

Soberly Julian gazed down at his wife, Stone's warning resounding through his head. *Remember what I said, Merlin. Macall's after ye—and he's got more ammunition now.* With that, Stone had paused, glanced at Aurora. *Don't let him use it.*

Stone didn't know just how accurate an assessment he'd made.

A near-violent surge of protectiveness shot through Julian, followed by a jolt of rage. Let that filthy bastard Macall try to hurt his wife. If he so much as touched her, he'd be dead before he blinked.

Sucking in his breath, Julian shelved his grand emotional proclamation for later, kissing Aurora again, this time purposefully rather than seductively. "Sweetheart, wake up."

She sighed, mumbling something unintelligible as she unconsciously lifted her face to receive his kiss.

"Soleil," he breathed into her lips. "It's time. We've got to dress, gulp down a hasty dinner, and ride to Fowey all within the hour."

Aurora's eyes snapped open. "I fell asleep," she announced.

A corner of his mouth lifted. "Yes, I know."

"Ummm, you feel good," Aurora murmured, wrapping her arms about Julian's neck, lifting her lower body to his.

"Do that again and we'll never find Barnes," he warned, fighting the urge to answer her body's invitation with his own.

Aurora stilled, moaning a protest. "What a wretched ultimatum."

"Not an ultimatum, *soleil.*" He threaded his fingers through her hair. "Only a delay."

"I hate waiting."

"I know." He chuckled, tracing the curve of her lips. "When it comes to you, so do I."

"Very well. If we must go, we must go." She hesitated, fully awake now. "Julian, will you give some thought to what I said before?"

"Oh, I already have." He withdrew from her reluctantly, kneeling to adjust her disheveled gown. "The whole time you were asleep." He smoothed her skirts back into place. "We'll talk later, after tonight's adventure is over."

"All right." Aurora searched his face as if seeking an answer she sensed hovered just beneath the surface. Her gaze dropped and fell on her rumpled gown, and abruptly her thoughts veered off in another direction. "I can't go out wearing this," she muttered, examining the gown's ripped layers and muddied hem.

"No, you can't." Julian's eyes twinkled as he refastened his breeches—which looked equally as pathetic as his wife's gown. "That's why I woke you. If we hurry, we'll have time for a quick bath and a change of clothes. I'll have Gin arrange for both. All we have to do is slip upstairs to our rooms."

"Room*s*?" Aurora tossed back her hair and laughed. "You scarcely let me peek into my new chambers, much less explore them. I hardly know where they are, or what they look like."

"They're pale blue and adjoining mine. That's all you need to know. Trust me, your chambers won't be getting much use." With a wicked grin, Julian unbolted the door. "Shall we?"

"Absolutely." Aurora crossed over, smoothing her palms up her husband's shirtfront. "You look hopelessly disheveled, you know. As if you've been making love all afternoon."

"Do I?" Julian caught her wrist, brought her palm to his lips. "That's because I have. What's more, if I had my way, the afternoon would be stretching into evening, then into night."

"I'll remind you of that later."

"I'm counting on it." His tongue traced a fine line to her thumb.

"Julian—stop," Aurora commanded, shivering. "Or we'll never leave this room, much less travel to Fowey."

"You're right." Sighing, he released her. "Are you ready to go upstairs?"

"Indeed. Maybe if we run fast enough, the servants won't notice our tousled state." Skepticism flashed in her eyes. "Never mind. Knowing your servants, I doubt we'll fool them." Aurora paused, her lips pursed as a sudden thought seemed to intrude. "Julian, that reminds me, I've been doing a bit of thinking of my own. I know this is a most unconventional household. But I am a duchess, and I do require a lady's maid, do I not?"

Julian arched a brow, wondering where this was leading. "Of course."

"And it is proper for me to select this person myself, isn't it?"

"If I remember my protocol correctly, yes, it is."

"Good." She gave him a dazzling smile. "Then I choose Emma."

"Emma?" Whatever he'd expected, it hadn't been this. "Sweetheart, she's barely fifteen. Further, she has absolutely no experience at being a lady's maid."

"True. But youth and inexperience do have their benefits. Emma will be a quick and eager study—not to mention the fact that she'll have no means of comparison and will therefore never know how unorthodox a mistress she truly has."

Julian chuckled. "I can't disagree with that."

"Then it's settled?"

Insight dawned. "How much of your decision is based on the reasons you've just given me and how much is based on the story I told you of how Emma came to be here?"

Aurora regarded him with her perpetual candor. "Equal amounts of both. Further, I can't stop remembering the way Emma looked at me when we met—as if I held all the wonders of the world in my hands. And not because I'm titled or even because I'm married to you— although she stares at you with utter worship in her eyes—but because I'm settled, happy, with a future that I embrace. I understand her better than she thinks. When I was her age my parents were gone, Slayde was constantly abroad, and I was sequestered at Pembourne like some trapped doe. I felt lonely and out of place, and despite the mass of kindly servants around me, I always felt alone, with a less than promising future. I imagine she must feel the same. I think I could help her, offer her a position she'd enjoy and a woman she can talk to."

"I agree." Julian caressed his wife's cheek, moved by her generosity of spirit. "Then Emma it is." His hand curved about her nape and he drew her toward him, lowering his mouth to hers. "Your parents' choice of names for you was most fitting," he murmured into her lips. "As was their reasoning for choosing it. You do fill the world with sunlight. Thank you, *soleil.*" He enfolded her against him, kissing her more deeply.

"You think Emma will be pleased?" Aurora whispered breathlessly.

"I think she'll be thrilled." With the greatest of efforts,

Julian raised his head, enjoying the dazed look in his wife's eyes—and the disappointment on her face. "I also think we'd best leave this room right now, before my resolve completely shatters and I take you right here, right now, and Barnes be damned."

With that, he inhaled sharply, and having regained a modicum of composure, he opened the door. "No one's about," he muttered, peeking into the hallway. He glanced back at Aurora. "Are you ready?"

"My knees are still shaking. Other than that, I'm ready."

Julian grinned. "Then I see but one solution." He swept Aurora into his arms, then strode out of the sitting room and toward the stairway. "So far, so good," he announced cheerfully, assessing the deserted hallway before taking the steps two at a time. "Perhaps we'll make it undetected, after all."

"Perhaps." Aurora was laughing so hard she could barely speak. "On the other hand, perhaps the servants are purposely avoiding us."

"Don't bet on it. My staff is anything but shy." Julian rounded the second floor landing, headed purposefully for his chambers.

"Safe," Aurora proclaimed as they crossed the threshold. "I never thought we'd actually succeed in getting past . . ." She broke off, her jaw dropping.

"As you can see, we didn't." Julian deposited her on the bed, then began unbuttoning his shirt, nodding at Gin, who squatted in the center of the room pouring pots of steaming water into a large copper tub. "Is that bath for me or the duchess?" Julian inquired nonchalantly.

"This one's yers." Gin rose, dragging his forearm across his forehead. "I prepared Mrs. Merlin's first. It's waitin' in 'er chambers. By the way—" He gave Aurora a questioning look. "It's all right if I call ye Mrs. Merlin, ain't it? I 'eard ye give it to Stone as one of 'is choices, and I like the sound of it a lot better than I do Lady

Aurora. I also 'eard Merlin mention somethin' about goin' to Fowey. I figured he meant tonight—Merlin ain't much on waitin'. Then I guess ye already found that out. Anyway, yer clothes were in no condition to go visitin', so I assumed ye'd be wantin' a bath. Course, I did mean to ask, but the sittin' room door was locked when I tried it, alertin' me to the fact that the two of ye wouldn't be wantin' company. So, I just went ahead and prepared the baths. All I need to know is, who ye'd like to assist ye?"

Sprawled in the center of the bed, Aurora gaped, utterly speechless.

"Now we're even, ain't we Mrs. Merlin?" A broad grin split Gin's bearded face. "Looks like we're both real good at surprises."

"Yes," she conceded, her eyes beginning to twinkle. "It appears we are."

"You're a bit much, even for my wife," Julian advised his valet. "Therefore, until she recovers from the shock of your actions—not to mention your eavesdropping, I'll answer for her." He tossed aside his shirt, sitting on the edge of the bed to remove his boots. "Aurora's decided she'd like Emma as her maid. Isn't that right, *soleil?*"

Aurora nodded, her shoulders beginning to shake with laughter. "Yes. Although I'm sure that comes as no surprise to your valet. Doubtless he's already heard that bit of news."

Gin emitted a whoop of pleasure. "No. That one I missed. I'll be a son of a . . ."

"Gin." Julian's reprimand sliced the air.

"'Cuse me, ma'am." The valet cleared his throat. "Emma's gonna be thrilled. I'll get 'er."

"By all means. And Gin—" Aurora held up her hand to delay his exit. "Thank you for your thoughtfulness *and* your attention to detail. To answer your questions, Mrs. Merlin is a perfect form of address and Emma, as you just heard, is indeed my choice for lady's maid. I have but one request: now that we're even, would it be possible for you to refrain from making any surprise appearances in my bedchamber—or Julian's for that matter—just in case I happen to be in a state of undress?"

Gin's dark eyes sparkled with humor. "It'd be more than possible. And I'd better stop those surprise appearances in more than just yer bedchambers, if my visit to the sittin' room this afternoon is any indication. Yup, I think I'll start knockin' on all the doors from now on, just to be safe. Ye see? Ye got nothin' to worry about. I might be rough around the edges, but I'm a gentleman through and through—and that alone will keep me honest." He cast a sidelong look at Julian, chuckling at the warning look in his employer's eyes. "That, plus the fact that if I walked in on ye Merlin would kill me."

"You look lovely, ma'am." For the fifth time Emma curtsied, this time as she slipped the final pin in Aurora's hair. "Can I do anything else? Get you gloves? A fan?"

Aurora rose from her dressing table and smiled. "No, thank you, Emma. You've done a wonderful job of arranging my hair and helping me dress—no one would ever know this was your first day as a lady's maid. As for gloves and a fan, they're too formal for where I'm going this evening."

"Very good, m'lady. Thank you." Another curtsy.

"Emma." Aurora lay a gentle hand on her shoulder. "'Tis I who should be thanking you. I'm as new at—" A twinkle. "—Merlin Manor as you are to the duties you just performed. I'm delighted to have a young woman to talk to, *and* one who can arrange hair so beautifully. I'm grateful you accepted the position as my lady's maid. But, given what I've told you about my propensity for getting into trouble, please—save your energy for extricating me, not for curtsying."

The young girl nodded vigorously. "Thank you, ma'am. I will." She smoothed the skirts of Aurora's beige muslin gown. "Would you like to wear a necklace? Some jewels would brighten up this dress."

"No, I think not." Aurora glanced down at herself and shook her head. "Given my destination, looking drab is appropriate—and inconspicuous. Jewels would only hinder things. But I do need my reticule." She walked over and scooped up the small satin bag. *"This* is a necessary adornment."

"Of course. You never know when you'll need a handkerchief or some hair pins."

"True." Aurora ran her fingers over the reticule's smooth, cool surface, then pulled the cords tightly closed, tucking the bag securely against her side. "A handkerchief, hairpins . . . or some other crucial item." Raising her chin, she assessed herself in the looking glass. "You just never know what you might need."

Chapter 13

It was just shy of eight o'clock when Julian steered the skiff into Fowey's harbor. Tying the craft securely to the dock, he leapt out, frowning as he assessed the unsavory types milling about the wharf in search of potential prey.

"Traveling by boat was much faster than by carriage, but it still took us too long to get here," he muttered, helping Aurora climb out beside him. "Dammit. If we'd only left Polperro with the last rays of daylight, we could have sailed more quickly, arrived before these lowlifes emerged from the bowels of hell."

"What good would coming earlier have done us?" Aurora reasoned, looking about with more curiosity than fear. "Barnes visits these taverns only at night. We had no choice about our timing. Besides, you're a superb navigator, day or night."

Julian was glaring at a slimy-looking wharf rat, staring him down until the menacing fellow slunk away. "Rory—remember what I said," he murmured to his wife. "Keep your head down and your eyes on the path. Stay close to me and walk." He turned his attention to her, drawing her mantle more closely about her shoulders, tucking a few loose strands of hair beneath her bonnet. "You can't help being beautiful," he grumbled. "Let's hope I don't have to kill anyone before we cross over and make our way to the Brine. Come."

He seized her arm, leading her away from the wharf and toward the small row of buildings across the road.

The path was rotted, the stench of ale more potent than that of fish and salt air combined. All around them, pairs of eyes watched their progress. Behind them, waves lapped lightly at the shoreline, rocking the few fishing boats that were anchored there, then receding into the chilly night sky.

A chipped sign reading The Brine told them they'd reached their destination.

"This makes Dawlish's look elegant," Aurora muttered, clasping her mantle higher about her as she and Julian took the remaining steps to a shoddy building that more closely resembled an abandoned shack than it did a tavern.

"Not exactly Carlton House, is it?" Julian returned dryly. He tensed, glancing back for the umpteenth time as if to verify that the rushing sound he heard was indeed the sound of the waves and not that of an approaching enemy or an audacious thief. His grip about Aurora's waist tightened as they reached the pub door. "Remember the rules, *soleil*. At no time are you to budge from my side or take matters into your own hands." His lips twitched. "And for heaven's sake, *don't* offer to join the sailors in a game of whist."

"Very funny." Aurora's fingers clutched her reticule, pressing it close to her side.

"You aren't carrying anything of value in there, are you?" Julian inquired, the sound of raucous laughter greeting their ears.

"Only the necessities," she assured him.

"Good. Then, let's see what we can learn." With that, Julian shoved open the door and guided Aurora in.

The pub was dark, reeking of spirits, filled with the most unkempt men Aurora had ever seen—men whose gazes snapped in their direction and whose conversation quieted, then stopped altogether as she and Julian made their way to the counter.

"Yeah?" The flabby-cheeked tavern keeper glanced briefly at Julian before openly assessing Aurora, his stare roving restlessly over her concealed figure, flickering from her bonnet to her face—where it lingered.

Julian's arm clamped about her like a steel manacle. "We're looking for Barnes," he bit out. "Is he here?"

"Who wants to know?"

"Merlin."

The tavern keeper blanched. "Ye're Merlin?"

"I am."

"Macall's lookin' for ye."

"So I've heard." Julian shrugged. "I'll catch up with him sooner or later. In the meantime, I need to see Barnes."

"Why?" One of the sailors chimed in. "'E sure as 'ell can't see ye—or anythin' else, for that matter."

A burst of laughter erupted.

"'E can't 'ear too well, either," a scrawny fellow added, tossing off a drink, then dragging his sleeve across his mouth. "So ye're wastin' yer time."

"No, *you're* wasting it," Julian returned smoothly. He leaned against the counter, casually extracting a wad of pound notes. "Let's see, he can't see or hear. Do you think he can count?"

The sailor's sleeve halted, his sunken eyes widening with interest. "I don't know about *'im,* but *I* can."

"Good. Then you can count this—*if* you tell me where Barnes is. I'd like to test his abilities to hear and see."

Julian peeled off two ten-pound notes and dangled them in the air.

It was the tavern keeper who lunged forward, leaning over the counter and trying to grab the bills.

"Don't even think of it." Julian snatched the money out of reach, his tone menacingly low. "Not unless you have information to give me. I don't like being swindled. It enrages me."

"Don't mess with him, Briney," another sailor piped up. "I've 'eard of this Merlin. 'E's not one to take on—not unless ye wanna get 'urt bad."

The tavern keeper took a step backward, holding up conciliatory palms. "Easy, fellow," he cautioned Julian. "I don't run that kinda place. No fights, no stealin', nothin'."

"I'm glad to hear that." Julian's smile was as pleasant as if he were greeting guests at a ball. "Now, to repeat my original question, does anyone know where I can find Barnes?"

"'E was 'ere earlier," Briney replied, wiping his hands on his apron. "I expect 'e's at the Cove. 'E usually goes there next, stays till ten. Then 'e goes 'ome to bed."

"Excellent. Thank you." Julian slapped the bills on the counter.

Eyeing the money, Briney hesitated, his hungry gaze once again sweeping Aurora. "'Ow about keepin' yer money and sharin' yer woman?"

Julian went deadly still. "How about taking the money and retracting your offer—or I'll break your jaw?"

"Okay, okay." Hastily the tavern keeper snatched up the pound notes, retreating farther behind the safety of his counter. "Didn't know she meant that much to ye. No 'arm intended."

That practiced smile was back in place. "Fine." Julian glanced about. "Enjoy your evening, gentlemen." He peeled off a few more bills, dropping them on the counter. "For your trouble—a few rounds of drinks for everyone, on me." He led Aurora to the door. "Oh, and Briney?" He turned. "Tell Macall I'm ready whenever he is."

Aurora stepped outside and breathed for the first time in fifteen minutes.

"Are you all right?" Julian tipped her chin up, assessing her ashen expression.

A shaky nod. "Just a bit taken aback. That . . . place wasn't at all what I expected. 'Twas nothing like Dawlish's."

"Dawlish's has a cleaner bunch of regular patrons. Half these sailors are smugglers, thieves—or worse. They're an entirely different breed."

"You were wonderful—Merlin through and through, without so much as a trace of Julian present. You even managed to intimidate *me.*"

Julian chuckled. "Now *that* is indeed an accomplishment."

Aurora didn't smile. "Daydreams and reality are far removed from each other, aren't they?" she asked in troubled realization.

"Indeed they are." Julian caressed her cheek. "Very different." He paused, studying her face. "Are you up for this, *soleil?* I could bring you home, return tomorrow night myself."

"No." Aurora seized the edges of his coat. "I'd be more frightened if you did this alone than I am now. At least this way I can look out for you."

A corner of his mouth lifted. "I'm honored."

"You're amused. Don't be. I haven't had ample opportunity to prove it, but I'm equally as determined as you to take care of those I love."

"As I said, I'm honored."

"And dubious."

"No, *soleil.* Never dubious when it comes to you."

Julian's head came up as a drunken sailor staggered out of the Brine. "Let's get out of here."

"How long will it take us to get to the Cove?" Aurora inquired, following close beside him.

"It's less than a mile away, right along the bank of the Fowey River. If we stay close to the shore, we should be able to sail upriver and dock within a half hour. We could go by foot, but I'd feel better if we avoided the riffraff we'd encounter along the way. We'll have plenty of time to deal with them once we reach the tavern itself."

"I can hardly wait," Aurora retorted.

Thirty-five minutes later, they left their skiff tied at the river's edge and climbed the rickety wooden steps leading to their destination.

The Cove, thankfully, was a bit less dilapidated than the Brine, but its patrons were equally as unkempt and a lot drunker than the others had been, probably because it was now almost an hour later, giving the sailors ample time to sink deeper and deeper into their cups.

Again Julian checked Aurora's appearance. Then, confident that she was as concealed as her layers of clothing would allow, he drew her close to his side, holding her tightly—and possessively—as he led her through the front door and to the counter.

"We got no rooms 'ere," the tavern keeper announced, his bloodshot gaze sliding from Julian to Aurora. "So ye'll 'ave to take this pretty morsel somewhere else." He leaned forward, his teeth so yellow, his breath so hideous that Aurora winced with disgust. "Unless, of course, ye want to share 'er with me. Then, we can take 'er to the kitchen and . . ."

"I don't want a room," Julian ground out, clearly battling back the urge to throttle the man. "My *wife*—" He emphasized the word. "—and I are looking for someone. We want you to help us find him."

"I sell ale, not information."

"I want both." Julian slapped a ten-pound note on the counter. "And I'll pay for them."

The tavern keeper's eyes gleamed. "That's a different story." He snatched up the money. "Who're ye lookin' for? And why?"

"A sailor named Barnes. He's old, gray-haired, with a gravelly voice. A reliable source tells me he spends his evenings at the Cove."

An assessing pause. "Ye still haven't told me why ye're lookin' for this fellow Barnes."

"He and I have a mutual friend I have some questions about."

"A friend? Or someone ye're plannin' to steal from or kill?"

"A friend. Someone I want to discuss."

"Nothin' more?"

"Nothing more." Clearly Julian sensed victory, for he withdrew two more notes, waved them visibly about like bait, then folded them neatly and tucked them into his palm. "As I said, I'll pay handsomely. No trouble, no fights, just information. After which—if Barnes should happen to be here—my wife and I will buy him a few rounds of ale, chat with him for a time, then take our leave. Period." Julian rubbed the pound notes between his fingers. "Well?"

The bloodshot gaze shifted hungrily to Julian's hand. "I guess a fellow 'is age can't be in any trouble," he rationalized aloud, reaching for the money. "'E's 'ere."

"Where?" Julian's fingers inched away.

"Over there." Scratching his bearded jaw, the tavern keeper leaned forward, pointing to a table along the side wall. "Ye can't miss 'im. 'E's tellin' 'is stories to who-ever'll listen. 'E's older than all the other men combined."

"Thanks—" Julian made a move to hand over the notes, then paused. "What did you say your name was?"

"Rawley."

"Rawley. Thanks." He slapped the bills into the tavern keeper's dirty palm, then seized Aurora's elbow, leading her across the room to the broken wooden table in question where four men—three elderly, one ancient—sat chuckling and drinking their ale.

Julian didn't have to guess which sailor was the one he sought.

"Barnes?" he inquired casually, looking at the stooped old man whose gnarled fingers clutched his tankard of ale.

"That's me. Who're ye?"

"Someone who needs to talk with you—alone."

"Sorry," Barnes said in that gravelly voice Stone had described. "I don't go nowhere with no one I don't know. 'Specially without a reason."

Julian blinked. "I'm not asking you to go anywhere. Just join me at that table way over there—" He pointed. "—for a drink."

"Nope. Can't. Talkin' to my friends. Tellin' 'em about the time my brig almost capsized when we was leavin' India."

"It'll only take a few minutes."

"Nope."

"Please, sir." Aurora's words emerged of their own accord. "My husband and I have searched everywhere for you. We lost a family member at sea—and no one but you can shed any light on the situation. Won't you please give us just a quarter hour of your time? I promise we mean you no harm." Gently she touched his arm. "It could make a world of difference."

Barnes scratched his gray head. "Ye two are married?"

"Yes, sir."

"And ye need to know somethin' about yer family?"

Aurora nodded. "About a relative of my husband's—someone you sailed with. We need your help; you're our only hope."

Shoving back his chair, Barnes stood. "In that case, I'll go." He glared at his friends. "Ye best not forget which part I was up to."

Judging from their blank expressions, Aurora noted with an inner smile, they already had.

"Over there?" Barnes asked, pointed a wrinkled forefinger.

"Yes. That would be perfect." Aurora glanced up at Julian, grinning at how impressed he looked at her accomplishment. "You're not the only man who succumbs to my charm," she teased under her breath.

"Evidently not." He guided them over to a corner that was as close to quiet and deserted as one could get in this pub. "Have a seat, Barnes; I'll get you another ale."

"Don't need it." The old fellow waved away the offer. "Just tell me what's on yer mind. For a minute I was afraid ye were another one of them pirates wantin' information on the black diamond. Lots of fellas used to ask me about it. Now it's just sometimes. But like I always tell them, I don't know nothin' about it. They was all just wastin' their time."

"Our questions aren't about the diamond," Aurora inserted with quiet candor. "But they are about the men who found it."

Barnes's shaggy brows shot up. "I thought ye said this was about yer family."

"It is."

A skeptical look. "Ye sure ye aren't some privateer lookin' for that stone?"

"I'm not a privateer," Julian assured him. "I'm Geoffrey Bencroft's great-grandson. And, while I never knew my great-grandfather, his actions have affected my entire life. I understand you sailed with him. And I'm eager to know anything you can tell me about him."

"So yer Julian Bencroft." Barnes's dark eyes turned bright with interest, his head veering slowly toward Aurora. "If what ye said is true and ye two really are married, that makes ye Aurora Huntley." He chuckled at her look of surprise. "I may be old, but I'm not dead yet. I hear all the local gossip, same as the next fella. And a weddin' between the Bencrofts and the Huntleys is big news in anyone's book."

"Yes," Aurora told him. "I'm Aurora Huntley Bencroft."

"Ye sound real proud of that fact."

"I am—for many reasons." Aurora drew a slow inward breath. "Neither of us believes our great-grandfathers were criminals, Mr. Barnes. We'd like to hear what you think, any firsthand information you can give us about Geoffrey Bencroft. We'll gladly pay you for your trouble."

"Don't want yer money." Barnes straightened his stooped shoulders, regarding them both through eyes grown wise with time. "Yer the first ones who didn't call 'em thieves. I can't speak fer Huntley, but I sure as 'ell can tell ye Bencroft was a good man, a decent man." He scrutinized Julian's face. "Ye got 'is eyes, ye know. Same restlessness. Same depth. Yup. Yer 'is great-grandson, all right. Maybe if I answer yer questions, it'll give 'im peace. What can I tell ye?"

"You were with Geoffrey on his trip home—the one he never completed?"

"Um-hum. I was a cabin boy on three of yer great-grandfather's voyages—includin' the last. 'E was real kind to me, told me all about the world, taught me 'ow to dream. I remember 'im standin' beside me on the deck durin' that last trip, puttin' 'is 'and on my shoulder and pointin' out to sea. 'Barnes,' he told me, 'there's a world of adventure out there, dreams to be lived and treasures to be discovered. Go after what ye want. Don't let anythin' or anyone stop ye. What they think don't matter. Be true to yerself and ye'll die an 'appy man.'" Barnes sighed. "Little did 'e know 'ow close 'is own death was."

"He died of a fever?" Aurora prompted.

"Yes, ma'am. 'Im and three-quarters of the others on that ship. But I made it my business to take care of Bencroft. I sat with 'im in 'is cabin, mopped 'is brow, and got 'im water. 'E was delirious with fever, talked about that bloody stone over and over again. Knew it was cursed, 'e did. Kept sayin' they 'ad to get rid of it. Begged 'is friend James to turn it over. Never said a mean word about the man, even though rumor had it Huntley stole the diamond right out from under 'im. Just kept beggin' 'im to give it over."

"Those were his words?" Julian leaned forward intently.

Barnes gave a raspy cough. "Ye're talkin' about a lot of years ago. I don't remember 'is exact words. Besides, 'e was babblin' mostly. The poor fella knew 'e was dying. 'E wanted Huntley to know it, too. Kept callin' out to 'im, tellin' him the end was near, the end was in sight, that 'e'd see James before 'e got there. I tried to calm 'im down, but 'e kept tryin' to get up, strugglin' to breathe. 'E never saw another dawn; died late that night. But ye should be proud of him—I don't care what folks say. 'E was a fine man. I'm 'onored to 'ave known 'im."

"Thank you." Julian swallowed. "Is there anything else you can tell us?"

"Nope. I think that's it. As I said, I 'ave no idea where James Huntley put the black diamond or if 'e really cheated 'is partner. But I don't see why Bencroft would be callin' out to 'im if 'e 'ad."

"Thank you, Mr. Barnes." Aurora covered his wrinkled hand with her smooth one. "You've been very kind and helped us a great deal."

"Yes." Julian extracted some bills, peeled off a hefty amount, and placed it on the table before Barnes. "We appreciate your time and your insight."

Ignoring the pound notes, Barnes leaned toward Aurora, gingerly touching a strand of her hair that had escaped from the bonnet. "Keep yer money, Bencroft," he told Julian. "But be good to yer wife. She's a real beauty—and not only on the outside." His face creased into a grin. "'Er 'eart is in the right place. Yer great-grandfather would be real pleased with yer choice."

Julian nodded. "I think he would, too."

"Please, Mr. Barnes." Aurora pressed the notes into his palm. "For the peace you've afforded not only us, but our great-grandfathers—please take this. It will buy you food, ale . . . and a chance to fulfill any of the dreams you've yet to realize."

The elderly sailor's eyes grew damp. "When ye put it that way . . . all right. And God bless ye."

Julian led Aurora out of the tavern and into the night. "That was a lovely gesture, *soleil,*" he said when they were alone. "The second one today, in fact. First, Emma, now Barnes." Tenderly he tucked her hair back into her bonnet. "Barnes was right. Your beauty transcends the mere physical. I'm indeed a lucky man."

"We're both lucky," Aurora amended. "You were as moved by Barnes *and* what he said, as I was. 'Twas no accident, that king's ransom you just left him."

"I won't deny being moved. It felt damned good to hear something commendable said about my great-grandfather—especially by a man who knew him personally. Still, from a more practical perspective, I'm not sure we learned anything of consequence."

"I suppose you're right." Aurora tipped back her head, frowning thoughtfully at her husband. "We already surmised Geoffrey's urgency to reach James before he died, presumably so together they could restore the black diamond to King George." A speculative pause.

"But . . . ?" Julian prompted.

"But I have the nagging feeling we learned something more, something we have yet to discern. Maybe it's because Mr. Scollard guided us in this direction, and he never does that without having a specific purpose in mind. So why would he want us to find Mr. Barnes only to learn what we already knew? No, I suspect there's more to this than we've yet . . ."

" 'Elp! Please 'elp me!" A smudged, scrawny boy of about eleven barreled down the path, nearly crashing into them in his haste. "Sir, ma'am, ye gotta 'elp me."

Aurora caught his flailing arms. "Help you? What's wrong?" She scrutinized the deserted path; then, seeing no one, she turned her attention back to the ragged urchin. "Is someone trying to hurt you?"

"No. It's me little sister. She's in that alley." He pointed. "She fell. She's bleedin' real bad. I can't get 'er to wake up. She's only four. Please . . ." He tugged at Aurora's sleeve. "Ye've gotta come."

"Where's your mother?" Julian demanded.

" 'Ome. Takin' care of me dad. 'E's sick. I was supposed to get bread and watch me sister at the same time, to bring 'er 'ome safe. And now she's 'urt—bad. Please—'urry." The boy started back, gesturing frantically for them to follow.

"Julian, we've got to help him." Aurora had already gathered up her skirts to rush after the lad.

"Wait." Julian caught her arm, eyes narrowed on the deserted path and the remote alleyway entrance that seemed to disappear into nothingness. "I don't like this. He could be a thief or Lord knows what else. We need more information before we go tearing after . . ."

"We'll have to take that chance. I can't leave a four-year-old child in that horrible alley, alone and injured." Wrenching her arm free, Aurora sprinted off after the boy.

"Dammit." Julian shot after her, unwilling to let Aurora out of his sight—although his instincts screamed their conviction that this whole situation smelled rotten.

A minute later his suspicions were confirmed.

Rounding the alleyway entrance just behind his wife, Julian had scarcely taken a dozen strides when the lad—

now twenty feet ahead—came to a screeching halt, spinning about to face them, an expectant look in his eyes.

There was no little sister.

In a rush Julian acted, grabbing for Aurora, simultaneously groping in his coat pocket for his pistol.

He never reached either.

Abruptly he was struck from behind, a sharp glancing blow between the shoulder blades that left him reeling. Before he could recover, he was shoved head-on against the brick wall. Reflexively his elbows came up to take the brunt of the impact, his ears ringing with Aurora's sharp cry of distress.

That sound was enough to supplant the pain lancing through his arms and back. Julian whipped about, only to see a glint of metal, feel the piercing point of a sword as it jabbed against his throat.

"At last, Merlin." The swarthy, venomous man at the other end of the sword was as familiar as his voice. "The day of reckoning has come."

"Macall," Julian acknowledged, noting that the bastard was grasping Aurora's arm with his thick, filthy fingers. Swiftly he inhaled, fighting back the instinct to lunge forward and snatch his wife away. It would be the stupidest move he could make, resulting only in getting her and himself killed. No, he had to stay calm, remain perfectly still as he tried to assess the extent of his enemy's irrationality. "I heard you were looking for me."

"And I found you." Macall spat at Julian's feet, then glanced at the restless urchin who hovered about, waiting. "There." He jerked his head in the direction of a small pouch of coins hanging from his coat button. "Take it," he ordered. "Then get out of here."

"Yes, sir." The urchin yanked the pouch free and bolted without so much as a backward glance.

"So this is your wife," Macall muttered, his gaze

flickering over Aurora. "Tell me, is she any good? Or did you marry her just for the diamond?"

Julian scarcely blinked. "Let her go, Macall. Your fight is with me, not Aurora." He swallowed past the sharp pressure in his throat. "You want to kill me? Fine. Release my wife. Then you can use two hands to drive me through."

"Julian—no." Aurora began to struggle, yanking violently but ineffectually at her arm, succeeding only in loosening her bonnet until it fell to the ground.

Macall dragged her closer, his grip tightening until she whimpered. "Brazen little thing, aren't you?" His taunting stare examined the fineness of her features close-up, took in the loose tendrils of red-gold hair that now tumbled down her back. "Do you know, I'm beginning to suspect Merlin had more than one reason for wanting this marriage," he said with a sardonic smile. "I'll have to satisfy my curiosity about that. Who knows? If you're skilled enough, it might persuade me to let you live."

"Think again, Macall," Julian countered icily. "What you have in mind requires two hands, one of which is currently occupied with holding a sword to my throat. Should you remove that hand, I'll find a way to kill you before you draw your next breath, much less touch my wife. So I suggest you forget whatever vile notion you have in mind. Let Aurora go and vent your rage where it belongs—at me."

"Oh, I intend to vent my rage where it belongs. After which *both* my hands will be free—as will your wife." With a sneer, Macall turned back to Julian. "You really have gone soft, haven't you, Merlin? Who would ever have thought a woman would mean enough to you to render you weak, ensure your undoing? After ten months of trying to hunt you down, I managed to lure you into what was obviously a trap simply by using her as bait. And now I'll get what I want by doing the same. How

unexpected—and how effortless." A harsh laugh. "Ironic, isn't it? As a result of your own stupidity, I'll soon
have both your prized possessions—the black diamond
and your bride." He jerked his chin in the direction of
Julian's coat pocket. "Take out the pistol, nice and slow.
Then toss it to the ground."

"Why should I? According to you, you plan on killing
me anyway." A deliberate pause. "Of course, then you'll
have only half of what you came for—your revenge.
What about the black diamond?"

"That won't work, Merlin." Macall's dark eyes glittered. "I don't need both you and your duchess alive to
get my hands on the diamond, not when she's Aurora
Huntley. I could easily kill you, then toss up your wife's
skirts right here in this alley and take her brutally and
repeatedly until she tells me where I can find the stone.
How would that be?"

Julian tasted bile. Slowly, knowing bloody well he had
no choice, he complied with Macall's demand, retrieving
his weapon and letting it drop to the ground. The bastard
was right. If Macall drove him through here and now,
Aurora would be at the privateer's mercy. Julian had to
stall for time, find a way to save her.

"Good." Macall kicked the pistol across the alley.
"Now we can get down to business." He pushed the
sword an iota deeper, pricking Julian's skin until blood
began to trickle down his throat. "As you yourself just
pointed out, I want two things: you—dead at my feet—
and the black diamond. The first is a fated reality, and
has been since the day you killed my brother. The second
is also a reality, but not quite as unconditional as the
first. You see, I can either acquire my prize easily or with
a bit of persuasion. That, Merlin, is where your choice
comes in. If you tell me what I want to know, you'll die
with a minimum amount of pain and the duchess here
will be allowed to live. If you refuse, your death will be

an excruciating one—as will your final memory: seeing me carve your bride into little pieces. The choice is yours."

"There's no choice to make," Aurora informed him, tugging again at her arm. "I'll opt for death if living means my becoming your possession."

"Such brave words," Macall replied. "And such naive ones. Fortunately your husband—unlike you—knows the agony a sword such as this can cause. I trust he'll decide accordingly."

Throughout Macall's tirade, Julian's mind had been racing. His alarm was for Aurora, though not because he gave any credence to Macall's threat to kill her first. The bastard knew firsthand how swiftly Julian struck. If Macall so much as inched the sword in Aurora's direction, Julian would be on him like the merlin on its prey. So that part of the threat was merely a ruse. However, the remaining part—Macall's vow to ravage Aurora cruelly and brutally after Julian was dead—*that* Julian believed with every sickened fiber of his being. Macall was evil to the core, and formidable as hell.

When he had the upper hand.

When he *didn't,* however, he panicked, became reckless. More times than not, that recklessness was his undoing. With a modicum of luck, it would be now.

Julian's hooded gaze flickered to Aurora, who was still trying unsuccessfully to free her arm—a futile effort, given that Macall was far stronger than she. However, the son of a bitch did have only a one-handed grasp on her. If there were a way to trick him into devoting both hands to his sword, maybe Aurora could break away and run to safety.

It was his job to provide that way.

Mentally, Julian gauged the distance between his wife and the alleyway entrance, trying to assess the amount of time she'd need to reach safety, finding he was unable to do so as a result of his increasing light-headedness. Dammit. He couldn't lose consciousness—not until Aurora was safe. He had to stave off his own fate long enough to create a diversion and allow her time to flee.

"Hurry up, Merlin," Macall prodded. "You're already sheet white and your coat's stained with blood. Any longer and you'll pass out cold. I want you conscious when I cut open your belly. Now what's it gonna be?"

"I don't have the stone," Julian managed, deliberately antagonizing Macall into action, praying the results would give Aurora the precious minutes she needed. "Neither does my wife."

"Where is it hidden?"

Julian stared right through him. "We haven't a clue."

"Damn you." Macall twisted the sword a fraction, deepening Julian's wound and drawing fresh blood.

Despite the excruciating jolt of pain that accompanied Macall's act, it was just what Julian had been awaiting.

With a choked groan—more real than feigned—he sagged, falling back against the wall, his head dropping to one side. *Let the bastard think I'm dying before he can find out what he wants to know,* he willed silently. *Let him do what he always does under pressure—panic and lose control.*

Macall didn't disappoint him.

"Don't you dare die yet, you son of a bitch," he bellowed, retracting the blade a fraction, as if by doing so he could lessen the severity of the wound enough to prolong Julian's life.

Julian seized his opportunity. Slowly, eyes shut, he sagged to the ground.

That did it.

"Merlin—get up!" Macall flung Aurora aside, grabbing Julian's coat to keep him from slumping farther downward, pointing the blade at his heart and shaking him. "Get up, you miserable bastard!"

Julian's eyes snapped open. "Run, Aurora!" he shouted over Macall's surprised roar of anger. "Get out of here!"

Aurora responded instantly, backing away from Macall and taking off like a bullet.

Relief—stark and absolute—coursed through Julian's soul.

His relief was short-lived.

Abruptly his wife slowed, and to Julian's astonishment and horror, she turned, stopping dead in her tracks a mere fifteen feet away. She stared at them, eyes widening with terror as she saw the demented rage on Macall's face, recognized his intent. "Wait!" she cried out as he drew back his sword, preparing to drive Julian through. "Don't kill my husband—I couldn't live with myself if you did. Julian doesn't know where the diamond is. Only I do."

The sword froze and Macall's head shot up, his pupils dilated with shock—and skepticism. "Only you?"

"Yes—only I." Aurora wet her lips, clearly struggling for composure. "As you said, I'm a Huntley. Since you're obviously familiar with the history of the black diamond, you know that 'twas *my* great-grandfather who stole the gem. The Bencrofts hadn't an inkling—either then or now—where it was hidden."

"Aurora . . . don't . . ." Julian rasped. "Do what I said . . . run . . . get away from here."

"Shut up," Macall ordered him. He inclined his head at Aurora, reason trickling back into his gaze, replacing the wild-eyed insanity of a moment earlier. "You're asking me to believe that Merlin married you without ever questioning you about where the stone was?"

"Of course he questioned me—many times. That doesn't mean I answered his questions. There are all kinds of ways of keeping a man's interest, Mr. Macall."

A flicker of suspicion. "Fine. Then if Merlin doesn't know where the diamond is, I can kill him right now."

"No, you can't. Because if you do, I'll never tell you the location of the stone. You can beat me, defile me, even kill me. It won't weaken my will." She raised her chin. "Surely you didn't expect a man like Merlin to marry a fainthearted woman, did you?"

Macall swore quietly, jerking to his feet, dragging Julian up with him. "All right, where is it?"

"Let Julian go."

Curbing his fury, Macall drew a harsh breath, ostensibly considering her request. "Fine. I'll let him go—*after* you tell me where I can find the diamond."

"I want your word."

A mocking nod. "Very well, you have my word."

Aurora glanced briefly at Julian, their eyes meeting for a split second before she looked back at Macall. Cautiously she studied him, as if judging the sincerity of his vow. Then in a rush of decision, she blurted, "It's hidden in my dressing table at Julian's Polperro manor. My brother dug it up from where it was hidden in the woods at Pembourne and gave it to me on my wedding day. The agreement was that I would share the stone with my husband—after he'd proven his fidelity over a period of one year. Given Julian's restless nature and transient way of life, it seemed prudent to ensure that 'twas me and not my possession that had incited his marriage proposal."

"A cunning plan," Macall acknowledged, his expression probing. "Still, I can't imagine you'd just toss a stone as priceless as the black diamond in a drawer."

"I wouldn't and I didn't." Aurora gave him an indignant look. "I didn't *toss* the stone into the drawer; I *concealed* it there. The drawer is locked. So is the jewel case which lies within *and* which houses the black diamond. I buried the stone at the bottom of the case, beneath all my other valuable jewels."

"It would take a lot of necklaces and bracelets to hide a stone that size."

"I assure you, my collection is more than large enough to accomplish the task. You must know how wealthy my brother is. He's also exceptionally generous. Between the gifts he presented me and the heirlooms left me by my mother and grandmother, I've amassed quite an array of costly and elaborate pieces—not only numerous enough to conceal the black diamond, but valuable enough to make you a very rich man. Rich enough to justify sparing Julian's life."

Macall's eyes glittered at the prospect of acquiring such wealth. "You say the case is locked?"

"The case *and* the drawer. Each has but one key—I allowed no duplicates to be made."

"Where are these keys?"

"With me." She held up her reticule, gave it an indicative pat. "I keep them in my possession at all times."

"Show them to me."

"If I do, *then* will you release Julian?"

"Once I know they're genuine, yes." Macall stared eagerly at her bag, the tip of his sword easing slightly away from Julian's chest. "Now show me."

"All right." Aurora lowered her lashes, tugging open the reticule and reaching inside. "Here." She extracted first one key, then another, holding them up for his inspection.

"Throw them over here."

"But . . ."

"Throw them at my feet. I'll pick them up and examine them. If I'm convinced they're real, I'll let Merlin go."

With apparent reluctance, Aurora tossed the keys to the ground. They landed a foot shy of Macall's feet. "I'm sorry," she said, her voice quavering as at last her courage seemed to falter. "I'm just so nervous, I . . ."

"Never mind." Impatiently Macall stepped forward to retrieve the keys, thereby easing his sword farther away from its mark and, more significantly, forcing him to release his grasp on Julian's coat.

Julian slumped to the ground the instant Macall's supporting arm was removed.

Macall froze, looking from his captive to the keys, uncertain which prize to seize first.

Aurora eliminated his choice the instant his attention was diverted.

Yanking a pistol from her still-open reticule, she aimed, and without the slightest hesitation fired a shot directly at Macall's heart.

The privateer crumpled silently to the ground.

Silence ensued, descended heavily upon the alleyway.

Julian recovered first, his unfocused gaze assessing Macall's lifeless body. Fighting back unconsciousness, he crawled forward, shoving the sword aside and groping for Macall's wrist. "He's dead." He raised his head, staring dazedly at his wife as she slowly lowered her gun. "When did you . . . learn to fire a pistol?"

"Just now."

"Just now," he repeated inanely. "Whose . . .?"

"It's Slayde's," she answered, walking over and dropping to her knees beside her husband. "I took it from his desk. I'm sure he hasn't a clue it's missing. That drawer is kept locked." She gestured toward one of the discarded keys. "I believe that's the key that opens it."

Julian followed her motion, wondering if he were more incoherent than he realized or if this were actually happening. He reached for his wife—the resulting pain inciting a harsh groan and assuring him that this was indeed reality.

"Julian—don't," Aurora whispered, easing him over onto his back. "You're hurt badly." She groped in her reticule, pulled out a handkerchief, and pressed it to his throat. "See what happens when you don't wear a cravat?" she teased, tears gathering in her eyes.

"It's not . . . that bad . . ." He caught her wrist.

"Rory, how did you manage this? How did . . . you arrange . . .?"

"I knew Macall was after you. 'Twas only a matter of time. Stone all but told you to expect him at one of these taverns. So I came prepared." She swallowed, watching as Julian's blood soaked through her handkerchief. "I'm going to get help—armed with my pistol," she added, warding off his protest. "Don't argue. We must get you inside, treat that wound." Pausing, she leaned forward, capturing Julian's hand and pressing his palm to her lips. "I told you earlier, Merlin—I protect those I love. You're an adventurer. I'm an adventurer's wife. You safeguard what's yours. I safeguard what's mine. It's that simple."

Julian stared from Macall's dead body to his wife's beautiful face. "Damn," was all he said before he lost consciousness.

"Gin—next time, heat this bloody water!" Julian ordered, shoving at the chilly wetness against his throat. "I feel as if I'm bathing in the snow!"

"Ah, he lives," Aurora quipped, leaning against the table and saying a silent prayer. Those were the first two coherent sentences Julian had formed since she'd left him in the alley to race back to the Cove and beg for help.

Once again, it had been Barnes who'd come to her rescue, ordering two burly young sailors to carry Geoffrey Bencroft's great-grandson into the tavern.

Throughout his transport, even after he'd been stretched out across two chairs and left to his wife's ministrations, Julian hadn't opened his eyes.

"'E's lost a fair amount of blood," Barnes had consoled Aurora as she'd bathed the wound, held clean cloths against it to absorb the still-trickling blood. "That sword I saw them men carry in 'ere looked real fierce. It musta cut yer 'usband pretty deep. But the bleedin' seems to be slowin' down now. Don't worry. 'E'll mend."

Aurora was thankful that Barnes appeared to be right.

"No more," Julian protested, shoving at Aurora's hands. "I'll wash later—*after* you've heated the water."

"I'm glad to hear that," Aurora murmured, leaning over Julian and smoothing his hair off his forehead. "Unfortunately, your wound requires cold compresses, not hot. So you'll have to endure the chill."

Julian cracked open one eye, then the other. "Aurora?" He turned his head a bit, frowning as he focused on his surroundings, the wooden table he was beside, the two chairs that held him. "Where are we?" he questioned over the sounds of clinking glasses and chortling men.

"In the Cove. Tending to your wound."

Recollection surged forth like the tide. "Macall . . ." he bit out, jerking to a half-sitting position.

"It's over," Aurora said softly, easing her husband back down. "Macall is no longer a threat. He's dead. I believe his body's been disposed of." A shudder. "In truth, I didn't ask nor do I care. All that matters is you."

"So it really did happen," Julian murmured, gazing up at her, his expression intense as he assessed her state of mind.

"Yes, it happened." Aurora rinsed out the cloth, returned it to Julian's throat with shaking hands. "Mr. Barnes was kind enough to ask two of his friends to assist me. They carried you in, placed you in the quietest corner we could find, then left me to tend to you." A worried frown. "Your wound hasn't stopped bleeding yet. It's slowed considerably, but it hasn't stopped."

"Don't be upset by that." Julian reached up, his knuckles tenderly caressing her cheek. "The blade on Macall's sword was broad and thin . . ." He paused, drew a breath that was still slightly unsteady. "It was able to slash a fairly deep cut with very little effort. But he hadn't gotten down to the serious business of killing me yet, so no real harm was done." Ever so gently, Julian's thumb traced her lips. "Stop looking so worried. I'll be fine." He made an attempt to rise, then thought better of it, sinking back into the chair.

"Stay still," Aurora instructed.

He flashed her a weak smile. "I don't dare disobey. Not when you're so adept with your brother's pistol." His smile faded, his brows drawing together as he felt her hands tremble against his throat. *"Soleil,* you're very pale. Are you all right?"

She nodded. "He didn't harm me. Other than a stiff forearm, I'm fine."

"That's not what I meant." Julian's hand slid around to caress her nape in slow, soothing motions. "You just killed a man. That's a very courageous and difficult thing to do."

Aurora met her husband's gaze, tears glistening on her lashes. "Yes, I did. And I'd do it again in an instant if your life were at stake."

Profound emotion tightened Julian's features. "Barnes was right. I *am* a lucky man—lucky to have you, lucky to be alive . . ." He drew yet another shaky breath. "Perhaps even a merlin has its limits. Perhaps it's time I stopped tempting fate."

"Perhaps it's time you rested," Aurora countered in a quavering whisper. She lay her palm against Julian's jaw, her voice barely audible over the din. "I need to get more compresses, anyway. Mr. Barnes is still here. He seems to be taking his role as my guardian very seriously, not only by offering his aid, but by warning the other men to stay away from me. Thus far, they've all complied. So I can move about in relative safety. You, on the other hand, had best lie still, else I'll have one of those sailors stand guard over you. I won't have you jumping up and undoing all my hard work by reopening your wound and worsening the bleeding."

"Aurora—" Julian seized her hand before she could leave him, bringing her fingers to his lips. "Thank you. I'm grateful to know my life lies in such beautiful, capable hands."

"And I'm grateful you're alive—more grateful than I can say." Aurora broke off, seeking the right words to convey how terrified she'd been at the thought of losing him, how fervently she'd prayed that her determination would make up for her lack of skill. God, if that bullet had missed . . .

"It wouldn't have," Julian murmured, reading her mind. "You're too bloody good a shot."

"I never held a gun before in my life."

"Trust me, *soleil*. You're not a woman who needs teaching—at anything."

With a watery smile, Aurora leaned forward, brushed her lips to his. "I love you, Julian."

Rising, she made her way across the pub, skirting the tables and halting when she reached the counter. "Mr. Rawley?" she summoned the tavern keeper. "Excuse me, but may I have a few more clean towels?"

Rawley shot her a disgruntled look. "I already gave ye a half dozen."

"The wound was worse than I thought."

"Listen, lady." The tavern keeper slammed a goblet of ale to the counter, leaning over to stare belligerently at Aurora. "I've seen a lot worse in my time. In case ye 'aven't noticed, this ain't exactly London's West End. The only reason I even 'elped ye out this much is 'cause I took pity on ye. But the Cove's a pub, not a sick ward. So get yer 'usband up as quick as ye can, and get goin'."

"I intend to." Aurora tried to control her anger—and her nausea. The tavern keeper's breath was nearly as foul as his temper. Still, she needed his cooperation for a short while longer. And that meant holding her tongue. "Mr. Rawley, I apologize for disrupting your routine. I'd like nothing better than if Julian were well enough for us to take our leave. But that can't happen until his wound stops bleeding. It's slowed quite a bit. Another few compresses should do it. So if you'll just allow me a few more towels and just as many minutes, I'm sure we'll be able to accommodate your request."

"Fine—ye want towels? Get 'em yerself."

"I'd be happy to. Where are they?"

Rawley jerked his head toward the rear of the pub. "Back there. In the storage room."

"Thank you. You've been most kind." Veering sharply about, Aurora stalked off, weaving her way through the rows of tables, pausing only to wave at Barnes as she passed.

"Where're ye goin'?" he called out.

"To get more compresses. Mr. Rawley's busy," she returned as loudly as she could.

Skirting the tavern's furthermost table, she reached the area in question, frowning when she saw there were not one but two doors to choose from. One of them had to be the door she sought.

It wasn't the first. Yanking it open, she was greeted with a burst of cold night air, informing her that she'd come upon the back entrance to the pub. Fine—then it was the other door.

Pulling it open, Aurora breathed a sigh of relief as rows of boxes and piles of towels told her that this was indeed the storage room.

"'Ey, duchess, ye need 'elp?" one of the sailors at the last table yelled good-naturedly. "I'll take on Barnes *and* yer 'usband if ye'll take me in that storage room with ye."

"Yeah, sure ye will," the sailor beside him chortled, giving his friend a dubious look. "'Er 'usband's Merlin. Even 'urt, 'e'd be able to thrash ye. Forget Merlin's wife and drink yer ale."

Both men dissolved into laughter and tossed back their drinks.

Aurora shrugged off the good-humored teasing, stepping inside the chamber and gathering up a small pile of towels—she hoped enough to finish treating Julian's wound so they could go home.

With that goal in mind, she retraced her steps, shutting the storage room door and turning to leave.

The cold hard object that was jammed against her ribs changed her mind.

"Good evening, Aurora."

Her head jerked about as she recognized the familiar voice, and she peered over her shoulder, requiring confirmation that her assailant was indeed who she thought it was.

"Drop the towels, my dear," the Viscount Guillford said with a pleasant smile. "You're coming with me."

Chapter 14

The towels tumbled from Aurora's hands. "Viscount Guillford?" she gasped, paralyzed with shock.

"Shh, keep your voice down, my dear. We wouldn't want to alert your husband to my presence. Not when you've just gone to so much trouble to save his life." Guillford pressed the gun closer against her as a purposeful reminder. "I needn't tell you what harm this pistol can do. You discovered that for yourself firsthand, not a half hour ago. So just do as I say and you won't get hurt. Nor will Julian."

Aurora sucked in her breath, aching to cry out, to alert some of the sailors to her plight in the hopes of ending it. Yet she couldn't—wouldn't—risk their lives, her own, and certainly not Julian's, before discerning the viscount's state of mind. Was he insane? Angry? What in God's name was his motive for holding a pistol to her, threatening to kill her and Julian? Would he in fact carry out his threat—shoot her, then rush into the room and shoot others?

She had to find out. "What is it you want me to do?" she asked cautiously.

"Do?" he murmured. "Merely looked pleased to see me, speak to me as if we were having a most enjoyable chat, then walk out that rear entrance as if we were leaving together."

"But why . . .?"

"Do it." Another jab of the gun. "Unless you want me to finish what Macall began."

Aurora forced a smile to her lips, half-turning to face Guillford, only too conscious of the pistol shoved into her ribs. "Why, Viscount Guillford—what an unexpected surprise," she managed. "'Tis delightful to see you, my lord."

"Excellent," Guillford commended under his breath. "Now turn and walk through the open door."

Still numb with shock, she complied, marching silently into the darkness of night. "Where are you taking me?" she inquired, her hand casually shifting to her side as they descended the steps.

"Don't bother searching for your reticule. It's lying on the table beside your husband. Be grateful for that. Because I assure you, I'm a far better and more experienced shot than you. As for where we're going, you'll know soon enough."

Reaching the foot of the stairs, Aurora whipped about to face him, her initial shock supplanted by anger and confusion. "I refuse to take another step until you tell me where you're taking me, and why. You obviously followed us here; 'tis not exactly your type of establishment. And you obviously want something in exchange for me. What?"

A flicker of a smile crossed the viscount's patrician features, and he paused on the bottom step. "Perhaps retribution," he suggested softly. "Has that thought occurred to you?"

"Yes—and I dismissed it just as quickly. Because unless you have another reason for seeking vengeance— one of which I'm unaware—I refuse to believe you were so totally devastated by our severed betrothal that you'd resort to violence. So why are you dragging me off like a pirate's prize?"

"An interesting choice of words, and a most intelligent conclusion." Guillford's smile faded, and he gestured toward the path with his pistol. "Both of which I'd be happy to address—*after* we're ensconced in my carriage and on our way. By the way, don't defy me again or test the limits to which I'd be willing to go. I assure you, I'm far more dangerous to you than Macall ever was. I have nothing to lose and everything to gain. So don't toy with me. Walk." He shoved her forward with his pistol, propelling her away from the Cove.

Instantly Mr. Scollard's words, his fervent warning, sprang to Aurora's mind: *Don't underestimate the dangers that await, from sources expected and unknown. They lurk in numbers, and in numbers must be undone. Greed is a great propellant. Vengeance wields more power still. And desperation is the most menacing by far, for it offers reward with no risk.*

Wisps of dread converged into abhorrent realization. The lighthouse keeper had been alerting her and Julian to the fact that not one, but two enemies loomed ahead to be faced: first Macall and then Guillford. Macall was the expected source, the one propelled by greed and vengeance.

Making Guillford the unknown danger, propelled by a desperation he himself had just described: he had nothing to lose and everything to gain—or, as Mr. Scollard had phrased it, reward with no risk.

But why? Based upon what? What had made Lord

Guillford so desperate that he'd resort to kidnapping, maybe even murder to attain his goal?

Don't underestimate the dangers, Rory . . . Mr. Scollard's voice seemed to urge. *Don't* . . .

That intangible reminder was enough to dissuade Aurora from pursuing the explanation she sought, at least for now. Later, she'd uncover her answers. First she had to escape.

Abruptly she came to a halt, sucking in air and weaving on her feet. "Wait," she managed. "I think I'm going to . . ."

"The only thing you're going to do is march toward the path," Guillford returned coldly, seizing her arm and pushing her along. "You're no more about to swoon than I am. If murdering a man doesn't render you squeamish, I doubt a mere abduction will. As I said, don't toy with me. Stop stalling for time. It won't work." He saw her start of surprise. "Did you think I wasn't aware of what you were doing? Never underestimate me, my dear. You might be a very bright and resourceful young woman, but I am a brighter and more resourceful man. Now hurry over to the path. My carriage is waiting just beyond those trees."

"So I was right—you are kidnapping me."

"Correction. I already have."

"For what reason?" she demanded.

Guillford's only response was to quicken their pace, shoving Aurora farther from the Cove and deeper into some ominous unknown danger.

Uneasiness tightened Julian's gut.

Aurora had been gone far too long to still be collecting towels.

Slowly he raised his head, testing the limits of his own endurance. The room spun for a moment, then righted itself. He swung his legs to the floor and pushed himself to a standing position. Another wave of dizziness claimed him, then subsided. Tossing the stained towel at his neck to the chair, he walked into the middle of the room, scanning the pub for Aurora.

No sign of her.

A bit unsteadily, he made his way to the counter, signaling Rawley over. "Where's my wife?"

"Good, yer better. Look's like the bleedin's stopped. Now ye can go home." The tavern keeper took one look at Julian's murderous expression and softened his words. "Maybe ye and the missus would like an ale before ye go? It'd do ye a world of . . ."

"Where is my wife?" Julian thundered.

Rawley backed off a half-dozen steps. "She wanted towels for yer wound. I sent 'er to the storage room to get 'em."

"You sent her alone?" Julian saw red. "Are you insane? What if one of your filthy patrons . . . ?" He broke off, squelching his rage. Choking this unfeeling bastard to death would only take time away from what mattered most: finding Aurora—a goal that was becoming increasingly more urgent by the second, given her conspicuous absence and the intensifying knot in his gut. "Where's the storage room?"

"Back there." Rawley pointed.

Wound and dizziness forgotten, Julian barreled his way through the pub, nearly knocking sailors down in his haste. He reached the rear of the tavern, noted the open door leading to the outdoors, and thrust his head out.

The littered grounds behind the tavern were deserted.

Veering about, Julian ripped open the storage room door, nearly tearing it from its hinges, and stepped inside.

No Aurora.

" 'Ey, Merlin, she left already," one of the sailors at the last table called out. "I guess this place finally got to 'er."

"Left?" Julian's insides wrenched. "When? Where?"

" 'Bout five minutes ago. Through that there door.

With one of yer kind. Real blue-blood type. Guess 'e gave 'er a ride 'ome."

Julian stalked over, grabbing the sailor's shirt and lifting him half off his chair. "Tell me what this man looked like. What he said. What my wife said. Anything you can remember."

"Sure," the red-faced sailor squeaked out. "But I don't think ye need to worry. She seemed real 'appy to see this fella."

"Yeah, she did," the other sailor concurred, nodding and scratching his beard. "She smiled and talked to 'im like they was good friends."

"Bencroft? What's goin' on?" It was Barnes, his weathered face creased with concern as he hobbled over. "Where's yer bride? Last time I saw 'er, she was gettin' ye some towels."

"That's what I'm trying to find out," Julian replied. "These men say Aurora left with someone."

"Left?" Barnes echoed in disbelief. "She'd never leave without ye."

"I know." Julian glowered at the sailor whose collar he grasped. "Talk to me," he demanded, giving the man a shake.

The sailor emitted a gasp, indicating that Julian's grip was choking him.

Shakily Julian lowered him to his seat, striving for control. "Tell me what you know."

"All right." He sucked in air. "Let's see—'e was tall, dressed real good. Kinda lean, not muscular, if ye know what I mean. Sharp features, dark hair. Yer duchess called 'im m'lord."

"She called 'im somethin' else, too," the bearded fellow added. "Before she dropped the towels and left with 'im. Viscount somethin' or other—pill or will—no! Gill, that's what it was. Viscount Gill-somethin'!"

"Viscount Gill-something," Julian repeated, the logical and heinous piece falling into place. "Guillford?"

"Yeah, that was it! Is 'e a friend of yers?"

Julian didn't answer. He was already halfway to the back door.

"Bencroft, wait!" Barnes called out. "Yer too weak to go after this fella by foot. Rawley's 'orse is tied out back. Take 'im. I'll deal with Rawley."

With a grateful wave, Julian rushed outside, bounding down the steps and around to the corner of the building, his own light-headedness forgotten. He had to rescue Aurora.

The mare was tied to a beam alongside the pub, just as Barnes had said. Freeing the reins, Julian vaulted into the saddle and took off toward the path, surveying the area as he rode.

He heard the hoofbeats echo from farther up the path.

Eyes narrowed, Julian peered into the darkness, spying the moving outline of an open carriage heading away from the Cove.

Its driver was tall and lean. Its passenger was small and slight.

A shaft of moonlight illuminated her hair as the carriage veered around a bend, revealing its red-gold color and heightening it to that of a burnished flame.

Digging his heels into the mare's flanks, Julian took off in pursuit of his wife.

"Now, what questions can I answer for you?" Guillford inquired, steering the phaeton along the winding road, the pistol close by his side, lest Aurora make any attempt to escape.

Aurora studied his profile, wondering if he were totally composed or thoroughly insane. "I have dozens of questions. Beginning with: What do you want? Why are you kidnapping me? How do you know of Macall? Where are you taking me?" She drew a breath. "Shall I continue?"

Guillford looked distinctly amused. "That won't be

necessary. I must admit, Aurora, you intrigue me. Had we wed, I believe you would have kept me thoroughly entertained. Taming you, however, that would have been a far more difficult task. Still, it might have been worth it. Your fire in my bed, your wealth in my keeping—perhaps I should have overlooked your indiscretion with Julian Bencroft and married you, tainted or not. The *ton* might have frowned, but only for a time. Eventually they would have forgotten the circumstances surrounding our marriage. Then I could have had it all."

"That doesn't answer my questions," Aurora retorted, ignoring his absurd fantasy. "Other than perhaps, the 'why.' Is it all for money?"

"Isn't everything? 'Tis either money or passion. And if you ask me, the former is far more valuable than the latter—and much harder to attain. But then, some men are fortunate enough to have both. Men like Julian Bencroft. Julian Bencroft and your brother, Slayde."

"Slayde?" Aurora started. "Where does Slayde fit into all this?"

"He's a Huntley. A wealthy, successful—damned lucky Huntley. That's how he fits into all this."

"You do business with him."

A harsh chuckle. "No, in this case, *he* does business with *me*. Or rather, *for* me. I reap a profit, he loses an investment. It works out quite nicely."

"I don't understand."

"Then let me explain. Did Slayde mention that splendid stallion I brought to his attention at our meeting the other day? 'Twas the reason I was at Pembourne—that, and to assess what I could learn about the whereabouts of that bloody black diamond."

The whereabouts of the black diamond? Aurora's head began swimming as she assimilated the viscount's words, more questions forming, tumbling over each other to be heard. But she stifled them, sensing that the only way to acquire her answers was to let the viscount maneuver their conversation in whatever direction he chose—beginning with the thoroughbred he planned to buy. "If I remember correctly, Slayde said you were interested in purchasing the stallion but couldn't, given that your assets were tied up elsewhere," she replied. "So he agreed to put up the money, then collect whatever profits were necessary to earn back his investment. After which you'd split all future profits equally."

"Ah, but the real truth is that your brother's investment will in fact become my profit the instant he places that draft in my hand."

"You're saying you have no intention of purchasing the horse."

"Quick as ever, my dear. And quite right. I plan to purchase nothing other than the cooperation of a greedy stable owner, whose allegiance costs but a few wretched pounds. My instructions to him will be as follows: should the Earl of Pembourne appear at his stables asking to have a look at our joint venture, show it to him—making sure he has no reason to doubt that the incomparable stallion does indeed belong to the two of us."

"What of the supposed winnings the stallion will earn?"

"Oh, the spirited fellow needs a breaking-in period, followed by weeks of training. He won't be ready to race for well over a month, which is more than enough time to keep your brother in the dark. After all, you and I both know Slayde is glued to his wife's side until the birth of their babe. By the time your brother becomes even mildly curious about the status of our investment, I'll have acquired a king's ransom from which I can easily pay him back—thanks to you."

Thanks to me? Aurora mused silently. *That certainly reeks of blackmail.* She inclined her head, studying the shadowed lines of Guillford's profile, the rigid set of his jaw. *Careful,* she cautioned herself. *Follow his lead. 'Tis the only way to learn all I can.* "So in effect, you're planning to steal Slayde's money—at least temporarily. Why? What is it you plan to do with it?"

"Extricate myself from debt."

Aurora's jaw dropped. "Debt? With your wealth?"

"My onetime wealth," Guillford corrected bitterly. "I'd hoped that between Camden's soliciting skills and Slayde's ready money, I could repay my creditors and regain a portion of my depleted fortune—the sum total of which is virtually impossible to recoup without benefit of the black diamond, thanks to Julian Bencroft."

"So that's why you were with Mr. Camden when we visited him," Aurora murmured. "You were seeking his help to . . ." She broke off, her chin coming up as the final part of Guillford's statement sank in. "Julian? Where does Julian fit into all this?"

"Your husband has undone every bloody thing I've attempted, from seizing that painting out from under me to snatching away my sole chance of acquiring the black diamond—you."

Aurora sucked in her breath, unable to restrain herself any longer. "That's the third time you've made reference to the black diamond. First you said that discovering its whereabouts was one of your reasons for coming to Pembourne the other day. Then you said you needed it to recoup your fortune. And now you've implied that I would have been your link to the stone. Am I to conclude I've just stumbled upon the true reason you asked for my hand—because you believed Lawrence Bencroft's ludicrous claim that the Huntleys truly did possess the black diamond? Is that why you were so devastated when my indiscretion made it impossible for you to wed me?"

"Of course. But don't make me sound such a cad. 'Tis also the reason why your beloved Julian compromised you to the point where you had no choice but to marry him." Guillford shot her a sidelong glance, his eyes glittering as he perceived her disbelief. "Come now,

Aurora. Don't let whatever feelings you have for your husband blind you to the truth. Your Julian knew just what he was doing when he took you to bed in that seedy pub. Just as he knew what he was doing when he publicly retracted his father's claim—which he did only after Lawrence's death when the inebriated fool could no longer defend himself—and only after securing your hand in marriage. That put a quick end to the widespread search that had recommenced as a result of Lawrence's accusation. *And* it ensured that the black diamond remained right where Julian wanted it: with his prospective bride, whose assets have now become his. The question is, where is the stone now? Did the wretched mercenary stash it at his manor in Polperro? Or did the two of you hide it somewhere, bury it away so as to safeguard it from scoundrels such as myself?"

Pieces were falling into place like rapid cannon fire. "When Julian and I left Pembourne for Morland—you were the one following us," Aurora realized aloud. "You thought we were en route to the black diamond, to either conceal or unearth it."

"So your husband *did* sense my presence. I was afraid of that when I saw him head for Morland Manor rather than continuing your journey to wherever the diamond is hidden."

"We weren't going . . ." Aurora stopped herself. There was no point in trying to convince the man; he was clinging too tightly to his groundless obsession. Besides, another implication spawned by his earlier statement was plaguing her too fiercely to ignore any longer. "A painting . . ." she muttered. "You said Julian seized a painting out from under you. What painting?"

"An incredibly valuable one. One that would have reversed my run of bad luck, restored my former way of life—my wealth, my stature. Why, I could have sold that treasure for ten times what I paid those two small-minded privateers to uncover it. Stupid fools. They uncovered the painting, all right—just as planned. But before they could transport it home and deliver it into my eager hands, the ever-scrupulous Merlin swooped down, confiscated the painting—to return it to its rightful owner, of course—and killed one of my men in the process. Damn Julian Bencroft. Damn those stupid fools for not being able to outwit him. And damn me for making the same mistake twice, hiring the surviving dolt yet again—this time to kill Bencroft and usurp the black diamond. I should have learned by now that to accomplish something of that magnitude, I can rely upon only one person—myself."

Aurora's hands were trembling violently in her lap, her worst suspicions confirmed. "The Macalls," she breathed. "Gerald and Brady Macall worked for you. You were the person who paid them ten months ago, sent them to Paris to abscond with that painting."

The viscount's brows were arched in surprise. "My, my. Your husband certainly has filled you in on a great deal of his colorful life, hasn't he? Now, that surprises me. From what I understand, the infamous Merlin is ever the loner, discussing no details of his adventures with anyone—or at least such was the case until now." A malevolent smile. "Excellent. He's even more smitten with you than I realized. That should bode well for my plan."

"You paid Gerald Macall to kill Julian," Aurora bit out, her insides churning with rage. "You're the reason that filthy pirate held a sword to my husband's throat and drew his blood."

"I wish I could take full credit for Macall's fervent resolve. But I can't. Macall wanted your husband dead as badly as I did—more so, from a personal perspective. He was avenging the loss of his brother, while I was avenging the less intimate but far more significant losses of my money, my future, and my reputation. Nevertheless Macall was a poor choice for me to have made. He's reckless and irrational. 'Tis just as well that you killed him; it forced me to do what I should have from the start: emerge from the shadows, take control, and wrest from Bencroft what I want—what's owed me."

"You're more insane than Macall."

"Am I?" Guillford swerved the carriage along the curves of the darkened road. "Tell me that when I've acquired all I seek. Which brings me to the answer to your original question: why have I kidnapped you? The answer is twofold. First, to procure vengeance—I want Julian Bencroft to suffer for what he did to me. And as you appear to be his first and only weakness, my holding your life in my hands—deciding whether to prolong it or dash it—will take care of that part quite nicely. And second, to acquire the splendid ransom I shall attain in exchange for agreeing to spare you—the one and only black diamond."

But you won't spare me, Aurora refuted silently. *I know too much; letting me live would be ensuring your own downfall. Moreover, if I realize that, Julian will realize it, too.*

Which means he'll be frantic to get to me, she reflected with a mixture of relief and terror. *Knowing him, he's probably on his way right now—his wound be damned.*

Fighting the urge to look back over her shoulder, Aurora asked Guillford, "May I know where you're taking me?"

"Certainly." Guillford pointed toward the west. "We'll ride beyond Falmouth until the roads become too steep for my phaeton. At which point, we'll abandon the carriage and take the remaining distance to the black-scarred cliffs by foot."

"We're going to the Lizard Peninsula?" Aurora gasped, real fear knotting her gut. "But that's . . ."

"That's . . . what?" Guillford taunted, clearly enjoying the fact that he'd unnerved her. "Hours away? Reachable only by traveling wretched excuses for roadways in the dead of night? Or were you about to say that the black cliffs are the steepest and most terrifying in all of Cornwall?"

"I was only surprised by the distance you intended to travel." Aurora forced her voice to remain calm, reflecting none of the dread that knotted her gut. "Especially by night. As for the roads, I've never traveled them, nor have I ever seen the cliffs. I know only that they're miles away. So I couldn't say whether they're terrifying or not."

"I keep forgetting how sheltered Slayde's kept you all these years, sequestered away at Pembourne like some fairy-tale princess. Well, my dear, before dawn you'll be getting a firsthand look at a savage section of the Cornish coast that's caused more death and destruction than I can recount."

"It sounds fascinating." Aurora looked away, Mr. Scollard's legends about the black cliffs running rampant through her mind: seamen flung overboard during brutal winter storms only to be engulfed by waves or dashed in the rocky coves; ships swallowed up by the mist or capsized by untamed currents; entire crews dragged under, never to be seen again.

She tried to push the dark stories from her mind, to focus on Mr. Scollard's more fanciful tales of the region—tales of mermaids and treasures, exciting rescues and booty. But somehow she couldn't—not this time. This time, all she could feel was a horrible sense of foreboding.

"Incidentally," Guillford added, urging the horses around a particularly sharp curve. "As I said, soon after we reach the peninsula, we'll be abandoning the carriage and traveling by foot—a perilous walk, to say the least. Between that and the formidable drive we're now undertaking, I'd abandon any thoughts of rescue. Your husband might be determined, but he's also wounded. Even if he's already realized that you're missing and somehow managed to come after us, he won't last beyond the first mile." A quick glance behind them. "I see no one now. But even if I'm wrong, even if Bencroft is following covertly in our wake, his pursuit will soon be ended. The two of you came to Fowey by boat. That means he'll have to pursue us by foot, since he doesn't dare take the time to seek out a horse or carriage. Given the fact that he can scarcely lift his head, how long do you think it will take him to pass out from exertion and loss of blood?"

Aurora kept her head averted, squeezing her eyes shut to block out the viscount's words . . . not only their truth, but the image they evoked: Julian unconscious, lying in the road, bleeding and alone.

Instinctively her hand closed around the scrap of gold encircling her finger, deriving inexplicable comfort from touching the cool surface of the ring that proclaimed her Julian's wife.

Besieged by worry, she prayed.

Dawn's first rays were slicing the horizon as Lord Guillford propelled Aurora up the rough path leading through the black cliffs. It had been miles since he'd dragged her from the phaeton, urged her along at gunpoint. Her body ached with exhaustion, her head pounded with worry over Julian's fate—and her own. Yet she forced herself to push onward, praying for a miracle.

Thus far, none had arrived.

She paused, tearing her skirts free of a protruding rock—the dozenth in as many steps. Her slippers were worn, her gown shredded, and Guillford and his pistol were mere inches behind her.

"How much farther must we go?" she panted, blowing damp strands of hair off her face.

"Until I say otherwise," Guillford returned icily, jabbing the pistol against her back.

Aurora glanced back over her right shoulder to assess

Guillford's condition—intentionally avoiding the dramatic coastal view to her left by doing so. If she allowed herself to explore that angle, to gaze downward at the jutting rocks and swirling waters below, she'd be sick.

"Don't build any false hopes that I'm going to collapse with fatigue." With a hard motion, the viscount yanked at his cravat, loosening the still meticulously tied knot. "I devised this plan weeks ago in the event Macall failed me. Therefore, I've already walked this entire path—not only to test my endurance but to locate the perfect cove to act as your temporary home. Both efforts proved successful. Now, move."

A twinge of hope—the first in seven hours—flickered in Aurora's heart as she continued on her way, teetering a bit as she ascended one of the cliff's ragged precipices. She wasn't surprised by the viscount's thoroughness; he was an exacting man by nature, most assuredly when his entire future was at stake. But now she knew something she hadn't before: he didn't intend to kill her immediately. Instead he meant to leave her here, presumably while he returned to Fowey, notified Julian of her plight, and bartered for her life. And while the thought of being abandoned here was frightening, it was infinitely more appealing than the alternative. Plus it might buy her some time, give her a fighting chance to escape.

Guillford's next words dashed that filament of hope.

"Lost in thought? Well, consider this: I don't trust you, Aurora. You're too damned resourceful. Thus, I won't be leaving you alone for too long—only long enough for me to travel to Falmouth and dispatch a missive to your husband. During that time, you'll be bound and gagged. When I return, I'll remove your bonds and—perhaps—give you a bit of food and water. I'd prefer to keep you alive and well until I get word from your husband, which should occur tonight."

Aurora paused. "How will Julian know where to contact you?"

"He won't. Nor will he ever know my identity, not if he hopes to live. My anonymous missive will advise him of my terms—specifically, to turn over the black diamond in exchange for your life. It will also instruct him when and where he's to leave the stone and, of course, collect you—a well-chosen location, incidentally, that's several shires away from here. As for how my missive will reach him, I've hired a most eager and discreet messenger who will track your Julian down and await his reply, then ride directly to Falmouth to convey that response to me."

"So you'll be returning to Falmouth after dark?"

"Yes. And once again, you'll be bound and gagged in your little cove. If things go as I expect, Julian's message will be an agreement to my terms. After all, what choice does he have? He certainly won't sacrifice your life, not even for the black diamond."

"But my life is already sacrificed, is it not? It was the minute I learned who my abductor was."

"Sadly enough, that's true. Julian will deliver the stone, but he won't be receiving his bride in return."

Aurora swallowed. "How do you plan to kill me?"

"That, my dear, depends on you. As I said, I don't trust you. On the other hand, I'm not an excessively violent man. So if you behave during my two trips to Falmouth, if you attempt nothing foolish, I'll go the merciful route and simply leave you to your fate."

"Which means flinging me, bound and gagged, in an isolated cove where I'll either suffocate or starve. How generous."

" 'Tis far more pleasant than the alternative, I assure you," Guillford said in a steely tone. "Because if you're difficult, if you make any stupid efforts to escape—including now—then I'll be forced to toss you over the edge of the cliff, to be dashed on the rocks below." He leaned forward, fingered one disheveled red-gold tress.

"Which would be a terrible waste for one as beautiful as you."

"Don't touch me," Aurora said quietly, yanking away her hair and walking forward.

He followed close behind, his sardonic chuckle chilling her blood. "How principled you've suddenly become. And at such an odd time. We're discussing your death and you're worrying about your virtue. Curious indeed. Well, fear not. While the thought of having you is tempting, I'm far more interested in your money than I am in your body—beautiful or not. Just remember what I said. How you die is up to you."

Again Aurora paused, this time pivoting to face her adversary. "I could refuse to cooperate. After all, you've just told me I'm to die no matter what. Why should I not just remain here, insist you shoot me where I stand?"

"Because my bullet would only inflict great pain rather than death," Guillford returned, his mouth thinning with anger. "I'd make sure of that. In fact, I'd make sure you were fully conscious and alert when you plunged over the edge of the cliff. Tell me, Aurora, are you that brave?" He strode forward, gripping her face and forcing it around and down, until her gaze swept the ragged coastline. "Are you?"

Peering downward, Aurora felt bile rise in her throat. The entire section of cliffs upon which they stood jutted out over the water, angled into a drop that meant instant death. Far below, the currents rushed wildly about, crashing into jagged boulders, lapping against towering columns of stone that loomed on every side, menacing in their domination.

God help her, she was too afraid to die this way.

Raising her head, Aurora stared off into the distance, spying the faraway peaks defining the western tip of Cornwall. *Land's End,* she mused vaguely, glimmers of Mr. Scollard's legends filtering through her mind.

Oh, Mr. Scollard, how I need you now, she reflected wistfully, realizing for the first time that she might never see her old friend again. *I need your wisdom. I need your faith. And dear God, I need Julian.*

In that instant, her gaze was captured by a faint object situated on a tiny island just off the coast of Land's End.

A lighthouse.

Graceful, tall, the stone structure brushed the newly lit skies with its presence, beckoning whoever craved its presence.

And oh, how Aurora craved.

Was it just her imagination or did the building much resemble her beloved Windmouth Lighthouse?

As if in answer, a tiny light flashed in the lighthouse tower. Just once—so fleeting one would hardly notice. Then it vanished.

Mr. Scollard, is that you? Aurora begged silently. *Are you telling me all hope is not lost?*

Another glimmer of light, fleeting—perfect.

Aurora had her answer.

Giving unspoken thanks, she regathered her strength, called upon her faltering reserves. So long as she was surrounded by her friend, his renewing faith, there was still hope a miracle might occur.

"Have you contemplated the scenery long enough?" Guillford demanded, his fingers digging into her cheeks. "Or do you require a closer view?"

"No," she replied with apparent submission. "I don't require a closer view. You're right—I don't want to die in such a horrid manner. I'm ready to continue our walk."

"Excellent." The viscount released her, gesturing a short distance away with the barrel of the gun. "We have only to go a bit farther—to the top of this peak. The cove is around back, a carefully hidden niche in the stone."

Aurora followed his gesture, noting that their goal was indeed nearby. Flanked by two towering cliffs, the top of the peak was narrow, the space separating it from the larger peaks narrower still.

"The path is quite cramped as it rounds back," Guillford announced. "Only one of us can pass at a time. I was a bit concerned about letting you out of my sight, even for those few seconds—but my concerns were put to rest by the little talk we just had. However, heed what I said and don't do anything foolish."

"I won't."

"Good. Now move." Another hard jab of his pistol.

Raising her chin, Aurora marched onward, taking the forty or fifty paces to the top of the ridge, then flattening herself against it, easing her way around the specified curve.

For a split second she was out of Guillford's reach.

It was enough time for her miracle to occur.

A flash of movement plummeted from the cliff overhead, small stones pelting the path as a dark figure crashed down, landing precisely where Aurora had stood not an instant earlier.

She heard Lord Guillford's shout of pain and surprise, and without hesitating, she scooted back around the curve, her eyes widening as they confirmed what her heart already knew.

Julian.

Having knocked Guillford down, he was in the process of kicking aside the viscount's pistol, sending it sailing across the ground.

The Merlin had struck.

"Get the gun, Aurora," Julian yelled the instant he spied her. "Shoot him."

Reflexively Aurora complied, rushing over and scooping up the pistol, positioning herself as Julian and Guillford rolled away, pounding at each other. Jaw set, she aimed, fully intending to put a bullet straight through Guillford's heart.

The problem was, he was not only a moving target, he

was entangled with the man she loved. The slightest error and she could fatally wound Julian.

She couldn't risk it. She had to wait.

The two men were a blur, a violent surge of pummeling fists and frenzied motions.

"Not this time, damn you," Guillford gasped, smashing his fist into Julian's jaw and propelling him to one side. "This time I'm going to win. This time you're going to die."

"You miserable bastard." Julian lunged for him again, slamming Guillford to his back, punching him once, twice, murder raging in his eyes. "When I think of what you intended for Aurora . . ." Another fervent punch.

Guillford groaned, turning his head wildly from side to side to evade the assault, then jerking upward, his forearm finding and connecting with the wound at Julian's throat.

Julian recoiled and doubled up with pain, and Guillford seized his opportunity, shoving Julian off him . . . sending him closer to the edge of the cliff. Then, he pounced, grabbing handfuls of Julian's shirt and dragging him toward what was obviously meant to be his death.

Aurora's warning scream froze on her lips as Julian retaliated, breaking Guillford's grip and sending him sprawling to the ground with one hard hurl.

Seeing her chance, Aurora aimed, but before she could fire, Guillford roared to life, coming to his feet and charging forward, clearly intending to thrust Julian over the edge.

Impassively Julian watched the viscount's approach, making no move to evade him—and thereby shattering whatever remained of Aurora's self-control.

"Julian!" she shrieked, terror cutting through her in rampant streaks.

It was too late. Guillford was upon him.

In a flash Julian acted, rolling directly toward Guillford, slamming the full force of his weight against the viscount's legs.

Thrown into motion, Guillford was catapulted forward. Briefly he grazed the edge of the cliff, grabbing wildly at nothingness. Then he went over—plunging downward, his piercing scream echoing through the cliffs, gradually fading away as it was swallowed up by the rushing currents.

A heartbeat of silence.

Abruptly Julian bolted to his feet, stalking over to Aurora and dragging her into his arms. "Tell me you're all right," he commanded.

The pistol slid to the ground and Aurora nodded, gazing up at Julian as if to verify that he was indeed here, safe, as was she. "I'm fine," she managed shakily, reaching up to touch his face, to lay her palm against his jaw. "Especially now that you're holding me. Oh, Julian, I thought you were . . . that he had . . ." Two tears slid down her cheeks. "That I was about to lose you."

"You'll never lose me." A fierce light ignited her husband's eyes. "Not now—not ever." He gathered her close, pressed her head to his chest. "I love you," he proclaimed, his voice tight, his lips buried in her hair. "God, how I love you."

Chapter 15

They spent all that day and night at a Falmouth inn—
first replenishing their bodies with food, then bathing
away the dirt and horrors of the past hours, and—
finally, finally—climbing into the warm, soft bed.

"This is heaven," Aurora murmured, sinking into the
mattress with a grateful sigh.

"No," Julian murmured, drawing her naked body
against his. *"This* is heaven." He caressed the delicate
line of her spine, his hands gliding down to cup her
bottom, lifting her against his straining manhood. "I
should let you sleep," he admitted, kissing her shoulders,
her neck, her throat. "But I can't. I need you. God, I
almost lost you." He threaded his fingers through her
hair, tugged back her head, and buried his lips in hers.

"We can sleep later." Aurora twined her arms about
Julian's neck, understanding and sharing his need to
reaffirm their life, their love. "Much later."

He kissed her deeply, hungrily, possessing her mouth

with bone-melting thoroughness and an equal amount of tenderness. "Are you sure you're all right?" he demanded between kisses. "That son of a bitch didn't hurt you, did he?"

"No, he didn't hurt me." Aurora's palms slid to Julian's shoulders, eased him away so she could gaze directly into his eyes. "As for how I am, I'd be totally renewed if you'd repeat those three wonderful words you said to me on the cliff."

A spasm of emotion crossed Julian's face, passion temporarily supplanted by something deeper, more profound. "Gladly," he said, his voice husky with emotion. "I love you. You can't know how much. God help me, even *I* didn't fathom how much—until this morning." He swallowed, cradling her face between his palms. "I've been a bloody fool, telling myself I was the same man I was a month ago; that I could control how much I allowed you to permeate my existence, my heart—that I even wanted to try. The truth is, my entire life changed the minute you walked into Dawlish's that night—*I* changed. And I wouldn't undo that change for all the world's adventures combined."

Tears glistened on Aurora's lashes. "When did you realize you loved me?"

"Yesterday while you were sleeping in my arms in the sitting room. But I wanted to wait, to tell you when I could savor the words, savor you. Then, that bastard kidnapped you . . ." Julian broke off, a muscle working in his jaw. "You have no idea how terrified I was. If I hadn't found you in time . . ."

"But you did," she interjected softly. "Deep down, I knew you would. Although how you managed, given your wound . . ." Her fingertips traced the narrow bandage at his throat.

"My wound is fine," Julian assured her, capturing her hand and bringing it to his lips. "Just a bit raw. As I told you, it was only a flesh wound. It stopped bleeding minutes after you went to collect the towels. But nothing short of death would have stopped me from going after you. As for how I managed, I borrowed Rawley's mare and rode as far as St. Austell, where I changed horses."

"How could you have taken time for that and still kept on our trail?"

"I know the terrain of Cornwall, *soleil.*" Julian kissed her wrist, his lips trailing up her forearm to the curve of her elbow. "Especially the woods and the inland hills, where one can travel by horse but not by carriage. I was actually ahead of you at one point. I also have quite a few contacts—one of whom has a stable in St. Austell. He gave me his swiftest mount and his assurance that Rawley's mare would be returned. When I realized where Guillford was dragging you, I rode on ahead, left my horse in Falmouth, and took a more direct route by foot, from Helston to the black cliffs. After that, it was only a matter of following you from the peaks above, and waiting."

"But . . ."

"Aurora," Julian interrupted, nuzzling the scented hollow at her throat. "We have a hundred things yet to discuss. And we will—later. But right now—" He raised his head, letting her see the naked urgency in his eyes. "—I've got to be inside you, to feel you all around me, to know you're here alive, safe in my arms. Can you understand that, *soleil?*"

Wordlessly Aurora nodded, drawing Julian's mouth down to hers.

He'd made to love to her countless times before, but never like this.

Solemn, intense, he worshiped every inch of her, his hands shaking as he caressed her, touched her with a reverence that obliterated all the day's ugliness and transformed it to beauty, warming their souls and heightening their passion tenfold.

Aurora's eyes slid shut, her nerve endings throbbing with excitement, clamoring for more.

Julian gave it to her—with his hands, his words, his mouth.

By the time he entered her, Aurora was frantic, her body on fire, her breath coming in wild, broken pants. "Please," she whispered, tugging at his shoulders. "Julian, please . . ."

"No earthly force could stop me," he rasped, his knees pressing her thighs wide apart.

Cupping her face between his hands, he crowded into her, letting her feel every glorious sensation as their bodies melded into one. "Aurora—look at me," he commanded, waiting until she'd complied before beginning the deep, slow rhythm she craved, rolling his hips in a way that drove him deeper, higher inside her each time. "Now tell me you love me."

Aurora was already unraveling, her legs tightly hugging Julian's flanks. "Oh, Julian—I love you."

His entire body shuddered at her words, sweat breaking out on his forehead. But he battled back his climax, refusing to let this moment end, refusing to tear his gaze from hers. "And I love you," he declared hoarsely. "My heart is yours, *soleil*. Always." He pushed into her, sealing his vow with the exquisite utter possession of her body.

A harsh cry escaped Aurora's lips, the pleasure too acute to bear. "Oh, God . . . Julian." Her body clenched frantically around his.

"Yes." He could barely speak. "Just like that—yes." He drove into her again, then again, his urgency splintering his control into fragments of nothingness.

"Don't stop."

"I won't . . . I can't . . ."

"Julian . . ."

"Yes, *soleil*—" He thrust forward one last time and

held himself there, jaw clenched against the vortex of sensation that was peaking inside him, pounding through them both.

"Julian!" Aurora screamed and shattered. Clinging to her husband, she dissolved into wrenching spasms of completion, feeling his answering tremor, the urgent swelling of his body inside hers.

With a feral shout Julian erupted, shuddering convulsively as he poured himself into her, the force of his release sending him surging forward again and again until he'd given her all of himself.

With a choked sound of awe, he collapsed, blanketing her with his weight, tremors of reaction still coursing through him. "My God—I want to give you the world," he managed, wonder lacing his tone.

As awed as he, Aurora caressed the bunched muscles of his shoulders, the damp planes of his back. "You already have," she whispered. "You've given me you. Oh, Julian, I knew you felt as I did. But I needed *you* to know it—and to say it."

"I know it to the depths of my soul. As for saying it . . ." Julian rose up but made no move to lift himself away, somehow needing to entwine the life-altering words around the magic they'd just made with their bodies. "I love you, Aurora Bencroft. I have from the moment you walked into Dawlish's. I will until the sun grows cold."

Aurora smiled through her tears. "I'll offer you a lifetime of passion, excitement and adventure—I promise."

"That I don't even question, much less doubt. In fact, I'm so certain your fire and spirit will pervade my life that I've made a decision. My days of solitary adventuring are over."

Her eyes widened. "Do you mean that?"

"I do." He rubbed one silky tress between his fingers.

"You, my love, are all the excitement I can handle. From now on, all our ventures will be embarked upon together—beginning with that extensive wedding trip I promised you. We'll be sailing off as soon as this mystery is behind us. And rest assured, the voyage I've planned will astound even you."

Excitement shimmered through her. "Where are we going?"

"To fulfill your dreams. To the sites of every legend Mr. Scollard has ever told you—plus a few additional sites of my own. The world is at our feet, Rory, and I intend to show it to you. How would that be?"

"That would be paradise." Aurora's mind was already racing ahead to the wonder of discovery, the exhilaration of seeing, experiencing, traveling . . .

Coming home.

She blinked in astonishment at the ironic direction her thoughts had taken.

"Sweetheart, what is it?" Julian questioned.

"I don't think you'd believe me if I told you."

A corner of his mouth lifted. "Try me."

"I was just thinking that our wedding trip sounds spectacular; a perfect beginning—and a perfect ending."

"Ending?" His brows drew together in puzzlement. "To what?"

"To a restlessness that is no more." Aurora drew a slow incredulous breath. "Oh, I'm sure I'll always embrace our journeys with open arms—as will you. But incomprehensible as this sounds, I'm looking forward to our homecoming almost as much as I am to our trip itself. Amazing, isn't it?" she said in wonder. "I've scarcely lived at Merlin Manor for one day, yet I've already begun to regard it as my home. Then again, that shouldn't surprise me. Your estate affected me as much—and as immediately—as you did, stealing my breath away and never quite restoring it. And your servants are the most endearing, albeit challenging group I've ever come upon. I can't wait to get to know them better. Most especially Emma, who's already reveling in her new job, and Gin, who's having a grand time *trying* to match wits with me—although I shudder to think how smug he must have been before I arrived." Aurora paused to inhale. "Also, the manor is but a shire away from Courtney and Slayde—and my new niece or nephew, who should be along very soon. Not to mention Mr. Scollard, whom I already miss and it's only been a few days." She broke off, eyeing the odd expression on Julian's face. "Am I upsetting you?"

"Upsetting me?" He shook his head. "No, *soleil,* you're making me incredibly happy. I saw the elation on your face yesterday as you explored Merlin Manor—strolling the beach, becoming acquainted with the servants—and I suddenly wanted nothing more than to transform my estate into the very home you just proclaimed it. At the time my reaction stunned me. But no longer. I realize now that ever since we met, I've been experiencing the perpetual and inexplicable need to do something I never fathomed doing, much less yearning to do: put down roots. Reconsidering Mr. Scollard's words in light of that fact, I begin to understand what he meant when he said you were a journey unto yourself, at the same time implying that my destination had yet to be reached." Julian caressed her face, his eyes alight with wonder. "He'll be proud to know that my journey is at an end—and the culmination is the greatest blessing I could ever imagine."

"The greatest blessing for us both," Aurora amended softly. She inclined her head, infused with a different type of joy. "You've pondered Mr. Scollard's words?"

"Thoroughly and repeatedly," Julian confirmed. "As I galloped toward the black cliffs, 'twas as if he were inside my head urging me on, reiterating the things he'd said two days past. I kept hearing his voice describing Barnes as having a wealth of resolution hovering at his feet, emphasizing the fact that Barnes possessed the ability to draw forth ghosts of the past that had to be silenced forever, else the future would remain out of reach. I believe Mr. Scollard was referring to *our* future, Rory, not merely that of the black diamond."

"And the ghosts we had to resolve—you think he meant Macall?"

"And Guillford."

"Yes, and Guillford." Aurora pursed her lips. "Sources expected and unknown—lurking in numbers, and in numbers were undone."

"So you heard Scollard's voice, too."

"I always do."

"We heeded his counsel," Julian pronounced. "You took care of me, and I of you."

"And now?"

"Now we do his bidding. We return to tell him of our discovery."

"He's going to have answers for us this time, Julian," Aurora realized aloud, somehow knowing it was true. "Or perhaps we'll supply those answers ourselves . . . with the aid of Mr. Scollard's magic."

"Perhaps." Julian cupped his wife's face between his palms. "In any case, the obstacles are behind us, *soleil.*"

Aurora nodded. "All but one."

"The black diamond."

"Yes," she concurred. "The black diamond."

Mr. Scollard emerged from the lighthouse the instant their carriage came to a halt. "Welcome back," he greeted them, his bright blue eyes suspiciously damp.

Aurora ran forward and flung her arms about him. "Thank you," she whispered fiercely. "You never left us, not even for a moment."

" 'Twas your faith that never left you, Rory," he declared, holding her away for a quick inspection, followed by a satisfied nod. "Your faith, your courage, and most of all, your love." With that, his glance shifted to Julian. "Your wound is healed?"

"Healed and well worth enduring." Julian gazed soberly at his newfound friend. "Thank you."

A hint of a smile. "And your destination—are the rewards all I envisioned them to be?"

"Even greater."

"Excellent." Mr. Scollard led them inside to the sitting room. "Then let us amass all your questions and put them to rest. 'Tis time for the ultimate resolution—and a most resplendent wedding trip."

That brought Aurora's head up. "You wouldn't care to tell me a bit more about that trip, would you?" she asked, settling herself on the settee.

"No, I wouldn't," Mr. Scollard retorted. "So you can stop staring at me like a hopeful pup awaiting a treat. That treat must be provided by your husband." He lowered himself to an armchair, shaking his head in exasperation. "Honestly, Rory, will you and Courtney never learn some patience? Between fending off her incessant questions about her babe's arrival date and now persuading you to stop snooping into your husband's surprise . . . 'tis a wonder I have enough strength left to climb the stairs to the tower."

"Do you know when the babe will come?"

Another twinkle. "Only the babe knows that."

That incited a worried frown.

"You'll have plenty of time, Rory," Mr. Scollard reassured her. "Resolve the past. Plan the future. By the time you embark upon it, you'll be an aunt."

"Very well." She leaned forward. "As you know, we spoke with Mr. Barnes. He told us nothing we didn't already know."

"Didn't he?"

Julian perched on the arm of the settee. "You're saying there was more to Barnes's purpose than leading us to Macall and Guillford?"

"I'm saying life's coincidences aren't coincidences at all, but fate."

"Like the sudden and essential appearance of a lighthouse that is a twin to this one?" Aurora inserted.

Mr. Scollard inclined his snow-white head. "No such lighthouse appears on any chart."

"I saw it, Mr. Scollard," she murmured, remembering that dark moment of despair when her friend's presence had sustained her. "I looked out toward Land's End and saw that miraculous beam just before Julian sprang down and attacked Lord Guillford. I wouldn't have survived my ordeal otherwise."

"Odd," Mr. Scollard replied. "Where you stood was Lizard Point, the southernmost tip of Lizard Peninsula. Land's End is miles from there. Then again, you were at one of Cornwall's highest peaks. That would explain your spying something so far away. But distinguishing the building's details, now that is an accomplishment."

"But not a coincidence," Aurora qualified, employing Mr. Scollard's philosophy. "That lighthouse appeared for a reason—to save my life. And distant or not, it seemed incredibly near. Why, I could see Land's End as clearly as if . . ."

"Rory." Julian's head whipped around, his eyes blazing with discovery. "Think about what you just said, and think about what Barnes told us."

Aurora frowned. "You've lost me."

"You said you could see Land's End, that it was incredibly near. Now consider my great-grandfather's last words, the ones Barnes said he uttered in feverish delirium."

Realization struck. "He said that the end was near, the

end was in sight, that he'd see James before he got there." Her eyes widened. "You think he meant Land's End?"

"Based upon Mr. Scollard's theory that life's coincidences are in reality fate—yes, I think he meant Land's End."

"Then by following that theory through, Geoffrey's saying he'd see James before he got there means the jewel is hidden somewhere relatively near Land's End." Aurora leapt to her feet and began pacing about. "That could be a dozen places—Penzance, Mousehole, Newlyn . . ."

"Might I remind you that there are still quite a few clues and apparent coincidences left unexplored?" Mr. Scollard suggested offhandedly.

"The clues." Julian snatched up the bag they'd brought from Cornwall, extracting both strongboxes— each bearing its key and contents—together with the sketch of Morland and the falcon text.

"Yes, the clues are all here, yet they're useless without the coincidences," Mr. Scollard proclaimed with but a cursory glance at the items Julian had displayed. "Each is integrally tied to the other."

"The coincidences. Fine." Julian prowled about, hands clasped behind his back. "A lighthouse that doesn't exist, examined clearly from a distant spot."

"Distant, yes, but seen nonetheless," Scollard clarified. "Seen at a moment of greatest despair, transforming it to a moment of greatest triumph. Seen by means of a miracle of nature—the same miracle that permitted you to rescue Rory from her fate."

Julian had stopped pacing and was pondering Mr. Scollard's words. "That miracle of nature was a peak in the black cliffs."

"Indeed. One of the shire's highest, I would imagine. Cornwall boasts many such peaks. Not all must be quite so towering or difficult to mount. It all depends on what is being sought and who is doing the seeking." One white brow arched. "Then again, I'm sure you know that. You are, after all, the Merlin—are you not? Or, at least, one type thereof."

"You're speaking in riddles." Julian eyed him speculatively.

"As did Rory's great-grandfather."

"The falcon book." Aurora nearly tripped over Julian in her haste to grab it. "You're alluding to the inscription in the book." She opened the front cover, pointing to the section she sought. "'As it is with the merlin and the kestrel, chart your path, then soar to the highest peak and the key to all life's treasures will be yours.'" She stared from the book to Mr. Scollard. "Wherever the black diamond is, we can spy its location from a peak close to Land's End." Again, she lowered her head, rereading the words as Julian stalked up beside her. "'Chart your path,'" she murmured. "I wonder if 'chart' refers to Geoffrey's sketch." She swept the diagram from the table. "Could it be there's more here than we've already used?"

"Possibly." Julian inspected his great-grandfather's sketch, then gazed pointedly back at the book. 'You are far greater than you appear—'" he read aloud, scanning the first lines of the inscription. "'A rock of strength, a giant among men.' If there is a connection between these words and the map, I'd guess that connection to be the word 'giant'—which leads us back to the legend that inspired Geoffrey's design. Is that what James is alluding to here? Is your great-grandfather sending us back to the Tamar River? If so, it negates everything we just determined."

"True. The Tamar is nowhere near Land's End," Aurora conceded. "Still, you're right about the blatant reference to a giant. It seems too glaring to be a coincidence. . . ." She caught herself using that word again, and her gaze flew to Mr. Scollard's. "Which it's not, is it? It's significant."

"As there are many types of merlins, there are many breeds of giants. Some are legendary, others tangible."

"A tangible giant?" Aurora frowned, totally at sea.

"If we follow the pattern, that tangible giant is a place," Julian reasoned aloud.

"Of course!" A soft gasp escaped Aurora's lips, fragments of memory falling into place. "Giant's Cave," she breathed, meeting Mr. Scollard's approving gaze. "How could I have forgotten?"

"You were little more than a tot when I relayed that particular tale to you, Rory," the lighthouse keeper replied. "It was sleeping in your memory, awaiting the right time to be recalled. That time is now."

"I know of no Giant's Cave," Julian inserted, brows drawn in puzzlement. "Given the fact that I've encountered many of Cornwall's most noted smugglers, I find that odd."

"No, actually, it isn't." Aurora turned to her husband. "You see, Giant's Cave is not a cave at all—it's a village."

"A village? Impossible. I know every village in . . ."

"As you know this one," she concurred. "Only you know it by another name: Mousehole."

Julian's jaw dropped. "Explain."

"Gladly. Giant's Cave is Mousehole's true name, although no one refers to it as such. It was coined 'Mousehole' by boatmen who recognized its inaccessibility by any means other than water—'tis near impossible to reach by land."

"As the giants pursuing Tamara spilled forth into the Channel, so does Giant's Cave," Mr. Scollard murmured.

"So that's the connection," Aurora breathed. "Another coincidence that's not a coincidence at all."

"I'll be damned." Julian shook his head in amazement, then glanced at Mr. Scollard, a new awareness dawning in his eyes. "That sheds light on another particular phrase you used. In referring to the black cliffs, you said that not all peaks must be quite so towering or difficult to mount. *Mount*—as in Mount's Bay, the cove of water surrounding Mousehole, spanning the distance between Lizard's Point and Land's End."

"That's where I spotted the lighthouse," Aurora realized, her mind streaking back over the details she could recall of the waters just east of Land's End. "But there are no cliffs arising from the bay. There's St. Michael's Mount, that magnificent old castle that sits amid the bay—but its location is all wrong. It's east of Mousehole, and as a result, even farther away from Land's End. It's also hardly what I would call a tangible peak. . . ." Abruptly she broke off and seized her husband's forearm. "The rocks—there were several formidable ones jutting out of the water." She pointed to James's inscription. "'A rock of strength,'" she recited. "It makes perfect sense. I should have thought of it immediately. One of the rocks in Mount's Bay is the tangible peak that will lead us to the black diamond." Another quick glance at Mr. Scollard. "And I know just which rock it is."

Julian's head snapped around. "Go on."

"'Tis the second part of the legend Mr. Scollard told me all those years ago—and it, too, has just awakened in my memory along with its counterpart." Aurora's eyes began to dance. "There's a legendary rock in the waters leading toward the village which, unlike the other jagged peaks in the bay, is submerged, revealed only at low tide. It's name is Merlin Carreg—or translated, Merlin Rock. *That's* the rock in James's inscription, the one upon which we must stand to find the treasure." She gave a little skip. "Many merlins, many giants, no coincidences—it's all falling into place."

"Indeed it is." Julian's face was taut with excitement as he scanned James's inscription one last time, then held out the book for Aurora's inspection. "Read the closing phrase of James's inscription. It provides us with the last piece of crucial information we need. James's instructions are now abundantly clear, as is our course. Mousehole is on the coast near Penzance, some eight miles east of Land's End. Both Mount's Bay *and* Merlin Rock lie directly at its feet. We must await low tide. When that occurs, we'll row out to Merlin Rock and climb out onto it. And then, we'll gaze across Mount's Bay in a direct line to Mousehole, keeping Land's End in sight."

"But what is it we're seeking?" Aurora asked, scanning James's words to determine what her husband knew that she didn't. "Surely our great-grandfathers wouldn't choose a hiding place that's within clear view of every passing sailor."

"They didn't. Mount's Bay is navigated mainly by fishermen, all of whom sail along the coastline so as to avoid the very rocks you just mentioned. And should a few ships actually pass close enough by Merlin Rock to offer their occupants the precise view our great-grandfathers meant for us to see, those glimpsing it wouldn't have a clue they were beholding something of great significance."

"What exactly is it they'd be beholding?" Aurora demanded.

"The final piece of the puzzle: the highest peak."

"Mousehole's highest peak?"

"Exactly."

"But Julian, Mousehole is a small fishing village. There are no soaring cliffs, ridges, or moors there."

"There needn't be. Keep in mind what Mr. Scollard said—not all peaks must be quite so towering or difficult to mount. The peak we're seeking could be no more than a modest hill. The important thing is that it will be visible from where we stand, and it will be taller than all else surrounding it." Julian tossed a grin in Mr. Scollard's direction. "Remember: 'It all depends on what is being sought and who is doing the seeking.'"

"You're an extraordinarily quick study," the lighthouse keeper praised.

"But of course. I am the Merlin, am I not?" Julian replied with a chuckle.

"Very much so," the older man concurred. "Very much so."

"So we stand atop Merlin Rock and gaze toward the highest point on Mousehole," Aurora interrupted, following Julian's reasoning. "And when we find it, we row in and begin our search."

"Right. We also bring a few things with us." Again he pointed at the inscription. "'Chart your path, then soar to the highest peak and the key to all life's treasures will be yours.' According to James, we've got to take Geoffrey's sketch and the strongbox keys with us when we row out to Merlin Rock."

"Our great-grandfathers must have stored their treasures in a third strongbox—one that requires both these keys to open it," Aurora said excitedly. With that, she snatched up the sketch. "Do you think this will help guide our way?"

"I do. My guess is it will chart out the area we'll eventually be exploring—it's doubtless some kind of map."

"How clever! A sketch with a double purpose: first, to lead us to James's strongbox, now to depict the location of the treasures that the Fox and the Falcon restored for King George."

"And among those treasures, my beautiful, brilliant Aurora, is the one that will remedy the past and make way for the future—the black diamond."

"At last," Mr. Scollard pronounced. "Your great-grandfathers' names will be untarnished. The clues they so carefully placed will be deciphered as they wished—by two whose lives and love will reunite families never meant to be divided. Thereby, all the seeming coincidences will be ascribed—and rightfully so—to fate."

Mr. Scollard rose, rubbing his palms together. "Low tide occurs late each afternoon. Plan to arrive at Merlin Rock just before sunset. Tonight, ride only as far as Polperro. Tomorrow, venture forth, and complete the voyage that will end your journey. In the interim, revel in your love—it is fate's greatest gift, as is the strength and perseverance that ensured it triumphed over all the obstacles and all the evil that threatened it." With that, he walked over to the sideboard, flourishing a pot and three cups that had definitely not been there an instant earlier. "But first, some tea. Enough to strengthen you— and to celebrate the most glorious of futures." Mr. Scollard poured, handing the first cup to Aurora. "Drink a great of deal of this between now and the commencement of your wedding trip," he instructed. "It will ease the seasickness you'll experience on your way home."

"Seasickness?" Aurora took up her cup, frowning. "I never imagined I'd suffer from that. I thought I'd adore sailing the open waters."

"You won't and you will."

"Then I don't understand."

"You'll only feel unsettled this once—and only on the last lap of your journey home. But fret not. There will be good reason for your short bout of sickness."

"A storm?" Aurora questioned.

Mr. Scollard concentrated on pouring the other two cups of tea. "A pending storm," he amended with a secret smile. "One that promises to bring with it an overwhelming amount of excitement, adventure, and passion."

Chapter 16

Julian's oars sliced through Mount's Bay, low tide having rendered the waters relatively smooth. Still, the small boat rocked from side to side—not due to the inefficiency of its navigator, but to the impatience of his passenger.

"I wish we could move faster," Aurora murmured, leaning forward to peer through the lingering filaments of light still flickering across the water.

"Yes, I know, *soleil.*" Julian grinned. "I'm as eager to reach Merlin Rock as you are. However, if you lean any farther forward, you're going to plunge into the bay, which will necessitate my diving in after you—*and* will slow us down considerably. Which would be a pity, given that we're almost there. So please try to stay still."

Reluctantly Aurora perched on the edge of her seat. "Very well, I'll try." She negated her own words at once, leaping up and pointing toward a faint gray mass that broke the surface of the water about thirty yards away. "That must be it."

"It is indeed. I spotted it five minutes ago and have been heading toward it ever since."

Glancing over her shoulder, Aurora tossed her husband a disgruntled look. "One day I'll best you, Merlin. Then we'll see about that bloody arrogance of yours."

Julian leaned forward, releasing an oar only long enough to tug Aurora backward until she tumbled onto his lap. "You've already bested me," he said huskily, brushing her lips with his. "You've conquered my heart, *soleil.*"

"Then we've bested each other," Aurora replied soberly, tracing the beloved lines of her husband's face. "Because I love you so much, it frightens me."

"Don't be frightened." He tucked her close against him, maneuvering the boat toward its goal. "I'm yours. Now. Always." He kissed her hair. "We began this adventure together. We'll finish it together. We'll deliver the stone to the Prince Regent, complete our great-grandfathers' mission—and ensure they're not only exonerated of all suspicion but celebrated as the heroes they were. Then we'll ride directly to Pembourne and stay until Slayde and Courtney's babe is born."

"After which we'll sail away to see the world." Aurora sighed, kissing Julian's throat. "I've never made love on a ship before."

"We'll rectify that before the ship even leaves port—I promise."

"I'm growing rather fond of your promises."

Julian tipped up her chin, kissing her until her bones melted. "I've a lifetime of promises to offer you, my love. An exquisite, wondrous lifetime." He bent his head to kiss her again.

The oar thudded as it struck something hard.

"Merlin Rock." Aurora jerked upright, exhilarated color staining her cheeks. "Julian, we're here."

"See how quickly the time passes when you're engaged in something enjoyable?"

A happy laugh. "You're welcome to distract me in that particular manner any time you want, Husband."

"Really? Then I doubt you'll be leaving our cabin to see any of the sights you crave during our upcoming trip."

"That's all right. I crave you more." With that, Aurora reached out, grabbing hold of the jutting stone and wriggling across onto its flat surface. "Care to join me?" Her eyes twinkled. "Although I must warn you, this stone is even more cramped and uncomfortable—and infinitely more public—than our carriage seat."

"Cramped, uncomfortable, and public don't deter me in the least. However, I wouldn't risk scratching that beautiful skin of yours," Julian proclaimed valiantly, tying the mooring rope about his waist and clambering across to where his wife was scrambling to her feet. "Still, there are ways around that particular problem." A challenging flame darted through his topaz eyes as he righted Aurora, tugged her against him. "I could take the brunt of the scratches," he murmured into the bright cloud of her hair. "Better still, we could stand. I'd support your weight, even drape your skirts around us so no one could see." A seductive chuckle. "Care to try?"

Aurora leaned back, stared at him in disbelief. "You're serious, aren't you?"

"When it comes to making love to you? Always. A more pertinent question is, are *you* serious?"

With a swift glance at their surroundings—the not-so-distant fishing boats, the nearby villages—Aurora gave it up. "Bested again," she grumbled.

Julian grinned. "You're welcome to retaliate. Later, you may best me to your heart's content."

"What an enticing notion. I look forward to it." She tucked loose strands of hair away from her face, her mood altering as she contemplated the smooth waters of

Mount's Bay, the picturesque shoreline that defined its boundaries, the huge white gulls that flew gracefully overhead. "To me, all this is a miracle," she admitted, awe lacing her tone. "Until now, these places were just wisps of dreams floating about in my head, fragments of Mr. Scollard's legends. Now they're real."

"They sound much like you," Julian replied in a husky whisper. "An unknown dream that's now reality—a miracle. *My* miracle."

Aurora curved into his side. "Thank you."

"No, *soleil*—thank *you."* His arm encircled her waist, keeping her close against him. "There's Mousehole," he told her, pointing straight ahead. "And Land's End wraps around to the west."

Following his gesture, Aurora gazed at the village that housed their great-grandfathers' secret, seeing naught but a tiny harbor dotted with fishing boats and a narrow stretch of beach that receded away from the shore to become green tracts of land. "It's lovely, but I'm not certain what I'm looking for," she said, peering beyond the coast to the rows of houses set before grassy hills. "As I said, there's nothing remotely towering . . ."

Her voice lodged in her throat.

The sun, now shimmering in the west, had poised over Mousehole, going utterly still as it bathed the village in a final blaze of color. Fiery rays swept inland, revealing a pair of gently rolling hills situated directly before Aurora's widening eyes. As she stared transfixed, the rays converged into one solitary beam that pierced the space between the two identical crests, illuminating a third hill nestled just beyond and directly between the others—a hill that soared taller than either of its counterparts, its grassy slope heralded by a line of hedges forming an arch at its base.

"Julian," she began, her heart hammering like a drum. "That hill . . ."

"I see it." His answer was a terse whisper, rife with excitement and discovery.

Aurora tore her gaze from the hedges, inclining her head to regard her husband. "It's more than the hill's height. Even more than the intense way the sunset converges upon it. There's something about it . . ."

"Such as the fact that those hedges are arranged precisely like the ones on Geoffrey's drawing?" Swiftly Julian extracted the sketch, unfolding it and pointing to the line of hedges his great-grandfather had sketched—hedges that opened into the thick maze of greenery that defined the grounds of Morland Manor.

The fading sunlight flickered over the drawing and Aurora stared from it to the hill and back. "You're right—they're identical." She inhaled sharply. "So it's true. This *was* our great-grandfathers' plan. What we're seeing now proves it. 'Twould be impossible for anyone approaching at a different angle to view the base of that hill. It's shielded by the slope of the land and the houses at its forefront. No one could spot it unless they were standing where we are, at precisely this time of day. And even if someone were to defy all those odds to stand upon Merlin Rock at low tide just as the sun set, they'd have no notion what they were viewing—not unless they held this very sketch in their hands."

"I'd be willing to bet there's an opening in that hill, Rory."

"And I'd be willing to bet you're right."

As if to substantiate the validity of their words and proclaim the fact that its mission had been achieved, the sun relinquished its hold on Mousehole, slipping slowly beneath the horizon, giving way to dusk.

"Let's row to shore." Julian tightened his hold about Aurora's waist, hoisting her onto the boat, and, after untying the rope about his midsection, swinging down beside her.

"We'd better hurry," Aurora advised, taut as a bow-string as they propelled the craft toward the coast. "I know we brought a lantern, but it will be far easier to find the opening in that hill with the aid of some daylight."

"Agreed." Julian rowed in quick hard strokes, taking them closer and closer to shore.

Aurora jumped out the instant she could, wading through several feet of ankle-deep water to tug the boat onto the sand. "Let's go," she urged her husband.

Julian needed no second invitation. By the time Aurora had wrung out her skirts he was beside her, seizing her hand to lead her onward.

They made their way across the sandy beach and through the narrow path leading inland. Once they passed the houses and reached the unbroken stretch of hills, they abandoned the path altogether, trudging over the rolling tracts of grass on a more direct route to their goal.

Dusk was giving way to darkness when they approached the twin crests flanking their goal.

Coming to a halt, Aurora squinted through the hills to the taller peak beyond and beheld the shadowy outlines of the hedges looming before her. She shivered— whether from excitement or the cold night air, she wasn't certain.

"Are you all right?" Julian asked, drawing her mantle more closely around her. Without awaiting an answer, he shrugged out of his coat, wrapping it about her for added warmth. "Better?"

"You'll freeze," she protested.

"Not a chance." He flashed her that devastating grin. "I promise. Besides, you can warm me later—at the same time that you best me." He captured her hand, guiding her to the base of the hill they sought.

Aurora caught her breath as Julian held up the lantern and scanned the hedges for an opening.

His answer came in the form of a dark hollow cloaked by greenery, hovering directly before them.

"There," Julian proclaimed, indicating the shadowy cavern with a triumphant flourish. "That's it, *soleil*. We've found it." His forearm shot out, precluding Aurora's immediate—and anticipated—rush forward. "Wait. Give me a minute to glance over this sketch. It will be dark in that cave—very dark. 'Tis best if I get my bearings before we enter, lantern or not."

Impatient though she was, Aurora recognized the prudence of her husband's actions. Forcing herself to stay still, she peered over Julian's shoulder, channeling her impatience into something productive. "Let me study the sketch with you. I know you're a superb navigator. But it can't hurt for us both to have a sense of where we're headed."

"Good idea." Julian lowered the drawing so they could both see it, angling the lantern to maximize their light. "For the first time in my life I wish I were more familiar with the grounds of Morland Manor," he muttered.

"You don't need to be." Aurora's forefinger traced the portion of the sketch depicting the area where they stood. "Geoffrey's drawing is very straightforward. These are the hedges closest to the manor. Behind them, the other rows of hedges sprawl back into a maze of sorts."

"The gardens are here, to the right," Julian concurred. "To the left are the tenants' quarters, the carriage house, and the stables."

"And look what's just behind the stables," Aurora exclaimed, eagerness lacing her tone. "Two barns—one large, one small. The large one is merely labeled 'livestock.' But the small one is specifically marked 'hunting dogs.'" Aurora raised ebullient eyes to her husband. "And we all know what hunting dogs pursue."

"Foxes." Julian gave his wife a quick, hard hug before

turning back to the sketch, scrutinizing the area surrounding the smaller barn. "Look. There's an opening in the hedges right here, alongside the dwelling. That's it, Rory—that's what we're looking for." Swiftly Julian reviewed the route they needed to take, committing to memory the curves and bends in the path.

"Now can we go?" Aurora demanded, shifting from one foot to the other.

"Yes, *soleil,* now we can go."

They plunged into the cavern, remaining still only long enough to assess their surroundings. The walls and ceiling were granite, the ground a rutted combination of dirt and stones. The ceiling, not more than five and a half feet high, cleared Aurora's head by a good five inches, but didn't come close to admitting Julian's towering frame. He compensated for that by stooping from the waist, keeping his head straight and his eyes fixed on their intended course.

"It's a natural cave," he announced, holding out the lantern so Aurora could see. "We've got a few feet on either side of us, which is good, but no room above us— or, I should say, above *me."* A frown. "That's going to make it difficult for me to maneuver the lantern and myself at the same time, not to mention consult the sketch. And *that,* unfortunately, means our progress is going to be slow."

"It doesn't have to be." Aurora gripped her husband's arm. "I have nearly half a foot of space over my head. I can move freely—even run, if need be. Give me the sketch and the lantern. Let me lead the way. You've already studied the drawing. If I take a wrong turn, you'll stop me."

"If I can catch you, you mean," Julian retorted dryly. Regarding Aurora's avid expression, he sighed, relenting with more than a touch of uneasiness. "Rory, I'll let you do this under one condition. Promise me you'll control that bloody reckless streak of yours. No running—the ground is rough and uneven, and you could trip and break your neck. No venturing more than a few feet in front of me. Most of all, no exploring unknown sites that pique your interest. Agreed?"

Laughter bubbled up in her throat. "You know me well, don't you, Merlin? All right, agreed. I'll be disgustingly boring and obedient."

"And I'll be right behind you to ensure that you are." He handed her the sketch and lantern. "Remember—go slowly. The ground is broken and embedded with rocks."

"I'm too excited to trip." Despite her quip, Aurora complied, knowing that to do otherwise would be sheer stupidity. Besides, they were so very close to their goal.

Clutching the lantern, she scanned the lower portion of the sketch, then struck off, veering to the left.

Their path wound in serpentine fashion as they walked past numerous passageways that led to parts unknown. Some minutes later, Aurora stopped to consult the drawing. "How much farther do you think we have to go?"

"If our course stays true to scale, we're more than halfway there," Julian supplied from just behind her. "Curve twice more—each time following the passage to the extreme right—then veer sharply left. Walk about ten or twelve feet, I should say. Then stop. The opening on Geoffrey's sketch is somewhere in that vicinity."

Aurora sucked in her breath. "Splendid." She continued as Julian had instructed her, following the precise course the drawing depicted, stepping gingerly over sharp pieces of rock and cracked sections of dirt. She could feel Julian's presence behind her, his excitement as palpable as her own.

"We're here."

Julian's terse words sent shivers down her spine and Aurora halted, holding out the lantern and surveying as much of the nearby area as she could. Below them, the same ragged path. Above them, the same low granite ceiling. And to either side of them . . .

A harsh gasp escaped Aurora's mouth. "Julian, look."

Even as she spoke, he was easing past her, seizing the lantern, and peering over her head at a spot where the granite wall adjoined the ceiling. A section of stone had been cut away, replaced by what appeared to be a grating of some sort—one that resembled an iron gate. From what Aurora could make out, the gate appeared to be approximately the size of a window, and there was an alcove behind it, although how deeply that alcove was set into the stone, she couldn't tell. What she could tell quite clearly by the light of the lantern was that the gate boasted a thick, hinged, vertical column that spanned its length dead center, and that opposite the hinge on the left and right-hand sides of the gate were carved two deep-slotted keyholes.

One keyhole was adorned with the image of a fox, the other of a falcon.

"This is it!" Aurora exclaimed. "We've found our great-grandfathers' hiding place!"

Exultantly Julian nodded, eyes narrowing as he examined the grating. "Geoffrey and James were ingenious to design this as they did. One alcove, one gate, two means of gaining entry. That way, either of them could get to the treasure if something should happen to the other. Clever as hell." Julian gave the grating a cursory rattle, confirming what they already knew—it was locked. "We don't need to guess how to open it."

"Can you see inside?"

"Only a glint of metal."

"I can't bear the anticipation." Realizing Julian's coat was still wrapped about her shoulders, Aurora dug into the pocket, extracting the keys one by one. "This key is Geoffrey's—it should coincide with the Fox." She pressed the key into Julian's palm.

Rather than inserting the key and opening the lock,

Julian merely glanced down at the scrap of metal in his hand, then placed the lantern on a nearby ledge and turned to his wife. "Do you have James's key ready?"

"It's right here—why? You only need one key to get into the alcove."

"True. Nevertheless we're going to do this together." Julian's knuckles brushed her cheek, equal measures of pride and tenderness lacing his tone. "We're partners, my love. Just as our great-grandfathers before us—only, as Mr. Scollard so aptly put, our partnership exceeds friendship. I'll act on Geoffrey's behalf, and you on James's." He wrapped an arm about Aurora's waist, lifting her off the ground until she was at eye level with the keyhole. "Shall we?"

With trembling fingers, Aurora inserted James's key into the slot where the falcon gleamed, watching as Julian glided Geoffrey's key into the notch embellished by a fox.

Simultaneously she and Julian turned—and with two telltale clicks, the locks released.

Both sides of the door swung open.

"Let me do this part," Julian instructed, staying Aurora's immediate motion to reach inside and lowering her to her feet so he could devote his full attention to the matter at hand. "Lord alone knows what might be crawling around in there."

That convinced her.

Still, she stood on tiptoe, eyes straining as Julian reached into the dark recess.

An instant later he tugged out a strongbox, lowering it down far enough so they could both have a full view.

The chest was unadorned but for two gilded images on top—one in the shape of a fox, the other in that of a falcon.

"Oh, God. Julian, this really is happening." Impulsively Aurora reached forward and seized the strongbox, only to discover just how heavy the iron chest was. With great reluctance she forced herself to release it, digging her nails into her palms to curb her impatience. "Open it—quickly."

A corner of Julian's mouth lifted. "Such admirable restraint—caution over craving. I'm proud of you, *soleil*. You've become a true adventurer." He held out the chest, gripping it firmly as he offered it to her. "Go ahead. Reap your reward. I'll hold it, you open it."

"I? Really?"

"You. Really."

Aurora needed no second invitation. She yanked up the strongbox lid, and together she and Julian gazed inside.

Atop the contents was a single slip of paper, its words faint and faded but still discernible:

Whether truth or myth, it is written: 'He with a black heart who touches the jewel will reap eternal wealth, while becoming the carrion upon whom, for all eternity, others will feed.' If neither Geoffrey Bencroft nor I return to complete our mission, 'tis the task of our chosen descendants to do so. For our families, for our King and country, and for whatever forces might possibly exist that are greater yet less palpable than we—I beseech you, restore this gem to its rightful home. Then, for all eternity, peace will abound. James Huntley, 1758.

Sweeping the note from its bed, Aurora and Julian stared into the strongbox.

An enormous black jewel glistened back at them.

"The black diamond." This time Aurora couldn't restrain herself. She reached in, her fingers closing around the stone. Snatching it from the chest, she stared in amazement at the gem's unwieldy size. "Dear Lord— it fills my entire palm. It's immense."

"Yes, it is." Julian transferred the stone to his larger hand, holding it out so they could both admire the smooth, multifaceted surface by lantern light. "We did it, Aurora." Tearing his gaze from the stone, he met his wife's radiant stare, triumphant flames blazing in his topaz eyes. "We bloody well did it." Abruptly he replaced the gem in its iron bed and set the strongbox on the ledge beside the lantern, swinging Aurora into his arms and kissing her fiercely. "Hell and damnation, we did it!"

Elation exploded inside Aurora and she laughed, flinging her arms about her husband's neck. "Yes, we did it! At last—the curse of the black diamond will be ended, along with all the hatred, the fear, the wrongful accusations." Realization sank in, sweeter than all the world's adventures combined, and the thrill of victory lulled into a more wondrous sense of peace. "Just think," she whispered, accosted by a fuller, richer kind of joy. "The past will truly be righted and finally, finally put to rest. And oh, Julian, the future will be ours."

"The future and the world," Julian concurred fervently, his own exhilaration tempered by the same deep-seated happiness reflected in Aurora's eyes. With solemn reverence, he stroked her face, a myriad emotions tightening his. "I love you, Aurora Huntley Bencroft."

"And I you," she breathed. "As of today—as of this very minute—we've truly melded the Huntley and the Bencroft names, not just legally but actually." A poignant pause. " 'Tis time for the peace James spoke of—and we shall commemorate it as he and Geoffrey would have wished." She raised her chin a notch, alerting Julian to the magnitude of her declaration. "I am now officially and proudly the Duchess of Morland." Her fingertips caressed her husband's nape. "And you, my darling husband, are truly the Duke of Morland—just as your great-grandfather before you. Chilton and Lawrence might have tainted the title, but they couldn't destroy it. Not when you're here to restore it to all its glorious, unconventional nobility."

A muscle worked in Julian's jaw.

"It's time, Julian," Aurora said with ardent conviction. "Let the anger and resentment go. Geoffrey would have wanted it that way." She never looked away. "So would Hubert."

That dissolved the last of Julian's resistance. Slowly he nodded, framing Aurora's face between his palms and making his own private peace with the past—and himself. "You're right," he acceded quietly, emotion darkening his gaze. "Very well then, the Duke and Duchess of Morland we are. Although I don't think I can ever bring myself to live in that mausoleum."

"You don't have to. I have splendid plans for your great-grandfather's estate. Plans that would make him and James very happy."

Julian looked intrigued. "Care to share those plans with me?"

"Later," she replied mysteriously. "Right now, all I want is to go home. Home—to Merlin Manor, our irreverent staff, and our soft, enticing bed." An impish smile. "Or have you forgotten my vow to best you?"

"To best me *and* to warm me," he reminded her, flashing that wicked grin Aurora loved so much. "The answer is no. I've forgotten neither. In fact, my beautiful wife, I think going home is an excellent idea. After all, before we ride first to Pembourne to flourish this stone before Courtney and Slayde, and then to London to turn it over to the Prince Regent, we owe it to ourselves to truly celebrate our new titles—and seal our family union—properly."

Aurora's eyes danced. "Need I ask what 'properly' means?"

"No. You needn't."

"Do you think Geoffrey and James would object to our delaying our trip a day or two?"

"I think they would applaud it."

"In that case . . ." Aurora wrapped her arms about her husband's neck, tugging his mouth down to hers. "I'd love to go home—*after* you provide me with an initial opportunity to best you. Would that be possible, given your assurance that our great-grandfathers would so heartily approve?"

Julian's lips curved against hers. "Here? In this cave?"

"Here. In this cave." Aurora cast Julian's coat to the ground, lowering herself upon it and gazing up at him with a seductive grin. "You wouldn't need to stoop over that way if you were lying down," she pointed out.

"True." He came down beside her, propping himself on one elbow. "Have I mentioned how much I love your sense of adventure?" he murmured, tunneling his fingers through the luxuriant waves of her hair.

"Ummm, once or twice." Aurora snuggled closer, wanting nothing more than to spend the rest of her life in her husband's arms. "Then you don't mind that this cave is somewhat primitive and more than a little uncomfortable?"

"Not a bit, *soleil.*" Julian tipped back her head, bending to cover her mouth with his. "I promise to make up for the less than optimum surroundings in the very best way I know how."

"How reassuring," Aurora sighed, her lips parting to the exhilarating pressure of her husband's possession. "Since I, better than anyone, know how diligent you are about keeping your promises."

With a husky chuckle, the new Duke of Morland proceeded to fulfill his promise, besting his duchess and being bested by her in return.

And thus, the Fox and the Falcon's long sought-after peace was consummated.

Epilogue

Merlin Manor
April 1819

For the fifth time in as many minutes, Julian stalked down the steps and paced the length of the hallway to the sitting room and back. He scarcely noticed the golden brown gangly limbed dog race by, fleeing for his life as a small dark-haired tot wobbled after him on unsteady legs.

"There you are, Tyler." Courtney swooped down on the child, scooping his wriggling body into her arms and cradling him against her. "Leave Tyrant alone, sweetheart. You've tortured him enough for one day, wouldn't you say?"

Huge jade eyes stared back at her. "No," her fourteen-month-old son replied solemnly.

"See what you're in for, Julian," Courtney teased, attempting for the umpteenth time to make her brother-in-law smile.

"What's taking that bloody midwife so long?" Julian demanded, coming to a screeching halt. "She's quick as a

347

whip when it comes to throwing me out. Why can't she deliver my child half as swiftly? Why?"

Courtney's gaze filled with compassion. "Julian, Aurora is going to be fine. I promise."

"You haven't seen her."

"Yes, I have. I left her chambers not twenty minutes ago. And the instant Slayde gets back, I'll be returning. She's a bit tired out, but she hasn't lost one bit of her spirit. In fact, you look equally as haggard as she." Courtney indicated Julian's rumpled clothing and tousled hair. "I don't expect you to sleep, but why don't you at least sit down and rest for a bit? You've been awake and pacing the entire night."

"She was crying out—in pain," Julian continued, scarcely hearing, much less complying with, Courtney's suggestion. "I heard her all the way from the landing. Aurora doesn't cry out in pain; hell, she doesn't even whimper. Why is she suffering so much?"

"You won't believe me, but the results will be worth every moment of pain."

"You're right, I don't believe you." Julian glanced about restlessly. "Speaking of Slayde, where is he? The last I remember he was dashing out of here, half-dressed. And that was hours ago, in the bloody middle of the night."

"He should be returning any time now. He left as soon as Aurora's pains began so he could go fetch Mr. Scollard. Aurora wanted to have her oldest friend here to share this miraculous occasion." A smile. "I think this will be one of the few times Mr. Scollard actually agrees to leave the lighthouse."

"Scollard—yes, maybe he can help her. He always seems to know what to do. He knew this babe would be coming. He as much as told us so when he spoke of our wedding trip. I wish he'd been there during those last few weeks at sea. Aurora spent half the time with her head in the chamber pot, and I had no idea how to ease her sickness. Can you imagine what that was like?"

"It sounds like every one of my sailing voyages," Courtney returned dryly. "I'm always seasick."

"Not Aurora. We sailed from the Far East to India, to the Continent, and not once during six months at sea did she become ill. Not until those last horrible weeks. Prior to that she was as natural a sailor as she is an adventurer. There were a few times when she was the *only* one on board who remained unaffected by the elements. Twice we hit storms that would—and did—turn seasoned sailors' faces green. The entire crew was retching, begging each other to switch shifts so they could retire to the berth deck. But not Aurora. I had to literally drag her below; she wanted to stay topside and ride the rolling waves, feel the ocean spray in her face. The ship pitched, the waters surged—and Aurora reveled in every moment. Then suddenly on our way back to England, everything changed. She became tired, queasy—hell, she could scarcely eat a morsel or stroll the deck without becoming ill. I was frantic. I thought she'd contracted some horrible disease as a result of our travels. I couldn't wait to get her home and examined by my physician. Why the hell didn't I realize she was carrying my child? How could I have been so stupid?"

"Julian, Aurora herself didn't realize she was with child." Courtney attempted to soothe him. "'Twas a natural assumption on your part that . . ." She broke off, whipping around as a ruckus erupted at the front door: loud pounding followed by sharp words and a purposeful slam.

An instant later Slayde strode through the hallway, Mr. Scollard beside him. Spying his wife, Slayde headed toward her, pausing once or twice to glare over his shoulder at Daniels, who was wandering about in disoriented circles, mumbling gibberish under his breath.

"I know your butler's a bit unusual, Julian, but doesn't he believe in opening the door?" Slayde demanded.

"Daniels is a bit unnerved by Aurora's discomfort." It was Courtney who answered, lifting her face to receive her husband's kiss and giving him—and Mr. Scollard— a meaningful look. "So is Julian. He was just berating himself for being unaware that Aurora was with child on their journey home."

Slayde arched an amused—albeit understanding— brow in Julian's direction. "No one realizes the moment a child is conceived—with the exception of Scollard, who knows about it beforehand. Stop being so hard on yourself." Leaning over, Slayde ruffled his son's dark head, transferring him from Courtney's arms to his own. "I'll watch Tyler," he murmured for his wife's ears alone. "Go to Aurora; she'll want you there." In a normal tone, he added, "I needn't ask if there's any news. Mr. Scollard assures me there isn't."

"Well, of course there isn't," the lighthouse keeper inserted with more than a trace of indignation. "If Rory had needed me sooner, I'd have been here."

Julian paled. "Does she need you now?"

"No. You do."

"Very amusing," Julian muttered.

"I wasn't trying to be amusing. But this is one adventure in which Rory is faring far better than you." Mr. Scollard patted Julian's arm. "She's tired. And, as usual, impatient. But she's strong, she's healthy, and she's very, very determined. She and your babe will do fine."

A flurry of footsteps sounded from overhead, and a minute later Gin burst down the stairs, sweating profusely and mopping at his forehead. "Spirits," he muttered, brushing past Julian to stalk into the sitting room.

"Spirits—yes, good idea." Relieved to be of some help, Julian gestured toward the side table. "Instruct Emma to give Mrs. Merlin whatever she needs to ease the pain."

"Mrs. Merlin?" Gin snatched a bottle of his name-sake, staring at Julian as if he'd lost his mind. "This ain't for yer wife. This stuff's fer me. My nerves are frayed." Without preliminaries, he lifted the bottle to his lips, tossing back five or six deep swallows. "All this waitin'—it's drivin' me crazy." Another swallow, followed by a frown as he studied the rapidly dwindling supply of gin. "I'd better stop guzzlin'. I promised Daniels I'd save 'im some. Don't know what good it'll do 'im, though. 'E can't stand still long enough to drink it. 'E's been wringin' 'is 'ands and whimperin' like a babe 'imself ever since Mrs. Merlin announced the babe was on its way. 'E didn't even 'ear the midwife when she arrived—she was knockin' on the door for ten minutes before 'e let 'er in. Not that I care. That ornery ol' witch should've been left on the doorstep instead of . . ."

"Gin!" Julian thundered. "You're supposed to be stationed outside Aurora's room in case she needs anything! Who the hell is watching over my wife?"

The valet blinked. "She ain't alone, Merlin. Emma and that wretched midwife Mrs. Peters are both there. Where the 'ell 'd ye find that shrew, anyway? She practically threw me out on my ear when I poked my 'ead in to see 'ow yer duchess was doin'—said somethin' about men only bein' good at makin' babes, not bringin' 'em into the world. She 'erself is guardin' that bloody door."

"She's just trying to keep all the well wishers out."

"No, she's tryin' to keep *ye* out. She said she's gonna take a strap to ye if ye burst in there like ye did earlier, raving like a lunatic. I don't think she likes ye much."

"What a coincidence," Slayde inserted wryly. "She made similar threats to me when Tyler was making his appearance into the world."

"Yeah, she bellowed somethin' about not likin' ye much, either," Gin confirmed. "But she said ye were a lamb compared to Merlin. She said 'e'd make a wounded bear look good, that never in all 'er years of doin' this 'as any man been as loud and domineering and downright unbalanced as Merlin . . ."

"That's it," Julian exploded, jerking about and storming toward the stairs. "I'm going up there and throwing the old crone out."

"Julian—don't." Courtney rushed forward, grabbing his arm and staying his progress. "I know Mrs. Peters is somewhat overbearing and more than a bit cheeky. But, trust me, she's extraordinarily competent despite her rather forward manner." Pleading tone or not, Courtney looked suspiciously as if she were biting back laughter. "She did a splendid job of helping me birth Tyler. Why, there's not a better midwife in all of England. So please, don't do something you'll regret."

Julian forced himself to comply, knowing full well that Courtney was right. Nothing mattered now but the well-being of his wife and child.

"I tell you what," Courtney went on in that soothing way she had. "I'll go up and check on Aurora. She'll want to know Mr. Scollard is here, anyway. Then I'll stay by her side until the babe is born. Would that make you feel better?"

"I'd feel better if I were with her."

"No you wouldn't," Slayde refuted. "Because not only would you swoon from the experience, but Mrs. Peters would then have to divert her attentions from Aurora and the babe to cheerfully toss your body out the bedchamber window. No, Julian, I'd say you were better off staying right here."

"Doing what?" Julian demanded as Courtney squeezed Slayde's arm and hurried off. "What the hell am I supposed to do while my wife is suffering?"

"Help Slayde watch Tyler," Courtney called over her shoulder. "My son will be delighted to introduce you to the joys of fatherhood."

Julian didn't smile. He averted his head, raking a

frustrated hand through his hair. Never in all his life had he felt so helpless, so terrified. Oh, somewhere in the dim recesses of his mind he'd realized there would be pain involved with bringing a new life into the world. But never had he expected Aurora—*his* Rory, who'd shot a privateer dead, been held at gunpoint atop the black cliffs, persevered through the long and dangerous discovery of the black diamond as well as its triumphant return to the Crown—to agonize like this, her slight body bathed in perspiration, racked with spasms of pain. Dammit. He should be able to help her. He *needed* to be able to help her. She'd given him so much: his heart, his inner peace, the spirit that lighted his days, and the passion that consumed his nights.

Marriage to her had been—continued to be—the most exquisite of adventures.

Immediately following Tyler's birth, they'd sailed off on their wedding trip, visiting every place Geoffrey's journal had cited as one of the Fox and the Falcon's destinations. First they'd journeyed to China and Singapore, next to Bengal and Ceylon. From there they'd traveled down to the southern coast of Africa, then west to Barbados and Trinidad, north to Canada and Newfoundland, and finally back to Gibraltar, Malta, and the Continent before returning home to England.

Each stop had been an awakening not only for Aurora, but for Julian, his wife's exuberance and sense of discovery more valuable than all the world's treasures combined.

The only puzzling part had been the inordinate number of purchases Aurora had made at each village they visited—mementos, she'd claimed, that would rekindle pivotal memories in the years to come. More baffling still had been her insistence that the purchases be shipped ahead not to Cornwall, but to Morland Manor.

It wasn't until their arrival in England, their brief stop in Devonshire, that Julian had discovered why.

When Aurora had said she had plans for Geoffrey's estate, she'd meant it. During their absence Morland had been converted into a magnificent testimonial to their great-grandfathers, each room dedicated to a different mission of the Fox and the Falcon, redecorated in the traditional style of whatever village, town, or city that expedition had taken them to. And in the manor's entranceway, a glass casing stretched the entire length of the marble hallway—a casing that displayed the very heart of the Fox and the Falcon: Geoffrey's journal and his sketch of Morland Manor, James's falcon text, and both men's daggers, strongboxes, and keys. Atop the casing, hanging proudly on the wall, was a letter from the Prince Regent himself, dated just after the black diamond's restoration, acknowledging James and Geoffrey for who they were, commending them for their loyalty and courage, and declaring them heroes.

The mausoleum that had haunted Julian's memories was no more. In its stead was a remarkable tribute to a pair of remarkable men.

Only two rooms at Morland remained unchanged.

The library, where Aurora had first told Julian she loved him, and one bedchamber: Hugh's. That room especially, Aurora had made certain remained as it was—untouched and undisturbed—a private haven for Julian to visit and to savor his personal memories.

Thus, Morland was at peace and Merlin Manor was home.

Julian had been totally overcome by what his wife had done. But his sentiments had paled in comparison to the ones he'd experienced when he learned she was pregnant.

Weak-kneed relief over her well-being had transformed to shock, finally evolving into a bone-melting combination of awe and joy.

Aurora was carrying his child.

The months that followed had been a miracle for him;

watching his wife's body change, ripen, and swell with his babe. He'd immersed himself in every glorious detail, loving Aurora to the very depths of his soul—and wanting her with an intensity that seemed to heighten with each passing day.

Still, when her pregnancy reached the stage that precluded lovemaking, he'd learned to endure celibacy— something he'd never imagined doing with Aurora in his bed. Hell, he'd even gone so far as to acquire a measure of patience, forcing himself to await the babe's arrival with a modicum of control.

Somehow it had all been bearable.

Until now.

Because now, Aurora was in pain—and there wasn't a bloody thing he could do to stop it.

"Soon, Julian," Mr. Scollard comforted, invariably reading his mind. "Very soon. In fact—" The lighthouse keeper pressed his lips together, glancing overhead as if he could see through the ceiling to the second floor. "— I'll give Courtney another quarter hour. Then I'd best go up. Shortly after that, Rory will be asking for you."

"The pain will become more severe?" Julian felt a knife twist in his gut.

"No. The pain will be rewarded with one of life's greatest blessings."

"I doubt I'll last."

"You will." Mr. Scollard smiled. "You and Rory have a long and wonderful life ahead. Filled with happiness, children, and—of course—adventure."

Julian groaned. "Don't even say that word. After this experience, I want nothing but a lifetime of complacency. Hell, even a London Season would look good about now."

"Which reminds me," Slayde interceded, "I learned something interesting while I was in Devonshire. Evidently the Prince Regent intends to give a ball in honor of Geoffrey and James—*and* you and Aurora for fulfilling their final and most vital mission. The ball will be held at Carlton House in June—giving Aurora more than ample time to recover from childbirth and feel strong enough to travel to London. I received a letter to that effect when I stopped at Pembourne. Siebert advised me that the Prince Regent's letter and invitation to you are on their way. I probably sped past his messenger on the road. In any case, it seems the ball will be the culmination of the Season, with hundreds in attendance to acknowledge our great-grandfathers and you and Aurora. The entire *ton* is already buzzing with the news." Slayde assessed Julian's glazed expression, and his lips twitched. "You look distinctly unimpressed by the prospect of this ball. I can assure you after twenty years of living with her, that Aurora will not share your lack of enthusiasm. She's spent more than a decade dreaming of taking part in a glittering London Season. And this will give her the opportunity not only to attend the grandest of balls, but to be at its very core. At last my sister is getting her wish—the *ton* is opening its arms in welcome, heralding you both, in fact, as heroes. As is all of England and much of the world."

"The privateers are none too happy with us," Julian amended, rubbing his bristled jaw. "We've deprived them of one of their most coveted prizes. With the black diamond safely ensconced in the temple from which it was stolen, they'll have to set their sights on a new, equally fascinating treasure." His gaze softened, shifted toward the stairs. "As for me, if Aurora will only endure this ordeal, I'll take her to every bloody ball in England—hell, we can even give one of our own, invite the entire fashionable world."

"Does that mean I'll 'ave to serve?" Gin asked, looking even paler than he'd been a moment ago.

"No. For that, I'll send for Thayer. He has little to do at Morland Manor these days, anyway—other than showing interested spectators around. He and the rest of the staff will leap at the opportunity to assume more traditional roles."

"Thank 'eavens." Gin sagged with relief. "It'll be bad enough 'avin' all those blue-bloods millin' around the 'ouse without 'avin' to wait on 'em." He scowled at the bottle in his hand as if arriving at some momentous self-sacrificing decision. "If it'll make Mrs. Merlin 'appy, I'll clean up a little and put on a uniform," he blurted out before he could reconsider and change his mind. "But I'm tellin' ye now, I'm not learnin' 'ow to bow or dance. And I sure as 'ell won't share my gin. Those blue-bloods can drink yer sherry and some of that pitiful punch that's got more fruit in it than spirits." With that, Gin snatched up a second bottle for himself and marched off to give the partially empty one to Daniels.

"I'm overwhelmed," Slayde chuckled. "For Gin to be willing to don a uniform? Aurora must have worked miracles."

"She has—with all of us." Julian resumed pacing, his brow furrowed with worry. "I wish Courtney would come down and tell us how Aurora is faring so I'd know . . ." He halted, having caught sight of Mr. Scollard heading for the stairs. "You're going to Aurora?"

"Yes." The lighthouse keeper never paused, his words trailing behind him as he ascended the staircase. "I'll be only five minutes. After that, I'll rejoin you. We'll have time for one brandy each. By that time, Courtney will be sending for you."

"Oh, God." Julian turned away, feeling as if someone had punched him in the gut.

"On second thought," Scollard called down from the landing, "you and Slayde begin without me. You'll toss off your first brandy in a few necessary gulps. I'll join you for your second."

"Come on," Slayde urged Julian, sitting Tyler atop his shoulders and gesturing toward the sitting room. "We've just been instructed to have a drink."

Julian followed, watching Tyler squeal with delight and cling to his father's neck, hearing Slayde's quiet chuckle as he knelt before the sofa and tumbled Tyler over his head and onto the soft velvet cushions.

A never-before-experienced lump formed in Julian's throat. "I remember how ornery and irrational you were during those long hours before Tyler was born," he commented, pouring two goblets of brandy and handing one to Slayde—after which, as Mr. Scollard had predicted, he downed his own drink in a few purposeful swallows. "Never having gone through what you did, I hadn't a clue as to the emotions you were feeling, the level of pain Courtney was enduring."

"The last was the hardest part," Slayde admitted, giving Tyler a plaything to amuse him. "Knowing how much Courtney was suffering nearly did me in. But afterward—seeing Tyler in her arms, knowing we'd created him together—" He broke off. "You'll see what I mean soon enough."

Julian nodded. "I hope so. I just keep telling myself that Scollard would know if anything were wrong." He shot Slayde a look of utter amazement. "Listen to me. Who would have ever thought I'd believe in a visionary, much less put all my faith in one?"

A grin tugged at Slayde's lips. "Face it, my friend. Your fundamental approach to life became a thing of the past the day you met Aurora. Trust me, I know. I'm married to her best friend, a woman who within a matter of weeks managed to convince me that the impossible is possible—and has kept me believing it ever since."

"We're very lucky men."

"Indeed we are."

"I concur wholeheartedly," Mr. Scollard declared, entering the sitting room. "In fact, I believe we should toast to that."

Julian jumped so high his glass nearly flew from his hand. "Is she all right?"

A proud smile touched Mr. Scollard's lips. "She's tired. But she's Rory—excited, courageous, and impatient. Therefore, weary or not, she's relieved that her impatience is about to come to an end."

"Dammit." A muscle worked in Julian's jaw. "I want to help her."

"Let nature be Rory's guide." Scollard took Julian's goblet, refilling it after he'd poured himself a drink. "Your wife is an extraordinary woman."

"I know." Julian seized his glass with a nod of thanks.

"Shall we have that toast?" The lighthouse keeper pursed his lips. "Quickly, I think. 'Twould be best if you downed that entire goblet before confronting Mrs. Peters. She's not entirely pleased with you." Abruptly Mr. Scollard halted, shaking his head as if to refute his own words. "No, I'll have to amend my timing. As things stand, 'twould be best if I lingered over my verbal tribute. Partly because I have much to extol and partly because Emma will use these extra minutes to wash everyone up and then to usher both herself and Mrs. Peters from the room. That way you'll have but one other person to encounter when you reach Aurora's bedchamber besides your wife herself—and I have a strong suspicion you wouldn't miss meeting that new occupant for all the world." So saying, Mr. Scollard raised his glass, waiting until the other two men had followed suit. "To two splendid men, Slayde and Julian, and to their exceptional wives, Courtney and Aurora. To Tyler—" He bowed solemnly at the tot, who stared at him with enthralled green eyes. "—whose welcome birth perpetuated the Huntley name in the most wondrous of fashions. To all the Huntleys and Bencrofts, reunited after sixty years, yet united wholly for the first time this day. And to the incomparable outcome of that ultimate union, an essential treasure conceived in love on a storm-tossed sea." Scollard's peaceful gaze swept from Slayde to Julian to Tyler, then rose to the ceiling overhead, clearly including the occupants of the second floor in his tribute. "Welcome," he said softly, a faint mist veiling his eyes. An instant later the mist was gone and he smiled, concluding his toast. "Here's to all of you. The joys will now abound, illuminating your lives and eclipsing the hardships of the past—now and forever."

Tyler made a cooing sound and clapped his hands.

Slayde and Scollard chuckled affectionately, then drank.

Julian didn't. "Something just happened, didn't it?" he asked Scollard quietly. "A moment ago, when you stared upward—you were sensing something. Was my child being born?"

Scollard arched a brow. "You haven't secured my toast with a drink. Do so, and fulfill its prophecy."

Taking a dutiful gulp of brandy, Julian continued to scrutinize Scollard's expression. "You haven't answered my question."

"No. *You* have." The lighthouse keeper met Julian's stare, conveying volumes with his gaze.

Eyes damp, Julian nodded, then bowed his head, giving silent thanks to the heavens.

"Your gratitude has been received and embraced," Scollard said with solemn assurance. "Now finish your brandy. But don't refill your goblet. You won't have time."

Julian complied, wondering when anything—other than Mr. Scollard's tea—had ever tasted this good.

"Julian?" Courtney hovered in the sitting-room doorway, her cheeks flushed, her eyes bright with happiness. "Your wife's patience is officially gone. She says to advise you she has no intention of savoring this prize alone. According to her, you embarked upon this adventure together, and together you shall reap its rewards. I'd suggest you go to her bedchamber posthaste."

Julian's empty goblet struck the sideboard with a thud. "Is Aurora well? And our babe . . . ?"

Courtney crossed over and squeezed Julian's hands. "Mother and child are both healthy and strong. Congratulations, Merlin. You're a father. Now, go. Your family awaits you."

Trembling with reaction, Julian bolted from the room, nearly knocking down Gin and Daniels, who were celebrating in the hallway, slapping each other's backs, and opening two new bottles of gin.

"We're proud of ye, Merlin!" Gin called, waving his bottle in the air. "Is it a boy or a girl?"

"I'll let you know." Julian kept going, taking the stairs three at a time, then rounding the landing and racing down the hall.

He paused before Aurora's closed bedchamber door, his hand shaking as he knocked.

"Come in." It was Aurora's voice, weak but clear, that beckoned him, and Julian nearly swooned with relief from the sheer joy of hearing it.

He entered slowly, cautiously, noting that the room was empty save Aurora—who was propped against her pillows—and the tiny bundle she clasped in her arms.

"Julian." She held out her hand, and Julian was beside her in a heartbeat, bringing her palm to his lips. She looked so pale, so drawn, dark circles casting shadows beneath her magnificent turquoise eyes.

"Thank God you're all right," he breathed, kissing her fingers, her wrist, her hand. "You look exhausted, *soleil.* I'm so sorry. Was the pain unbearable?"

"Only until Mrs. Peters put our daughter in my arms," Aurora replied softly, watching her husband's expression.

Julian's breath caught and his head came up. "Our daughter?" he repeated.

"Come meet her." Aurora caressed his jaw, urged him closer as she tucked the blanket away from the sleeping infant.

Julian stared, emotion knotting his chest in tight

irreversible fists as he feasted his eyes on the miracle he and Aurora had created through their love.

Tiny features met his scrutiny—eyes closed in slumber, dark lashes sweeping fine-boned cheeks, a straight upturned nose, and a pink rosebud mouth—Lord, it was like seeing a miniature Aurora, only with a small cap of his ebony-colored hair. "She's you," he said in a choked voice.

"Not entirely," Aurora demurred. "Her hair color is yours. So are her eyes. When she awakens you'll see. They're like fiery chips of topaz. Isn't she beautiful?"

"Beautiful isn't a strong enough word," Julian managed, touching the babe's downy cheek, the warm curve of her chin.

"She bellows like you, too. Even Mrs. Peters said so. She said we should have expected such a loud yell and such a stubborn arrival—given the unpleasant but most likely prospect that our daughter would take after you. According to Mrs. Peters, you're the most thunderous, willful, and domineering man she's ever met. And you doubtless wouldn't hesitate to pass those traits on to your child."

At that moment, not even Mrs. Peters' caustic remarks could shatter Julian's euphoric state. "There's another reason for our daughter's turbulent nature," he murmured. "According to Mr. Scollard, she was conceived during that storm at sea."

"I know. He told me so when he left my chambers— just a few minutes before she was born." Aurora kissed the infant's silky head. "Julian, let's call her Marinna. It's derived from the Latin phrase meaning 'from the sea.' That way, the love in which she was conceived will surround her, stay with her all her life."

"Marinna Bencroft." Julian smiled, bending to brush a kiss to his daughter's brow, then shifting to cover his wife's mouth with his. "It's perfect. So is she. Thank you, *soleil."* He framed Aurora's face between his palms. "I love you more than you'll ever know."

"And I you," she whispered.

As if to remind them who was the true champion of the day, Marinna stirred, her lashes fluttering then lifting to reveal the brilliant topaz depths beneath. Squirming, she opened her rosebud mouth and emitted a loud, ear-piercing squall that defied her delicate beauty and made her new father jump to his feet.

Blinking, Julian gaped from his daughter's now-alert, wide-eyed appraisal to his tired, laughing wife. "She takes after *me?"* he demanded, amazed that so tiny and fragile a creature could make so deafening a sound. "Perhaps. But there's quite a bit of you in her as well." He grinned as Marinna demonstrated that fact, groping at her mother's nightrail in furious, determined motions that vividly stated she had no intentions of being detained or deterred—then bellowing until Aurora moved the offending garment aside. "Quite a bit of you," Julian repeated, his chest tight with emotion. "Such as your decided lack of patience. And your uncanny resourcefulness," he added in an aching whisper as Marinna unerringly found her mark, latching onto her mother's breast, her tiny fist clenched beside it.

"You have a point," Aurora agreed, tenderly cradling their daughter as she drank. "You, little one, are an impeccable combination of Huntley and Bencroft," she apprised the infant. "And I can't imagine anything more ideal than that."

Silently Julian agreed. Feeling more blessed than he'd ever imagined, he watched the two women he loved, Aurora's damp mane of red-gold hair sweeping over Marinna's fair skin.

My daughter. My daughter, he echoed inwardly, besieged by a fierce sense of possessiveness as he drank in the wondrous combination of himself and Aurora: his topaz eyes and dark hair blended with his wife's exquisite features, his own strong-willed intensity melded with Aurora's fire and spirit.

Abruptly Mr. Scollard's toast sprang to mind, and Julian realized that once again, the intuitive lighthouse keeper had been right.

Through Marinna, the Huntleys and the Bencrofts were now truly and wholly united.

And from this day forth, their joys would abound.

Author's Note

I hope you reveled in Aurora and Julian's exciting search for the black diamond; I think you'll agree they discovered far more than even they anticipated!

The "Black Diamond Series" was both a challenge and a joy to create and, as always, I'm wistful at having to bid my characters good-bye. I hope Courtney, Slayde, Aurora, and Julian brought you all the magic they brought me and that you'll be inclined to reread their stories again sometime soon. If so, you've given me a gift worth far more than the black diamond itself.

And now . . . it's time to switch gears again!

My current project, *The Music Box,* takes us to Victorian London and its nearby shires, where a devastating loss and a long-hidden deception bring together two wonderful and deserving people.

Gabrielle Denning, orphaned at five, is taken in and raised by Lady Hermione Nevon, an eccentric noblewoman with a heart of gold and a deeply buried secret.

Bryce Lyndley, a brilliant and successful barrister, is at the core of that secret. Gaby and Bryce's meeting is an accident of fate—or is it?

Either way, what they discover in each other is even more beautiful than the haunting tune played by Gaby's treasured music box—her last remaining memory of her parents.

I hope the preview Pocket Books has provided you of *The Music Box* whets your appetite for the romantic and mysterious tale I'm in the process of creating. As always, I'm delighted to receive your notes and letters. You can write to me at:

P.O. Box 5104
Parsippany, NJ 07054-6104
(Include a legal-size SASE if you'd like a copy of my latest newsletter.)

And visit my exciting new web site at:

http://www.andreakane.com

E-mail address: WriteToMe@andreakane.com

With love,

Andrea

Pocket Star Books
Proudly Presents

The Music Box
Andrea Kane

Coming Soon
From Pocket Star Books

The following is a preview of
The Music Box. . . .

Violent coughing tore at her lungs, jarred her awake.

She sat up, rubbing her fist across her face as she tried to clear the cobwebs from her head, the burning mist from her eyes.

Where was she?

Not in her room. Not safe. Not tucked in her bed as she'd been when she last recalled.

The robins. The nest.

The shed.

She remembered now.

A bright glow slashed the room, along with a fierce surge of heat. She scrambled to her knees, her pupils wide, dilating with bewilderment.

Sunlight? It couldn't be. It was night. An unusually cold night. That was why she'd sought shelter. She'd been shivering when she slipped into the shed and snuggled into the pile of old blankets. Yet now she was unbearably hot, her hair plastered to her nape, her nightgown clinging to her skin like a soggy piece of candy. Why?

The glow intensified, a wall of flames leaping at her like a predatory tiger.

Fire.

The shed was on fire.

Whimpering with fear, she cowered in the corner, pressing a blanket to her cheek for comfort. Her harsh rasps mingled with the flames' ominous crackling, the sound a terrifying contrast to the lilting melody that had lulled her to sleep.

The music box. Her stomach tightened with dread. *Where's the music box?*

Frantically she groped on the floor. There, she thought, snatching it up with trembling fingers. Just as she'd left it, only silent now, having performed its customary miracle earlier that night. The silvery tones had danced through the treetops, soothing the newborn robins, then accompanying her into the shed, nestling beside her and serenading her to sleep.

Only to awaken to a nightmare.

As she stared across the flame-lit room, the full horror of the situation struck home. Not even her music box could protect her from this. If she stayed here, she'd die.

She didn't want to die.

"Mama," she whispered instinctively, only to realize how foolish she was being. How could she pray for her mama to save her when neither of her parents had a clue where she was?

No—it was up to her to save herself.

Small chin set, she struggled to her feet, clutching the music box and casting the blanket to the floor. Her eyes stung with tears, but she dashed them away, knowing she had but a brief time before the fire took over, robbing her of any chance for escape. It had to be now.

She made her way across the shed, bumping into one storage crate after another, wincing at the resulting pain but refusing to allow herself to cry out. To do that would mean to stop holding her breath. And that would mean inhaling the smoke that clamored at her nose and lungs.

Stubbornly she kept her lips pressed tightly together, biting back the silent sobs that shook her.

After twenty steps that felt more like a hundred, she reached the door.

The handle was scalding hot, burning her fingers so badly she yanked them away. She tried again, but it was no use. She couldn't withstand the pain long enough to open the door.

Her lungs were bursting. She had to get out.

Her gaze fell on the sleeve of her nightgown, and an image sprang to mind of her mama using kitchen cloths as aids to remove hot pie pans from the oven. Perhaps her nightgown could serve that same purpose.

Determinedly she yanked down her nightgown sleeve until it covered her entire hand. That done, she grasped the door handle, feeling the heat radiate through the fine linen as she gave the handle a frantic twist. At the same time, she flung her slight frame against the wooden door with every ounce of strength she possessed.

The door swung open, releasing her from her fiery prison.

Cold night air slapped her face, laced with the scent of musk and burning timber, and she stumbled outside gasping in one grateful breath after another. Unsteadily she made her way across the grass, one slippered foot at a time, until her strength gave out, her knees tumbling her to the ground—and to safety.

Still clutching the music box, she managed to turn her head, shaking her wild tangle of hair from her face so she could see the full impact of the blaze from which she'd just escaped.

Flames were everywhere. They seemed to gobble up the entire row of structures that led from the shed to the outdoor staff's servants' quarters.

The servants' quarters . . .

God—no.

"Mama!" White fear descended like a monstrous dragon from a fairy tale. She battled her way to her feet, tripping over the hem of her nightgown and falling to the ground. Shoving herself upright, she abandoned the music box, cupping her hands to her mouth and calling, "Papa!" Dizziness swam through her head, but she ignored it, taking three tentative steps toward the wall of smoke and flame.

She never reached it.

"Mama . . ." She began to weave, her movements dragging strangely, everything unraveling in a series of slow, eerie motions. Abruptly her legs refused to obey the commands of her smoke-veiled mind, and then the grass was rushing up toward her at an alarming rate. She called for her parents again, but her voice sounded funny, and it seemed to come from somewhere far away. "Mama . . . Papa . . ." This time what emerged was a croak.

Her eyes slid shut, unconsciousness stifling her pleas and her resistance, wild flames completing their deadly mission as she slumped just beyond their portals.

One by one, the buildings were swallowed up by the raging inferno.

Spared from its hideous destruction, she lay insensate, the music box resting in the grass behind her.

Secure and unscathed, it lay, its mother-of-pearl uncharred, its gilt trim untainted.

Its melody utterly silent.

Look for
The Music Box
Wherever Paperback Books Are Sold
Coming Soon
from Pocket Star Books

An All-New Collection of
Heartwarming Holiday Stories

UPON A
MIDNIGHT CLEAR

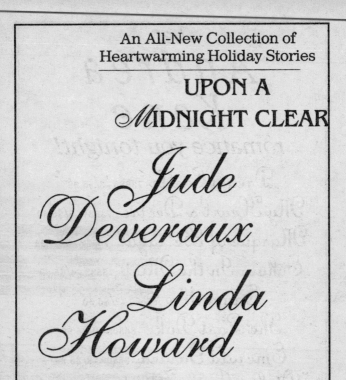

Jude Deveraux

Linda Howard

MARGARET ALLISON
STEF ANN HOLM
MARIAH STEWART

Available in Hardcover
From Pocket Books

POCKET
BOOKS

1405-01